A SIMPLE CHOICE

DAVID PEPPER

A SIMPLE CHOICE

G. P. PUTNAM'S SONS
NEW YORK

PUTNAM
—EST. 1838—

G. P. PUTNAM'S SONS
Publishers Since 1838
An imprint of Penguin Random House LLC
penguinrandomhouse.com

ISBN 9780593419731
eBook ISBN 9780593419748

Printed in the United States of America
1st Printing

BOOK DESIGN BY KATY REIGEL

To Mom—keep fighting

And Nate—for a lifetime of fighting

A SIMPLE CHOICE

PART ONE

CHAPTER 1

Pemaquid Point, Maine

THE GRAY GROOVED rocks and the old lighthouse atop them had served as center stage for Senator Duke Garber's most pivotal moments. So there was only one place to do what he needed to do now.

He parked the old black Ford pickup in the dirt parking lot at the bottom of the rocky hill. With the sun inching above the horizon, wisps of yellow and orange streaking north and south, he'd counted on being alone.

But a white station wagon sat parked at the far end of the lot. No doubt it was that of the tall woman who walked her two chocolate Labs here most days. She'd often arrive later in the morning, as he was leaving. They'd share polite nods as they crossed paths.

He peered up the hill toward the lighthouse. Nobody there. She must've been on the dirt path that hugged the shoreline, the same trail where he'd walked his golden retriever, Max, for years. Or, in later years, where Max had walked him.

The good news was that she would recognize his car and think nothing of it.

He turned off the engine, left the key in the ignition, and opened the truck door. He grunted as he lifted the heavy work boot off the floorboard and onto the rider along the truck's side. He lugged his right foot over, then lowered both boots to the lot's dusty surface.

Leaning against the truck, he stood upright to his full, wiry six feet two inches—two inches shorter than the peak height that had served him well, apart from his three years as a paratrooper in Vietnam, where his size made him a juicy target. The 3.5-liter engine went silent, and he swiveled his head—his right ear was the better one—to enjoy the full symphony of the Atlantic crashing into the craggy Maine coast. Above the steady breeze came the percussion: first the thundering crash of waves against rock, then the fizz of the water receding.

He opened the truck's rear driver's-side door and pulled out the gray backpack. He'd bought it in nearby Bristol the day before, then filled it with gravel from his driveway in New Harbor. Every bone in his torso must've creaked as he hauled the thirty pounds onto his back and cinched two nylon straps tight around his shoulders. He buckled two more sets of straps at his sternum and waist.

He trudged up the slick striated rocks. Like the rings of an ancient redwood, horizontal streaks of white, rust, black, and gray marked different minerals piling up over passing eras. Droplets of frigid ocean spray kissed his cheeks and forehead. The pungent whiff of salt water and fish wafted into his nostrils, a stench only a lifelong Mainer could love.

With each labored step, memories rushed back in pinpoint detail. As a kid playing with his two sisters under the watchful eye of his mother. As a teenager making out with Maude Fletcher in his souped-up Dodge Charger in the spot where the station wagon was now parked. Exchanging vows with Kay at the very top. His own kids climbing every inch of these rocks, year after year, before they moved west. Walking with Kay, then with Max, then alone.

But notable moments at Pemaquid Point spanned beyond the personal.

Whenever things got tough—close elections, tough decisions, moments calling for thoughtful deliberation—the senator had paced these rocks in silence.

Goose bumps pricked along his forearms as he stepped out of the glow of the rising sun into the long, cool shadow of the lighthouse. Shrouded in a similar shadow, he'd called President Bush to let him know he opposed the Iraq war. He grinned, recalling the machine-gun spray of Texan profanity the commander in chief had fired back his way. His decision, wildly unpopular at the time, had aged far better than he had.

Higher up the rocks, he passed a weather-worn cedar bench. A decade before, sitting on that bench, he'd pulled the plug on a nascent campaign for the White House. He'd second-guessed himself ever since. President Robinson had been a huge disappointment. He could've beaten her that year, and he would've done better by the country. He could've been one of the greats.

Past the bench, up and to the left, an exceptional slab of pearl-gray granite jutted out amid the flat sandstone surrounding it. As long as his truck, it burst upward several feet in the air, folding over at its top like a thick blanket over the back of a couch. Geologists explained that it, too, was once horizontal, but that extreme pressure and heat created the distinct fold of rock millions of years ago.

Whatever the cause, Duke considered it Mother Nature's perfect lectern. It was where he'd launched his first campaign for the House decades earlier, along with his first Senate race ten years later. And it was there, on a spring morning three years past, that Duke had stood proudly next to Colorado governor Janet Moore and endorsed her for the presidency.

It was a decisive moment in the campaign—many said the final nail in the GOP coffin—given that Duke was a Republican and Moore a Democrat. He and the president had been close ever since. She offered him the secretary of defense post months later, but he declined. His chairmanship was the better job, a perch from where he guarded every one of America's most valued secrets—and knew more than any other elected official in the nation short of the president herself. Plus the diagnosis had just come in.

As he climbed farther, the waves thundered loudly enough that they even penetrated his nearly useless left ear. Usually therapeutic, the ocean's roar now churned his stomach. The higher he stepped, the tighter his chest squeezed, allowing only short, quick breaths.

Still, he kept plodding up the hill. Sills of multicolored rock, some with edges as sharp as knives, now towered over him on one side. Crevices and creases at his feet grew wider and more perilous.

After years of back pain and endless steroid shots, his withered legs didn't move the way they used to. He concentrated on each step as if navigating an obstacle course. If he tripped or hesitated in any way, it might tempt him to reconsider. And reconsidering would be a mistake.

He'd made the choice, eyes wide open. This had always been one of the possible outcomes. And delaying would make things worse for so many.

He passed the lighthouse, absorbing its simple grandeur one last time. The white stone. The antique lens. The flashing red light. The quaint keeper's house behind it, now a museum that preserved the region's story—and would soon tell his own. Pemaquid's lighthouse had become his anchor, a source of serenity in a world buffeted by chaos. Of many major accomplishments with nationwide or worldwide implications, he was just as proud of his quiet work to keep this little gem open all these years, squirreling money into the Coast Guard's budget to sustain it.

As he neared the highest rock, roundish and creamy gray, gulls circled overhead. One landed on the cliff's edge, squawking loudly and flapping its wings, as if warning the town's most famous resident that he was getting too close. Through the breeze, the muffled sound of dogs barking echoed from the far side of the lighthouse. Probably the old lady's Labs on the trail below.

He ignored it all.

Instead, he pulled the backpack's straps even tighter, as he'd do before jumping out of an airplane decades before.

With the edge now only feet away, both legs shuddered as if pleading for him to turn around.

He clenched his jaw. He'd made his choice long ago. There was no stopping now.

He focused all his energy on his right leg, the stronger of the two. He lifted it up, forced it forward for a long stride, then planted it firmly onto the steeply angled rock.

His left took more effort—a dragging motion more than a true step.

Then back to his right. The workhorse. His longest stride yet landed on the mercifully flat top of a rounded boulder.

He drew a breath, then pulled his left leg even.

From the final rock of Pemaquid Point, he could see the surf below, a violent maelstrom of white, black, and blue. A splash of icy water nipped his cheeks.

Staring straight at the horizon, he flung his right leg forward one last time and plunged into the churning ocean.

CHAPTER 2

——

Mansfield, Ohio

AN HOUR NORTH of Columbus, Amity Jones pulled her black Jeep off the highway, skidding a few feet into the intersection at the end of the long exit ramp. The snow-caked stoplight overhead turned green seconds later, and she took a left to head into town.

Not a lot had changed since she'd left home for good fifteen years back.

But the short drive west from the highway was more jarring now than it had been back then. Maybe because some blocks of her old stomping grounds looked more like the bombed-out towns she'd patrolled in Afghanistan than the modern buildings of D.C. and Columbus, where she'd lived more recently.

She passed shuttered factories and warehouses on Mansfield's outskirts, then aging brick buildings, more gray than red, as she entered the compact downtown. Empty storefronts and decaying edifices betrayed the deep economic challenges the town faced. Yet the occasional new retail store, coffee shop, or restaurant attested to the grit of a community fighting back.

The same grit Amity had long considered her greatest strength.

Mansfield's was the story of too many Ohio towns—a proud manufacturing hub a generation ago, now struggling to find its place in the fierce twenty-first-century economy. While a major state prison provided solid jobs, it was not enough to replace thousands of lost auto jobs, or the others that disappeared when plants and factories closed decades back. And anyway, locking people up was a sad replacement for making things the rest of the country bought.

Amity turned south, then passed some modest houses and the stark remains of an abandoned Dairy Queen. She turned left into the next driveway, pulling into the newly paved parking lot in front of the Mansfield Hospital, the rugged town's nicest and most modern building.

After a quick elevator ride, Amity took a seat in the third-floor waiting room. She pulled out her phone to check her Twitter feed, her usual fix when passing time. But, getting no reception, she instead grabbed a copy of the *Mansfield News Journal* from the low wooden table in front of her.

Two articles dominated the front page. Across the top, a large headline and sizable article described the disappearance of Senator Duke Garber in Maine two days before. Amity's recent boss had been close to Duke—same generation, both larger-than-life veterans who went on to acclaimed public service careers. The senator had stopped by the chambers once and couldn't have been more of a gentleman. So when the Pemaquid Point story first broke, she'd absorbed every word. The *News Journal* article offered nothing new.

The paper's second major story was local but also familiar. Nine-year-old Colin Gentry had overcome a bleak cancer prognosis. The disease had started in his liver and spread to his lymph nodes. When it invaded his bones and blood months ago, they'd given him weeks to live. Now he was cancer free, back at school, and even playing basketball again.

Exactly as Mom had described. They even had the same doctor.

But if Morton Stumbo had performed the miracle for Mom's young neighbor, he hadn't been nearly as successful with Mom, which was why Amity was here today.

She scanned the article for details about young Colin's path to recovery. Nothing stuck out that she and Mom hadn't already tried. She'd do just about anything to help Mom, but the problem was, there wasn't much else to be done. Unless she happened to win the medical miracle lottery young

Colin Gentry had, Mom's fate was sealed. Plus, Mom was far less inclined to help herself at this point. Just like always, Amity was the family problem solver. In many ways, the parent of the duo.

"Ms. Jones?" a voice called out minutes later as Amity checked out high school basketball scores on the back page.

"Yes," she said, looking up at the young receptionist who'd checked her in.

"She's ready. The nurse is wheeling her out now."

Two doors swung open as Amity stood up, paper in hand. A short man in scrubs walked slowly behind a silver wheelchair.

As she'd trained to do in a courtroom, Amity forced a neutral face to conceal her shock.

It had been only two weeks, but Mom, slumped low in the chair, looked even grayer and thinner than before.

Time was running out.

CHAPTER 3

Pemaquid Point

PALMER KNIGHT HAD spent a few summers in Maine in his early teen years, at a camp for the kids of the rich and famous near Kennebunk. While he couldn't stand most of the other campers, he'd loved both the lakes and the coast. He'd always wanted to come back.

But not for work.

And definitely not for an occasion like this.

"Step a few feet to your right, Palmer. The senator's truck is behind you, but the other news vans are still in the shot."

He did as told, his cameraman swiveling his lens in the same direction. He glanced around as three other reporters stood before their own cameras, preparing for the same noon update. All three had crammed themselves into his live shot, and it was clear why. They still didn't take him seriously. Just a rich kid trading on his family connections—not a real journalist. It was a rap he was always trying to beat, even if milking those connections had so far been the key to his success.

He tucked his wire-rimmed Ray-Bans into his pocket, then rubbed his hand through his wavy sandy-blond hair.

The small light flashed green. Go time.

"It's been over fifty hours since Senator Duke Garber parked his pickup truck here on the scenic Maine coast, by this historic lighthouse," Palmer said into the camera, gesturing behind him with his left hand.

His somber expression and tone were part of the show, but the news had truly hit him. In the three interactions they'd had, Senator Garber—a protégé of Palmer's grandfather—had treated him well. He was one of the good ones.

"And he hasn't been seen since. The fear is that he fell into the ocean while walking on the rocks above."

The anchor's baritone voice chimed in with the question they'd agreed to.

"What do the authorities think happened?"

"They don't want to speculate at this point. They say there's no sign of foul play. The senator knew this place well and took this walk a lot. But he was also getting older, so may have slipped and fallen. At this time of year, it can be slick up there."

A plausible theory. He'd witnessed the senator hobbling into and out of hearings over the past year. And he'd almost fallen himself, ten minutes prior, on the wet, craggy rock.

The anchor chimed back in.

"The senator held a lot of important posts in Washington, including chairing the Senate Select Committee on Intelligence. People say he knew more secrets than anyone in Washington. How can the authorities be so sure there wasn't foul play?"

Palmer nodded. This was the question he'd been asking all day. Garber's committee's agenda was chock-full of hot-button topics, and those were just the ones they could reveal.

"So far, that's what they've said. But you're right about the senator. He was a vault of top secret information. Which is one reason he was one of the last people left whom all sides in Washington respected."

"But they're sure there's no sign of foul play?" the anchor asked.

"That's the word so far." He let his voice rise, signaling to his viewers that he didn't believe it either.

And of course he didn't bring up the other obvious question: Was it suicide? The media hesitated to mention it on air as a general rule, but especially with someone as prominent as "Senator Duke," as all of Maine and most of Capitol Hill called him.

Palmer wrapped up his live shot a minute later, then watched as the other reporters signed off.

Political deaths didn't often amount to the top story for any network, let alone all of them. But Duke Garber was an institution. For a generation, presidents and foreign leaders had sought his counsel. And no one more so than President Moore, even though the two were in different parties.

So Palmer and the other networks were all there for the same reason.

Sure, the senator might've fallen off a cliff. Or jumped.

But with everything that the old senator knew, there were all sorts of reasons someone might have wanted him dead.

CHAPTER 4

—

Mansfield

"WELL, I'LL BE. Amity Jones!"

Dexter Mills's deep, gravelly voice hadn't changed in two decades.

"What brings you by?"

Amity had driven Mom back home, ten minutes southwest of downtown Mansfield. Exhausted and heavily medicated, Mom had changed into her old robe and dozed off in twenty minutes. Never comfortable in Mom's bedroom, Amity spent the next hour straightening things up around the house and cooking her an early dinner. Mom's best friend then arrived to keep an eye on her. Dr. Stumbo had said she'd be much stronger by evening, after some rest.

On the way back to the highway, Amity had stopped at the two-story brick building that housed the *Mansfield News Journal*.

"Just passing through, Dexter. Mom needed a ride back after a small setback in her treatment."

Dexter, the paper's editor, frowned. It was a small town, and folks knew Mom was sick.

Except for some wrinkles and flashes of gray in his sideburns, Dexter looked no different than when Amity had interned for the paper as a high school senior. Wiry and tall, he even donned a tan fleece jacket, blue jeans, and leather boots, just as he had back then.

Amity's *News Journal* internship had propelled her into journalism at Ohio State, where she became editor in chief of the *Lantern*. Her Army service and law career took her in other directions, but she'd always credited those early years in journalism for the development of some of her best skills as a lawyer and interrogator. She checked in with Dexter, her first mentor, about once a year.

Amity sat down in the empty chair facing his cluttered desk. After filling Mills in on her move back to Columbus, she held up the paper she'd snagged from the hospital.

"I saw your story on the boy who miraculously recovered from cancer. Incredible."

"A miracle for sure," he said.

"I mention it because Mom could use something just as miraculous. Between us, it's getting pretty desperate."

Neither Amity nor Mom liked to talk about her health, but the day's update had doused the last glimmer of hope.

"Don't you guys go to Dr. Stumbo as well?"

"Sure do. But he can't say anything."

"HIPAA?"

The federal law that keeps medical information private.

"Yep," she said, nodding. "Do you know anything more about the treatment?"

He shook his head. "We all know Stumbo well. Hell, we go to the same church. But he clammed up on this one. You'll see he wasn't quoted in our story once."

"I noticed. No family quotes either."

"They're hermits. Wouldn't talk."

Amity nodded. They'd lived next door to the Gentrys for years. Since Colin had gotten sick, Mom had barely seen them.

"Well, how'd you get the story, then?"

"You know Mansfield, Amity. The poor boy went in with weeks to live late last fall and walked out of that hospital three weeks ago with a clean bill of health. Half the hospital was talking about it, which meant the whole town was talking about it the next day."

"But you had so many specifics."

"If you read closely, the quotes were from people who'd observed him back out in the community: his coach, a friend's dad, a neighbor. But the family itself steered clear, and hospital officials wouldn't say a word. They're livid we ran the story at all."

"I don't get it. Why so quiet on such a positive story?"

"Some people are private that way. The Gentrys even more so. Always have been."

"Dexter, I knocked on the Gentrys' door a few weeks back."

She let the sentence hang.

"You did?" he asked, leaning back. "And what happened?"

"They shooed me away like I was contagious."

"Who's 'they'?"

"Mrs. Gentry."

"A nosy neighbor knocking on the door? Wouldn't you have done the same?"

"Maybe, but Simon and I used to swing on their swing set with their oldest—before Colin was even born. And when I stopped by, I had flowers in my hand. Even so, Mrs. Gentry wanted me gone."

Dexter exhaled, visibly uncomfortable at Amity's prying.

"They probably wanted their privacy. Pretty understandable."

"My mom said Mrs. Gentry and Colin were gone for months. Mr. Gentry would also disappear for weeks."

"Well, the poor kid was near death. He likely needed world-class treatment and went out of town. That happens a lot."

"But read your own story. The public narrative is that Dr. Stumbo saved the day."

Dexter nodded. "Maybe they went to Cleveland, Columbus, or Cincinnati. All have great children's hospitals. And they're close enough that Dr. Stumbo could still have been involved."

Amity shook her head emphatically. "If you're in those cities, you'd go back and forth every few days. She was gone longer than that, and packed accordingly. Large suitcases, prepared for a long trip. They'd leave at night, but Mom doesn't sleep well and saw them go."

Dexter leaned forward, preparing to stand. She'd failed to pique his interest.

"Amity, sending kids to the best treatment a family can find is common. What parent wouldn't do that?"

"Exactly." She dropped both hands on his desk. "So why keep it a secret?"

CHAPTER 5

——

Pemaquid Point

LIKE A SPIDERWEB strewn across the senator's final steps, yellow police tape crisscrossed the rocks leading up to the lighthouse. And with those rocks blocked off, Palmer Knight had been walking a trail along the shore, learning nothing new of what had happened.

An old woman who stopped by remembered seeing the senator's truck two mornings before as she walked her dogs but hadn't seen him on the trail. She also recalled her dogs acting strangely for a few minutes, barking into the air, but hadn't known why.

To keep his bosses happy, Palmer recorded her describing how she'd often see the senator there and how kind he was. Her eyes welled up as she spoke.

The FBI had arrived at the scene around noon the day before, but the lead agent, who'd driven up from Boston, remained mum.

The helicopter circling overhead never paused for long, meaning it hadn't spotted anything.

And shifts of divers from local and state authorities searched the coastline for hours. If they'd found him, there would have been commotion. But they remained subdued all afternoon, even as shifts changed.

Palmer couldn't track down any close family of the senator to talk to. A widower, he lived alone down the road in New Harbor, keeping to himself in a town whose primary focus was lobstering. His kids had left Maine decades ago, and they weren't taking calls from the press.

If any of the other reporters had learned anything useful, they weren't letting on.

The only official who would talk was the local fire chief. With thirty minutes before Palmer's next live update, he coaxed the chief to talk on background.

"Chief, if he fell in by accident, wouldn't he have been swept up against the rocks somewhere nearby?"

The squat firefighter squinted as sunlight beamed into his face. "Either that, or he sunk straight to the bottom. I've seen 'em go both ways in these types of incidents."

"What types of incidents?"

"People falling off the point—or jumping off. It happens more than you'd think." He gestured toward all the news vans. "But usually no one cares."

"But if he'd sunk, wouldn't the divers have found his body at the bottom? They've been down there for hours."

"You never know. The tides and underwater currents toss things around down there, including human bodies. They're covering a lot of ground, but these things can take a while."

"'A while,' as in more than two days?"

The chief's weathered skin wrinkled across his square, grim face. "It certainly can be."

His voice cracked as he finished his sentence, betraying his outer confidence.

CHAPTER 6

——

Cambridge, Massachusetts

"So HE SIMPLY stepped off the cliff?" the bearded man asked.

The two men were huddled in a corner of the small, shadowy tavern on the seedy edge of Cambridge, each with a full stein of dark beer planted in front of him. The bar had opened at four, just minutes ago. Only one other couple was there, making out sloppily in the other back corner. Still, the two men spoke quietly, each with a slight accent.

"Indeed he did."

Although the younger of the two, the respondent was the one with no hair. His was an intense baldness, his scalp shining. His other prominent feature was a pointed, twisted nose—no doubt the result of at least one bad break—which converted each breath he took into an audible wheeze.

Although few interacted with him directly, the team knew the bald man as Quinn. And he was proving to be incredibly resourceful.

"I've watched it four times now. He struggled physically, but there was no hesitation at all."

He lifted his stein a few inches off the table, then took a hearty swig. Thick from head to toe, his torso was shaped like a triangle. Even his neck was laced with muscles, which flexed as he drank.

The older man nodded, then wiped away a speck of foam from his white beard.

"Given the news we delivered, there was no alternative for him. I'm just relieved we didn't have to spill blood."

Quinn smirked. "Sort of the same difference, if you ask me."

Another sip.

"And you searched his house for any connection back to us?"

"Every inch. The man was a pack rat, but I disposed of anything that left even a hint."

The older man placed the stein down on the grooved and pockmarked maple of the tabletop.

"Still, we owe him." Looking around the dark room, he was talking to himself more than to Quinn. Remembering. "He started it all."

Another pause.

"And he knew."

"Knew what?"

A grin appeared through the old man's beard as he looked back at Quinn.

"That they wouldn't be able to say no."

CHAPTER 7

Pemaquid Point

IT STARTED WITH the FBI agents.

And their phones.

For hours, three of them had been pacing in the parking lot, getting in and out of their cars, talking quietly among themselves. Restless and bored like everyone else.

Then, shortly after Palmer's recent update, the calls came in rapid succession. Each of the three received a call, then made their own. Amid the chatter, the looks on their faces told Palmer something was breaking. Body language, too—the way they leaned forward, into their phones. They weren't bored anymore. Something was up.

Twenty minutes later, as the sky and waters darkened behind them, the afternoon shift of divers scrambled back from the rocks with an energy they'd lacked before. The last two divers were carrying an object in a large black plastic bag.

Palmer and three other reporters jogged in the divers' direction.

The lead FBI agent and two local police officers blocked their path.

"Whoa," the lead agent yelled in his thick Boston accent. "Give 'em room."

"What is it?" Palmer yelled out at the divers. "What'd you find?"

One of the divers carrying the bag glanced in his direction, then turned away. But the momentary look—the dilated eyes and pained grimace—told the story.

Behind the wall of beefy authorities, the two divers lugged the dark bag to the van, then placed it in the back.

As Palmer deciphered every detail, he texted his cameraman, who was sitting in the van: Set up right away.

The fact that two people were carrying the bag meant whatever they were carrying had some heft to it.

The fact that they were spread several feet apart meant it had some length as well.

They weren't struggling, which meant it was not a whole body.

But when they laid it down in the van, they did so gently. Carefully.

Not the kind of respect you'd show an inanimate object.

As one of the agents slammed the van door shut, Palmer's phone rang. He wasn't shocked by who it was, but it also meant the story was about to get a lot bigger.

CHAPTER 8

———

Mansfield

Two cardinals fluttered between the trees, flashes of red darting among the snow- and ice-tipped branches. Dancing from tree to tree, headstone to headstone, they were always there, adding life to the little cemetery where Dad lay.

In her younger years, Amity had convinced herself that Dad was watching the cemetery cardinals with the same zeal they'd spotted birds from their kitchen window. A small manual in hand, they'd identify all variety of winged visitors to their small backyard. But they didn't need the manual to recognize their favorite and most frequent guests. Dad went so far as to give the cardinals names, drawing from the best of the Buckeyes and Browns.

As she aged, the cardinals brought her peace for a different reason. They were watching Dad when she couldn't be there. When no one else came by.

Fifteen minutes south of town, the small cemetery was tucked between rolling fields that were drab in the winter, plush and green with soybeans in the summer. Stopping here guaranteed a late return to Columbus, but the report on Mom's condition had compelled her to visit.

She laid down a bouquet of pink and red carnations at the foot of Dad's gravestone, adding needed color to the otherwise white and gray ground.

Then she leaned down and wiped away snow from his name with her bare right hand.

AUGUST D. JONES

"Big Gus," all his work buddies had called him. Led a good life.

A high school wrestler and baseball star, Dad had had the brains to go to college but didn't. Like most, he dedicated his body and mind to making cars—specifically, stamping the sheet metal that formed the backbone of every car GM made. The work paid a decent wage back then, thanks to the union, which he served as a shop steward. And he gave every ounce of his big, generous heart to raising a daughter who looked up to him as Superman—big and strong and gentle all at the same time.

She closed her eyes.

The scene returned as it always did but carried special meaning today:

"Make sure to take care of your mother for me. She's gonna need you."

"I will, Daddy. I promise I will."

They were the last words they'd ever shared alone. Father and daughter were sitting in Mansfield's sole hospice, Mom having taken a break from his bedside to get some fresh air and a glass of water. As weak as he looked—hairless, his face gaunt and pale—his hand gripped hers firmly as he whispered. His inner fire was still burning.

He meant every word.

Mom came back through the door moments later. That evening Dad passed away. The peaceful expression on his face masked massive organ failure.

The commitment she'd made that day had shaped her entire life since, those final words molding a pledge permanently into her conscience. An eleven-year-old taking on the responsibility of a grown-up.

Her mom never knew of it. And her younger brother, Simon, only six, wasn't part of it. Her and Dad's secret. The last link of an unbreakable chain they'd forged in their eleven short years together.

She began fulfilling the pledge immediately, sitting at her inconsolable mother's side to plan Dad's funeral, then speaking for the family in the small church where his open casket lay. It was the first time she'd ever spoken to a large group of grown-ups, but she hadn't been nervous. Telling the world about her superhero was the easiest part of a horrible weekend.

Amity boosted Mom the rest of her childhood. She took on many of the household chores and worked jobs to help pay the bills. She worried about the things that are usually left for mothers and fathers to stress about. And she looked out for Simon as he grew. Even as her studies and service took her all over the world, she returned home often. Mom grumbled about both kids leaving her in Mansfield by herself, but Amity's own guilt—that her helpless mom needed her—was the stronger voice calling her home.

When Mom got sick, the pledge meant Amity had to move home permanently as soon as her clerkship ended. Yes, that foreclosed other rare paths of opportunity laying right before her. But the promise at Dad's bedside echoed louder than ever.

A gust of wind blew her hair in front of her face, a strand catching below her eyelid. She opened her eyes to free it.

The scene faded from her mind, but his name was still before her.

AUGUST D. JONES

She kneeled down, dampening her right knee, then lowered her head.

"I'm doing the best I can, Daddy. It's gonna be a fight, but I'm doing the best I can."

She stood up, turned around, and walked back to her car.

CHAPTER 9

Washington, D.C.

"Do y'all buy it?"

Tennessee senator Shepherd Logan, the most senior member around the dark mahogany table, studied his three colleagues as he posed the question. They looked as shaken as he had in the mirror ten minutes before. Even Senator Gigi Fox, Logan's always tan and cocksure colleague from Florida, was sapped of her usual fire.

Their slumped postures felt unbecoming against the backdrop of tall Corinthian columns that surrounded them. The small bipartisan gathering was taking place in the storied Marble Room, a stately hideaway available only to members of their exclusive hundred-member club. Not even top staff could set foot within its doors. Good thing just now.

Their informal caucus met there monthly, but that late afternoon meeting had come about at the last second.

"That Duke just fell off a cliff? Not a chance," said Byron Blue, the portly, affable Alabama senator with a bad comb-over, hard-right worldview, and far thicker drawl than his Tennessee counterpart. "We were warned."

As he always did before talking, Colorado's Sam Ireland—at six-four, the tallest man in the Senate—cleared his throat. Years of smoking had ravaged the moderate Democrat's lungs and throat.

"Duke was getting up there. We could all see it. So let's not jump to conclusions."

"C'mon, Sam," Gigi Fox said, waving her tiny, speckled hand dismissively. As they often did, the silver and black bangs that plunged to the tops of her eyes shook as she spoke. Most of her remaining hair was wrapped into a tight bun angled back from the top of her small head. "There's no way it's a coincidence."

"Let's not get carried away, Gigi," Ireland said back, using the nickname all of America called Florida's longtime senator, by far the most recognized figure of their little group.

"We all knew this was a possibility when we first agreed to all of this," she shot back, crossing her arms. "Duke knew it better than anyone. No use playing dumb now."

"So if you're right, what do we do?" Ireland asked.

Logan leaned forward, eyeing each colleague intensely as the tendons in his wiry neck drew taut.

"Stick with the plan. And remember how Duke ended every meeting: 'This is much bigger than us.'"

But even as he said the words, his own guilt screamed the truth: in the end, it *was* all about them.

CHAPTER 10

Pemaquid Point

A RISING MOON illuminated the fog that hung low over the Atlantic, providing an appropriately eerie backdrop to Palmer's update.

"We break in from the Maine coast with some terrible news," he said into the camera. "About an hour ago, divers recovered a human leg a few hundred yards from the cliffs behind me. They have now identified it as that of Senator Garber. Needless to say, this confirms that the respected Maine senator has died."

His fingers tingled as he gripped the mic, not from chill but nerves. He was scooping everyone, thanks to the incoming phone call thirty minutes before. And it was that rush of a scoop—of beating everyone to a story— that had pushed him into journalism in the first place, as opposed to the higher-paying Wall Street and venture capital gigs most of his prep school and Columbia buddies had opted for. Jobs he could've landed with his family's connections.

Days like today, all that sacrificed income was worth it.

Authorities on-site had not yet shared the details, so other reporters could only mention that an object had been found as they awaited an update. But he could go further. A lot further. As they often did, his connections were paying off handsomely. So much for the scorn of his competitors.

"Palmer, that's awful news," an anchor said through his earpiece. "I know it's difficult to discuss, but what do they think happened?"

"The authorities here are speculating that a shark got ahold of the senator's body after he'd already drowned."

"Terrible. And is there any more speculation on how he ended up in the water in the first place?"

"They're treating it like an accident . . ." He paused for effect, highlighting the second part of the tip. "But in Washington, they're digging deeper."

"Digging deeper how?" the anchor asked, melodrama in his voice.

"Our sources are telling us that while they have no reason to suspect foul play, intelligence agencies are looking into the nations with the most reason to harm the senator."

"Any word on which countries those might be?"

Palmer's stomach fluttered. What he was about to say would create waves across the world. But his source had been clear: Name these three, in this precise order.

"Yes. They're focused on Russia, China . . ."

Another pause.

". . . and Saudi Arabia."

CHAPTER 11

———

Washington

"How's MARY DOING, Shep?" Senator Gigi Fox asked, grasping her old friend's trembling right hand.

As they usually did after Marble Room meetings, the two senators took a car over to the Mt. Vernon Grill for martinis and a late meal. The Tennessee and Florida senators, octogenarians both, had been friends across party lines for years. With their spouses, they'd traveled the world for both business and pleasure. Before his wife, Kay, had passed five years before, Duke Garber had been the third member of their travel clique. And he'd still share steak dinners with them at the Mt. Vernon Grill, including one three weeks ago. They'd had a great time then—reliving old war stories and remembering friends who'd passed away long ago. Duke hadn't dropped even a hint of a problem. So his death not only hit them harder than the others; it came as a shock.

Shepherd Logan's eyes moistened as he pictured his wife Mary's shriveled body. Her hair was finally filling back in, but she remained so frail. They had both been varsity athletes in their youth and stayed active all their lives, so it was especially difficult to see her in such a weakened state.

"You know she's a fighter, Gigi. And despite the tough odds, she's beating it. She really is."

She squeezed his hand again.

"That's wonderful. Wally and I are heading to the Baltics this summer. You'll need to join us."

Logan chuckled. Measured both by distance and luxury, Fox traveled like no one else on Capitol Hill.

"If she's up to it, we'll be there for sure. Like old times."

The waiter dropped a plate in front of each of them, a rare twelve-ounce filet mignon for her and charred grouper drowned in butter for him.

"Gigi," the white-haired Tennessean said as he lifted his martini, "as small as you are, you can out-eat every man in the U.S. Senate." He made the same joke at most of their meals, in response to her always vigorous orders.

She held up her fork, a large piece of bloodred steak speared on its end. "Shep, you know I'm a Midwesterner at heart, and with that comes a robust appetite."

They savored their entrées for a few minutes before Gigi turned back to business.

"You really think we should keep moving forward?" she asked in her no-nonsense tone, the same one she used in Senate hearings, where no one was tougher than the former Florida attorney general and prosecutor.

"Absolutely. There's no turning back now. Duke knew this was the right thing to do despite the risks. We're talking the most basic of human rights."

She nodded slowly.

"Don't we know it."

CHAPTER 12

—

Damariscotta, Maine

"SAUDI ARABIA? REALLY?"

Driving the narrow, slick Maine highway back to his inn, Palmer Knight checked back in with National Security Advisor Sandra Ellrod. His cell phone was on speaker mode so he could grip the wheel with both hands.

"No doubt about it," she said.

It almost didn't feel fair.

Ellrod was the mother of one of Palmer's closest friends at Lodge Academy in Rhode Island. He'd known her since ninth grade, when she was ambassador to NATO but had kept her oldest son, Tyler, back in the States for school. But Tyler's mom's fancy title didn't stand out at Lodge. Other kids' parents were senators, congressmen, judges, Wall Street and private equity bigwigs, big-time lawyers, and the like.

Many of those connections came in handy now, boosting Palmer quickly in the competitive world of D.C. cable news. Yes, for many in the business, this rendered him an "access journalist," as if there were something wrong with having a broad, high-rolling network. All Palmer knew was that he scooped his competition like clockwork.

Ellrod had first thrown him a tip after he'd signed on with CNN. He'd aired it, which led to another. Over time, that trickle grew into a steady stream of national security exclusives that served them both well.

"How do you know?" Palmer asked, leaning toward the windshield, struggling to make out lane markings through the blowing snow and flapping wipers.

"Easy," Ellrod said. "Neither Russia nor China would be reckless enough to assassinate a sitting U.S. senator. Plus, relations with them are on a slow boil—nothing that would lead to this. Things are far more volatile with the Saudis, and that new king wouldn't hesitate to do it."

"'Volatile,'" Palmer said back, chuckling at the understatement. "More like explosive."

In her campaign, President Moore had vowed to pursue a robust human rights agenda. When she followed through as president, the relationship with the Saudis soured. She imposed sanctions on the kingdom in her first one hundred days, exacting deep damage on its economy. The king soon claimed to be in compliance with a new human rights protocol, only to be caught in violation once more. At the UN two months ago, the president had vowed that another violation would trigger the most stringent sanctions possible, including targeting the Swiss bank accounts of the royal family.

"So what—"

Bright headlights suddenly blinded him. A large vehicle was headed directly his way. He grunted as he twisted the steering wheel to the right, veering from the fast to the slow lane. A truck raced by, just to his left.

"Palmer, you okay?"

After a few swerves, he straightened the car out in the right lane.

"I almost joined the late senator, but all good now," he said, taking a few breaths. "I was going to ask: What comes next?"

"We listen in on the embassy, and in the kingdom, and see what we hear."

"And you'll let me know?" he asked.

"I'll do what I can," Ellrod said. "But let's get you off this call so you get back to D.C. in one piece."

CHAPTER 13

Columbus, Ohio

IT WAS A simple rule that one of Amity Jones's Supreme Court co-clerks had taught her: Get to work before the boss arrives, and leave only after he leaves.

Up for her daily Potomac run at five, in before seven most mornings, Amity had beaten Justice Gibbons to his chambers all but three days of the term. She now followed the same morning routine for Struggles & Heinz, the boutique appellate firm she'd joined after the clerkship, making a splash across Columbus's legal community. After her first day, no one had arrived before her. And as her co-clerk had promised, it was the most productive time of her day. Impressing the bosses was a side benefit.

So this morning, having walked in at six forty-five, Amity finished one Ohio Supreme Court brief, drafted a motion for a pending district court deadline, and still was the only one in the office as she emailed the draft motion to the firm's head partner.

Looking out at the snow-covered Ohio Statehouse grounds, now beaming bright under the rising sun, she called home.

"How you feeling, Mom?"

"Amity, you worry about me too much. I'm feeling fine."

But her halting voice and raspy breaths confirmed she wasn't fine at all.

She'd been suffering for close to two years and had looked as rough yesterday as Amity could remember.

"How was your date last night?"

Mom hated talking about her health. She preferred figuring out ways to marry Amity off, and her one concern about Amity moving home had been that it would kill her daughter's prospects—romantic ones—after she was finally liberated from the crushing schedule of a U.S. Supreme Court clerkship. But Mom's concern was nothing new. She'd been equally worried at every rung of Amity's career ladder.

Last night was supposed to have been Amity's second date since arriving in Columbus. An associate at another firm had asked her out. She'd even tamed her usually unruly ginger-colored hair with a salon appointment the night before last.

"It didn't happen."

"Aw, why not?"

"I canceled."

"Why would you cancel?"

"I didn't feel up to it." The truth was, meeting Dexter Mills and stopping by the cemetery had derailed her plans. "Plus, I had to get back here for work."

"Amity, life is about so much more than work. No one knows that better than you. Than us."

It always came back to this. Amity's professional success had never impressed Mom. It got in the way of the things Mom wanted most, and she never hesitated to say so.

It was also a not-so-subtle reference to Dad. Losing a father at eleven was as painful a blow as a shy, doting daughter could suffer. Which was why she didn't appreciate the reminder. The picture to her monitor's left provided it every day. The four of them together: Dad, Mom, Amity, and little Simon. Dad died two years after it was taken, and that perfect little family was never the same. The smiles never returned.

Simon now topped her by four inches, so the photo also served as a good reminder of how young he had been when things fell apart. The five-year gap between them had rendered their lives entirely different. He'd been too young to appreciate the difference before and after Dad's passing—the change in Mom. In the family. After high school he never looked back, going away to college and then moving out west. Rarely visiting. Starting his own family. He now cheered for Stanford over the Buckeyes, and the 49ers over the Browns, the ultimate sign that he had truly left Ohio behind.

Whenever Amity resented shouldering so many of the family burdens, she reminded herself that Simon had not been at Dad's bedside that day. He hadn't made the pledge. She couldn't blame him for something he'd been too young to be part of. Plus, her childhood had been shaped by Dad in so many positive ways—something Simon had missed out on. If that meant a heavier load for her now, so be it.

Amity turned away from the photo, shifting to the topic she'd thought about all morning.

"Anything else happen next door?"

With Mom out of it, they hadn't talked about it the day before.

"At the Gentrys'?"

"Yes."

"You know, it was busy as ever the other day."

"Thursday again?"

"Yeah. Like I told you, always Thursday. The dark van shows up. They move the equipment in and out. This time there was a car that came too. Two extra people, it looked like."

Mom spoke nonchalantly as Amity coaxed her along. She wanted to get back to dating.

"And still no Dr. Stumbo?"

"No. He's never with them."

"How's little Colin look?"

"Like a kid again. Playing in the backyard. Riding his bike. Amazing for him."

"That's great. But why these intense visits? If he's better, what could they be doing?"

"Who knows, honey. Keeping an eye on their patient, I guess. We should be happy for them. That family's been through so much."

"Of course we are." A long pause. "So they're there every Thursday?"

"Yes. Eight in the morning, right after Chet drops the mail off."

"And when do they leave?"

"Around four." She yawned through the phone. "Amity, dear, you're wearing me out being a busybody. Can we talk about your next date?"

"Sure thing, Mom."

Amity opened up the calendar app on her phone.

Good.

Thursday morning was free. She typed "Home" next to the 8:00 a.m. slot. She'd have to postpone the rescheduled date, which she'd already downgraded to morning coffee.

CHAPTER 14

Washington

"WHY ARE YOU calling us about this?"

Odd response, Palmer thought. Washington politicians jump at any chance for national press. But here a senator's press secretary was pushing back on an interview.

He'd have to sweeten the pot. But because he was tired from his early morning flight back from Portland, he didn't feel up to a big negotiation.

"Senator Ireland is ranking on Intel, right?" Palmer asked.

"He sure is."

"So he would've worked closely with Senator Garber."

"Of course. Our office was devastated by the news. The senator especially."

"That's why Senator Ireland would be the perfect person to talk to. We're looking for leaders of both parties to share their memories of Duke. To talk about how sometimes, even in Washington, friendships can cross party lines."

When it came to good press, he was lobbing up an alley-oop pass no senator could refuse.

"Let me check," the press secretary said.

But even with the noncommittal words, his eager tone gave him away. The interview would happen.

———

"DUKE WAS ONE of a kind. Democrat or Republican, we all admired and respected him, as a public servant and a friend." Senator Sam Ireland paused, then cleared his throat. "A lot like your grandfather."

It was late afternoon, the day's hearings and other business were done, so the senator was relaxed and garrulous. Palmer and he were seated in his private Senate office, surrounded by photos and Colorado landscapes. Elder statesmen on Capitol Hill like Ireland always spoke highly of Palmer's granddad's tenure there.

He nudged the interview forward.

"You served on one of the nation's most important committees together, Senator. You both led it at different times. Tell us about that."

"That's a little open-ended, Palmer," interjected the press secretary, sitting off to the senator's right. "Do you have a more specific question about the deceased senator?"

Palmer clenched his jaw, irritated. One Beltway rule he'd learned quickly was that the older a senator was, the more protective his staff became. Dread often in their eyes, it was as if the old-timers were always on the verge of saying something that would instantly destroy their careers. So, no surprise, from the moment Palmer asked his first question of Ireland, the young flack had shielded his boss like a well-trained guard dog. This was the third interruption so far.

"I'm okay," Ireland said nonchalantly to his aide.

The senator coughed for a few seconds, hacked into a handkerchief, then swallowed. He leaned forward over his solid oak desk. Even seated, Ireland towered.

"Duke was a vault of information. He knew more than anyone else in this town about our nation's most important secrets and greatest vulnerabilities." He thought for a second. "And every other country's as well. In many respects, it made him the most important person in this building."

He coughed three more times.

Palmer cringed. They could edit out the interruptions, but the fits were so severe, he wondered about the poor senator's health.

"Other countries' vulnerabilities?"

"Palmer," the flack said in a disapproving tone, as if Ireland weren't even there.

But Ireland didn't hesitate. "Yes. He knew them all cold."

Perfect. He'd walked right down the path. Time for a big step further.

"Do you think that could be connected to what happened to him? All that he knew."

If the old senator was surprised by the question, he hid it well. His bushy white eyebrows angled down toward his nose, but that was it.

The press secretary shifted uncomfortably in his chair. "We really shouldn't go down—"

"You know . . ." the senator said, interrupting.

Palmer braced for a scolding.

". . . I thought about that last night. And I'm going to encourage Duke's successor to look into that. I trust that the president and intel agencies already are. It would be irresponsible not to probe it."

Palmer's heart beat faster as his interview struck gold. The senator had said far more on camera than he'd expected. So he went for broke.

"What do you think about the speculation of who might've done it?"

The press secretary now stood, lifting his chubby left hand as he did. "This type of speculation is not what we agreed to."

"Angus, sit down."

The senator shot the man a brutal glare while lifting his long, lanky arm in the aide's direction, index finger jutting straight up in the air. One corollary to the Beltway rule was that senior senators hated being coddled as if they were teetering inches from a land mine.

The senator looked back at Palmer with an easy smile.

"Now, you understand that I can't share any classified information."

"Of course."

He leaned forward.

"I saw your report last night. I don't know who your sources were, but that's where I'd be looking as well. Especially the Saudis. I don't say that lightly, but that possibility must be pursued."

CHAPTER 15

Washington

FOR A RITZY embassy, the room could not have been less hospitable. Three dark, windowless walls and a huge mirror taking up most of the fourth. Only two high, uncomfortable stools to sit in. With no signal for his phone and no cameraman allowed, time ticked by slowly as Palmer waited.

Two raps joggled the door.

Palmer stood up to his full, rangy six feet, one inch as a small man entered. Palmer recognized him from past television appearances, where he always came across as pleasant and professional.

"Greetings, Mr. Knight. I'm Nasser Ahmad, the embassy's public affairs liaison."

Unlike the man who'd politely escorted him to the room, Mr. Ahmad glowered.

"Nice to meet you."

Palmer reached out to shake his hand, but his host just stared at it.

"I've seen you a number of times on television," Palmer tried. He grinned as he said it, but the man didn't return the pleasantry.

"Mr. Knight, how may I help you?"

He remained standing, so Palmer did as well. This would apparently be a short meeting.

"I wanted to ask you about the speculation—"

"And this is all off the record." A command, not a question.

"Of course. There is speculation that Senator Garber had recently learned important secrets about Saudi Arabian human rights abuses, both in neighboring nations and against dissidents in your country . . ."

Senator Ireland had expanded on his suspicions in their meeting.

". . . and now he has died mysteriously on a cliff he's walked on for seventy years. What do you say to those who suspect your government may be behind his death?"

As he ended the question, Palmer eyed every inch of the man's face, from his broad forehead to his narrow eyes to his pencil-straight mustache, thin lips, and drawn-in chin. You could only gather so much in an off-the-record interview, but smoking out lies was something you *could* do.

No part of him budged. Not a hair. Not a droplet of perspiration.

"Mr. Knight, I met with you today to inform you that your suggestion—repeated on the air twice—that we were involved is pure anti-Arab calumny. And we will take any and all action necessary to stop you from speculating further."

He reached out and handed him an envelope. "Please read this carefully and pass it along to your bosses."

Palmer had heard words like this before. Some had even gone to his bosses previously. After about a year in journalism, he'd come to recognize such subtle or direct threats as confirmation that he was onto a real story. Which only made him pursue it more aggressively. Plus, his network and his family's standing formed a robust shield, making him more or less untouchable.

But the fierce look in this man's eye, and the angry tone in his voice, were as intense as any he could remember.

He opened the envelope slightly, the seal of the kingdom emblazoned on the top of a yellow piece of paper. No doubt some formal letter of protest. He closed the envelope and tucked it into the small bag hanging over his shoulder. He'd need his glasses to read the fine print.

"Mr. Ahmad, as you know, the First Amendment protects us in pursuing our stories. We get to ask questions here."

"*Here?*" Ahmad looked around the room, raising his hands. "You must know you are sitting in Saudi territory at the moment."

For the first time the man smiled, his teeth a gleaming white. But his eyes flared with scorn.

As he always did when confronted, Palmer stiffened his stance. He'd been a scrawny kid, only filling out in his college years through hard work. So he'd learned from his youngest years that you always push back against bullies.

"It's no secret you kill opponents of the regime in other nations. Does this represent the expansion of that approach to the United States?"

Ahmad glared back, smirk gone.

"So you are denying involvement in the senator's disappearance?"

The man shook his head.

"Mr. Knight, I am instructing you to cease mentioning our involvement again. Or disseminating speculation from unnamed sources with an anti-Saudi agenda. Not one more time on your station. Or we will act."

"This is not the way it works in—"

"This *is* the way it works in our kingdom. We have a different culture from yours." He turned around. "You have been warned."

He walked out the door and shut it behind him.

Palmer donned his Ray-Bans, opened the envelope, and glanced at the letter, nearly laughing out loud. Diplomatic gobbledygook stating almost the exact opposite of what he'd said.

Seconds later the man who'd escorted him to the room reentered, along with his warm smile.

CHAPTER 16

———

Washington

"SAM, YOU SHOULD'VE filled us in before doing that interview with the Knight grandkid. You're playin' with goddamn fire."

Tennessee's Shepherd Logan glowered at his colleague, Senator Sam Ireland, as the other senators looked on. They were back in the Marble Room for another late afternoon meeting.

Ireland coughed into his napkin and glared back.

"This isn't my first rodeo, Shep. We all know what I said about Saudi abuses was absolutely true. Hell, someone's already leaked most of it. Duke would've wanted it out there, and as the committee's ranking member, I fully intend to pursue it now that he's gone."

Byron Blue chortled from across the table. "As the committee's next chairman, I'm with you all the way, partner."

An angry Logan shook his head, preparing to spit fire their way. But Gigi Fox laid her hand over his wrist, calming him. The Florida senator was the only one in the chamber who had that effect on him. She may have been the most fiery advocate in the entire body, but she also had a disarmingly tender side.

"Shep, it'll be fine. Lighting a fire under the Saudi angle might help matters."

But then she turned to Ireland, lowering here voice to the rumble they all knew so well.

"Sam, no more going rogue. We are all in this together."

CHAPTER 17

—

Adams Morgan, Neighborhood in Washington, D.C.

"CAN YOU HOLD for NSA Ellrod?"

They always asked it this way, as if it were a toss-up question. When the national security advisor wanted to talk to you, you didn't say no. Especially when she's been feeding you scoop after scoop.

"Of course," Palmer said, sitting at the kitchen table in his Eighteenth Street row house, recovering from a long run.

"Palmer?"

"Yes."

"I can't say much over this line, but the story triggered what we expected."

The Saudis must've been reacting internally to all the speculation he'd aired, but she couldn't just come out and say it.

"So it was helpful?"

"It was helpful."

"Chatter?"

No doubt they had the embassy wired every which way.

"Oh, yes. Lots of it."

"The third country?"

Palmer stood up and walked to the large bay window that looked out onto the bustling street below.

"Indeed."

This Saudi scoop was turning into one of his best stories yet. The entire D.C. press corps was trying to play catch-up but didn't have a clue where Palmer was getting his material. And Ellrod had promised that neither she nor others from the administration would talk to anyone else.

Palmer grinned as he remembered the other reporters butting into his live shot up in Maine. Now they were nowhere in the picture.

"We'd like to share more. See where it goes."

As always, she was calling for a reason. But serving her interests aligned with his.

"I'm all ears."

CHAPTER 18

Washington

THE EMBASSY VISIT weighed on Palmer as he looked into the camera.

Not so much the nasty words. Those weren't new. It was the look on the attaché's face that wouldn't fade. Pure rage, from a guy who was used to getting everything he wanted back at home. This was not idle talk.

The countdown began in his ear. "Ten . . . nine . . . eight . . ."

Palmer guessed that the regime was attuned to the press corps chatter that he was a lightweight. A pretty boy who'd back off when bullied.

". . . five . . . four . . . three . . ."

But in that, they'd be wrong. He *always* stood up to bullies.

". . . two . . . one . . ."

And he was about to stand up in a big way.

"Well-placed sources tell me they've heard nonstop chatter between Saudi officials here in Washington and back in the kingdom. Which only makes our national security folks more suspicious about their involvement in the senator's death."

The late afternoon meeting with the national security advisor had lasted thirty minutes. Just the two of them, walking through what their embassy taps were picking up.

And it was a lot. The Saudis were in an all-out panic. The ambassador was in the dark, demanding to know if leaders back in Riyadh had ordered a hit without telling him. And it was clear that Senator Garber had indeed gleaned reliable intelligence of new Saudi atrocities—and the regime knew it.

Now the anchor turned to Palmer.

"Did the senator have information they were willing to kill him for?"

"My sources tell me he was about to open hearings about new Saudi war crimes in villages in Yemen and other neighboring countries."

"Really?"

"Yes, but it gets even bigger. The senator had been raising alarm bells about the kingdom's use of new tactics to cloak those atrocities from UN and U.S. monitors, and the public."

"So they killed him before he could get this out there?"

"Unclear, but that's one theory they're pursuing."

His mouth dried, forcing him to take a sip of water with the camera rolling. Ahmad would be watching.

"Is that an act of war?" the anchor asked.

Palmer put down his glass and took a deep breath.

"If they can prove that it happened, they'll treat it as one."

CHAPTER 19

———

Washington

PALMER ALWAYS PUT his phone in silent mode overnight. Colleagues said it was nuts, but he valued his sleep enough to take his chances. He slept for only six hours anyway and woke up enough in between to see if he'd missed anything.

On Wednesday morning he rolled over at the sound of his alarm clock and checked his phone.

He jolted straight up.

The small screen told the story: seven missed calls and twenty-three new text messages. Almost all from the studio.

WTF? screamed the first text message, from eight minutes ago, sent by one of his producers. The messages below that, arriving throughout the night, all repeated that same theme. His agent had been the first to text him, at 12:08 a.m.: Palmer, call me right away. This is bad.

Before responding, he looked to see who else had called. A few friends. Mom. Then Dad. And several numbers that looked like they were from CNN, but not from the news side. Then another from Mom.

He checked the most recent CNN message first. It was a man's voice, one he didn't recognize.

"Palmer, this is Jason Joffe, CNN's chief counsel. Please call right away."

He walked into the kitchen in search of coffee as he dialed the number Joffe had left. A man answered on the first ring.

"This is Palmer Knight. Is this Mr. Joffe?"

"It is. Before we discuss anything, know that I am CNN's attorney, not yours."

Which set the tone pretty clearly.

"Um, that's what I assumed. What's going on?"

"Do *you* have an attorney?"

"I have friends who *are* attorneys, but I can't say they are *my* attorney."

Except for a DUI in college, he'd never needed one.

"My advice is to make one of them yours right away."

"Mr. Joffe, what's going on?"

"Mr. Knight, this isn't going to work for you. Get your attorney, then get in here by ten a.m."

"But I'm supposed to start working at nine."

"You're not working today."

"What?" he asked, almost yelling. "What the hell is going on?"

The man muttered something to someone else.

"Turn on your TV."

Palmer picked up the remote from the kitchen counter.

"CNN?"

"Any channel. You're the star of all of them right now."

CHAPTER 20

Columbus

NESTLED INTO THE small coffee shop a block from her law firm, Amity Jones had stopped sipping her pumpkin-flavored latte, glued to the bizarre story now airing on the TV screen for the third time in fifteen minutes.

What a twist to the Duke Garber story.

She recognized the surprising center of the scandal: Palmer Knight, that reporter who always seemed to be a step ahead of the Washington press corps.

She'd always thought he was good-looking, if a little thin. He had a natural charm. Cocky, with an air of entitlement that gave her flashbacks to the silver-spoon elites at Stanford Law School. But even so, his sandy-blond hair and chiseled jaw made for good television.

He'd covered the Court a few times during her term, getting the inside scoop on some big decisions hours before anyone else. He clearly knew someone on the inside, maybe even one of the justices. According to her old boss Justice Gibbons, Knight's grandfather, a longtime senator from Rhode Island, had shepherded several of the older justices onto the bench.

Knight had also been the one all over Senator Garber's death. But the video that kept running made it clear he now was the one in serious trouble.

REPORTER CAUGHT IN SCANDAL, blared the chyron across the bottom.

The video was grainy, but the key elements came through clearly. Dressed casually, Palmer Knight was standing in an alley, a gray building behind him, talking with a shorter man. Seconds into the clip, the man reached into his pocket, pulled out an envelope, and handed it to Knight. Knight opened the envelope to look at what was inside, then placed it into a small handbag hanging over his left shoulder.

"Of course we don't know what's in the envelope," an anchor's voice said as the video ran again. "But when do sources ever pass reporters envelopes like that? In an alley, of all places. Palmer Knight certainly has some explaining to do."

The voice of a woman piped in. "Actually, if he opened the envelope far enough, our people are saying that we might be able to get a better look at its contents. But what I don't understand is why he'd be meeting with a man like that in the first place. Someone that infamous."

On cue, a different photo popped up on the right side of the television screen. Although not a mug shot, it looked like one. A dark-haired man with a broad nose, high cheekbones, olive skin, and stubble on his face to match his buzz cut. Below the photo were the words "Abu Nadel."

Amity recognized the name but couldn't place it.

"Viewers may recall that Abu Nadel is the Yemeni militia leader whom the Saudis have complained about for years. Destroying towns on both sides of the border. Slaughtering women and children indiscriminately. Nadel's militia has blown up countless Saudi transport convoys as they've crossed back and forth over the border and executed anyone they captured."

As the anchor spoke, several video clips of burning villages and trucks filled the screen. The final clip showed five men kneeling in a line, blindfolded, two armed men behind them. Nadel's face then reappeared on the screen alongside footage of Palmer's rendezvous.

Amity took the last sip of her latte. Most days she missed the faster pace of Washington, whether juggling Army Judge Advocate General's Corps cases or Supreme Court briefs. But D.C. could also be rough. Cutthroat, even in the rarefied air of the Supreme Court. You never knew who would blow up on any given day. Today it was Palmer Knight's turn.

On days like today, Columbus felt just fine.

Amity stood up and dropped her empty cup into the garbage. She had another brief to write.

CHAPTER 21

——

Washington

"Please explain what the hell you were thinking."

It was two minutes past ten. Five people were seated around the glass-top conference room table on the corporate wing of CNN headquarters. Palmer had been here twice before: to sign his initial contract, thanks to some high-flying references, and to sign his big re-up after proving his worth.

Those meetings had been all smiles and glad-handing. This was the opposite.

Palmer's heart had been pounding away since he'd first flipped on his kitchen TV. Heat flushed through his body. Distracted by knowing that millions of people were now watching footage of him consorting with a terrorist and by a high-pitched buzz ringing through his ears, he asked Jason Joffe to repeat himself.

"Please," the lawyer said before a long pause. "Explain to us what the hell you were thinking."

Palmer gripped the edge of the table as he leaned forward. But before he could protest the hostile statement—an unnecessary pile-on—his lawyer's hand shot in front of him, nudging him back in his chair.

"Mr. Joffe, it is our contention that Mr. Knight never met with Abu

Nadel. This is a total fabrication, and we fully expect you to stand by your employee."

Several friends he trusted had recommended her, but when they'd met thirty minutes before, Pauline Simko's youth had at first unnerved Palmer. However, a quick wit and palpable confidence had erased his doubts in their brief introductory meeting. She was erasing them further now.

Blond and tan, Joffe looked like a surfer in a dark suit. Two brown-haired men, younger than he was, sat on either side of him, also dressed in dark suits. One was taking notes.

Joffe leaned forward. "Never met with him? Are you kidding? Watch that video."

Outnumbered, Pauline rose higher in her chair. "It is our contention that that video is a fake. Doctored. You're in this business, so you know better than most that it's not difficult to do. We have already hired a specialist to examine it."

Joffe chuckled as Palmer continued to squeeze the table, a better outlet for his anger than blurting out something he would regret.

"Trust me, *we* have an entire building of specialists here, and they've studied every millisecond of that video. The movements. The lighting. Everything's legit. We even looked through past clips of Palmer to see if the image of him here matches any appearances he's made on CNN."

He stopped talking, building momentary suspense.

"And?" Pauline asked.

"Nothing. He's never appeared remotely like this on any broadcast. This looks absolutely real."

"How about in studio?" Palmer asked.

"No. You're almost always seated in studio. Not once have you engaged in a standing conversation from the side."

Palmer caught himself about to nod.

Pauline changed the subject. "Mr. Knight never met with Abu Nadel. He was covering the story *you* asked him to cover, and pursuing leads from reliable, high-placed sources. Hell, you guys ran the stories and aired him live in the studio just last night."

"What's your point?" Joffe asked.

"This is punishment for his coverage of the Saudi angle on the senator's suicide. This is a blatant attack on the free press. You know as well as I what the Saudis are capable of. You should be *defending* your reporter, not throwing him under the bus."

Joffe shook his head as he gestured toward the frozen image of Palmer with Abu Nadel. "C'mon."

"What do you mean, 'C'mon'?" Palmer shot back. "The Saudi embassy guy threatened me when I interviewed him."

Joffe leaned back in his chair, exaggerating a groan.

"We've talked to him as well. He said he was fully cooperative with you even as he told you they weren't involved. You did get to interview him, right?"

"Yes. On background and alone. But he only met with me to issue a threat, not to pursue the story. He clearly made good on his threat."

Joffe reached into his pocket and pulled out an envelope. The seal of Saudi Arabia was emblazoned on its corner.

"But that's not what he wrote in the letter he gave you."

Palmer leaned forward. "Wait—was that the one on my desk?"

"Yes, it was." He shook his head. "Mr. Knight, did you ever read this letter?"

"I did. But it didn't reflect at all the way he talked—"

He took the single piece of paper out of the envelope and pushed it across the desk, laying it flat between Palmer and Pauline.

"Maybe you can edify your lawyer on what it says."

Palmer took out his glasses, put them on, and skimmed the first two sentences again: "While we object to your suggestion that Saudi Arabia was involved in the tragic death of Senator Garber, we will cooperate fully with any reporting you choose to do. As temporary citizens of your country, we respect your First Amendment and the freedom it provides to the American media to pursue the stories you choose."

He looked up, waving the letter in the air. "Like I said, this is a joke."

Pauline grabbed it and started reading, shaking her head.

Joffe glared at her. "I don't see the humor here. They gave you an interview, pledged to cooperate, yet you still blame them for that video?"

Losing ground, Palmer's muscles tensed.

"That letter is a crock. The guy threatened me. Said I was forbidden from running the story. And when I brought up the First Amendment, he said that our constitution didn't apply at their embassy."

"Was anyone there to corroborate your story?"

"No. They said no cameraman."

"And you didn't tape it?"

Taping every conversation was the best practice, so reporters had proof of their work when challenged.

"They wouldn't allow it."

"And did you report to anyone that you were threatened?"

Palmer shook his head. "I didn't. They happen more—"

"So all we have is a letter that you personally accepted, promising full cooperation with your story? Why in the world would they have given that to you if their plan was to do the opposite?"

"For this very moment."

Joffe rolled his eyes.

But it was a good question. Why give him a letter at all? He recalled the room at the embassy. The long wait. The mirror, no doubt of the one-way variety. The fact that the attaché had stayed standing. The handing over of the letter from the attaché's pocket to Palmer's hand. Then placing it into his bag.

Palmer took a deep breath, calming himself.

"Can you play that video one more time?"

Joffe pushed "play" on a small remote.

This time the video looked familiar in a new way. Both men standing. Talking. The handing over of an envelope in a way that looked like a payoff.

Palmer's stomach clenched as he figured it out.

"The video!" He jumped six inches out of his seat. "That's why!"

"Excuse me?" Joffe said.

Pauline lifted an eyebrow as she looked over at her client.

"We were talking, standing up, and then he handed me that letter. Just like in the video where the guy hands me the envelope. They're the same exact set of motions. There was a one-way mirror in that room; they clearly taped the whole thing."

"Taped it? Why?"

Now Palmer gestured toward the screen.

"To generate the content for the concocted scene in that damn video. They didn't take it from old clips of mine. They shot their own clip while I was in that room. It was their own little studio."

Joffe smirked. "Do you know how unhinged you sound right now? We're going to—"

Pauline, now standing up, interrupted.

"We believe any action you take now is premature. This needs to be investigated more deeply."

Joffe sliced the air with the side of his palm.

"Consistent with his contract and our HR policies, we've done enough of an investigation to take preliminary steps. We even gave him his chance to explain himself. But rather than giving me something credible to take to the CEO and the public, he's doubled down on crazy."

He glanced to his left, at the associate who wasn't taking notes. The young man took the hint, picked a manila folder up from his lap, and slid it across the table to Pauline.

"I'm sorry, Mr. Knight, but we must suspend you indefinitely. Please sign here and hand us your materials."

CHAPTER 22

Washington

Shepherd Logan and his wife, Mary, hobbled down the right side of the Washington National Cathedral, stopping at the third pew from the front.

As they slid into the two final spaces in the pew, it was as if their mini-caucus had called another meeting. Next to Mary sat Gigi Fox and her husband, Wally; next to Wally towered Sam Ireland, a lifelong bachelor; and next to Ireland sat the tiny, gray-haired Amanda Blue, who was seated next to her husband, Senator Byron Blue, who dwarfed her.

Gigi reached over and grasped Mary's hand, whispering loudly enough so they both could hear her.

"Mary, it's wonderful to see you. Duke would be so happy knowing you were well enough to be here."

Mary nodded, lips pursed. "Like you, he was always there for all of us." She looked back at Logan and smiled. "So of course I should be here for him."

As she finished her sentence, a murmur crescendoed from the back of the cathedral up to where they sat. Then, like a wave rolling through, everyone stood and looked to the rear of the cathedral. The nation's last four presidents and their spouses—two husbands, two wives—were making their way up the center pew.

Gigi turned to the Logans.

"Even in passing, Duke proves to be one of a kind. This is the first time these four have been together since Janet became president."

Logan chuckled. "And *your* funeral might be the only event that will bring them back together again."

Gigi dismissed the comment with a wave of her hand. "What do you mean by that nonsense?" she asked, winking. "Like Mary, I'm going to out-live them all."

The cathedral's organ blasted its opening notes, and they took their seats again.

Logan frowned as he leafed through the long speaking program.

CHAPTER 23

Washington

"So you believe me, right? I mean, it was your tip, after all. You *know* me."

Palmer found himself on the ground floor of the West Wing, one room past the vice president's office. He had engaged in brief formalities with National Security Advisor Sandra Ellrod and her deputy before cutting to the chase. She had called him minutes after the meeting at CNN.

She smiled.

"We believe you. And you're right: it *was* our tip," Ellrod said. "The story was right on the mark."

"Great."

Palmer leaned back in the chair and exhaled. To have her on his side was a game-changer.

"When are you going to say something?"

"No time soon," she said.

Palmer smiled, waiting for an indication that Ellrod was putting him on. Nothing came but a stern expression.

She was serious.

"What do you mean, 'No time soon'?" he asked, temper mounting.

"Palmer, we simply can't weigh in right now."

"Why the hell not? My entire career—not to mention my good name—is being flushed down the toilet!"

Her grim look didn't flinch.

"This is bigger than you, Palmer."

His body tensed. That damn video was replaying nonstop, and no one was willing to back him up.

"I'm confused. What good could possibly come of my career being destroyed?"

Ellrod leaned forward over her desk.

"The lives of hundreds of thousands of people might be saved. And perhaps the answer to why the great Senator Garber is no longer with us."

There was no way to respond to that.

"So why did you bring me here?"

"The president felt you were entitled to know. And she thought you might be willing to help further."

"Help further?" he asked, exasperated.

Ellrod ignored him and stood up. Her deputy followed suit.

"Come with us. We'll explain."

———

BURIED DEEP WITHIN the White House, the room felt like a CNN studio, but with even more monitors and space-age tech, along with two three-star generals operating them all.

After brief introductions—the two, it turned out, led the Pentagon's cyber war efforts—they played a series of disturbing videos.

The first monitor showed what looked like a wartime rally. Hundreds of masked men hoisting weapons in the air—handguns, rifles, AK-47s— even some swords. On a stage was a smaller man, speaking, yelling, pacing back and forth as the crowd cheered and waved their weapons.

Subtitles appeared below the footage: "We will never stop fighting the kingdom," the man yelled. "And for every life the kingdom takes, we will take five of its women and children." A roar from the crowd. Arms and weapons in the air. Then more militant red meat.

Apparently that speaker followed through on his threats. Because on the next screen over, huts and small homes burned as armed men and boys rushed to and fro. Bodies lay on the ground amid the flames. Others huddled near the ground.

Three other screens aired similar footage: militant rallies, charred towns, injured and dead victims. A close-up on one screen revealed blackened limbs and gleaming organs spilling out. Some of the dead were children.

Palmer leaned away, averting his eyes from the final images.

"What monsters!"

The generals, stone-faced, looked at Palmer. They were either heartless or had seen the videos so many times, they'd become desensitized.

"We agree," Sandra Ellrod said, as stern as before. "If they're real."

Palmer looked back at the bodies. The kids. The armed men.

"They look damn real to me."

"To us too. Many aspects may be. But we're not sure anymore what's real and what's not."

"You're not?"

If this crew didn't know, who the hell did?

One of the generals spoke up. "You ever hear of 'deepfake' videos, sir?"

The term had popped up a lot over the last year.

"Sure. Want to make a politician or celebrity look bad? Make a fake video of them saying something stupid. Or a video of them naked. But they never fool anyone. Too obvious."

"Think bigger, Palmer," Ellrod said. "If weaponized, deepfake videos can go way beyond individuals or politicians."

"Like how big?"

"Think entire countries." Ellrod gestured at the two generals. "The reason you're looking at six stars operating these keyboards is because the weaponization of deepfake technology will soon impact relations between entire nations and carry enormous consequences for our national security."

Palmer looked back at the monitors. "And you think these might be fake?"

"We're highly suspicious. These are now running all the time on Saudi media, in Saudi living rooms, daily. They're being used to justify so much of their hostile activity over the past year."

"But you don't know if they're real?"

"Even a year ago we could tell. As you said, early generations of deep-fakes were easy to spot: they were sloppily doctored videos that were already in the public domain or left some other obvious traces. With artificial intelligence, the Saudis have developed new techniques that are much tougher to detect. We think that's what we're seeing here, but we have no way to prove it."

The general reached for the mouse he'd been operating and moved it slightly. The footage of the war rally froze, and the face of the man on the stage—the one rallying the crowd—took up most of the screen.

"Until perhaps now," he said. "Recognize him?"

Palmer leaned forward and squinted through his lenses, zeroing in on the man's face. He had more facial hair, and was dressed in fatigues, but the resemblance was clear.

"The guy in the video with me. Giving me that envelope."

"Yep."

Palmer recalled the name. "Abu Nadel."

Ellrod shook her head. "Well, that part is less clear. We don't even know if such a person exists."

"An actor?"

"Or an artificial intelligence creation. Make up a bad guy out of whole cloth, create fake videos of atrocities he caused, and use it as a justification for ethnic cleansing and human rights violations on a broad scale."

The second general sat up more stiffly than before. "Or worse: blame atrocities the Saudis themselves are committing on him and his made-up militia group."

Ellrod nodded. "That too."

"So the entire Nadel story line may be false?"

"The entire *insurgency* may be false. But again, it's hard to prove."

Palmer's head spun as the people who were supposed to know every-thing kept using such mealymouthed language.

"Okay. And what does this have to do with Senator Garber's death?"

Ellrod looked back at him gravely.

"Duke was all over this. He was convinced the Saudis were using deep-fakes to justify killing thousands while evading responsibility, and he was about to hold hearings and then hit them hard with sanctions. He wanted us to move more quickly and was about to go public."

Palmer nodded. So the original tip was solid.

"When were the hearings going to be?"

"Next week."

"And who knew about this? The whole committee?"

"No. Only Garber and a few of us. We pushed him to hold off, but he insisted. These hearings were going to be a bombshell."

CHAPTER 24

Washington

A SEA OF more than two thousand faces stared up at Dr. Paden Blackwood from the pews of the Washington National Cathedral.

An awesome sight.

Not only the sheer size of the crowd but the quality. A president, three former presidents, their spouses, eight prime ministers, dozens of foreign members and ambassadors, and hundreds of members of Congress sat before him.

The world's leaders in one room, listening to his every word.

Still, the professor had delivered so many lectures at Harvard and at universities around the world that not a bead of sweat formed as he took in his audience.

There was so much he wanted to tell them. One speech to this gathering could change the planet. Could change the course of history.

But he kept his focus on his lifelong friend. He'd get back to changing the world later.

"Two lads," he declared loudly, followed by a long pause. "A young Mainer from a tiny harbor town and a young Scotsman from a small hamlet on the North Sea. Both sons of simple lobstermen, thrown into the complex and erudite world of Harvard Yard, among hundreds of Andover,

Exeter, and St. Paul's grads. *They'd* grown up reading the *Times*; *we'd* grown up barefoot, fishing and reading with our mums."

Another pause. A few smiles came from what was no doubt a heavy Andover and Exeter crowd.

"Of course, Duke and I hit it off from the start. But I quickly learned that I wasn't unique. He hit it off with everyone he met."

As he ended the sentence, Blackwood looked down at the front row. President Janet Moore, in all black and holding her husband's hand, stared back.

Duke had introduced Blackwood and Moore twice, first during her campaign, then months after her inauguration. He'd urged Duke to run, which would've unlocked huge opportunities for both of them. But it had never happened. So his next hope had been that Duke's close connection to the new president would open up equivalent opportunities.

But it had only taken one conversation for him to know. She was a lightweight. Rigid, with no vision. No long view or sense of history. Not surprisingly, their brief meetings had led to nothing.

He politely smiled as their eyes met. She looked so much older now, with graying hair and exhausted eyes. Much thinner too. Did she even recognize him as he stood before her on the world's biggest stage? Likely not. Beyond her narrow mind, she lacked Duke's interpersonal gifts.

It didn't matter. She'd remember him soon enough, and not because of today's speech.

"From those days, Duke soared, as all his friends knew he was destined to do."

He lifted his hands high in the air, as he did every week in Harvard's largest lecture hall. He reveled in his reputation for spellbinding lectures. Even though he was a med school professor, undergraduates, law students, and others flocked to his course. So broad and pathbreaking was his work— so mind-blowing the subject matter—that credits were doled out even to philosophy and ethics majors who took his class. The world-famous Dr. Blackwood. Harvard's most inspiring orator. Its giant.

He continued.

"A man of his intellect, of his courage, of his commitment to greatness, of his vision, cannot be held back by any obstacle."

As in his lectures, the crowd sat frozen except for their eyes, which followed his long arms as they rose. He recognized the look; even the president appeared spellbound.

"And of course Duke, our great friend, faced obstacles. Again and again. While most at Harvard avoided the war, he enlisted and was badly wounded. When most who were wounded went home, Duke insisted on a second tour. When he lost his first few elections because he told the truth about the war to a country blind to that truth, he never quit. And when he won, he quickly rose to become the nation's most respected senator. And soon after, America's most respected statesman."

Audience members nodded their assent. Even the row of presidents, sufficiently full of themselves to discern the slight, had no choice but to go along.

Blackwood now spread his long, thin arms wide. He aimed to look as large as possible, a technique that pulled his audience further in while also propelling endorphins throughout his own body. He could feel the rush as he reached his full wingspan—a surge of energy for his final burst.

But first, importantly, he lowered the volume. This forced his audience to lean in. To listen more carefully. And as with all the words he spoke, he purposely maintained a trace of a Scottish accent. To Americans, it made him sound more intellectual. More authoritative. Like a king. The same reason he'd always maintained his trimmed white beard.

"And then came the greatest obstacle of all: he lost his sweet Kay." He slowed down, separating each word with a pause. "Far too soon."

He glanced to his left, at the pew of senior senators Duke had introduced him to. Senator Ireland, the tall one with the Rhett Butler mustache, coughing. Senator Shepherd Logan and his recovering wife. Senator Fox, looking at him sternly. The fat one, Blue.

"And then he battled illness himself . . ."

Unlike the president, these senators knew him well, and the role he'd played in their friend's life. They wouldn't like this performance, or that he was speaking at all. Overly careful senators didn't appreciate audacity of this scale.

Then again, they wouldn't say a word. They couldn't.

". . . one that would have ended the lives of most, but one that, like everything else in Duke's life, he conquered."

He upped his volume again while speeding up his pace.

"And how he conquered it. Conquered it all."

He fixed his gaze to the back wall of the cavernous chamber. He let seconds pass. Total silence.

"Duke was a simple man. He never moved from his New Harbor home. Even in his Senate office, there was nothing fancy for visitors to see. No plaques. No honorary degrees. No fancy photos to tout a gold-plated network. No, Duke didn't need those."

He smothered a grin as dozens shifted in their pews, uncomfortable hearing about their own vainglorious furnishings.

"Only images of his beloved Kay, his beloved Maine, and a simple message above Duke's desk. Many of you have seen it: five short words etched into the birch bark and wood he had removed from his Maine woods decades before, early in his journey."

Another pause.

"Five words: 'The obstacle is the path.'"

Seconds more of silence. Then a whisper as he lifted his hands a final time.

"'The obstacle is the path.'"

He lowered his gaze to the flag-draped coffin ten feet in front of him, addressing it directly.

"Friend, paratrooper, senator, statesman, Mainer . . . what a path. What a brilliant path."

As with the end of every lecture, he let his hands fall lifelessly to his sides.

He looked straight down, eyes closed, as if so exhausted, not an ounce of energy remained.

CHAPTER 25

Washington

"EXCUSE ME."

One of the generals picked up the old-school receiver of a beeping desk phone and listened for a few seconds.

"Got it," he grunted, then hung up.

He turned to Ellrod. "We've got sound, ma'am."

She nodded back.

"You've got what?" Palmer asked.

The general didn't answer, instead turning back to his keyboard. After a few keystrokes a new video appeared on the desk's largest monitor.

Palmer slumped in his chair, seeing that he was again at center stage of a concocted setting.

The video was less grainy than the first. Although Palmer didn't recognize the clothes—jeans and a loose-fitting brown parka—it was clearly him sitting in the corner of what looked to be a restaurant or café. He appeared jittery, glancing around the restaurant—toward the counter, the back wall, the main door.

Seconds later, a man walked through the restaurant and sat down across from him. He leaned forward, eyeing him intensely, then uttered some words. Palmer listened, saying nothing back. As quickly as he entered, the visitor got up and left. Then the video ended.

"Who is *that*?" Palmer asked.

"Looks to be Abu Nadel's right-hand man," the general who'd answered the phone said. "One sec."

He pulled up several videos of rallies, zooming in on one man who always stood ramrod straight within feet of Nadel. Definitely the same guy. No doubt the media would make the connection soon too.

"And what's he saying?" Palmer asked.

"Hold on."

The general typed on the keyboard, bringing the video back to the beginning. He replayed it at full volume.

The words the man whispered in Palmer's ear came through clearly: "It's time to proceed."

"They're killing me," Palmer said, his head spinning. "Just killing me. You need to say something."

"We can't," Sandra Ellrod said. "This is a critical opportunity, especially now that they've added sound."

"Opportunity?" Palmer shot back. "Thanks to me! You should thank me by bailing me out."

"Not yet, Palmer. We need more of this if we can get it."

"More?" he asked, forcing a laugh.

"Yes. The more, the better." Ellrod looked at one of the generals. "General, please explain."

The general on his left piped up. "The problem with all the videos we showed you before is they're so well done, we can't be certain as to what's real and what's fake."

Palmer was catching on now. "But we know that *my* videos *are* fake."

"That's the whole point, son. The 'opportunity' is that we are observing a sophisticated deepfake operation as it happens. It's a gold mine of information."

He looked at his colleague, who took over the explanation.

"Our engineers can detect distinct traces from these videos. Not only how they're produced but the precise appearance and movement of Nadel and his colleague, who we suspect are AI creations. We can then match these traces up with other recent videos to affirm that they, too, are fake."

"And you couldn't do this without letting my reputation go up in flames?"

Lips pursed, the general shook his head.

"I'm afraid not. We need videos that we are one hundred percent sure are deepfake. The fact that they included both men is a gift. Sounds too. They're clearly threatened by your story. These videos alone may allow our guys—"

"—and women." Ellrod sat up as she said it.

"—and women . . . to pull the thread out of everything else they're doing, or do so in the future."

"So we just wait?" Palmer asked, throwing up his hands.

"Yes, we do."

CHAPTER 26

—

Mansfield

ALTHOUGH MOM'S BEDROOM provided the best vantage point over the Gentrys' driveway, it could not have been a less comfortable perch for Amity.

Even the first fifteen minutes in the small room spun up painful memories of Mom's struggles. After Dad had died, mired in a deep depression, she'd rarely left home outside of work, forcing Amity and Simon to navigate the ups and downs of childhood—school, boyfriends and girlfriends, sports—on their own.

And her isolation within their small home was even worse. For hours each afternoon and evening, Mom would seal herself in the bedroom, door locked behind her, leaving the two children alone all that time with no inkling of what was happening inside. By the time she was twelve, Amity was making dinner for the three of them every night, leaving Mom's serving outside her door. When she heard the door open and close a second time, she'd gather up the dishes and clean them. Then she'd put Simon to bed.

Mom finally received the help she needed as Amity entered college. And Simon had sworn things were fine all through his high school years. But the bedroom always brought back the darkest moments of those early years.

Mercifully, an unmarked black van pulled up at 8:00 a.m. on the nose. A sedan followed it into the driveway. New York and Ohio plates.

"Told ya," Mom whispered as Amity peered through the thin bedroom curtain that had been hanging there since before she was born. "Same time every week."

"Good work, James Bond," Amity said, relieved she could get to work.

Using her phone, she snapped as many photos as she could. Three people got out of the van—two men and a woman—and a man and a woman climbed out of the sedan. One man from the van and the woman from the car wore lab coats, the bottoms of which fell below their dark parkas.

"You don't recognize any of these people from the hospital?" Amity asked, repeating herself from their phone calls.

"Nope. They're not from around here."

Mom had been a teacher at Mansfield Middle School. Thirty-nine years. Even with her sheltered existence, she knew everyone.

For the next fifteen minutes, two of the men walked back and forth between the house and the van, carrying and wheeling a number of pieces of equipment into the modest two-story home.

"Do they ever leave during the days they visit? Lunch breaks or anything?"

"Not that I've seen. Once they get that equipment in there, we won't see them again until four p.m. Are you really going to stay here all day?"

She removed her phone from her pocket.

"I sure am."

CHAPTER 27

—

Boston, Massachusetts

"WE ALL CHEERED you from the faculty lounge, Dr. Blackwood. You were wonderful."

Dr. Paden Blackwood slowed his pace as the wide-eyed assistant professor with the big glasses and short brown bob opened the door for him, beaming. Side by side, they passed through the grand Harvard Medical School entrance he'd been entering for half a century.

"Why, thank you, young lady," he said, grinning.

He'd met her a number of times, and beyond her shapely figure and attractive smile he remembered being impressed by something she'd said once. But her name escaped him.

"It was a labor of love. He was a good man."

Unfortunately, they were walking at the same pace. With class starting in five minutes, he wanted a moment to himself to gather his thoughts. Despite his eloquence, he was at heart an introvert, so time alone gave him his energy. But she remained over his left shoulder, chirping away.

"I remember seeing him when he visited here," she said, looking up at him through her thick lenses. "It was clear how close you were. So touching."

He maintained a smile even as his stomach knotted. He'd made few mistakes in his life, and her comment reminded him of one. A big one. But at the time, he'd had no way of knowing.

Almost three years ago, Duke had reached out, asking to stop through on the way back to Washington. So they'd made a half day out of it. Duke sat in on one of his lectures, then Blackwood hosted an informal gathering of administrators, faculty, researchers, and graduate students to meet his friend. Given how much money the senator had funneled Harvard's way for a generation of scientific research, they greeted him like the large benefactor he was. Even Harvard's president dropped by.

After all that exposure, the two old friends lunched alone, looking out over Boston from the top of its tallest building. There, Duke told him about the relapse and bleak prognosis. Blackwood was just the second person to know, after the senator's oncologist. And he made sure that there wouldn't be a third. But given what followed, the fact that they'd had such public interactions on campus still haunted him.

Now, walking down the medical school building's corridor, Blackwood forced a full-blown guffaw. "Yes. I was honored to have a U.S. senator sit in on one of my classes. Although I'm not sure he understood a word of it."

"Well, it was a delight to meet him in any case. I'm so sorry for your loss."

"Thank you. But it was the world's loss."

He kept waiting for her to veer away, but she didn't. They both turned a corner, facing down another long hallway.

"How is your latest research going?" she asked. "We're all so excited about it."

"Incredibly well. We are seeing breakthroughs on a weekly basis."

The auditorium was only yards away. With all three sets of double doors open, the hubbub from within the crowded room spilled out into the hallway. More than eight hundred students took his survey course.

"Of course," she said. "I'm doing a few new trials myself. Making some progress as well."

"Good for you," he said as he entered the doorway, not looking back.

He loped down the aisle, students taking their seats as he passed by each row. Once at the bottom of the room, he jogged up five steps onto a small platform and stood behind the classic cherrywood lectern he'd used for years. "Blackwood's pulpit," they called it.

He raised his hands high and wide. The remaining chatter ceased immediately.

"Okay, class," he said, chin out. "Who's ready to change the world?"

CHAPTER 28

——

Cambridge

TWO HOURS AND a quick lunch later, Paden Blackwood sat in the small conference room, huffing.

Even in winter, and at his age, he preferred walking the route between the world's most storied med school and its most concentrated cluster of biotech companies. Going by foot to Cambridge's Kendall Square released energy built up over his ninety-minute lecture, calming him enough so that he could shift his mind and mood to business. The walk also reminded him how far he'd come since he'd first opened BioRevolution thirty years ago. Back then, rent was cheap and the square was nothing more than a few diners, a Laundromat, and a hair salon. Now it was its own small city, teeming with people, sleek glass edifices, and all the trappings of exploding profits.

With a large monitor on one end of the oval glass-top conference room table, two men and two women looked at him as they presented data one at a time. Snow flurries fell outside the room's large, tinted windows.

Neena Vora, BioRevolution's senior research director and Blackwood's star student from two decades ago, kicked off the reports.

"Trial group one continues to show great promise, Doctor. Eighty-five percent of the group displays a recovery level between five and ten. Averaging seven-point-two. That mix works on any number of pathogens."

"And the control group?"

Unlike his lectures, Dr. Blackwood managed meetings with short, clipped sentences and rapid-fire questions.

"Not well. Only one has lived, and she has only weeks left."

"Side effects?"

"Severe in the short term. Two didn't survive them. But we still anticipate that they will fade for most subjects."

"That is wonderful news, Neena." He sat up and grinned as he scanned all four researchers. "What was once called a 'moon shot' will be basic treatment within a year."

He looked to the next figure down the table, his newest researcher. The large man with the boyish face and blond hair peered back nervously through his square, thick glasses.

"Nathan, how proceeds trial group two?" Blackwood asked.

"It's been a struggle, Professor."

Blackwood shook his head. "Still? How so?"

"Counts are decreasing among most—"

"Well, that's good. What's the struggle?"

"It's the side effects. We haven't figured out how to avoid permanent changes to the strands, which might have unpredictable next-generation impacts."

Blackwood hunched over, grunting.

"Young Nathan, how many times have I told you: I'm the one to worry about those impacts. Your job is simply to make sure the treatment eliminates the pathogen in the present."

"It does that. But, Professor, the complexities of the change—"

Bang.

Blackwood banged his fist on the table to cut Nathan off in mid-sentence. Blackwood wasn't angry. Getting angry meant he'd lost control, and his therapist had taught him techniques for maintaining control. But this was a pivotal moment. With three others looking on, his newest researcher was questioning him. Second-guessing a critical component of their work. Indeed, the raising of such doubts in the broader community was the primary reason people were suffering and dying. Needlessly dying.

The four researchers stared in his direction, saying nothing. Nathan had never seen the fist slam before. Neena had, a number of years ago. She'd pushed back far more forcefully than Nathan had just done. But after a long harangue she'd learned. She never second-guessed again.

"Nathan?" Blackwood said quietly, interrupting seconds of silence.

"Yes, Professor," the researcher said, his lips quivering.

"Do you know who I am?" he asked calmly.

"Of course, Professor."

"Do you know what I teach? All that I've published?"

"Of course."

"And you knew all those things when I offered you this position, correct?"

"Of course, Professor."

"And you are here to learn from me?"

"Yes, sir."

"Well, do you think you have the knowledge, the experience, the sensibility, to question me?"

Nathan paused before answering. The tone of the question meant that there was only one correct answer. But that answer also would alter his future work. And the nature of the discussion in meetings like this.

Which was why Blackwood savored the pause. He wanted the young man's response to come after proper and thoughtful deliberation about all that was at stake. To assure what had just happened would never happen again.

"No, Professor." Nathan's thin blond hair shook as he answered, then he looked down. "I do not."

Blackwood smiled. "Thank you, Nathan. Please continue with your successful work."

He looked at the other woman sitting at the table.

"Now, Susanna, tell me about the third trial group."

CHAPTER 29

—

Mansfield

"Haven't you gotten enough by now?"

Amity rolled her eyes. Over the course of the morning and early afternoon, from the two windows overlooking the Gentrys' driveway and front door, she'd captured photos of every aspect of the odd visit. And throughout it all, she'd had to tamp down Mom's concern that they were being too nosy.

"No, Mom, I haven't. Please, just let me do my thing."

The task brought Amity back to her first mission in Afghanistan, on the outskirts of Kabul, where she conducted extensive surveillance. Hours of boredom interrupted by seconds of excitement and terror, week after week, all coming only months after graduation. While her target here wouldn't fire back, several times a visitor looked in Amity's direction, forcing her to duck beneath the windowsill or leap to the side.

Helpfully, the war zone experience had disciplined her to maintain focus through both the monotony and Mom's tut-tutting. And she knew to study and document every detail of a scene—details most would look right over. So, from the bedroom window, she snapped close-ups of the two vehicles and their license plates. She captured the faces of each visitor from a number of angles. She zoomed in closely on their clothes. She took a picture of each piece of equipment they lugged into the house and shot another round of photos as they packed up to leave.

"What are you going to do with all this?" Mom asked after coming back into the room shortly before four.

"Figure out what's going on, that's all. Wouldn't it be nice to get you some of whatever treatment he's gotten?"

As with everything else, Amity was more eager to help Mom than she was to help herself. Amity was the one who began scouring the country for experimental treatments, to no avail. Then after Mom first mentioned that their young neighbor had undergone some type of miracle cure, Amity had obsessed about learning more. The more hush-hush things got, the more she wanted to get to the bottom of it. Dr. Stumbo himself had looked nervous as hell when Amity first asked about Colin Gentry.

"And how are you going to do that?"

The wooden front door of the neighbor's house slammed shut.

"Hold on," Amity said, peering above the windowsill.

A large blond man in a white lab coat wheeled a bulky piece of equipment back to the van. As he passed its rear bumper, he looked up, squinting.

"Shit." Amity ducked back down.

"Great. Did someone see you?" Mom asked from the rear of the bedroom.

"I don't think so, but I guess we'll find out."

Metal crashed into metal as the van doors closed. An engine started, followed by another.

"They must be done. Gotta run."

She pecked Mom on the cheek, pulled her hair back into a ponytail, and jogged down the stairs.

———

AFTER AN HOUR of driving, Amity had only seconds to make up her mind.

Near Columbus, the car shifted over a few lanes, looking to turn off I-71 in the direction of the airport.

But the van hadn't budged from the fast lane. It was still heading south.

They were splitting up.

The van had out-of-state plates and contained all the equipment. The car was less unique. With Ohio plates, it could even be a rental.

She went with the van.

Several car lengths apart, they headed south, curled west around downtown Columbus, then veered south again, still on I-71, and headed toward Cincinnati.

CHAPTER 30

Washington

"WE CAN'T THANK you enough for your patience, Palmer."

Even with all his contacts, it was the first time Palmer had been in the Oval Office. Or in any intimate meeting with the president of the United States. Which meant things were serious.

They were seated on cream-colored couches facing each other, with NSA Ellrod standing and one of the generals from the Situation Room seated in a chair to the side.

The president continued.

"Duke was one of the last of a generation who believed politics is public service. Your granddad's generation. And he was such a resource to me and so many others. What a loss to our nation."

A spiderweb of wrinkles emanated from the president's eyes, and streaks of gray peppered her otherwise raven hair. She was a good deal thinner than when she'd been elected. But while Janet Moore may have aged noticeably in recent years, her energy and intensity had never faded, just as her stately posture had never slackened.

"This can't go on for much longer, Madam President," Palmer said, repeating the demand he'd made the prior afternoon that had led to this face-to-face meeting. "It sounds like you've learned all you need to call the Saudis out for what they're doing and shut it down."

She shook her head, her blue eyes piercing Palmer's. "Not quite. We're not ready yet."

Another cryptic line.

"Now what?" Palmer asked, more sharply than he'd intended.

"Sandy, tell him."

Ellrod took a step forward, gripping the wooden back of the chair in front of her.

"There's one more thing our intel folks picked up about the Saudis' use of deepfakes."

"Worse than slaughtering people?"

"No, but related." She paused, looked at the president, then looked back. The chair creaked under her weight as she gripped tighter. "*We're* next."

"'We'?"

"Yes. They're working on a plan to use deepfake to do great harm to the United States."

"How?"

"We're not sure yet. It could be targeting the president and political leaders here. Or our military. We're desperately trying to figure it out. So was Senator Garber. Their goal is to destabilize us so we can no longer challenge what they're doing."

"Including," the president interjected, "making sure I don't get reelected, because I've stood up to them."

Palmer waved his hand. "C'mon, people will see through bullshit like that. They can't harm the United States—or *you*—with fake videos."

The president sat up straight, now glaring.

"Mr. Knight, are you paying attention to the world we live in?" Her harsh tone made it clear she didn't want an answer. "Timed right, a video making it look like our troops are committing atrocities in some foreign country, or that police are doing so here, or that I'm doing God knows what with a man or woman, will have been viewed millions of times before we can intervene. People believe what they see, and running around screaming

'Fake video!' after something goes viral doesn't convince them otherwise. Just look at your own predicament!"

Leaning forward, her eyes blazing with intensity, she didn't look tired anymore. And she was damn persuasive. With partisan deadlock in Washington, her reelection was going to be a tight race. The foreign enemies she'd tangled with could very well interfere. And, in a close election, that could make the difference.

So Palmer changed topics.

"And you still think they killed the senator over this?"

Her shoulders sagged. "We can't say. The timing of it all is highly suspicious. We have no smoking gun from the chatter following your stories. Yet."

For the first time it dawned on Palmer. "So I'm being deepfaked about a story that might not have been accurate?"

"I said 'yet,' Mr. Knight. I can tell you that they're panicking about the fact that they're being connected to his death so publicly."

"Hence the attacks on me."

"Right."

They sat in silence for a few seconds. Then Ellrod stepped away from behind the chair.

"Palmer, we can't do exactly what you want. We need more time. But we can get you out of the spotlight."

The president and general both nodded. They had clearly discussed this before Palmer arrived.

"Anything will help. I'm all ears."

CHAPTER 31

Ohio/Kentucky/Tennessee

AMITY HAD DRIVEN to Cincinnati a number of times in college and once since she'd moved back. Knowing the Queen City as she did, and that she was already a hundred miles from her Columbus apartment, she hoped that the van was heading to the world-class children's hospital there, ten miles north of downtown. That would allow her to get back to Columbus at a reasonable hour.

But the van sped right past the exit, then past the entire city.

She followed it into Kentucky across the decaying double-decker bridge that spanned the Ohio River. With the sun setting downriver to her right, the van switched over to I-75 as it left the outskirts of metropolitan Cincinnati and entered the rolling snow-frosted hills of rural Kentucky. Maybe they were headed to Lexington, as there were major hospitals there as well.

But an hour later the van sped by all the Lexington exits.

With no moon out, the black sky darkened the steep hillsides along the highway.

Amity was hours from home. If she was going to make it back in time for work the next morning, this was her point of no return.

She'd already driven so far. She'd already sacrificed a day—at a time when Mom had only months to live.

So she kept going.

Maybe they'd stop in Knoxville, the next big city off I-75.

She hoped so, anyway.

———

SO MUCH FOR Knoxville.

Twenty miles from the Tennessee border, in what felt like the middle of nowhere, the van pulled off the highway.

A small town called Corbin.

At first Amity assumed they were stopping for the night. A Motel 6 and a Ramada Inn sat right off the exit, along with a Cracker Barrel, a Taco Bell, and some gas stations. But after the driver filled up the van, it headed past both motels and right out of town. Amity, still at half a tank, had idled at a gas station across the street, then followed well behind.

They wound their way along a state highway, up and down steep hills, heading generally southeast by way of endless curves and more towns the size of tiny Corbin. She kept her distance, worried that the smaller highway would make her pursuit easy to detect.

Through the darkness, the small sign announcing the Tennessee border emerged at the last moment. The more impressive welcome came from the large tunnel cutting through a miles-long mountain. After the tunnel and a town called Tazewell, the road narrowed further as its curves and hills intensified.

Amity prided herself on her long-distance driving stamina, but she was fading, yawning every few minutes. She'd finished her last Diet Coke before Cincinnati and desperately needed another one.

After another thirty minutes, the van finally pulled off the highway.

She looked twice at the sign.

Bean Station.

Odd name for a town.

Her car's digital map indicated it sat on the edge of a body of water named Cherokee Lake. It was too dark for her to see it in detail, but Bean Station was at best a small resort town. Definitely not the site of a major hospital doing the type of cutting-edge research that would have saved Colin Gentry's life.

A few hundred yards off the exit, the van pulled into the driveway of a ragtag one-story motel. A large sign on its roof displayed its name: the Cherokee Inn. After parking, the two men and the woman walked across the small lot to the lobby, each carrying a duffel bag. They were done for the night.

Amity got out of the car, phone back in camera mode.

CHAPTER 32

Bean Station, Tennessee

A BRIGHT LIGHT warmed Amity's eyelids.

Strange. She always kept the shades of her apartment shut tight to keep the room pitch-black. Light never seeped through.

She opened her eyes, the initial view as blurry as always when her glasses were off. In seconds the contours of her windshield came into focus. She wasn't in her apartment at all.

She looked to her left. A mostly empty parking lot and a long one-story wooden building with a red roof. She squinted at a sign at the roof's center but couldn't make out the letters. She reached for her glasses in the center console, put them on, and looked again.

The Cherokee Inn.

The long drive was a blur, but now she remembered its end point. A small town in the hills of Tennessee, near a lake, in the parking lot of a motel. Then she recalled why she'd driven all those hours.

She glanced to her right. Good. The van was still there.

She looked at her phone: 6:50 a.m. An hour later than her normal wake-up time.

One text from Mom: Where are you? Hope you're safe.

It was in response to a text she'd sent around 11:00 p.m.: Good night.

Mom was a worrier, so Amity texted her back right away.

`All good. Safe and sound.`

The thoughts that had consumed her as she'd fallen asleep rushed back now: this van had been making some type of house call at the Gentrys', in Mansfield, every week. They started their work at 8:00 a.m. each time. And whatever they did inside took about eight hours. Given its remote destination, this drive was not destined for a hospital or medical facility, as she'd first assumed.

It was another house call. Likely at 8:00 a.m.

Her stomach rumbled with hunger and she craved a Diet Coke. But she didn't want to risk losing the van. So she'd wait until 8:00, watch where it went, then take her break.

Minutes later the motel's front door opened. Amity slumped lower in her seat to avoid being seen. An elderly couple hobbled out, a man exiting first, followed by a woman using a cane. They walked to the first car in the lot, an old station wagon parked in a handicapped space. The man opened the door for the woman, then climbed in the driver's seat and drove away.

Ten minutes after that, a young couple bounded out the front door, hopped on a Harley, and roared off the lot.

Minutes passed without the door moving again.

Seven thirty.

Seven forty.

She was so famished, the swirling of fluids inside gushed louder than her breathing.

Seven fifty.

Maybe she was wrong. No 8:00 a.m. house call after all. She'd have to risk grabbing a bite to eat.

Another minute passed, then the motel door opened.

Amity slumped down in her seat again.

The two men and the woman walked out briskly, duffel bags in hand, straight to the van. A minute later they drove off the lot. Amity waited thirty seconds to start the car, then exited the lot as well.

A couple blocks down, the van turned left, heading up a small road into the dark green mountains looming above. She followed, but slowly, keeping the van in sight as she navigated a series of tight, steep curves through dense woods of white pine, walnut, oak, and hickory. Occasional breaks in the trees revealed stunning views of the sun-kissed lake below.

After several miles, the road leveled out for a few hundred yards before plunging back into a steep descent—same curves, same woods, same views.

Minutes later, with the lake not far below the road, the van's brake lights blinked several times. Amity pumped her brakes as well. The van, now at a complete stop, waited a few seconds, then took a left off the road.

With no traffic coming the other way, Amity stayed still, guessing that a security gate had been opening as the van waited.

Once the van disappeared, she angled her rearview mirror to the left and drove slowly down the hill. She squeezed the steering wheel tight to combat the butterflies in her stomach: she'd invested an entire day and risked the ire of her bosses for this moment. Rather than turning, or even pausing, she passed at a steady speed, affording a long look in the mirror.

As she'd assumed, there was a black-and-yellow security gate blocking the small road. To its left was a wooden guardhouse, along with a sign in front.

Cherokee Terrace.

It wasn't an individual driveway but an entire gated community.

Her breaths slowed as she navigated two more curves before the road dead-ended at a bank of large pines. She turned around and put her car in park, taking a moment to think through the mounting obstacles.

———

AMITY STEPPED INTO the dense forest of pine trees, making her way from the road, parallel to the lake. The damp ground soaked through her sneakers and caked the lower half of her blue jeans.

She pushed forward.

A quick view of Google Maps showed that the fancy homes of Cherokee Terrace sat close to the lakeshore, so at some point her off-road trek would intersect with them.

Sure enough, after fifteen minutes, the red angled roof of the first lake house came into view through the trees. She picked up the pace, weaving between trunks, rocks, and thick bushes, concentrating to maintain her footing on the wet leaves and loose ground. It all felt like the rugged-terrain training courses she'd endured in boot camp.

The moment of excitement ended instantly as she spotted a twelve-foot-high metal fence running from left to right all the way down to the lake. Even worse than its height, a wire ran along the top of the fence. Electrified, no doubt.

Fifteen minutes later she was back on the road, brainstorming.

Plan A was dead. Now what the heck was plan B?

CHAPTER 33

Washington

IN A NEARLY empty hearing room, it felt like such a hollow gesture.

But Chairman Shepherd Logan, a stickler for formality and tradition, banged the gavel hard against the wooden desk to call the morning subcommittee meeting to order.

Only three of his colleagues had even bothered to show up. Even Gigi, the ranking member, wasn't there: a memorial event in Florida had pulled her away. Duke's seat, immediately to his right, sat empty. This left only a few of the more junior senators in seats to his far left and right.

Appropriations. Armed Services. Judiciary. Foreign Relations. Intel. Those were the glamour committees whose meetings always packed the room, usually accompanied by rows of television cameras. They were the assignments members clamored for. The committees where it took decades in the trenches to emerge as chair.

Not this subcommittee. A dozen people in the room actually constituted a decent crowd. No media and no one from the general public. Just Senate and administrative staff—and lobbyists with monetary interests in the various topics of the day.

Logan cleared his throat and kicked things off.

"First on today's agenda is an update on the USDA's Animal and Plant Health Inspection Service request for the year."

Because it was part of the Appropriations Committee, the subcommittee he chaired allocated billions of dollars. But because so much of its jurisdiction involved mundane topics, the scale and gravity of its work was cloaked beneath painfully dull presentations and reports.

Looking no older than forty, a deputy assistant secretary of agriculture spent twenty minutes walking through the Department of Agriculture's Animal and Plant Health Inspection Service process and budget needs. After she was done, a first-term senator from Iowa read a scripted statement, then asked a series of questions, making clear he was in the pocket of some corporate seed interests. Senator Logan looked on patiently until the senator's time was up.

"Thank you for that presentation and for your excellent questions, Senator." He looked to his left and right as if he was surrounded by colleagues. "Next on our agenda is the rural utilities division's budget request for next year."

A gray-haired, bespectacled man in a tacky tan suit approached the table and began his presentation. After ten minutes, as the presenter was wrapping up, Logan heard shuffling behind him. A first-term senator from Oklahoma scrambled to his seat, a young staffer in tow.

"Mr. Chairman," the senator said as he sat down, far too loudly, because his mouth was an inch from the mic.

"Thank you for joining us, Senator," Logan said with an eye roll. Showing up late, listening to nothing, then reading a statement to satisfy the interest group that drafted it was beneath the dignity of the Senate. But to the newbies, that was standard operating procedure. "Go right ahead."

"Thank you, Mr. Chairman. I'd like to make a statement on this topic."

"I'm sure you do, Senator," Logan said.

The curly-haired Oklahoma senator read prepared remarks for six minutes, not a question in sight, before Logan dismissed the witness. The senator left as noisily as he'd entered.

The two topics that followed involved an update on the Department of

Agriculture's buildings and facilities across the country and its foreign marketing plan for the coming year. Ten minutes of comments for each, but so dry and apolitical, no senator offered even a comment.

After those wrapped up, only one senator remained in the room, along with five people in the gallery.

When he was younger, Logan likely would've left as well. But now he knew better.

Of all the topics within this subcommittee's jurisdiction, the final one on the agenda was the biggie. The one with national and global consequences that would last far beyond any of their lifetimes. The one that attracted offers of big campaign money that he was always turning away. The one that had convinced him to accept what was viewed as a dreary backwater subcommittee chairmanship and that had kept Gigi and Duke and Sam and Byron on board despite far better options.

The one that had been at the heart of the deal.

"Good to see you again, Dr. Driscoll," Logan said, a rare smile lifting jowls that had grown more prominent with age. "Please come forward and let us know what the good folks of the FDA are working on."

FDA director Don Driscoll—as thin a man as Logan had ever seen—hobbled up to the table. After taking his seat and offering a polite Texas greeting, he opened a thick binder and presented his usual bone-dry overview of his agency's work.

The remaining senator ducked out in the first half of the presentation, but Logan took in every word. Pleased.

Everything was still moving forward.

CHAPTER 34

———

Bean Station

Tackle box. Fishing rod. Hat. Windbreaker.

With a quick stop in a run-down bait-and-tackle shop not far from the inn, Amity picked up enough supplies to look the part. Only her sneakers were out of place, but all the boots for sale would've slowed her down.

Donning the gear took her back to the good old days at North Lake Park, only minutes from home and the site of their perfect Sunday afternoons together. Dad would tie a line around a rubber worm for Simon but let Amity fish with a real hook. They'd haul in mostly bluegill with an occasional bass, then hit the Dairy Queen on the way home.

With that memory in her mind, Amity lowered herself into a twelve-foot angler's kayak and shoved off from the state park where she'd rented it for fifty dollars cash.

She had four hours.

Cherokee Lake was a long, narrow reservoir snaking diagonally northeast, so the paddle to Cherokee Terrace was a lot straighter than the drive.

The early morning wind having died down, the glassy water now created a mirror image of the tree-lined mountains surrounding the lake. A park ranger had explained that all boats were pulled off the lake in the winter, so each stroke of her paddle broke the otherwise perfect silence.

Twenty minutes in, after a long section of thick woods, the same house she'd seen from her abbreviated hike emerged on her left side. Red roof and cedar walls, with a wide wooden deck overlooking the lake from high above. A well-kept yard sloped down to the water's edge, bisected by a stone pathway leading to a long dock.

Lights were on in the large bay windows behind the deck, so she kept paddling while angling toward the shore. Her new fishing rod hung out the side of the kayak, its baitless line trolling behind.

Another dense pack of trees followed the yard, then a second house identical to the first. Its lights were also on.

She kept paddling.

The fifth lake house was smaller and older than the others and sat far closer to the water. It was pitch-black within.

Nobody home. Finally.

She eased the kayak ashore at the next bank of trees.

———

AFTER TRUDGING UP the tree line, she reached the paved private road connecting the lake houses. From the map online, she knew there were five houses to the right, farther down the hill, along with the five houses she'd paddled by.

She headed to the right, in the opposite direction of the guardhouse, looking for the van or any sign of who lived here.

The street was empty and all five yards spotless. Worse, there were no identifying marks on any of the houses she passed—neither names nor numbers. And no mailboxes to snatch mail from. No van, either—not parked on the street or in a driveway.

Past the last house, on the other side of the street from the lake, were two tennis courts and a small clubhouse. The lights looked to be out inside, presenting the best opportunity she would get. She glanced in both directions and, seeing nobody, approached the clubhouse door. She turned the silver knob, opened the door, and went inside.

The small lobby within had three doors, one dead ahead, one on the right, one on the left, each with a square window at eye level. The right door's window revealed a small workout room inside—some treadmills, a variety of weight machines, and a few exercise bikes. The other two doors opened into locker rooms. The one on the left was larger, so she entered it.

A dark hallway led past a set of showers, toilets and urinals along the left side, and ended in a square room with lockers on three of its walls. Like the houses outside, the lockers were numbered but with no identifying names. They were all locked.

She stepped back into the hallway and toward the door, when the click of a doorknob broke the silence, followed by male voices. Twenty feet in front of her, the locker room door cracked open.

———

"HOPIN' IT'S NOT too slick to play."

In twin Tennessee twangs, the two men had caught up on family and politics as they shaved. Then they turned to tennis.

"Oughta be fine. This new surface dries pretty fast."

Amity huddled in the shower only feet from them behind a thin plastic curtain, not making a sound. The curtain was mercifully opaque.

"I hope so. The added fees weren't cheap."

"No, they weren't." The man laughed as he said it. Country club humor.

Amity looked down, first noticing a thin trail of brown water spiraling from her mud-stained sneakers into the drain. Had she tracked mud along the bathroom floor and up to the shower? The hair on her arms stood on end.

"Well, it better be ready, because I need to get some strokes in."

"That's right, you got the quarters this weekend, don'tcha."

"Sure do."

"Nice. I bowed out last weekend."

"I saw that. Two sets and done, huh?"

"Yep. Don't let his age fool you: the old man still has a wicked forehand."

"Yeah, I know." He laughed again.

"And he moves quick when he needs to."

"You wouldn't know it. I swear he needs a walker."

"Not on the court, he doesn't."

The rush of water ceased, leading to seconds of silence. Amity held still, her heart thudding against her rib cage.

"Hey." The voice was louder, making clear the speaker was facing the shower, not the sink.

She crouched down, bracing for the curtain to open.

The other man gargled, then spit out loud.

"What?" he answered, water or mouthwash still in his mouth.

"Look."

Another long pause.

She clenched her fists, poised to jump through the curtain and run past—or through—whoever was there. One key lesson from hand-to-hand combat drills had been that the first mover almost always wins.

"You dragged your backyard into this place. Might want to take your boots off next time."

"Whoops. How did . . . ? Ah, I'll get it when we're done . . ."

Then came another gargle, followed by more forceful spitting and some butchered words she couldn't understand.

"By the way, who else is left in?"

"I know Winters is. Jacobs too. But I'm not sure who's playing who. Check next to the big board."

She typed the words into her phone.

More silence, followed by the rush of aerosol.

"Speaking of the old man, how's *she* doing?"

"Who?"

He gargled again while uttering a word, presumably a woman's name. The initial syllable was inaudible, but the name sounded like it ended in *ree*. Carrie? Terry? Sherry?

"I hear good."

"Incredible. Six months ago they thought she was a goner."

"I know. Hard to believe. She looks as sick as she did then, but they say she's doing better. Back to her daily walks, even. I saw her yesterday before dinner, hobbling along the road like a zombie."

"Be nice, man. It's truly a miracle she's walking at all."

"Miracle? More like the best connections you can find. Membership has its privileges."

Another laugh.

"True."

"Maybe you should take it easy on the old man this weekend in case you ever get sick."

———

THEY CHITCHATTED MORE in the locker room as they donned their tennis attire, then walked back past the showers and out the door.

Amity waited another five minutes before stepping out of the shower. The guy on the left had been right: the dirt she'd left on the tile floor was a speck compared to the sludge dragged in by the guy at the second sink.

The "old man" . . . His sick wife's daily walk . . . The "big board" . . .

Enough nuggets to give her some direction.

Amity peered out the clubhouse door. Seeing no one nearby, she stepped back outside.

The rhythmic pop of taut racket strings striking a tennis ball echoed from the side. She followed a thin, tree-lined path around the small building toward the sound. Fortunately, as she turned the corner, the trees to the left obstructed the view from the courts.

To the right, a sloped roof angled down from the side of the building. Under it were three rows of long benches facing the courts. A few yards behind the benches were some high round tables surrounded by tall stools. Beyond the tables, a drink and snack bar hugged up against the building, with a smattering of posters—tennis stars in action—on the wall itself.

All in all, a typical tennis clubhouse. But based on what the two men in the locker room had said, she was looking for something specific.

Amity narrowed her eyes and scanned the wall more closely. Between two of the posters, there it was: the familiar bracket of a tournament. And below it, the "big board": a club challenge ladder, with the competing tennis players numbered one through ten.

Finally.

Names.

Standing on the path, she took out her phone to photograph the two lists, but the writing was too small to capture.

Amity looked back to her left. The two men were so consumed with their game they weren't looking her way. She tiptoed another ten feet along the path, reaching the last point before the row of trees ended.

She raised her phone again, zoomed in, and grabbed separate shots of the tournament bracket and the club challenge ladder.

"Hey!"

The loud, grating voice howled from the left. She whipped her head around to see one of the tennis players kneeling over to pick up a ball. From the low vantage point, he'd spotted her through gaps between the thin tree trunks.

"Hey!" he yelled again. "Who the hell are you? What do you think you're doing?"

With no good answer, she shoved her phone into her pocket, whirled to her right, and sprinted down the path.

"Some redhead was standing there taking photos," the man yelled back at the other player. "Call Security."

She raced past the clubhouse and toward the road. With her head start, she knew she'd outrun the two tennis players; she'd always outrun most of the guys in her unit, whether on a flat surface or through rough terrain, and she'd been religious about staying in shape.

Her bigger worry was getting back to the kayak before security from the guardhouse cut off her path. Pursuit was all about geometry: good angles topped speed every time.

She sprinted across the road and past the first house. Not a person in sight but loud yelling from behind her. Seconds later, tires screeched from up the hill. She darted into the yard of the second house, then ducked into the first line of trees just as a black pickup with a flashing yellow siren flew down the hill. She ran farther into the woods as the truck's tires squealed again, followed by more shouts back and forth.

"She ran that way!"

The wet leaves, mud, and steep angle forced her to half run, half slide down the hilly woods. She twice slipped to the ground, soaking her jeans all the way through. While cutting through the woods was slower going, it kept her out of sight.

She slid to a stop a few feet from the lake's edge and scanned the sloping yard in front of her. Nobody there. The kayak was three houses away. Still worried they could cut her off, she made a break for it even though she'd be exposed.

"There she is! Down there."

At the top of the yard, a tall man dressed in a black and yellow outfit sprinted at an angle of attack down the grassy hill. Fast. The tennis players lagged behind.

She reached the next patch of heavy woods, then dodged trees and some large rocks before entering the next yard. Mud squished and sticks crackled behind her as the tall guard entered the woods she'd just exited.

As she ran full speed across the second yard, only feet from the lake's edge, she heard a noise.

She glanced over her right shoulder.

Only feet from her, a much bigger man, bald and with a hooknose, raced her way.

Unlike the guards, he was as fast as she was, and aiming in precisely the right direction to take her down.

His thick shoulder collided into her right hip with brute force, knocking her legs out from under her and sending the left side of her body—from her head down to her ankle—crashing to the lawn.

CHAPTER 35

—

Cambridge

"HISTORIC!"

Paden Blackwood rarely laughed out loud, but back at BioRevolution's headquarters after a morning seminar, he couldn't contain his elation about their best outcome so far.

Neena Vora, his research director, flashed a wide smile back.

"It truly is, Doctor," she said, gesturing at the papers in the manila folder he'd just reviewed. "The last set of scans are encouraging."

"Encouraging?" He cackled, waving the case file in the air. "The boy is one hundred percent clean. Once only weeks away from death, and now all the malignant cells are gone. We are a step closer to altering the human life cycle."

Neena nodded before her expression hardened.

"Neena, what's wrong?"

"Something else has come up from the visit."

"What is it?"

"They were followed."

His good mood cratered. He closed his eyes, taking three deep breaths to diminish his volcanic temper in the way his therapist had suggested. He laid the file on the conference room table so as not to throw it.

"Followed?" he asked, baring his teeth. "Where? By whom?"

"It looks like a nosy neighbor followed the team from Mansfield to Tennessee."

"A nosy neighbor, you say?" He controlled his tone to subdue his anger. "How could they allow themselves to be followed?"

"I don't know, Doctor. But Quinn has her now."

"Good. Who is she?"

"It looks like she's a lawyer from Columbus. An accomplished one."

"Accomplished how?"

"Our research found that she clerked for the Supreme Court last year."

His pulse quickened.

"Neena," he said through a tight smile. "A former Supreme Court clerk is not a mere nosy neighbor."

"Understood. But her mother lives next door to the Gentry family. And she must have asked her daughter about it."

"And then this daughter followed the team from Mansfield to Tennessee?"

"She did."

"Five hundred miles?"

Neena stared back in silence.

"Does she know where they went?"

Neena's round, blinking eyes answered his question. "She got inside before Quinn apprehended her."

"And do you know if she relayed that information to anyone?"

"We know she had pictures on her phone."

"Pictures of what?"

"The inn where the team stays there. The van and our research team. And she took some from Tennessee. But we found no messages or phone calls relaying that information to anyone."

"No messages at all?"

"She texted her mother this morning. But only that she was safe. No location."

"And you say Quinn has her now?"

"Yes. They're heading back but want to know what to do with her."

"Good. Tell them to bring her here."

"Okay," she said, letting out a long breath.

Blackwell knew his top researcher well, her strengths and weaknesses. Neena was a true believer, committed to their research and willing to ignore government obstacles if it served their mission of finding cures. For her, the greater good of healing people justified skirting rules and laws shaped by a flawed political system.

But she was too prudish about violence. She was a doctor through and through, so harming people could not be justified. It was the one thing that might drive her away from their work.

So he kept the worst of what he and Quinn did hidden from her.

CHAPTER 36

Tennessee

TENNESSEE'S BACKROADS WERE a lot rougher when you were tied up in the back of a van.

With thick rope binding Amity's ankles and plastic zip ties wrenching her hands behind her, every swerve rolled her back and forth across the floor of the vehicle, behind the rear seat. The sharpest curves tossed her into the sides of the van, and every brake or pump of the gas pedal sent her tumbling forward or back.

After the brutal tackle by the big bald guy, there'd been no way to resist. He'd walked her back up the hill to a van—a different van than the one she'd followed—as the two tennis players and two security guys watched. The way the bald guy was now driving, ignoring every thud and groan as her body bounced around, made it clear he cared less about her getting hurt.

Amity never got carsick, but the violent ride, blindfolded, was roiling her empty stomach. Even after the road smoothed out, she could feel the nausea churning in her abdomen, then curdling up into her lower throat. As a law clerk, she'd once handled a police misconduct case in which a woman suffocated on her own vomit. And that very thing had happened to several prisoners in Afghanistan. Now, with her mouth gagged, that prospect haunted her.

She screamed through the tape wrapped over her mouth.

"Please be quiet back there!" a voice replied from up front.

She screamed again even louder, then kicked her legs against the metal van door.

"Please stay quiet!"

"I'm going to throw up!"

Although the words were clear in her mind, the tape over her mouth converted them into muffled gibberish. But the henchmen up front would at least know she was trying to tell them something.

A different voice yelled back. Higher-pitched, with a slight Irish accent.

"Shut the *fook* up, lady!"—"fook," like "look."

She screamed the words even louder.

"Go see what's wrong with her," the Irish voice said.

Amity swallowed hard, the intensity of the nausea building by the second.

"Are you serious?" the other man asked.

"Shut up and do it."

The driver was clearly in charge.

A seat belt clicked open as the van shifted lanes and slowed.

Amity swallowed again.

After a few grunts, a large hand gripped her right shoulder and rolled her onto her back.

"What do you need?" a deep voice asked, more politely than she expected.

"Take the tape off," she said. Although the words again came out muffled, it was clear what needed to happen.

She braced for the sting of tape being ripped off her mouth, but the man pulled it off gently.

Her mouth free, the buildup of vomit exploded out violently.

"Jesus," the man barked, clearly hit by some of it.

She spit more onto the floor before speaking.

"That's what I was trying to tell you. I needed to puke."

"Yeah, I figured that part out." His voice was now half-annoyed, half-sympathetic. "Are you done at least?"

She took a deep breath through her nose, calming herself.

"Maybe if you slow down a bit. And my stomach is empty. Get me some water and some food and it should settle down."

"Let's get her some water," the man yelled up at the driver. "And I think we can sit her in the back seat like any other passenger, don't you?"

"Fook that." The Irish accent again came through.

"Trust me, if you don't get this lady some water and quit rolling her around back here, this van won't recover for a month."

CHAPTER 37

Washington

As THE MEETING came to order, butterflies fluttered in Senator Shepherd Logan's stomach—a rare occurrence. He had no idea what his colleague Byron Blue might do, now that he had the chairman's gavel.

He knew his colleague from Alabama too well. They were both Southerners. Both Republicans. And they had both won every election they'd ever waged. But that's where their similarities ended.

Blue was a hot dog, and he'd have a hard time holding back on his first day in the chair occupied for so long by Duke Garber.

To make matters worse, there was a full room there to observe it. The public, the press, key State Department, NSA, and Pentagon staff—all there, waiting to see what he'd do. Blue had clearly dropped enough off-the-record hints that they all suspected something big was coming. But Blue hadn't let his colleagues in on it.

It was one of the worst-kept secrets of the Senate. For decades Blue had dreamed of becoming the nation's secretary of state. With a new president a distinct possibility next year, this chairmanship gave him that chance. But there was a lot of competition from the next generation of right-wingers, so Blue would have to play things right. And Logan feared that meant he'd unleash his worst instincts now that the whole nation was watching.

"I want to begin with a standing moment of silence for the man who so ably chaired this committee for so long. Let's say a prayer for Duke."

Chairs squeaked and knees creaked as a roomful of people stood in unison. Logan watched the second hand of his small desk clock tick away for an entire minute of silence. Duke deserved every second of it.

"Please be seated," Blue said.

As a sign of respect, Logan had kept Duke's nameplate on display at his subcommittee meeting earlier that morning. But here at Senate Intel, Senator Blue made sure it was gone. And having sat one seat to the right for years, he now occupied Duke's old chair.

With cameras rolling, he took a sip of water, then cleared his throat.

"To begin, today I am announcing that we will advance Senator Garber's human rights agenda as a key element of this committee's work. It is no secret that those matters consumed him. Atrocities anywhere in the world, but especially the deplorable activities we've seen of late in Saudi Arabia."

He paused, hamming it up.

Logan stared straight ahead, jaw clenched. He, Blue, ranking member Sam Ireland, and Gigi had agreed that this was the right step, even though they worried it risked the ire of the president and leaders of the intel agencies. But for Blue, Logan knew, that was the whole point.

"It is also no secret that this week—at today's very hearing—the senator planned to examine the most recent tactics by the kingdom to advance its troubling agenda. And now he has died mysteriously."

He paused again.

"This committee's first priority will be to investigate whether there is a connection between the two. We will get to the bottom of it. And if we do find a connection, what has occurred is no less than an act of war."

Both TV and print reporters looked down, furiously scribbling notes. This was news—both the direction he was announcing and the belligerent rhetoric.

While Blue sat perfectly still, Logan stirred uncomfortably, as did their other, more seasoned colleagues. This was not the tempered, careful tone that Senator Garber always set. Such bellicosity usually came from a loony House member on the fringes of power, staving off a primary. Not the chairman of the Senate Intelligence Committee, whose every word sent a signal to the world about American intentions.

Blue continued.

"Today we begin that journey. Whatever is classified, we will present in a classified setting. But whatever we can share, we will share publicly. The American people deserve to know exactly what is happening."

He took another sip of water, then lifted his horn-rimmed glasses from the desk and positioned them on the end of his nose. He gazed down at the witness table, where a thin, black-haired man in a navy blue suit and gray tie sat ramrod straight, looking back up at him.

Minutes before, in a private room, Logan had seen Director of National Intelligence Mike Morino and Blue arguing. But in the end even Morino couldn't stop the chair of the Senate Intelligence Committee from doing what he was about to do.

"Director Morino?"

"Yes, Mr. Chairman."

"Please get us started. Explain to the American people all the ways that the Saudi government is violating human rights in their own country and beyond their borders."

"Yes, Mr. Chairman."

The director opened a small folder and began his presentation.

CHAPTER 38

——

"Stay down back there," the driver barked at Amity. "Don't move and don't say a damn word."

They were inching through a McDonald's drive-through line after pulling off the highway. The ride had been far better from the comfort of the back seat, but they'd moved her back to the floor to hide her for the stop.

She'd heard every conceivable accent in the Army. So Amity listened closely to the voices they encountered along the way. Unlike the first drive-through hours before, the voice over the McDonald's intercom was not a Southern twang. A Midwestern accent, maybe? Or mid-Atlantic? And even blindfolded, Amity could tell it was getting dark out. They were clearly heading east and north. Maryland or eastern Pennsylvania. Maybe New Jersey, but still a ways from New York City.

As she'd requested, they ordered her a Diet Coke, a grilled chicken sandwich, and fries. Ten minutes later they were back on the highway and the passenger joined her again.

"Here you go," the man in the front passenger seat said, holding the sandwich up to her mouth. Amity leaned her face forward into the sandwich and started chewing.

They'd kept the tape off for the ride but had ignored her attempts at conversation. Still, she was learning a lot.

"Thank you," she said after taking a long sip of the soda through the straw he'd tilted her way.

"You're welcome," the man said. He continued to be polite.

The two men did not know each other well. Most of their conversations were about mundane topics. At every turn, the driver was cocky. Aggressive. Coarse. The passenger, passive and civil. And at times uncomfortable. His size had hidden it when they'd grabbed her. The driver was an experienced henchman. A pro. The passenger was not. This was not his usual assignment.

"Fries, please."

He lifted her arms and placed the cardboard container in the fingers of her left hand.

"I can't eat them this way," she said, shaking her bound wrists.

"Okay." He pulled the container away. "Here you go."

A single French fry touched her lower lip, prompting her to lower her jaw. He then placed it in her mouth.

She chewed, then swallowed.

"No one makes fries like McDonald's. Yum."

Seem as human as possible, the Army had always drilled in them about being a hostage. Make them like you.

"True," he said in the friendliest tone yet.

He fed her several more.

"That's enough making friends, Doc," the driver yelled from the front. "Get back up here. We're almost there."

Doc? That explained his more civilized approach.

The vehicle slowed again, exiting the highway.

"Here are the last two," he said back to Amity.

She leaned forward and ate them.

"And I'm putting the soda right in front of you. There's still some left."

"Okay."

"Thanks for being so nice to me."

"Enough with the happy talk!" the driver yelled, although Amity sensed it was aimed as much at the doctor as at her.

The van made a sudden and hard right turn, throwing her against the side wall.

Before she could complain, a low-flying jet roared overhead.

CHAPTER 39

Washington

"WELL, YOU SURE riled the whole world up with that meeting today, Byron."

After a long day of hearings—with Gigi having just flown in from Florida—the foursome were back in the Marble Room. Shepherd Logan sat at the head of the table, turning to Senate business after he'd filled them in on Mary's steady improvement. Today was her checkup, so he'd know more in a few hours.

"I did my best." Senator Byron Blue's fleshy jowls shook as he laughed. "And Lord knows the Saudis deserve all we can throw their way."

"Well, let's not start World War Three in the process," Logan said, not returning the good humor.

"What's happening to you, Shep? You sound like the White House," Blue said, still enjoying himself. "They're pretty hot about that meeting, too, but they're Democrats."

He and the president had battled since the day she was sworn in. And he was already hard at work to make sure she was defeated next year.

Gigi cut in.

"Okay, boys, enough playtime. Please keep it under control, Byron. You might even try working with the White House sometime. You'll have the

opportunity next year to cause trouble, but right now we have more important things to get done."

She turned Logan's way.

"You make your progress?"

Logan nodded, pleased that the FDA's budget request had been approved
without a word of questioning.

"You bet. Full speed ahead."

"Have you told him?" Gigi asked.

"Not yet. We have a call scheduled for tonight."

CHAPTER 40

—

Location Unknown

IT DIDN'T TAKE long for Amity to miss the van, bumps and all.

As she'd witnessed up close in Afghanistan and advocated in a major case last spring, solitary confinement was cruel and unusual punishment.

Sure, she was sore all over from the bumpy ride. But hours in the small, dark room where she now sat, bound to a chair, were making her claustrophobic, combining hunger, dizziness, and a racing heartbeat that wouldn't slow down. Except for one visit with a glass of water, the polite doctor whom she'd warmed up to—who'd driven the final few hours after dropping off the Irishman—was now gone.

Brightness exploded into her blindfolded eyes as a light flipped on. The door opened, followed by the clicks of a woman's heels approaching her.

"Ms. Jones?"

It was a kind voice. Refined, like the van's passenger. Foreign. British.

Amity was not in the mood to return any civility.

"Who are you? And why are you keeping me here?"

"Ms. Jones." The voice was even calmer. Again, like a doctor talking to a patient. "I understand our security man was rough with you. Let me apologize. You must know—we only want to understand why you were following our team."

The woman was right. Amity did know, and she'd pondered for hours how she'd answer.

"I am, by military and legal training, a researcher. I had no agenda but to learn more. But I know nothing. There's no information for me to share with anyone. And my mother knows nothing."

"Your mother?"

The woman was a poor dissembler. Amity had stewed about Mom the entire trip, certain that these professionals would connect her involvement back to Mom's house.

"Yes. As I said, she knows nothing. She's just a sick woman looking out a window all day."

"But you took photos. Why?"

"Look through my phone. I document everything I do. Who doesn't these days?"

"Yes, we see that. But our uniforms, license plates, equipment? Driving hundreds of miles? This appears to be more than innocent curiosity."

"I was curious. That's my nature. But that information rests only on my phone. Delete it, for all I care. Keep my phone. I will walk away and not breathe another word."

She'd long ago set up her phone, always low on memory, so photos were instantly uploaded to the cloud.

Amity felt a slight tugging on her arms, along with the woman's warm breath against the back of her neck.

"Ms. Jones. It's very late."

The woman stepped backward.

"You are free to lie down and rest. But don't move until I've left."

Her heels clicked again as the woman exited the room, the door creaking shut behind her. Things turned dark again.

Amity jiggled her arms. While her wrists were still tied together, they were no longer bound to the chair, which allowed her to lie down on the cold floor.

She rolled onto her side—arms twisted awkwardly behind her—and shut her eyes.

CHAPTER 41

—

Washington

"How was the call?"

They rarely met early in the day, but Gigi was eager to know where things stood. So they were grabbing coffee a few blocks north of the Capitol.

Senator Shepherd Logan took his time to answer, first getting in two slow sips of straight black coffee.

"He was as spirited as always—crowing about more progress. We are on the verge of major breakthroughs."

"Don't we both know it. And thank God for that." She took her own long sip. "Was he satisfied with the new support?"

"You know he's *never* satisfied. He takes the financial support for granted at this point, so we hardly talked about that. Now he wants to speed up approval."

Tucked into the final report of yesterday's hearing—that of the FDA director—was a $2.5 million allocation for additional research. Only deep within the appendix did the report spell out where those dollars were headed, and even then it was well disguised. And the description of the precise research had been intentionally vague.

"And he's not worried about Duke?" Gigi asked. "Or upset?"

"Worried? Not a mention. It's like they never knew each other."

Gigi shook her head as she took another sip. "Scary. And to think they were best friends."

"Scary and *sick*," Logan said, nodding. "When it comes to geniuses, you have to take the good with the bad."

"Geniuses?" Gigi scoffed. "Try sociopaths."

CHAPTER 42

Brussels, Belgium

ON EITHER SIDE of Dr. Paden Blackwood sat a doctor and an ethicist. But the professor was the main draw, as two thousand medical professionals, thought leaders, and journalists from around the world listened attentively only blocks from the European Union headquarters.

Dr. Anika Reddy—a former student of Blackwood's, now a respected Oxford professor—sat to the side of the table in an oversized wooden chair, teeing up the first question after introductions.

"Dr. Blackwood, the techniques you are pioneering could cure some of the most pernicious diseases afflicting humankind. How many years before you turn that potential into a reality?"

He took his time. This simple question was the reason he had drawn the largest crowd of the annual gathering of the world's greatest medical minds.

How many years away? The truth? None.

That reality had already arrived.

Over the past year, he had successfully spliced and edited human DNA strands to create what he termed "genetic bullets," each precisely designed to kill a specific type of cancer cell by sabotaging that cell's own genetic makeup. And he'd done it not just in petri dishes or lab rats but in live bodies. Real people were already being cured. In Ohio. In Tennessee. In Maine. In towns across the country.

But he couldn't tell this crowd that. No one outside his team and his benefactors knew.

Oh, how he wanted to announce the history-making news right there. Major newspapers across the world would have no choice but to scream it out in headlines the next day. His place in history would be sealed. But beyond his inscrutable grin, he couldn't drop the slightest hint.

"Several years, at least. What works in a laboratory with isolated strands is important, and those tests are showing promise. But applying it to real cases is another matter entirely."

"And either way," Dr Reddy jumped back in, "no government has yet approved doing so with humans."

"Of course not," Dr Blackwood agreed, nodding soberly.

The tiny, bespectacled woman to his left leaned forward toward her microphone, looking out to the audience before speaking.

"And for good reason."

Blackwood smiled tightly, fixing his gaze straight ahead. He'd scolded Dr. Reddy backstage that an associate professor from a mid-tier public school had no business sitting on a panel with him, commenting on his work, let alone questioning it.

"Why do you say so?" Dr. Reddy asked.

The woman rose in her seat as she spoke.

"Altering the human genetic code, as the good doctor's breakthrough does, implicates the future of our species. Millions of lives can be saved, of course. But the genetic makeup of generations to come will be impacted in profound ways. We need consensus on what is appropriate and what is out of bounds before we alter human genes across the planet."

"Please be specific, Doctor. What's the risk?" Dr. Reddy asked.

Anxious to charge back into the conversation, Dr. Blackwood leaned forward to speak.

But the woman spoke up first, removing her glasses as she answered.

"Let's take cancer. With Dr. Blackwood's techniques, we may have the ability to remove, alter, and then re-inject immune cells to fight cancers we've never been able to fight before . . ."

He strained not to look her way. This was hitting too close to home—and where he was seeing his greatest success. But, like his own research-ers, younger generations didn't appreciate the incredible breakthroughs he was forging, and the miracle of alleviating the pain and suffering of so many.

". . . And we may very well defeat a particular cancer with a procedure now," she continued. "But altering immune cells to fight one form of cancer also permanently changes the genetic code, promising consequences we can't yet understand. We may set a ticking time bomb that explodes in fu-ture generations. Or even current subjects."

"After it's too late?" Dr. Reddy asked.

"Far too late," the woman said, "and after disseminating it worldwide. And there are other risks. What if some geneticist decides she wants to splice genes to alter a patient's moods? Or change other fundamental as-pects of a human being that have nothing to do with a deadly disease? That's all possible through the techniques the good doctor is perfecting. We should all shudder at the directions this could go in and demand a robust, global regulatory regime before we lose control."

Temperature rising, Dr. Blackwood sat up stiffly and cleared his throat.

"May I add a perspective?" he asked, in a tone so menacing the audience murmured uncomfortably.

"Of course, Doctor."

"'Too late,' as you put it, is letting a single patient die needlessly, which also wipes out all her progeny."

Dr. Blackwood went silent to let the words sink in.

"Please say more, Doctor," Dr. Reddy said.

"Not to put too fine a point on it, but the future lives you say you worry about?" He glared at the woman next to him. "By definition, they wouldn't exist unless we'd saved the original life in the first place. You, young lady, are saying, 'Let those people die.' Millions of people who are alive today—just let them die . . ."

A look of disgust came over his face while the eyes of the crowd shifted to the woman.

"I propose the opposite: Let us save the lives of the present. As many as we can. And let us be bold and confident enough in human ingenuity to manage the speculative risks you point out, most of which border on the paranoid."

"But are you prepared to play that role?" Dr. Reddy asked, interrupting.

"Excuse me?" Dr. Blackwood asked.

"You are talking about striking a balance that will impact millions of lives over generations across the world. In the end, the direction of the human race—all in your hands. Is that a role you are prepared to play?"

He looked out at the crowd, allowing their anticipation to build.

"Ladies and gentlemen, when we all took our oaths to enter this profession, that is the role we vowed to play, is it not? Saving human lives is the highest purpose any of us can serve—the most awesome power one human being can possess—and we are on the verge of possessing it on an unimaginable scale. And believe me when I tell you, this world is desperate for us to use it."

He stood up. More murmurs.

"So I ask all of you: Are *you* prepared to play this role?"

The crowd answered with spontaneous applause, the vast majority leaping to their feet.

————

AFTER THE PANEL discussion wrapped up, after the line of well-wishers and junior professors and other supplicants dwindled to zero, Dr. Blackwood walked behind the stage.

He looked at his phone, eager for an update from Boston.

Two messages from Dr. Vora, who'd canceled her trip to keep an eye on matters.

We have the girl, and her mother.

CHAPTER 43

Location Unknown

THE HEELS RETURNED, striking against the hard floor and waking Amity.

Even as she opened her eyes, everything remained pitch-black. The blindfold was still wrapped tight around her head.

Her hands still bound, triceps burning, she rolled onto her back and lunged up into a seated position.

The footsteps halted only inches behind her.

Amity's skin prickled as the visitor's breath rushed past just above her head, tickling the top of her hair. A quick tug from behind pulled her arms up and away from her back, but then the rope that had bound them fell away, liberating her wrists.

"You'll want to stretch them out." It was the polite voice from earlier.

Her arms were so stiff, she could hardly move them at first. But over the next minute she was gradually able to extend them to either side, then straight up in the air, then out in front. As she brought them to the floor, she gave them a spirited shake.

"Good. Here you go."

Amity could sense an object in front of her. She reached out and touched a cold cylinder. Either hard plastic or glass.

"Take a drink. You need to rehydrate."

She gripped the object and lifted it to her mouth, swallowing the cold water so quickly, she almost choked.

"Thank you."

She drank more, gulping down half the container.

"Ms. Jones, we have some good news."

"Good news? You're letting me go?"

The woman laughed.

"No. That can't happen right now. Better news than that."

Amity fidgeted, clueless about what the news might be. The blindfold put her at a deep disadvantage. She couldn't read the face of the woman speaking to her, while the woman could study her every expression and body movement.

"Better than freeing me?"

"We're confident you will agree." She stopped talking, leaving Amity hanging for a few seconds.

"What is it?"

More silence.

"It's about your mother."

"My mother?" Amity's temples throbbed as her mood swung from confusion to anger. If they threatened her mother . . . "What about her?"

"She's very ill."

"Yes. She's battled for years."

"And survived longer than most in her condition."

Another pause, one Amity didn't interrupt.

"We've looked at her closely."

"*You* looked at my mother?" she asked, almost screaming. "How? Where is she?"

"She's here. Right down the hall."

Mom? Down the hall? Ridiculous. Pure manipulation. Some type of psychological game to wear her down.

"Here?" she asked, then interrupted herself. "Where's here? And who's 'we'?"

"Our team. You know, the world-class team that saved her neighbors' boy."

World-class.

The two words sent a jolt through her body.

All she'd ever wanted for her mom was world-class care, the type of treatment she'd seen Justice Gibbons receive when he'd gotten ill. The type Colin Gentry had gotten right next door.

This woman was goading her. Mocking her.

"Please stop. My mom is back in Mansfield. Leave her out of this."

"I'm happy to show her to you if you calm yourself."

Such a soothing voice. Without a trace of the discomfort that accompanies lying.

Amity took two long breaths.

"If so, what right did you have to bring her here?"

"I believe you know Dr. Stumbo in Mansfield. He asked us for a second opinion on her condition."

A second opinion. Again, all they'd ever wanted.

Amity stilled. Maybe it was true.

"And what did you find?"

"A steady, unstoppable decline. On her current path, she has no more than four months to live."

Four months was the best-case scenario.

"So what's the good news you referred to?"

"The good news is that we can change that path."

Amity ground her jaw, shutting out any false hope this woman was conjuring up.

"Change it how?"

"As you and your mother have seen firsthand, our team works miracles."

"You sure did with Colin Gentry," Amity conceded. "But that's just one case. And he's young, not like Mom."

"There have been others. And the good news is your mother is the perfect candidate for the technique that saved Colin's life."

"As in 'cure her'?" Amity asked, shuttering her eyes.

A cure. There'd never been hope for a cure. From Mom's first diagnosis two years ago, from the first meeting with Dr. Stumbo, only two questions were discussed. How long could they prolong her life? And how much could they relieve her pain?

Not once had Dr. Stumbo mentioned a cure.

"Yes. A cure."

Another long pause.

"But whether it happens is up to you."

CHAPTER 44

Bethesda, Maryland

HOLED UP IN his suburban Maryland hotel room, Palmer Knight first saw the video on the motel's flat-screen TV. It hit so close to home, butterflies stirred in his stomach.

Senator Byron Blue, the brand-new chair of Intel, was having a horrible day. The footage was as clear as the videos of Palmer. An outside camera captured the rock-ribbed Deep South conservative entering a dark movie theater with a young woman. A young woman who was clearly not his wife.

Even worse for Blue, a camera inside the mostly empty theater captured him petting and kissing his companion throughout. Judging from the right-wing cable coverage of the videos, this was not going to go over well with Blue's base. Not one host defended him.

Palmer took a closer look at the videos on his laptop. They appeared absolutely real, even when replayed frame by frame.

Palmer immediately dialed NSA Ellrod.

"Looks like another deepfake, huh?" Palmer asked.

"It would fit the pattern, since he went after Saudi Arabia the other day. He's definitely denying it."

"Yeah, we victims will do that," Palmer said sarcastically. "So what are you going to do about it?"

"There's not a lot we can do right now but study it closely," Ellrod said. "If it *is* fake, it adds to our library, which will be helpful down the road. This is exactly what the president was worried about."

"Yeah, for herself. But what about the senator?"

Palmer smirked. They didn't mind having Blue hanging out there. He'd long been a thorn in the president's side, and Ellrod was clearly livid about his first meeting as chairman.

Deepfakes were clearly weapons as powerful as the president had suggested.

"For now, he's going to have to fend for himself."

CHAPTER 45

Location Unknown

It took a few seconds for Amity's eyes to adjust to the light. But when they did, there she was.

Through thick glass, in a separate room, Mom lay on a wide bed. The upper half of her body was tilted up slightly, surrounded by tubes, wires, and electronic devices that looked far more advanced than anything back in Mansfield.

World-class, Amity recalled as her heart rate spiked.

"Only look forward," the woman's voice warned from behind, just as Amity turned her head to the right.

"Okay. Okay."

Mom's eyes were closed, and she appeared shades paler than she'd been Thursday morning. Her chest rose and fell in a slow but steady rhythm.

"Why are her eyes closed?" Amity asked. "Is she all right?"

"She had a close call the other day. A real meltdown. Dr. Stumbo got her back to this point, and we're waiting for her to come to. But she's stable."

"Why the meltdown? She was fine when I was with her."

"That changed quickly in the twenty-four hours after you left. As you know, she's been in a delicate state for months."

There was no point in arguing.

"But you still think it's curable?"

"We know it is. She's at a better starting point than others we've saved in the past year. Colin Gentry included."

Amity's mind raced.

"Why didn't Dr. Stumbo call you guys before this? If you knew each other. If he knows what you're able to do."

"He knows very little. We reached out and notified him that we could save the Gentry boy, and that's all he understood. What we do is highly experimental."

"So he called you about my mother?" Amity asked.

"He did."

A lie. She'd been begging Stumbo for an experimental approach for months. Anything to change Mom's trajectory. He'd never done so.

"And how was Colin Gentry so lucky to get on your list? Along with whoever you visited in Tennessee."

Small hands patted her gently on both shoulders.

"Ms. Jones, I suggest that you limit your concerns to your mother's condition."

She watched her mother breathe for a few seconds. Her head tilted back, lips slightly open. The poor woman had suffered for so long. Mostly alone. On her current path, her fate was set.

But turning her over to this mysterious group, under these conditions, was clearly reckless.

"What do you want me to do?" Amity asked.

"Tell us everything you know and who you've told."

The way she said it turned Amity's stomach.

"So this is blackmail?"

"Amity," the woman said softly, "we would like to help your mother. Save her life."

Clearly blackmail. No wonder they were having this conversation only feet from Mom's hospital bed.

"I followed you guys on my own. Didn't tell a soul."

"Then why the photos?"

"I told you: I document everything."

"Amity, I'll only ask once more. Who did you tell beyond your mother? What did you send?"

Amity took a deep breath as she recalled her conversation with Dexter Mills, the one person she'd talked to.

Mom's chest rose slightly, then eased back down.

CHAPTER 46

Old Town, Neighborhood in Alexandria, Virginia

"There art thou, Romeo!"

As Shepherd Logan looked on from deep in his leather recliner, Senator Gigi Fox goaded their Alabama colleague in a way that only she could.

Senator Byron Blue, who'd just slumped down in a recliner across from the couch Fox was occupying, turned beet red.

"This ain't no laughing matter, Gigi," he said in an uncharacteristically weak voice. "You may know it's bullshit, but back in Tuscaloosa I'm getting killed over this fucking video. We're getting flooded by calls demanding I resign."

"Well, she was cute at least." She winked Blue's way.

"Stop. It's one of those deepfake things the media's been talking about. Probably the Saudis."

"I recall you dismissing that concern not long ago, Byron. I had a bill to deal with it and you voted no. Remember?"

The door to Logan's personal library cracked open and Colorado's Sam Ireland sauntered in.

"Sorry I'm late, fellas—Georgetown's an icy mess." His eyes twinkled as he spotted Senator Blue. "Hey there, Tiger. Surprised you're here."

Blue frowned. "Nowhere else to go, to be honest. Amanda is sick of it all and furious, and I'm being hounded by the media anywhere near Capitol Hill."

Ireland sat down next to Gigi, stretching his long legs out while still looking at Blue.

"What are you—"

Logan sat up straight.

"Enough! We can talk about Byron's problems later. We've got some decisions to make about the more pressing matter. Mary's by herself in Bean Station so we could even have this meeting."

The other three looked his way. His reference to Mary brought them to attention.

"The doctor is losing his patience."

Ireland shook his head. "Losing patience? He just got another couple million without a soul knowing it but the four of us."

"I reminded him of that," Logan said, "but he says it's no longer about the money. He's got enough results; he's ready to go. He needs a green light from the FDA before anyone else catches up. Or catches on."

Gigi leaned forward.

"That's a hell of a lot harder than appropriating money no one's paying attention to."

"I told him that. But he insists that's part of the agreement we all made. First research support, then the approvals."

Blue's chin folded into thick wrinkles as he nodded. "Well, that was our end of the deal. And he's done his end, so he's got all of us by the sack. He knows it. *We* know it."

"Shep, is your relationship with the director still solid?" Gigi Fox asked.

"With how much money we've been throwing at the FDA? Better than ever." He leaned back in his chair. "The man hugged me after the hearing the other day."

Blue spoke up again. "But the guy's a Boy Scout. This is a much bigger ask than throwing money his way."

"We were all Boy Scouts not long ago," Ireland said. "But now look: we're all caught up in this thing."

Logan gestured toward a photo of Mary and him in their tennis whites, old wooden rackets in hand, when they were in their twenties. "Some things are worth cutting corners for."

"That's my point," Ireland said. "Let's find out if Don Driscoll might do the same."

Logan leaned over his desk, eyeing his colleagues one at a time.

"Funny you should say that. Blackwood says he already has the answer. Just needs to make the offer."

While Logan delivered the words with a grin, the fluttering in his stomach he'd felt on and off for the past year returned in force.

"Offer" didn't quite describe the conversation that would take place. But Don Driscoll might face the same choice they'd all made.

CHAPTER 47

—

Location Unknown

"I DIDN'T THINK anything like that was approved yet."

After Amity had insisted on hearing the details of the treatment, the woman behind her walked through the basics. Amity had done enough of her own research to recognize the technique the woman described: splicing and editing DNA strands to design and unleash cancer-fighting immune cells. The trick was to create a precise DNA strand that served as the perfect kryptonite for each type of cancer.

"We've gotten narrow government approval for what we're doing."

"In humans?" Amity asked.

"In humans. We're the only ones. It's highly experimental—and confidential."

"A few years back, I read that a Chinese doctor did something like this—"

"He was a quack. We're legit, with government support."

She was reacting too defensively for legit.

"What's the risk of side effects?"

"Well, your mother is both elderly and unwell, so she certainly might not survive this. That's the biggest risk."

"No, I meant from editing genes. They haven't approved it yet because of the risk of unintended consequences. Long-term ones."

"We've minimized those."

"Minimized?"

"Ms. Jones, your mother isn't going to be passing on her genes to anyone anytime soon. She's entirely risk-free."

"But what about the Gentry boy? I can't imagine that's been approved."

A long pause.

"Again, let's stick to your mother's case. We can save her life, with no consequences long-term. Versus four months. We simply need you to promise not to say a word and tell us everything you know."

As the words sunk in, a queasiness swept over Amity's stomach.

It was a grotesque offer. Wrong on so many levels. She'd spent years in the JAG Corps cracking down on corrupt schemes far less consequential than what the woman was proposing here.

But as she thought of Mom being cured, her eyes welled up. How could she say no? Everything she'd wanted for Mom since she first got ill was there for the taking. And she could keep her pledge to Dad. This was the entire reason she'd followed the van in the first place. Mom being better— being pain-free—was such an unimaginable outcome that contemplating it made her giddy. She bit her lip to keep from smiling.

The truth was, there was almost nothing to tell anyway. They'd seen her photos, so they knew what she knew.

And there was nothing to lose.

Just need you to promise not to say a word.

She'd said the words so politely, like an eloquent mobster.

Your mom lives if you shut up.

She closed her eyes, puffed out a sharp breath, and balled her fists.

Ashamed.

Years of touting a commitment to the rule of law. Holding others to it, all the way to the highest court in the land.

But here she was, on the verge of flouting it the first time it would serve her own ends.

CHAPTER 48

Cambridge

"What did Quinn say?"

Blackwood's eyelids drooped and his head ached. The long flight home had taken a toll in a way it had not in his younger years. But before heading to bed, he wanted a full update on the Ohio girl and her mother. So even though it was past midnight Brussels time, he was back in the dark corner of his preferred Cambridge pub, seedy enough to host private conversations without the constant interruptions that occurred on campus.

"The same thing I did," Dr. Neena Vora said back, arms folded. She wasn't comfortable here. "The daughter's fine. She made the right decision. She cares too much about her mother and won't tell a soul."

He smiled. No one had ever resisted the offer. They made the same choice every time.

"So she bought it?"

She sighed. "She did. She's back home, keeping to herself."

Seeing her pursed lips, Blackwood exaggerated a scowl. Still too much softness on his team.

"Neena, if there's nothing we can do, there's nothing we can do."

"I understand, but to knowingly give false hope? It goes against everything we are taught. And we take an oath to—"

"Neena, this is bigger than one person. This is about thousands. Millions."

"I understand. But can't we simply try to help her?"

"She is well beyond help, Neena. And we need proven successes, not failures. We both know that."

CHAPTER 49

—

Columbus

AMITY JONES STARED at the computer monitor, her fingers frozen above her keyboard.

A major brief was due with the federal district court—which meant filed electronically by midnight—and she was confident she had the winning argument. But she couldn't concentrate, and it showed. Her bosses were leaving not-so-subtle hints of displeasure, clearly expecting more from a Supreme Court clerk.

She'd been unable to sit still from the time her flight took off from LaGuardia, following another long van ride. The entire reason she'd asked questions about the Gentry case was to find a cure for Mom. Now Mom was in the same hands as the doctors who'd saved Colin. Apparently even the same location. Still, she was suffocated by stress and nerves, knowing that the deal she'd struck represented a sickening form of bribery or blackmail. And she'd agreed to it.

There'd been two calls from the woman so far, both at 8:00 p.m. She seemed to take her medical charge seriously: the soothing British accent, the consistency of her calls, the encouragement. But all she'd tell her was that Mom's treatment was under way. No word yet on whether it was working. And who knew if she was even telling the truth.

Amity suddenly missed Dr. Stumbo, whose bedside manner was far rougher but who at least kept them abreast of every unsatisfying detail.

She also got jittery thinking about her phone. Her abductors had had access to it for hours, so it was certainly tapped. The only question was how deeply. From both her military service and legal work, she knew technology existed to track not only her calls, texts, and internet searches but every movement she made. Sophisticated hackers could even grab every image captured in the camera lens, whether she was taking a photo or not.

The only good news was that no one appeared to be following her in person. And she knew how to look.

Her desktop monitor timed out for the third time in ten minutes, the screen going black.

As she dropped her index finger to tap a key, her desk line rang.

The firm's managing partner.

"Amity, where's your draft?"

He sounded even more annoyed than when he'd scolded her for the previous week's absence, which she'd blamed on Mom's health.

"Almost done, John."

"I'm sure it'll be fine, but you know I don't like to review things at the last second. And this is one of our biggest verdicts in years. We need it upheld."

"I know, and it will be. I'll send it by six."

"Make it five thirty," he said, then hung up. They were losing confidence in her by the day.

As she put down the phone, her somber reflection stared back at her through the resting monitor. It was a startling site. Her eyelids drooped halfway, while dark semicircles hung below her eyes. Her lips curled down, forming wrinkles diagonally downward where her chin and cheeks met. Her red hair was an unprofessional and tousled mess.

She closed her eyes.

The image said it all. This wasn't sustainable.

The arrangement was eating away at her. The deal she'd cut—hideous.

Once the brief was done, she'd do something. She'd be careful, but she *had* to do something. She had to learn more.

She touched the space bar and the screen lit back up.

———

AFTER EMAILING THE final draft of the brief, Amity retrieved her Tennessee photos from the cloud.

And as she clicked through them—images of the van, the doctors, the Cherokee Inn—the conversation from the tennis club locker room played back in her mind.

One of the men had said there was a woman there, really sick, but undergoing a miraculous recovery. She hadn't heard the name, but it was something like Terry or Carrie. And that woman's husband was still in the tournament. That was the couple Amity needed to find.

She retrieved the photo of the tournament bracket and blew it up on her screen.

After one round, eight players remained in the tournament. They were written in large print with a thick Sharpie, each name easy to read.

Players named Minor, Shuler, and Plasse were all in the top half of the bracket along with Jacobs. Symmes, Logan, and Coolidge were in the lower half with Winters.

She recognized two names from the locker room conversation: Jacobs and Winters. The conversation had made clear neither was married to the sick woman, so Amity skipped over them.

One at a time, Amity googled the six remaining names.

Nothing showed up on Minor.

The Shulers—Gord and Erma—were the parents of a retired football quarterback and congressman. The county newspaper—*Grainger Today*—published a profile on all their good works for Bean Station, including a photo with their famous son. Gord looked like the guy who'd spotted her from the tennis court.

Larry Plasse was a retired millionaire and easy to find. He had an active

Facebook account and had won the Cherokee Lake fishing tournament each of the past three years. But Amity found an obituary detailing his wife's death two years ago, and there was no sign that he'd remarried. So she took him off the list.

Clay Symmes was the top seed of the tournament. He had been the name partner of a major Knoxville law firm until his retirement. But his Facebook page was plastered with photos of a young wife, the most recent shot from only two days before. If she was going through some type of intense treatment, she was hiding it well.

The only Coolidge she found near Bean Station was a Tyson Coolidge, whose LinkedIn account provided few details except that he was forty-three years old. Too young.

Finally, she looked on social media for the names Logan and Bean Station. Nothing came up. No personal Facebook page or Instagram account. Nothing on Twitter. Not surprising for an old man. So she did a broader internet search.

Her heart skipped a beat as a number of articles from a decade ago popped up. It had been big news when the Logans had moved to the small resort town from Knoxville. The articles quoted the couple about why they'd decided to settle there. And local officials crowed about how much the new residents would mean to the Bean Station community. That it would put the whole region on the map.

But after the opening fanfare, the excitement had worn off. Not a single article appeared in the last ten years. Apparently the town had adjusted to the presence of two such prominent citizens. In recent years, you'd have no idea they were even there—which was probably why they'd relocated in the first place.

Amity dug further. The Logans had both played tennis at the University of Tennessee, which was where they'd first met. And they'd been together ever since. Fifty-six years.

More recent stories also revealed the wife's pancreatic cancer diagnosis. The articles read like obituaries, giving her only months to live while people lavished praise as if she'd already died.

It all checked out.

Ironically, Amity not only knew the name, but she'd seen the husband's face before. In person.

She'd stood a few feet from him less than a year ago. Justice Gibbons was the ultimate Beltway political insider, and his annual holiday party in Old Town was *the* event of the holiday season. Amity had seen Logan at the previous December's party.

He was as high-profile as it got—not only for Tennessee but for the country.

Senator Shepherd Logan lived at Cherokee Terrace.

As did his wife, Mary.

PART TWO

CHAPTER 50

——

Bean Station

LEANING AGAINST THE marble island in his kitchen, Senator Shepherd Logan hobbled to the old plastic phone hanging from the wall.

Senate security staff had warned him to use his secure landline. They'd meant that advice for classified conversations, but he'd also heeded it for calls to and from Cambridge. And he knew that was where this call was from.

He reached out and held the phone to his right ear.

"Doctor?"

"Yes. It's me."

"What did your man learn?"

The neighborhood was still abuzz about the tennis club trespasser. She'd kayaked there in the dead of winter and hiked up the muddy hill. She'd made no attempt to break into any of the houses and left both players' wallets untouched in the locker room. Why would anyone go to all that effort to photograph the tennis hut? The security team was baffled, as were all the residents.

But Logan knew. Even before they'd called to warn him, it was clear what the intruder had been after. His nerves had been raw since Mary had described it all.

"She was a neighbor of an Ohio patient. Her mom has terminal cancer. She followed the van south."

"You think they know who I am? Who Mary is?"

"We don't think so. She was just hoping to cure her mother . . ."

Logan could sympathize. That's what had gotten him into this mess in the first place.

". . . but she's got a pretty impressive background, so we can't be sure."

"Impressive how?"

"She just finished clerking for Justice Ernest Gibbons."

Logan shook his head, his mood sinking further. Ernest was a friend, of course. But he was also the most respected jurist on the Court, which meant each year's law clerks represented the sharpest law grads in the nation.

"Was she a former Army JAG Corps lawyer?" Logan asked, recalling the intruder's entry by kayak and hilly sprint.

"She was. How'd you—"

"Ernest cut his teeth as a JAG lawyer. He thinks it's the best training out there, so he selects the Army's top JAG officer every year to clerk for him. Cream of the crop. She'll figure it out; you can bet on it."

The old senator lowered his body onto a wooden stool next to the phone, leaning most of his weight against the wall. His torso and legs suddenly felt so heavy. Unwieldy and sluggish. The room around him fogged up. He was exhausted. Queasy.

He thought of Mary, asleep in the bedroom. So weak. So tiny. But getting better. Thank God, she was getting better. Even though she hadn't asked for it, this was all for her. And whatever happened, that made it worth it.

He'd made the right choice.

But the cost was sure adding up.

He'd spent his political life staying out of the swamp of Washington. Avoiding the traps and trappings of power, rejecting the graft and special favors that were there for the taking. That discipline, passed down from a father who'd spent his life behind the pulpit, had been one of his secrets to success while so many others came and went, often stained forever.

He'd followed all the rules because it was the right thing to do, but it also carried an enormous benefit: no one had leverage over him. And, owned by no one, he was liberated to best represent the people of Tennessee.

Until now.

"Jesus? I can't afford to have—"

"We're monitoring her closely, Senator. We won't let her get in the way of our progress."

The offer to cure Mary had been different than all the other offers that had come his way. How could he say no? Especially when the goal was to advance a breakthrough that would help countless others just like her. And of course the proposal had come from Duke Garber, the straightest arrow in Washington. If Duke was good with it, it had to be okay. Heck, Gigi had jumped at the chance. As private as she was about it, she couldn't hide how thrilled she was by her beneficiary's recovery.

"Oh, Doctor, I have no doubt you will make your progress—"

He'd come to learn that "progress" was all the professor cared about.

"—but you assured me that this work would never be found out. I've spent my life building a reputation for integrity. If the end of my career is tainted by scandal, it would be—"

"Scandal?" the professor asked, an edge of anger in his voice. "Senator, as we've discussed many times, what you are doing now will be your greatest legacy."

The conversation always returned here. The professor was a true believer. To him, on the verge of curing millions, big-government bureaucracy posed an illegitimate obstacle to saving lives. It was too slow. Too unsophisticated. Too corrupt. The doctor could be persuasive on this point. It was one way the members of their small caucus reassured one another that they were serving the greater good.

But, deep down, Logan knew.

It was the promise of Mary being cured that had always been his central motivation, dousing any qualms that arose. He'd finally done what he'd always avoided: a deal, in exchange for the most direct and overwhelming personal benefit imaginable. And if it got out, that would taint him forever. A crooked, twisted deal would be his legacy.

"When you say you're monitoring her, what does that mean? Will it come out or not?"

"We have several points of leverage to start. And we can take it further if we need to. It will not come out. But . . ."

Logan rolled his eyes. The doctor always wanted something. He was always pushing for more. And he knew—they knew—they could never say no.

". . . it means we need to move more quickly than ever."

"It's happening, Doctor. I have the meeting scheduled for next week."

"Good."

They wrapped up the call.

Logan rose from the stool and returned to the bedroom. He wasn't tired yet. And he was too on edge to sleep either way.

Still, he wanted to watch over Mary as she slept.

CHAPTER 51

_____

Columbus

"THOSE MUST BE flukes, Amity."

Needing fresh air, Amity was jogging along the snowy banks of the Olentangy River when her younger brother, Simon, called back, using the new phone number she'd given him.

With the sun making a rare appearance, she'd slowed to a walk to describe the mysterious van of doctors delivering lifesaving treatment to patients in Ohio and Tennessee. Without mentioning her name, she walked through Mary Logan's miraculous recovery.

"Flukes how?" she asked Simon. "Aren't all sorts of breakthroughs happening that are leading to new cures?"

"In the lab, yes. And we're funding a lot of that work. But not in humans. That's still a few years away."

Simon had visited Mom for a weekend after her initial diagnosis, but that was it. Sharing the responsibility more evenly would've been a huge help, but their small family had never worked that way. As the older sister, Amity had always been the glue. As the baby brother, Simon had happily taken that for granted. Then again, Amity reminded herself, she'd made the promise to Dad. Simon hardly remembered him.

On a few occasions Simon had pushed back on Amity's doting. "She's a lot tougher than you think she is," he'd say. "Stop babying her." After an especially intense argument, they'd called a truce and never spoken of it again.

But Simon's professional focus—investing in biotech research—was suddenly far more relevant to Amity's life. Maybe he could step up this one time.

Amity pictured the van going house to house, saving lives on each end of the five-hundred-mile trip. One fluke, as Simon put it, would beat long odds. Back-to-back flukes would be like winning the lottery. A lightning strike.

"Well, maybe someone's getting a head start."

"Amity—"

She could practically hear the eye roll through the phone.

"—that wouldn't happen. Not in this country, at least. Nothing beyond lab and some animal research has been approved. Editing kids' DNA is still years away from being approved. Without those approvals, there's no money to do the work—from either firms like ours or the government." He paused. "And without that funding, it doesn't happen."

Amity remained skeptical, but moved on.

"Can you at least tell me who's capable of doing that kind of research? In labs, at least?"

"Of course. We get all the proposals that are out there and fund a lot of that work."

"Is it a big universe?"

"There were some big breakthroughs a few years ago—a new way of modifying DNA with far more precision, which opened the door for cures to previously incurable diseases. But it's mostly theory right now. Labs are popping up all over the world to explore just how many forms of cancer can be tackled."

She looked out over the icy river, still holding the phone to her ear. Not what she wanted to hear: too many to narrow down.

"Simon, I don't have time to look into all those."

He paused, holding her in suspense.

"Well, at the end of the day, there are only about a dozen or so with the capacity to do anywhere close to what you're describing. Most are linked in some way to a major research university."

Amity grinned. That was more like it.

"Can you send me the list of those companies?"

"Sure. That's easy. I pretty much hear from them all."

———

AMITY SPENT THE rest of the morning researching Shepherd Logan.

It turned out he was a rare thing in Washington: a Boy Scout.

Even as chair of the Senate Banking Committee, he took no PAC money. Not from banks, energy companies, pharmaceutical companies, or others. Almost all of his support came from everyday people back in Tennessee, mostly in small amounts. And nothing from groups tied to medical research or anyone who worked for them.

While well beyond his prime, like Duke Garber, Logan had always struck Amity as a statesman. And a gentleman. Apparently she'd read him right.

She tried a new line of inquiry.

Maybe one of his committees oversaw medical research. He chaired Banking, but what else? What committees would preside over health research like this?

"The Senate Committee on Health, Education, Labor and Pensions," she said out loud, reading from the top of the screen. She typed again, and waited.

It definitely had jurisdiction over biomedical research. And it looked like they'd held hearings on this type of research.

She leaned in closer, looking up and down the roster. Shepherd Logan didn't sit on the committee.

She typed some more.

He sat on Homeland Security and Government Affairs, Appropriations, and Veterans' Affairs.

All important committees, but none with jurisdiction over medical research.

———

SIMON'S EMAIL ARRIVED later in the day. At the risk of another talking-to by the managing partner, she closed the motion she was working on and opened the email.

Boston dominated the list, with four different labs conducting gene therapy research; three had spun out of Harvard, one from MIT. A Baltimore firm had sprung out of Johns Hopkins, and there were also world-class labs emerging in Chicago, Raleigh-Durham, and New York, along with labs associated with the Mayo Clinic and the Cleveland Clinic. Then the scene jumped 1,500 miles west, with a cluster of labs in Palo Alto, along with labs in San Diego and Los Angeles.

She called Simon to learn more.

"They're all at about the same stage of research, exploring different types of diseases to cure," he explained. He still sounded bored by it all, unconvinced that anything notable was happening.

"Are any focusing on cancer in particular?"

"Actually, the ones on that list *are* the cancer labs. I didn't include the ones that weren't. You wouldn't believe how many are popping up all over the place for so many different diseases."

"And how far along are they? The ones focused on cancer."

"Still early. Baby steps, really. I can assure you no one's anywhere near driving around the Midwest, making house calls on people they've cured. Hell, they'd be locked up if they were."

Amity spent the next few hours looking into the people associated with the labs listed in the email, checking if they had any political connections or history of giving.

Nothing.

They were predominantly ivory tower professors and researchers, and not political at all. A good number weren't even U.S. citizens, so they were barred from contributing to politicians. A few gave dollars locally, but that was it. Definitely no pattern of giving to Senator Logan or other members of Congress.

Overall, these people were focused on their lab work, not politics. Unlike the rest of the world, they didn't look to be buying access on Capitol Hill.

CHAPTER 52

Bean Station

"FOLLOWED? HOW IN the hell . . . ?"

Shepherd Logan hadn't slept but an hour. The heavy rain washing across the mountains hadn't helped, but his churning stomach was the far greater culprit. He felt as ill and as empty as he had after hearing that the final step of Duke's life had been off the Pemaquid Point cliff where he, Mary, and the Garbers had spent so many good moments together. Right past the lighthouse and little museum that he and Duke had kept open all those years.

Without sleep, his ulcers had acted up by sunrise, and a roasting from Gigi Fox would only make things worse. But he had to tell her.

"I'm afraid so," he said, then slumped back on the same stool where he'd sat when he talked with Dr. Blackwood the night before.

"Do you think she found out Mary is being treated?"

"I think we have to assume that."

"Damn. How in the hell . . . ?"

"She followed the van, apparently. Then snuck onto the grounds here. But that Quinn fella is on it."

A long pause.

"Quinn?" Her low voice pierced through the phone. "We're not a third world banana republic, offing people, especially someone who clerked for Ernest."

They had both served with Ernest Gibbons in the Senate before he'd become a Supreme Court justice, and remained friends.

"Of course not, Gigi. Don't lecture me. You and I have both spent our lives building reputations for integrity. At this point, that's all we have. Duke wasn't willing to lose that, and I'm not either. So we've got to do something."

Silence on the other end. No one talked back to Gigi Fox. He could envision her seething—the same squinty eyes and jutting jaw that had almost shut down the Senate to stop his banking deregulation bill.

"Shep, I have as much to lose as you. But we need to set some boundaries before this gets out of control."

Seconds passed. She usually calmed quickly.

"How's Mary feeling?" she asked in a much softer tone.

"Better this morning than I've seen in a year."

"Wonderful, Shep. Doesn't that make it all worth it?"

He took a deep breath, recalling Mary's smile an hour before as he'd brought her coffee—something he'd done every day for nearly sixty years.

"It really does."

He reflexively returned the polite question her way.

"And how's—"

He cut himself off, having momentarily forgotten. She'd made the same choice he had. But she never talked about it.

CHAPTER 53

———

Mansfield

"SHEPHERD LOGAN? As in, the senator?"

Amity nodded as Dexter Mills stared back at her.

"You got it. What are the odds that the next stop after Mansfield was the home of Shepherd freakin' Logan?"

"Senators and their families get sick like everybody else, Amity," Dexter said from the other side of his desk, still poo-pooing it all.

"Oh, they get sick. But a miracle medical team making weekly house calls is definitely *not* like everybody else. Especially when they're working so hard to keep it a secret."

She left out the fact that they'd kidnapped her. And that she'd had to leave her cell phone back in Columbus in case they were still tracking it.

"What did you say the survival rate was for what Mrs. Logan had?"

"Bleak. Ten percent. But lower for her age."

He nodded. "Same as the Gentry boy."

"Exactly. That van I followed is basically the 'Miracle Express.'"

Amity didn't want to come out and say it, but she was back to learn more about the Gentry family. She'd found no tie between Shepherd Logan and any biotech research operation. But if she could find a connection between

Mary Logan and young Colin Gentry—two beneficiaries of the van's good work—it might reveal who was behind it.

"Dexter, you may be sitting on a huge national story right here in Mansfield. Some kind of Manhattan Project for curing cancer, with Colin Gentry as one of its first success stories."

"You think?" Dexter asked, the first tinge of interest in his gravelly voice.

"You bet. But we need to know more about Colin. And the family. How did a kid from here win the treatment lottery?"

He looked up thoughtfully. "Wouldn't it be because of his condition? That was my impression."

"Sure. But who knows if any other connection helped get him selected? You know how Washington works."

"Washington? We're in Mansfield, Amity. No one has connections here. And that family? No way."

That family.

Mom had explained the basics a few times. The Gentry family had once been among Mansfield's wealthiest but had plunged from grace several generations back. But that was about all Amity knew.

Dexter would know the details.

"You're probably right. Either way, tell me more about them."

He leaned back in his chair.

"Colin's parents are the salt of the earth. His mom works at the grocery store and sings in the church choir. His dad works as a supervisor at the prison and has coached little league for years. His real claim to fame, though, is he was an extra in *Shawshank*."

The famous movie had been filmed at the old Mansfield jail, five minutes from where they were sitting.

"But that Gentry clan has been through a lot," Dexter pointed out. "Way before Colin got sick."

He reached down to his desk's left side and rolled out a drawer of files. He pulled out a manila folder, took a sheet off the top, and laid it on the desk. It was a copy of a black-and-white photo.

"Here. I dug this up when I was doing the Colin Gentry story the other week."

An old factory. Like dozens of photos she'd seen before—grand fortresses from a past era, always some combination of brick facades, dark smokestacks, conveyor belts, with railroad tracks curling around the outside. Steel mills, ironworks, and plants that made everything from brake pads to soap. Back when manufacturing was the beating heart of Mansfield, these factories churned away day and night, three shifts employing hundreds or thousands of workers at each site.

This photo was right out of central casting. And on top of it, in understated print, were the words "Gentry Stove Company." Handwritten at the bottom was the year: "1924."

"A couple generations back, the Gentries were Mansfield royalty. They founded and ran one of the country's largest stove manufacturing plants before selling it to Westinghouse. So for several generations, in Mansfield's heyday, they were one of the old-money families—loaded, but also well respected, generous, and active in the community."

Amity recalled the modest house where Colin Gentry now lived. Not even as nice as Mom's small two-story.

"So what happened?"

"After the sale to Westinghouse, the biggest name of the next generation of Gentrys—the leader of the clan—was a larger-than-life character named Elvis Gentry. Educated out east, with his inherited wealth, he became a real man about town. Elected county commissioner in his twenties. Then served as mayor for years. Beautiful wife and big family—five kids. He sprinkled money around the town, both from his government perch as well as his own private fortune. He became very active in state and national politics. People thought he'd end up as governor—or in Washington."

Amity had driven Ohio enough to know that many small towns had a figure like this. Some rose to national prominence. In Fremont, near Lake Erie, it was Rutherford B. Hayes. Down the road, in Marion, Ohio, it was Warren Harding running his newspaper before ascending to the U.S. Senate, then the presidency. These proud towns plastered the names of their ascendant citizens all over the place. Streets. Buildings. Parks. Even presidential libraries and statues.

But Amity hadn't seen the name Gentry anywhere as a kid.

"Interesting. Was he Colin's grandfather?"

"No. His great-grandfather."

"*Great*-grandfather. The story goes back that far?"

"You know us small towns. We talk about this stuff as if it all happened yesterday."

"I think that's why I left," Amity said, chuckling.

"Well, Elvis got serious about running for governor. People around the state expected big things. But right before the big announcement, one of his opponents outed his secret—"

"Opposition research even back then," Amity chimed in.

"Of course. And someone hit the mother lode. Elvis Gentry had a mistress—a much younger woman, who worked at City Hall."

"Can't imagine a sex scandal would've played well back then."

Dexter shook his head. "Not well at all. It exploded."

"And that ended his campaign?"

"A lot more than the campaign." He patted the stack of papers on his desk. "When Colin first got sick, I looked through the paper's archives and talked to a few old-timers. This was front-page news for weeks, here and across Ohio. He was finished, as was the family's good standing. Elvis skipped town with his mistress, leaving his wife, Alma, to raise the kids by herself, including Colin's grandfather. But she kept the shame of it all largely to herself."

"Shame?" Amity asked, mouth falling open. "She didn't do anything wrong."

"Back then it didn't matter. Especially not in a family of their standing. They fell to nothing almost overnight."

"Well, at least she had more resources than most to deal with it," Amity said.

Dexter shook his head. "Somehow Elvis took all the money with him. If he was sending her money, it wasn't much. He must've changed his will while he was at it, because none of the kids ever saw much of it."

"What a swell guy," Amity said. "Let me guess: She died penniless?"

"Pretty much. Decades ago. Penniless and close to a hundred. In a retirement home up the street."

He pulled out another piece of paper from the stack, handing it to Amity.

"Here's her obituary. Barely a paragraph for the former first lady of Mansfield."

Amity glanced at it, shaking her head.

"So sad. And her and Elvis's kids?"

"Colin's grandfather lived a good life here, working at the GM plant and raising Colin's dad and a daughter. He was laid off like everyone else when the plant closed and died a few years after that."

"And the siblings?"

"Sad to say, Colin's granddad was the only one who stayed. The stain on the family must've been too much to bear, because the other kids all left after high school and never came back."

"Did you track any of them down?"

"I tried, but no luck. They scattered all over. The oldest son died in Korea. The other's in a nursing home in LA after living his whole life a bachelor—apparently has severe Alzheimer's. The daughter got married and had a couple kids, followed by a bunch of grandchildren. She's a widow. Lives in some retirement home near Tampa."

"And the fifth?" Amity asked.

"She's a mystery." He shrugged. "I never found anything on her. The rumor was she died young, but there's no trace of that either."

Amity looked back at the obituary. "That's right. It says here she preceded her mother in death. "And what happened to the guy who ruined all their lives?" she asked.

"Rumor is Elvis Gentry and the mistress ran off south. There was a short news story years later when he died. No trace of her, and apparently he took his own life. Lived in New Orleans at the time, but the information on that is sparse as well. You'd never know he once was the king of this town."

"And all the money?"

Dexter shrugged. "Who knows? But if he didn't squander it, it went somewhere—and definitely not here. In today's dollars, it'd be a fortune."

"What a fall from grace. Merciful of you not to mention any of this in your story on Colin."

"Why put them through that again? My guess is that's why the Gentrys don't want to talk. They've moved on from the past and led good, humble lives, but have always kept to themselves."

He looked out the window—snow was falling in thick clumps—then looked back at Amity.

"So you see why I said this is not a family with the type of connections you're looking for?"

Amity nodded, but her instinct was the opposite.

What were the odds that a family with such a moneyed history would happen to be *the* family to benefit from a miracle cure doled out to the well-connected?

Not high.

She gestured at his short stack of papers. "Can I look through those?"

"Actually, I'll make you copies. But there's a lot more in the archives downstairs."

CHAPTER 54

Mansfield

THE ANCIENT ELEVATOR bumped to a stop. The metal gate clanked loudly as Dexter Mills pulled it to the side. Amity stepped into the dark basement of the *News Journal*, taking a trip back in time even before reaching the archives.

She'd loved studying this equipment as an intern. Amid the grunge and dust emerged the skeletons of old hulking printing presses, complete with cases of movable type. Huge rollers lined one end of a long open room, where reams of paper once raced through, imprinted with gallons of ink as they went. Past the rollers was a storage area, then a large depot that connected to a driveway outside. Back in the day, dozens of trucks would have arrived there early in the morning, loaded up with bound stacks of fresh papers, soon to deliver them to tens of thousands of locations across the region, beating the good people of a teeming Mansfield to their morning coffee.

Like Gentry Stove Company, the GM plant, and other shuttered factories around town, all that activity was now gone. All those jobs, lost. In the paper's case, replaced by a website.

After the brief walk, Dexter took Amity to a dark, square room in one corner of the basement that housed shelves of thick bound volumes of the *News Journal* from its heyday.

"The golden years of newspapers," he said as he walked her through one volume that was lying on the table. A thick, full-sized newspaper—not the mini-versions in most cities today. Lots of stories—local ones, not just pulled from wire services. Lots of reporters. Columnists. Multiple sections, each loaded with content. And pages and pages of ads and coupons.

"I barely recognize them," Amity said. "The Dexter Mills era of print journalism."

"Hardly," he laughed. "But when my era started, it was a lot closer to this than what we put out there now."

Dexter pulled out the 1938 bound volume and handed it to her.

"Gotta finish a column," he said as he walked out. "Holler if you need anything."

Amity laid the heavy book on the table and opened it to the first page, crinkled, creased, and yellow.

The new year started with a blizzard that shut down most of Ohio. Worries were growing about events in Europe and a still anemic global economy. FDR and Governor Davey promised better days ahead.

While Elvis Gentry was mentioned a few times prior—a few quotes and some public appearances—it was the January 20 paper that kicked off intense coverage of his campaign.

First good, then bad.

MAYOR GENTRY PLANS GOVERNOR RUN ran across the top of the page. It was a glowing story about Elvis, the family, and the difference they'd made in Mansfield. The photo couldn't have been better if Elvis himself had handpicked it. He was a smaller man, handsome and trim, with high cheekbones, a thin mustache, and prominent jaw. His dark hair was parted neatly to the side, and he sported a sharp three-piece suit. Even on the now dull newsprint, an energetic confidence burst from his pose—arms crossed, big, toothy smile, standing outside City Hall as if he owned the place. Which he clearly did.

An editorial ran in the same day's paper praising Gentry for his able stewardship of the city and listing his accomplishments as he entered the latter half of his third term. It closed with the simple line "Gentry has led Mansfield well. He will do the same for Ohio."

Two days later, the fall began.

The top left of the paper read: LOCAL PARTY LEADER: GENTRY CAN'T BE TRUSTED.

In the era before tabloids, the paper was gun-shy about going right out front and saying it. But amid a number of run-of-the-mill criticisms, eight paragraphs down, a single sentence delivered the bombshell in muted language: "Chairman James even suggested that Mayor Gentry has been unfaithful to Mansfield's first lady." No detail or context followed the charge.

Two days later, that changed: EVIDENCE MOUNTS OF MAYOR'S INFI-DELITY.

For the first time the paper mentioned that the alleged mistress worked at City Hall. The front page featured a recent photo of the mayor, his wife, and their five kids—the youngest an infant in Alma Gentry's arms—dressed to the nines and all smiling.

That photo had to hurt, Amity thought to herself.

Then things got worse.

In the weeks that followed, the sordid details streamed across the top of the fold.

A few stories in, the mistress was named: Abigail Bryant. She was single and twenty-eight, ratcheting up the scandal, given that Mayor Gentry was fifty-one. Several people, quoted anonymously, said they had been together for years. And everyone at City Hall knew it.

Today, a politician caught in such a scandal would be shrouded by a crisis communications team expertly guiding him on what to say and do. Elvis Gentry had none of that and did everything wrong. From the outset he gave interviews on the record, clearly confident that his family's years of goodwill would protect him. He lashed out, blaming "bloodsucking leeches" for "staining the good Gentry name" while offering blanket denials. He left himself no wiggle room for when evidence surfaced. As the articles and questions kept coming, cameras flashing in his face, his tone grew more defensive and his expression more desperate. One of the front-page photos captured him with his mouth open, eyes squinting, jaw jutting out as he yelled. He looked both angry and guilty.

As the stories mounted, he stopped commenting on the scandal, instead plunging ahead with his statewide run. A quote on one front page summed it up: "I remain committed to leading the state as its Governor and will not let these gutter accusations get in my way."

Amity shook her head. She'd met kids like this at Stanford Law and on the Court. A guy like Gentry, from a family like that, had been living above scrutiny his whole life. He had no clue how to deal with a true crisis.

The paper turned on him in weeks. The second Sunday of February—peak readership—an editorial called on Gentry to resign: "The Mayor should not only end his run for Governor immediately. He must allow Mansfield to start afresh. He must step aside."

He soon retreated to a fallback position: he wouldn't run for governor but would stay on as mayor to continue the progress in Mansfield. And he would run for reelection the following year.

But that wasn't good enough. Three more editorials followed, delivering the same message while dialing up the temperature each time. The final one was the bluntest: "For the good of our great city, so we can move on and he and his family can move on, it is time for Elvis Gentry to go."

Two days after that, in late February, the best-known figure in Mansfield hung it up.

The front-page headline ran: MAYOR GENTRY RESIGNS; COUNCIL PRESIDENT MURRAY TAKES REINS OF CITY. An editorial the same day praised the decision and welcomed the new mayor.

Six weeks later came the story, buried deep in the paper, that Elvis Gentry had left town, providing few details.

That was the final mention of him. And the family.

"What a fall," Amity said out loud.

She returned to the front of the bound volume. She reread the first story, then paged through the volume again. She'd taken good notes but wanted to be sure she hadn't missed anything. On the second go around, what stood out the most was that a single writer had written every story.

She jotted his name down in her notebook: Woodrow Solomon.

Mr. Solomon had pursued the story relentlessly but also had been pretty humane about it. He'd left the family out of it all the way through.

And while he'd mentioned the mistress's name in two initial stories, he never did so again.

Not a single photo of her appeared.

CHAPTER 55

Mansfield

QUINN PUFFED A long, loud breath into his clenched fist as he entered his third hour of waiting. A lengthy stakeout would have been standard in his early years as an agent, but not for someone of his current skill and experience.

He was parked two blocks from the *News Journal*, opening up a perfect line of sight to the newspaper's main entrance. It was bitterly cold outside, so he occasionally turned the rented Dodge Caravan on to reheat it. Wary that an idling car would raise suspicion, he'd turn it off when the internal temperature hit 65 degrees. He was now on his third round of the routine, the temperature having just hit 62.

The drive north on the interstate had been rough—black ice, at least three accidents slowing things down, semis caking his windshield with slush every few minutes. The only benefit of the treacherous conditions was that Amity Jones never noticed the Dodge Caravan trailing her for an entire hour.

And now another three-hour wait in the bitter cold.

Yes, he was being paid well for this gig—a payday amounting to three years of his public salary—but he was too old for this shit.

The temperature gauge flipped from 64 to 65, so he turned the ignition off.

His phone vibrated. A new text message.

The professor.

Keep an eye on her. But don't hurt her.

Quinn shook his oversized head. A senator was dead and they'd made him kidnap the girl and her dying mother. But now they were getting squeamish?

Says who? he texted back.

Says me. No harm comes to her unless instructed.

His phone vibrated again.

Copy?

He was definitely getting too old for this shit. He couldn't return to his day job soon enough.

He typed back.

Copy.

CHAPTER 56

Mansfield

"Woody Solomon?" Dexter Mills asked, standing in his office doorway as Amity prepared to leave.

"Yeah," she answered, holding a manila folder containing the papers he'd copied for her. "The reporter who covered the Elvis Gentry meltdown in 1938."

"That's right. He must've been a rookie back then. Not an assignment the old guys would've wanted, I imagine."

"You know much about him?"

"Old Woody . . ." He looked up as he trailed off. "Woody became an institution. He _was_ the _News Journal_ for half a century. Gave me my first job in his later years. Most of us here, and in a whole lot of other places, owe our careers to him. All of us wanted to be the next Woody Solomon."

"When did he pass away?"

"He died about twenty years back. The whole town showed up for the funeral. The governor and both senators spoke."

"That good, huh?"

"He was. Tough but always fair. But his secret sauce was building deep relationships and treating everyone with respect, even when they screwed up. He was a good man personally and a good man professionally."

"Yeah, he could've been a lot tougher on old Elvis Gentry. The ed board here sure was."

"That wasn't his way. He didn't like the cheap stuff. Never did. He had a deep commitment to this community, and that's what drove his journalism. Bad news and scandals disappointed him. They felt like setbacks to the hometown he loved. He covered them by the book, but it's not what he enjoyed."

Amity nodded, her mind whirring. Her gut feeling from the archives was that young Woodrow Solomon had been holding something back. Dexter Mills just confirmed it.

"He still have family around here?" she asked.

"Sure. The Solomons are great people. His oldest son is the high school principal."

"Wait, Coach Solomon is his son?"

"Yes."

"Well, why didn't you say so?"

CHAPTER 57

Mansfield

"AMITY JONES, HOW the hell are you?"

Sam Solomon wasn't only the principal of Mansfield High but also its basketball coach. So Amity approached him on the sideline of the school's old gym in the middle of practice, leading to a big bear hug.

"Jeez," he said. "You're in even better shape than back in the day."

He hadn't coached the girls' basketball team, but the boys' and girls' teams often traveled together. So he'd watched her will her team to a lot of victories as the school's star point guard.

He was as intense now as he'd been back then, so their conversation advanced in spurts amid the repeated thuds of basketballs bouncing on the hardwood.

They caught up on her move back to Ohio and then Amity's mother's health. The two had overlapped for years as faculty at the school.

"Your mom's a tough woman, Amity. I watched her up close for a long time when we were dealing with all sorts of issues. If anyone can pull through this, she can."

"Thanks," Amity said, letting the hopeful words bounce right off her before turning the conversation toward his dad, Woodrow.

"My dad wouldn't have thought much of journalism today."

"Who could?" she asked, playing along. "Your dad's generation set a high bar."

He grabbed the whistle hanging by a cord around his neck and blew forcefully into it.

"Dribble drill two," he yelled. "Dribble drill two."

All twelve players sprinted in unison to center court before dribbling up and down the court, straight one way, then zigzagging all the way back.

"It looks like you've got some talent," Amity said, laughing.

"Not bad for a shrinking public school," he said. "But not like your heyday."

Driven more by her grit and speed than her talent with a ball, Amity had led the team to two state championships. And the boys' team had been runner-up her junior year.

Coach Solomon blew the whistle twice more, piercing her ear.

"Sprints," he yelled. "Sprints."

Each player rolled his ball to the side of the court and ran up and down the gleaming floor.

He looked Amity's way.

"So what do you need from Dad?" he asked, his directness embarrassing her.

"Dexter Mills at the *News Journal* told me that when your dad passed away, you came into possession of all his old newspaper stuff."

He looked back at practice, hands now on his hips. "Sure did. Boxes and boxes of it."

"Notebooks too?"

If Woody Solomon had held back information about the Elvis Gentry scandal, Dexter Mills said they'd be stored in a bunch of small spiral-bound notebooks. Woody was famous for them, filling up thousands over his career. Off the record. On the record. On background. Observations. Everything. And he never threw them out.

"Of course. That was most of it."

Amity tiptoed into the most important question. "You still have them?"

Another shriek of the whistle. "Free throws!"

Most of the boys lined up behind the free throw line, the first one taking a shot while two gathered under the basket to rebound. The shooter made his first seven shots, then missed one, then made his last two.

Then they rotated.

"Good!" he yelled without turning her way.

The next boy started shooting.

"Do you still have the notebooks?" Amity asked again.

He mumbled to himself as the kid missed four straight free throws. Then he looked over.

"Of course. Dad's old notes probably contain the most complete history of Mansfield over the fifty years he was in journalism. At some point I hope to put some kind of book together from all those little notebooks."

"Great idea. I was hoping I might review some of them for something I'm looking into with Dexter."

"Guys! At least seven out of ten or we lose games . . . Rotate!"

Amity waited a few seconds.

"It's an important and timely issue, and your dad's notes may be the key."

Amity braced herself as he pulled the whistle to his lips and unleashed the longest and loudest blast yet.

"Hit the lockers, guys! We'll talk in ten."

The boys placed the balls onto metal racks on the far sideline, then jogged through the door to the locker room. This was a disciplined crew. Like their coach.

Coach Solomon's chipper attitude faded as he turned back toward Amity.

"Amity, I want to help you, but Dad protected his years of notes like an armed guard. People trusted him. They shared things in confidence they wouldn't tell anyone else, and he protected those secrets like they were his own. I'm sure you understand."

Of course Amity did. From a legal standpoint, the reporter-source privilege disappeared when the parties passed away. But Coach Solomon probably wasn't interested in that technicality.

"I understand your respect for your dad and his commitment to keeping confidences. But I wouldn't be here asking if it weren't important. Lives might be at stake."

He stepped onto the court, heading toward the locker room.

"Including my mom's," she called after him.

CHAPTER 58

Mansfield

"REMIND ME AGAIN why we're doing all this?" Dexter asked, a twisted scowl on his weathered face.

Even with multiple light bulbs glowing from the ceiling, Sam Solomon's basement was as musty and dark as the *News Journal*'s, with the bonus feature of a mildewy stench. It was freezing cold to boot, so they left their winter coats on.

Amity exhaled.

"Because finding some connection to the Gentry family could tell us who is behind these miraculous recoveries."

"I know, I know."

They were standing in front of stacks of cardboard boxes that lined one wall. Before heading back upstairs, Solomon had directed them to those, saying they were chock-full of his dad's old notebooks.

Their dismal storage space aside, the boxes themselves attested to a truly impressive career. Dozens of them, each representing a year of hard work. They were stacked from oldest to newest—the oldest boxes lying on the floor, next to the wall; the newest boxes stacked on top, several rows away from the wall.

"Wow. He kept plugging away into the eighties," Amity said, lifting two boxes from the closest row and moving them off to the side.

"Sure did," Dexter said. "He's a better man than I intend to be."

Amity reached into the gap Dexter had left to get to the next row. She moved the boxes for 1963 through 1966 out of the way, then did the same for some boxes from the 1950s and 1940s.

"Here we go," Amity declared moments later, leaning over. "Nineteen-thirty eight."

She carried the 1938 box over to the basement's best-lit corner and sat on one of the closed boxes. She used the serrated edge of her car key to slice open the box's top, which unleashed an even more noxious odor.

"Yikes," Dexter said, his weathered face wrinkling even more. "I hope we find something good in there."

The notebooks were stacked neatly in four rows, a dozen across. Amity picked up a handful on top and flipped through them.

Woodrow Solomon took copious notes, so each notebook covered two or three days of interviews. Occasionally, just one day. Fortunately, he was highly organized: each of his notebooks was labeled on the front by the dates of the conversations within. Less fortunately, they were stacked in reverse chronological order, the oldest at the top, so they spent another ten minutes carefully removing each notebook and stacking them all off to the side.

Finally, she got to February, then January.

"Geez, what language was he writing in?" Amity asked after opening the first notebook she had, from January 20, 1938.

"The same one I write in," Dexter said. "Write shit down as fast as you can and hope you remember it later."

Amity laughed. She had waited tables all through college, so she understood. "Guess he didn't have anything to record with at the same time, like you guys do now."

"Yep. This was definitely pre-Dictaphone days. Well, look for the highlights, anyway. Then we can try to decipher the rest."

Finding nothing in the January 20 book, Amity set it aside.

January 21 was a busy day for Woody Solomon, because the next two notebooks were labeled with that date. A quick review of her notes from the archives revealed why: the twenty-first was the day after the paper had announced Gentry's statewide run and the day before the first negative story.

The first page of the first notebook contained the name Chairman Andrews, underlined. Andrews was the party leader who ripped the mayor in the January 22 story.

Amid page after page of chicken scratches, a few words stuck out, often circled: "drinking," "steered contracts," "wasted dollars," "blizzard response." This guy was dropping all the dirt at once. And the amount of scribbling between the headings meant he was providing a lot of details.

Well into the notebook, at the top of the page, the word "Mistress" appeared.

"Here we go," Amity declared.

But unlike the other headings, not much scribbling followed, just a list of names. And a large question mark appeared at the bottom.

"It doesn't look like Woodrow was interested in the affair to start," Amity said out loud. "Or at least he didn't buy it."

"Like I said, that wasn't his thing."

"Nope. But he did write down a bunch of names."

"Makes sense. If I didn't buy a story, the first thing I'd do is ask for other sources with firsthand knowledge. I bet these are the people who could confirm the affair."

Dexter dropped his notebook and moved behind Amity, pointing at the names listed.

"Five confirming sources. Not bad."

The last name on the list rang a bell: Wiley Murray.

Amity looked at her notes from the archives.

"Murray," she said out loud. "That's the council president who replaced him when he resigned."

"Wow. Same party and all. What a snake."

"Well, who knows if he ever talked."

Amity reached the end of the first January 21 notebook, then paged through the second. It contained a series of shorter interviews, including with two of the people listed on the "Mistress" page. Pages of notes followed each name. And one page included the name Abigail Bryant, circled, with the number "28" written next to it.

"Looks like he followed up and got a lot more details in the afternoon," Dexter said, now absorbed by Amity's notebook.

"Yep. Apparently good enough to at least mention the alleged affair in the next day's story."

"Yes. But he didn't mention her name yet. Or her age."

"Not yet. He probably wanted to verify those too. Good discretion."

Dexter laughed. "Ol' Woody wouldn't last a week in the current media environment."

For the next hour they went through notebook after notebook, walking in Woody Solomon's footsteps as he followed his trail of sources.

CHAPTER 59

—

Mansfield

AN HOUR INTO waiting on the residential street, Quinn called the professor.

"What is it?"

"Doctor, she's up to something here. She's a dog chasing a bone."

"Tell me exactly what, please."

The professor's impatient tone rankled Quinn. He'd worked for the nation's finest, something this megalomaniac certainly was not. No matter the circumstance, others never talked down to him. They respected his years of service.

"She didn't go to her mother's at all but started at the newspaper. Spent hours there. Then she headed over to the high school and spent another forty minutes there, watching a basketball practice—"

"She watched a high school basketball practice?"

"Yes, sir. Then she followed the coach back to the school building. Came out twenty minutes later."

"Okay."

"And now she and some reporter are at the coach's house."

"And where are you?"

"Parked four driveways away."

Silence on the other end.

"Professor?"

"Stay there. I'll see if anyone can figure out what she might be up to."

"Okay. She's close to something. I could—"

"Do nothing unless I say so directly."

Quinn hung up and made a second call. Same update. But, as always, a far more respectful response.

CHAPTER 60

Fort Myers, Florida

"SEE YOU NEXT week, Senator."

Like always, Gigi Fox was the first person off the United Airlines flight from D.C. into Fort Myers, the closest commercial airport to her Naples home. Seat 1A, which her staff reserved every week, guaranteed a quick exit.

She had taken the two-hour flight ever since United launched the direct route a decade before, saving her tens of thousands of dollars in jet fuel and pilot time each trip. The handful of crew who flew the route had long ago dubbed it the "Senator Fox Express." She now saved the private jet for West Coast and overseas trips.

"Thank you, Captain. Have a great weekend."

Pulling her small bag behind her, the senator briskly walked up the jet bridge. Entering the terminal, as tired as she felt, she forced a smile. She knew what was coming.

Within feet, eyes followed her.

"Hi, Senator," a voice from her right called out.

She looked in that direction and waved at a curly-haired middle-aged woman waiting to board a flight at the next gate over.

"Hey there. How are ya?"

"Great." The woman giggled. "Thanks for all you do."

"Thank *you* for giving me the opportunity!"

The woman whispered into the ear of a pimply-faced teenager standing next to her, who then stared as well. Others in the line murmured as they watched her walk past.

Years back, when Gigi Fox won the big case that put her on the national map, people began recognizing her in public. Some, particularly African Americans, would say hello as if they knew her. But once elected as Florida's second ever woman senator—and its first Democratic woman—people pointed her out wherever she went. Especially back home. And as she unleashed her signature populist rhetoric on the buttoned-up Senate floor, everyday Americans saw her as fighting for them. They greeted her like they were old friends.

At first, she'd assumed modesty was the appropriate response. But she learned quickly that people mistook that for rudeness. A hearty smile and warm reply to the attention proved far better.

"Welcome home, Senator."

The man's voice came from her left. A United Airlines gate agent who'd worked there for years.

She waved back.

"Good to be home, Johnny. How's the family?"

"Wonderful. Yours?"

"Great. We're blessed."

She kept walking.

A few more greetings and thank-yous followed—more travelers, another gate agent, a kiosk worker, and a shoe shiner—before she stepped onto the escalator descending to the baggage claim.

A few seconds to think.

Shepherd was right: things were getting far too dicey.

Duke leaping off a cliff.

The professor, idiotically, speaking at the funeral. Looking at them as he did.

One of Ernest's law clerks following the van to Tennessee. Now on the hunt back in Ohio.

She recalled Shep's words. Like him, she'd spent her career burnishing a reputation of integrity. Breaking barriers. Fighting for justice. As every walk through every airport terminal reminded her, her fight for everyday people was noticed.

As Shep fretted about *his* standing, it had never occurred to him that to get to the rarefied air they both now occupied, *she'd* overcome far more. And having climbed so much further, she had so much more to lose.

As a kid, she'd moved from town to town throughout Florida, her single mom bouncing from one job to the next, waiting tables while staying under the radar. Outside of the love of her doting mother, her only assets as a teenager were her street smarts and book smarts, which fueled her success at each of the seven schools she attended before graduating high school. Top grades earned her a full ride to the University of Florida, where she graduated second in her class. Then she became one of the first women ever to attend Duke Law School.

Back then, law professors were far tougher on the two to three women in each classroom than the dozens of men who surrounded them. Whether intentional or not, that treatment helped immensely, preparing her for the most antagonistic questions while teaching her that a sharp retort beat a long-winded answer every time. The tactic would later serve her well in the courtroom, in campaign debates, and in the well of the Senate.

But there had still been more barriers to overcome before she'd lead those opportunities.

Second in her law school class, she couldn't land a job at a major law firm. Couldn't even land an interview. Which was when she began her work as a low-paid public defender—and even then it took her a year to convince her male boss to let her argue before a jury. Three years later, after she'd beat them time and again in court, the local DA cherry-picked her by doubling her salary. After a decade of locking up criminals, she then ran for office herself.

First as DA, when her boss retired.

Then attorney general.

Then . . .

"Take a load off, Senator. You're home!"

A cherubic bearded man rose from below. He was riding the up escalator as she neared the bottom.

"Couldn't come soon enough," she said, smiling back. "From the swamp to paradise."

"Amen," he said as he lifted past her.

She stepped off the escalator and passed the baggage carousel, heading straight outside. After days of Washington cold and gray, she squinted under the bright Florida sun.

The black Escalade with tinted windows idled where it always did, first in line. Airport security knew the car and its passenger.

She opened the door and sat down in the back.

"Welcome home, Senator," the driver said.

"Thank you, Thomas." Hearing Thomas's Australian accent brightened her mood. Having worked for the family for years, he'd become a member himself. "Home never felt so good."

She stewed the entire drive home.

Yes, the treatment was working. They were making so much progress. But the risks were growing just as quickly.

As Thomas drove south along the coastal highway, low Gulf waves lapped against the white beach for miles on end, interrupted only by palm trees and the new, gaudy mansions that dotted the Naples coastline. The sun had already dropped a third of the way toward the horizon along its rapid wintertime descent. She'd traveled the world many times over yet still didn't know of a better view.

The Escalade slowed, veered right into an exit lane, then stopped. The turn signal clicked as Thomas waited for the two sides of the iron gate to open.

"We're here, Senator. Wally is excited to have you home."

"Wonderful," she said. "That makes two of us."

When the gate opened, the Escalade passed between two large alabaster columns and entered the fanciest seaside estate in the area.

CHAPTER 61

———

Mansfield

THE DOOR CREAKED as light flooded the basement from above.

A voice yelled down from upstairs. Coach Solomon.

"Guys, we're gonna head out soon. Girls' basketball game. You're going to have to wrap up."

"We're almost done," Amity yelled back into the air.

But they weren't even close.

Thirty-two notebooks were laid out across the cement floor. Every one from January 21 until the late February day when Mayor Gentry resigned.

After an hour, she and Dexter had mostly deciphered Woodrow Solomon's shorthand. And they'd come up with a good system: Amity would skim through the notebooks to find pertinent details, then Dexter would take photos of the relevant pages in case they needed them later.

Amid the notebooks, eight different sources confirmed the Gentry affair. Some political operatives with axes to grind. Two members of the Mansfield City Council. And Council President Murray, in particular, lived down to Dexter's hunch. His interview was the longest, and he didn't hold back in castigating the mayor with 1930s-style personal insults, some of which—"cur," "wretch," "scalawag"—they understood.

Several City Hall staff talked off the record, coming across as especially credible. They had witnessed things up close and had no obvious agenda.

But for all Amity and Dexter found, few details emerged that hadn't been reported in the paper. Most of the sources simply confirmed the same facts.

The affair had gone on for years.

Abigail Bryant was twenty-eight years old when it was discovered.

She had some type of administrative job in the mayor's office and was good at it. The City Hall staff complimented her for her hard work and professionalism.

They were never seen together in public but were known to spend time in his office after business hours. Several witnesses had walked in on them while they were embracing.

Abigail joined the mayor on several official trips, including to Columbus and to Washington. One City Council member once spotted the two in a room together at the Great Southern Hotel in Columbus at a far later hour than appropriate.

If Woodrow Solomon left some of these details out of the paper because they weren't germane to the story, Amity couldn't blame him.

"Hey," Dexter said, not looking up from a notebook he was leafing through. "Here's another guy who said they thought it had ended a year or so before. That she had left town for some time."

"Interesting. That's what the deputy clerk said as well. But then she came back and it started up again."

"Maybe they tried to break it off but failed."

An interesting tidbit.

The door creaked again.

"Guys!" Solomon yelled from above, using his coaching voice. "Three minutes!"

They had already moved all the other boxes back into place, along with all the 1938 notebooks they hadn't used into their box.

"You get all the photos you need?" Amity asked Dexter.

"Sure did."

She started placing the thirty-two notebooks back into their box.

"Not sure there's any breaking news in what we found here," Dexter said, verbalizing Amity's own disappointment.

"Well, we can go back through the photos and see if we missed anything."

But Dexter was right. If Woody Solomon had buried some bombshell in 1938, he hadn't written it down in these notebooks.

As Amity laid the January and February notebooks back in the box, her eye caught the dates of the notebooks they were covering: April and May.

She stopped stacking.

"Wait a second."

"One minute to go, guys!" Solomon yelled from above. "I can't miss tip-off!"

"Just putting everything back how your dad had 'em," Dexter yelled back before turning to Amity. "What?"

"We forgot one story."

"We did?"

"Yes. Late April. When Gentry skipped town."

Amity reached into her pocket and looked again at her notes from the archives. April 26 was the day the paper had reported that Gentry and Abigail Bryant had left.

She grabbed eight notebooks from late April, handing four of them to Dexter. They started paging through them furiously.

Suddenly the room went black, as if a kid was playing a prank on them.

"Sorry guys. Time's up."

The lights turned back on as Sam Solomon's winter boots appeared at the top of the stairs. Amity half expected a loud whistle next.

"You can always come back."

Amity shoved four notebooks inside her coat.

Dexter did the same.

They closed the 1938 box and placed it with the others.

"All done!" she yelled back. "On our way up."

CHAPTER 62

—

Mansfield

Leaving Solomon's house at the southern tip of the county, Amity and Dexter headed back to the paper.

With Amity behind the wheel, Dexter read aloud from the April notebooks they'd grabbed. He set aside the first six, having found nothing relevant. But the seventh caught his attention.

"Looks like Gentry left days before the April story ran. Woody was late to it, playing catch-up."

"Makes sense," Amity said. "That's not the kind of thing you'd announce. Who told him?"

"A council member. Not one of the ones from before. An ally, I believe . . ."

He turned a page.

"Rumor was he was heading south. Unclear where."

"Anything about Abigail Bryant joining him?"

Amity turned her left-turn signal on and waited in the left-turn lane into the North I-71 highway entrance, one exit down from the Mansfield exit.

"Nothing."

Dexter held the notebook closer to his face.

"Hold on. There's an address here. Underlined. One Twenty-Four New-man Street."

He turned the page as Amity began to turn left.

"Wow!" Dexter yelled out.

"What?"

A startled Amity swerved back into the turn lane, as a semi sped past the other way. The sudden change forced the driver of a black BMW behind her to brake to a screeching stop. He blared his horn for a good five seconds.

"The next interview is with a 'Mr. Bryant.' And that address is written again. Woody went to their home."

Distracted, Amity sat in the main road, frozen in place as cars sped past on both her left and right.

"'Mr. Bryant'? As in a husband?"

"Or a dad. Who knows?"

"Good find! Let's track it down."

With the next oncoming car fifty yards away, the BMW circled around Amity's left to enter the highway, honking one more time.

The next vehicle back—an SUV—slowed down, giving her space to turn left onto the highway.

Helpful, although not because he wanted to be.

The driver was keeping his distance. Staying hidden. But his large bald head was unmistakable.

Amity gripped the steering wheel tightly, trying to calm her nerves.

"Dexter, we're being followed."

———

AMITY TURNED LEFT and drove five miles up 71 before getting off at the Mansfield exit. But rather than turning the usual left into town, she headed into a village of gas stations and fast-food restaurants that survived off the highway traffic and were much busier than Main Street in Mansfield itself. After a few turns, she pulled into a packed Applebee's parking lot.

The bald guy was damn good, staying well back. If it weren't for dumb luck, Amity never would've noticed him. The question was whether he knew that she'd seen him.

"Now what?" Dexter asked as she parked.

Amity looked back in her mirror before answering. The gray Dodge Caravan pulled into a BP station several properties away, but the driver didn't get out.

"*Now* we surround ourselves with other people and figure out what the hell we're gonna do."

Minutes later, food ordered and oversized plastic cups of Diet Coke in front of each of them, they brainstormed from a booth off the bar.

"The fact that he hasn't tried to stop us means they want to know what we're looking for."

"That's rather optimistic of you, Amit—"

A loud clang cut him off as a young server dropped a large plate of potato skins, drowning in melted cheddar cheese, onto the table.

Famished, Amity ignored her fork and knife and grabbed the first potato skin with her fingers.

"So what do we do next?" Dexter asked.

As Amity took a bite into the first potato, the piping-hot cheese singed her lips and tongue. A quick swig of Diet Coke temporarily soothed the pain.

Mouth still stinging, she took another sip.

"We split up."

Dexter cocked his head.

"Split up how?"

"I'll go to that Bryant address and check it out. You stay here and go through the rest of the notes. If he sees me, I'm sure he'll stick with me."

"But we only have one car."

"I know we're in Mansfield, Dexter, but you do have Uber here, don't you?"

Mom had taken an Uber to the hospital the other day, among other trips.

Dexter nodded sheepishly. "True."

She took out her phone and ordered one.

———

AFTER WATCHING AMITY climb into a silver Toyota Prius, Dexter dove back into Woody Solomon's April notes.

Just a few words made clear that "Mr. Bryant" was the proud father of Abigail Bryant. He'd spent most of the short interview complimenting her. Supporting her. Defending her. As any father would.

"Beautiful person." "So dedicated." "Supervisors loved her work." "Compassionate." "Conscientious."

Then came confirmation that she'd left town.

"Gone three days ago."

"Two suitcases."

"Left warm clothes behind."

"Didn't ask for money."

"Family devastated."

But Mr. Bryant didn't know where she'd gone.

The fact that they'd left on the same day, that she hadn't asked her family for money, and that she'd left her cold-weather clothes suggested she'd indeed gone with Gentry. South. Woody appeared to agree, writing: "Together."

The pages that followed included fresh conversations with the two City Hall workers interviewed months before. She had left City Hall within days of the scandal breaking, they explained. But now these workers, who had kept up with her personally, confirmed she had skipped town earlier in the week.

The final page of the notebook was cryptic.

It was the City Hall deputy clerk, who appeared to know both the mayor and Abigail Bryant well. Most of Woody's notes here were inscrutable. But apparently he was the only person who knew where they'd gone. Because, below everything else, one word was written clearly, on its own—circled and underlined.

With an exclamation point next to it.

"Virginia!"

CHAPTER 63

————

Mansfield

DARKNESS SET IN as the Uber driver took Amity back past the old brick buildings of downtown Mansfield. Then they headed north, navigating among abandoned buildings of various shapes and sizes—ghosts of the town's industrial past—while bouncing over multiple sets of railroad tracks. The silhouette of the old state prison known as the Ohio State Reformatory—the site where they'd filmed *The Shawshank Redemption*—emerged like a medieval fortress in the distance. They turned right, bounced along a bumpy road between some run-down homes, and stopped.

This was a pretty shabby part of town, a place Amity never went as a kid.

"Here you go, ma'am."

The beam of the car's headlights lit up the near-empty remains of an old strip mall. The only functioning businesses were a check-cashing shop and a dollar store separated by three empty storefronts.

"Are you sure this is the right address? I was looking for a house or an apartment."

"You said One Twenty-Four Newman Street, right?"

"Yeah."

He pointed to the electronic map on his center console.

"This is One Twenty-Four Newman."

She looked out the window again. It was the kind of place she'd escape to as a kid when Mom was burrowed in at home. These little outdoor malls still felt new back then, bustling with latchkey kids with a few dollars to spend and hours to kill after school. Shoes. Video games. Candy. Stickers. All right there, up and down the mall. The closest she and Simon got to an amusement park.

But big-box stores, then online shopping, had delivered a crushing one-two punch to little malls like this. The better shops couldn't compete, leaving dollar stores and check-cashing operations as the last gasp of commerce.

She looked at the Uber driver's pudgy face in the rearview mirror. White beard. Gray hair. And lots of wrinkles in between.

"You from around here?" she asked.

"Sure am. Born and raised. Seventy-two years and counting."

Perfect.

"Do you remember when this little mall was first built?"

"Sure do. Maybe forty years ago. Forty-five, I'd say. They knocked down a whole lot of old homes to build this and some other new stuff around here. They also added Route Thirty up over there. Just like that, the old neighborhood vanished. Only the Reformatory is left."

"Was that controversial? When they tore it down."

"Not really. They forked over good money to the residents to leave. Looks like a bad decision now, but at the time people happily took the cash and moved elsewhere."

"What was it like before that?"

His shoulders shrugged.

"Uh, they said it was pretty nice. Tight-knit community, from what I hear. Lots of history."

"You know people who lived there?"

"A couple kids from school and one teacher, but not really. Actually, never went to the neighborhood at all."

"Never? Really? It's not like Mansfield is all that big. Only a few minutes from downtown."

He shrugged again, then darted a glance in the rearview mirror.

"Ma'am, times were different then. Like they were everywhere. Kids like me . . . we didn't go to the Black neighborhoods."

It took a moment for his final two words to settle in.

"Excuse me?" Amity asked, leaning forward as her stomach quivered.

He chuckled awkwardly, sensing that she was judging him. That he needed to explain himself.

"They called this place Company Line. It was the first real Black neighborhood of Mansfield, ma'am. They say it grew pretty fast in the thirties and forties, not far from the Reformatory and the steel mill. Some of the old families and a bunch of new ones moved in. But we kept pretty separate back then. I guess we still sort of do, but it was worse then. I wouldn't have ever gone there as a kid. We didn't mix much. Though, like I said, we heard people were pretty nice over there . . ."

He paused.

". . . before it all went away."

Amity stared out the window.

Mr. Bryant.

Company Line.

A historic Black neighborhood chopped up by new development and highway construction. It had happened so often around the country, around the same time. She'd reviewed several housing discrimination cases with similar stories, only to have the displaced families resegregated elsewhere.

Suddenly it all made sense.

The family shame, so deep that Mrs. Gentry became a lifelong hermit and her kids all left town.

A scandal so salacious that Elvis Gentry didn't just quit but fled Mansfield and never returned.

Woody Solomon barely mentioning Abigail Bryant. As Dexter Mills said, he didn't enjoy the big scandals.

And he didn't even write it down—in his notes or in the newspaper itself.

But he didn't need to. Everyone would've known.

Abigail Bryant lived in Company Line. With her family.

She was Black.

Amity sat in stunned silence for a few seconds.

"What's the word, ma'am?" the driver asked. "You getting out?"

"You can take me back to the Applebee's now."

CHAPTER 64

Naples, Florida

"Honey, you've got nothing to hide. You're doing so much good."

If Gigi was the shooting star of the couple, Wally Fox had been its solid, stable rock for almost sixty years. The one who lifted her when she had doubts. The one who steeled her when she faced criticism.

So he played that role again now.

They were sitting on the upper balcony of the mansion, sipping cocktails Thomas had prepared, watching the slim arc of orange and pink shrink over the Gulf. A light breeze cooled the evening air.

They'd met in law school. She was second in her class. He was first. Wally Fox from the hills of North Carolina, near Boone, not far from Asheville. Tall and thin, an easy smile, with mutton chops, curly blond locks—all of them gone now—and a thick Appalachian drawl. Dreamy as could be, he even strummed the banjo. He swept her off her feet, and they married in their third year.

"Wally, I think I made a mistake," she said, leaning back in her wooden chair. "I should've left well enough alone, and now it's too late."

While she hadn't landed a single interview out of law school, he'd gotten outright offers from the top twelve white-shoe firms on the Eastern Seaboard. But to be with her, and to punish those who'd rejected his whip-smart wife, he rejected every last one and settled for a corporate law boutique in Tampa. He quickly rose to be the town's top lawyer and, soon, one of Florida's best.

The timing of his rise in legal circles had been ideal. No one really knew how much corporate lawyers made. Some became millionaires. Others barely made ends meet. People just assumed Wally Fox was raking it in, which was why he and his firebrand progressive wife were able to live so well. After all, she was a public servant, making peanuts, so he must've been the breadwinner while she did her thing.

But if anyone had done the math, it didn't add up. Their wealth was too substantial—their estate too grand—for a guy who started with nothing who now billed hours at a Tampa-based law firm.

But no one did the math.

"Since when have you left well enough alone, Gin?" Wally asked. He'd called her "Gin" since law school, even as "Gigi" had taken hold with every-one else. "If you'd left well enough alone, you'd still be defending drunk drivers in muni court."

"Hey," she said, squeezing his hand in hers. "I still wonder if that wasn't the most important job I ever had: sticking up for the little guy—the one with no one in his corner."

He was needling her. More than anyone, he knew how important that work had been to her. It reflected her core, shaping the rest of her life's work even as they'd come into their wealth. And it was why he loved her.

"Well, you still do that every day, just on a bigger scale."

She smiled.

"I do my best."

"Gin, if your only mistake was that you're helping the little guy one more time, that's not something to ever regret."

She nodded. He was right. She'd make the same decision again. It was the right thing to do.

When the time had come to choose, Shep had chosen to help Mary. Sam

Ireland and Duke Garber each faced their own physical battles, so they'd helped themselves. She still didn't know who Byron Blue had helped; he was as secretive about it as she'd been.

For her, the choice had been as obvious as it must have been for Shep. The guilt had hung over her for years: life for them had been so unfair, while she had been so fortunate, arguably at their expense. So when she'd faced the decision, it felt like the most meaningful way to make things whole. Especially after they'd stubbornly refused to accept financial help. After she'd failed to help the last time.

This time they'd accepted, and, thank God, it was working. They were all joyous about the news.

The pink sliver on the horizon had disappeared, replaced by only the faintest orange glow.

"I won't ever regret it. But as remote as it seemed then, the risk I most feared is now playing out."

The door cracked open behind them.

"Senator," Thomas said gingerly. "I hate to interrupt."

"What is it?" she asked, leaning forward, their moment of peace ending. Thomas would interrupt only if it was important.

"You have a call. From Boston."

CHAPTER 65

——

Mansfield

"STUNNING" WAS ALL Dexter Mills could say after Amity explained what she'd found.

About Company Line.

About Abigail Bryant.

"There wasn't one hint of Abigail's race in any interview," he said after taking a few sips of his Diet Coke. "Not in a single story. And not one photo of her."

Happy hour was in full swing, packing people into the Applebee's bar and jamming some right up against their booth. Rather than talking over the din, they scooched as far into the booth as they could and leaned over the table only inches from each other.

Amity leaned in as she replied, "I guess in a small town, back then, it wouldn't even need to be written down."

"No need. Everyone would've known. And that explains the intense re-action to the scandal for years to come."

"Yes, it does."

She glanced at the notebooks sitting next to Dexter's still untouched silverware. "Did you find anything else in those?"

A woman in the bar yelled out, drawing Amity's gaze. Then she froze.

The back of a bald, round head gleamed only feet away, reflecting the bright lights overhead. The figure was thick and tall, like the man who'd tackled her back in Tennessee.

"Look down," she said to Dexter as a chill ran down her back.

"What?"

"Just look down. Hide your face. Now."

She grabbed the drink menu off the table and held it in front of her.

"What?" Dexter said impatiently.

The bald head was even closer now.

"I think he—"

The man took a step to his right, his head turning enough to reveal a short goatee and straight nose.

"Forget it," she said, exhaling as she laid the menu back down. "False alarm."

"Well, that's good," Dexter said as he looked back up. "And to answer your question, no, I didn't find much. Nothing like yours."

"Nothing at all?" Amity asked. Realizing they were sitting ducks while crammed in the back of the booth, she scanned the crowd as they spoke.

"Just confirming the basics. Oh, and one person said they'd run off to Virginia."

Dexter flipped to the page and showed Amity the notation: *Virginia!*

"Strange. Woody was awfully enthused about that fact—exclamation point and all. Wonder why?"

"Don't know. He never mentioned it in any stories or anywhere else. Must not have panned out."

Amity stared down at the open notebook, racking her brain while trying to drown out the noise.

"Wait a second."

She looked straight at Dexter, her pulse quickening.

"Do you have those copies from before? Of the papers from your drawer?"

"Yeah."

He took the folder from a small satchel and laid it on the table. Amity grabbed it and quickly flipped through the pages.

"Hey, Red!"

Having been called that too often over the years, she looked up. A bearded man, late thirties or forties, was leaning against their table.

"Yes?" Amity said.

"Isn't he a little old for you?" the man asked, swaying as he laughed.

So many retorts came to mind, but she decided that the best one was to ignore the drunk. She looked back down and continued flipping through the folder. The man stepped back into the crowd.

"What are you looking for?" Dexter asked.

"Here it is."

She pulled out a page and scanned it.

"I knew it. I'd glanced at it before, in your office."

"What?"

"This is Alma Gentry's obituary."

She rotated the piece of paper so it faced Dexter.

"Why would her obituary mention where Elvis Gentry had gone?"

"It doesn't." She paused a beat. "But, like any obituary, it mentions her kids. *Their* kids."

"Well, what do they—"

"Just read it!" she said, louder than she meant to.

Dexter looked down, his eyes dancing from left to right, still unsure what he was looking for.

Amity pointed to a couple of lines.

"'Alma Gentry (née Gabriel).'" A few sentences summarized her life, cleansed of the scandal. Then came her kids, and two sentences that Amity read out loud.

"'Alma is survived by her sons Jerry and Melvin and daughter Camille. She was preceded in death by her son Elvis, Jr., and her daughter Virginia.'"

"Virginia!" Dexter exclaimed.

Amity's heart beat so hard she could hear it despite the crowd.

"Exactly. Virginia wasn't where they went. It was a name. The name of their youngest daughter."

"The one who disappeared."

"Exactly! So why would she end up in Woody's notes, with an exclamation point, as he interviewed people about Elvis Gentry and Abigail Bryant skipping town?"

Amity clamped her hands together. It was clear now.

Several City Hall employees had said Abigail Bryant had disappeared for some months. They assumed it was for good. But then she'd come back.

"Because they took Virginia with her."

"And why would they do—"

"My God."

CHAPTER 66

Mansfield

QUINN SAT IN the gas station parking lot, waiting for the duo to get back on the road. But he needed direction on what to do.

They'd clearly seen him. Pulling into the Applebee's, staying there that long, splitting up, using Uber to do so. They knew he was watching.

Splitting up was the right idea, but it hadn't worked. He'd followed the Prius with the drone he always had on him. The woman had headed back into town, then slightly north, all well within range. It was slightly windy out, but far less so than the Maine flight where he had hovered yards beyond the lighthouse, offering a perfect view of the senator's final walk. This pocket-sized drone could do just about anything.

It had been an odd visit. Whatever she was looking for, she hadn't found. Pulling up to a lifeless strip mall, sitting in the car for two minutes, then heading straight back. Weird all around.

The professor had demanded every detail. The newspaper visit. The school stop. The principal's house. So now Quinn reported the strange drive to the strip mall.

Minutes later, the professor followed up with one question.

What is the exact address of the mall?

A quick online search found it.

In the 100s on Newman St., he texted back. Between Mulberry and Bowman. Near that old jail where they made the movie.

No response.

His phone rang.

"It's time," the professor said.

"Time?"

"Yes. They're getting too close."

CHAPTER 67

——

Mansfield

AMITY FORGOT THE noise around her as she thought it all through.

Virginia Gentry.

A name buried eighty-odd years ago in a small Ohio town. And almost everyone who knew had a good reason to keep it buried right there.

Elvis Gentry and Abigail Bryant had run off in part to make it all go away. Taking Virginia Gentry with them.

Alma Gentry would've known the truth. Which meant she'd been part of it, knowingly raising the offspring of her husband's affair as her own daughter—a mixed-race half sister of her own children. Together, a hell of a reason to keep it all buried.

Woody Solomon had likely discovered the truth. But he didn't relish scandal. And this was as scandalous as it got.

Better to let it die.

And it did.

Even if someone had been looking, back then, a young girl, hundreds or thousands of miles away, might as well have been living in a foreign country. Given the mystery of her departure, no one would've known where to look. Or how.

But in the days of the internet, all you needed was a name.

And now Amity had one.

Amity took out her laptop and searched for women named Virginia Gentry.

Through Google and Facebook. Then Instagram and Twitter.

Hundreds of matches emerged. All over the country.

Far too many to be useful.

Lawyers. Housewives. Students. Dentists. A model. A few journalists. College kids. A city council member in Memphis. A mayor of a small town in Montana. Some were wearing bikinis, others pantsuits, others everything in between. Most were white, some Black. All shapes and sizes. Most anonymous. None famous beyond their own community.

She narrowed her search to women born in the 1930s, but the search grew even more fruitless. Grandmothers and retirees, gray- and white-haired. Inactive or slowing down. None felt remotely close to the elite world of Shepherd and Mary Logan and miracle cures.

She conducted the same drill with the name Virginia Bryant. Even more names to sort through. A tiny needle buried amid acres of haystacks.

"Nothing," Amity said, frustration in her voice after an hour of looking. "She probably got married and changed her name."

"Or they might have changed her name from the outset," Dexter said. "Still, you'd think it would show up somewhere. At least as a first name and maiden name."

Amity looked up, seeing that it was now fully dark outside.

She stood up.

"We've been here long enough. And he must have left by now. Let's call it a day."

———

EVEN THOUGH THEY didn't see the Caravan at the gas station or anywhere else, Dexter insisted on accompanying Amity back to Columbus.

Driving through a steady snowfall, exhausted, they stewed for thirty miles—long silences followed by fits of brainstorming, then Dexter doing some quick searches online in the passenger seat. But they kept coming up empty.

Twenty minutes from Columbus, Amity pulled off at a state-run rest stop, boulders of plowed snow piled up on both sides of the turnoff. Amity used the bathroom, then bought a Diet Coke and a Kit Kat from the vending machines.

As she walked through the lobby, the large, smiling faces of Ohio's new governor and lieutenant governor beamed at her from the back wall, their perfect white teeth accentuated by the sheen of the new photos.

The duo had been sworn in only a few months ago. Yet, here they were, already featured at rest stops.

Amity chuckled. Government moves as slow as molasses when constituents are the ones waiting. Basic services. Public record requests. Contracts and refunds. Long lines for license plates. All so slow.

But the updated photos of governors and other politicians sprung up almost overnight after an election. Amazing how the levers of government work so well to serve the politicians at the top who pull them.

She turned and walked toward the main door, cold air rushing in as she pushed it open. Then she stopped, looking back at the photos one last time.

She froze as it dawned on her: they were going about their search all wrong.

She'd gone to the trouble of looking into the Gentry family because she suspected a deal at the highest levels. Because a well-connected person—perhaps a ranking politician like Senator Logan—had secured the miracle treatment for Colin Gentry.

So, in looking for Virginia Gentry, it made no sense to start where she had—at the bottom, with broad searches of every Virginia Gentry in the country.

No, she should start where the dealmaking would have taken place—at the top. And that was a far more manageable universe. A needle from a handful of needles. Forget the haystacks.

"You mind driving the rest of the way?" she asked Dexter when they got back to the car. "I've got an idea."

A minute later they merged onto the highway. Once back online, Amity didn't go to Google, Facebook, or any other broad search tool. She went straight to the roster of the one hundred members of the most exclusive club in the world.

The United States Senate.

And things narrowed down quickly.

There were only fourteen women in the body to begin with.

But Virginia Gentry would be in her eighties now, while almost all the women in the Senate were newcomers, part of a new generation rising in politics. Only five were over sixty-five. Only three over seventy-five.

Of the three, one was native Hawaiian. Amity took her off the list.

The second was the four-term senator from Minnesota. She hailed from a family that had dominated Minnesota politics for three generations. She was definitely not Virginia Gentry.

Only one senator remained.

Amity pulled up her website.

No birth date was listed, but she was definitely in her late seventies or early eighties. Her steely, narrow eyes bore into Amity. Dark complected, leathery skin, with black and silver bangs falling close to her eyes, the rest of her hair pulled back in her signature bun.

The great Florida firebrand.

Amity had been a fan of the senator since law school. Awed, really. A pistol amid dozens of bland, buttoned-up men, she could shake up the entire place in a single three-minute speech. Always on a mission. Always righting wrongs. Never backing down.

"Gigi Fox," she said out loud.

"From Florida?" Dexter asked.

Heart pounding, she started researching the Florida senator.

"It's gotta be her."

Amity had never looked into it, but she'd always imagined the aging icon had a hell of a life story.

CHAPTER 68

—

Naples

GIGI FOX HATED it, but she and Wally had slept in different rooms for years.

He'd battled throat cancer in his mid-sixties, escaping with a clean bill of health. The only long-term consequences were that he had to pay close attention to his diet and that he snored so loudly she called him her little jet engine. They'd tried everything to muffle the harsh raking of his throat that accompanied every breath while he slept, but nothing worked.

So, after dinner and their evening drink, they'd prepare for bed in their joint bathroom, kiss good night, then part ways to sleep.

Usually she fell asleep before nine and slept soundly. But on rough nights she despised the separation.

Tonight she couldn't even close her eyes.

The most recent update from Mansfield scared the hell out of her. Visits to the newspaper and the school meant the woman was digging deep into the Gentry lineage. And the car ride to the site where Mother had once lived meant that research was making headway.

For most of her life, all she knew about Mansfield was that it was a struggling town in Ohio. A victim of the failed economic policies she'd fought so hard to change. Still, a world away.

But not long after being elected senator, after a call out of the blue, she'd learned the truth.

Mansfield, Ohio, was her hometown. Her father had once been its mayor. And her father and mother had left in disgrace, in large part because of her.

In short, she'd learned her entire life had been a lie.

Her name growing up had been Ginny Milburn. According to her mother, Milburn was a drunk who'd left them when she was an infant. There were no photos of him, and Mother never talked about him, so young Ginny never asked.

As she came of age, she just assumed Mr. Milburn had been white. Mother's skin was a striking olive gold; Ginny's was lighter—a light pecan brown—and, unlike Mother, she had straight hair. Her pallor was so light that Mother had succeeded in getting Ginny into white schools from the outset. With that initial success, Mother had made sure that she passed as white in all other endeavors, shielding her from the discrimination she battled on a daily basis. Since her father was white, for most of her childhood Ginny had assumed this was normal. Only later did she realize how hard Mother must've worked to pull it off—how much it had twisted Mother's life into knots. This was why they'd moved so often.

Two years after Mother died, on Ginny's twenty-first birthday, she'd learned even more. A letter arrived in her college mailbox from a fancy New Orleans law firm. A week later, its author—a well-coiffed mustachioed man with a deep Cajun accent—visited campus to reinforce the letter's simple message. A trust had been set up in her name and would disburse funds every five years for twenty-five years as long as she was living a good and productive life.

Ginny had peppered the lawyer with a lifetime of questions, but he demurred.

"All I can tell you," he'd said in a small law office near campus, "is that your father was named Gentry. He was a deeply troubled man—so troubled that he took his own life. But before he did, he named you the beneficiary of his estate."

"Why me?" she remembered asking. "Was I his only child?"

"I've said all I can. Now let's open up an account and get you started."

They never met again. But everything the lawyer had said that day came true.

The first payment had arrived the next week and was enough to get her through the rest of college and then law school. Over the next twenty-five years, at the promised five-year intervals, the payments escalated far beyond anything she had expected from that one-hour conversation. And only Wally knew.

After an hour in bed, she finally closed her eyes. But her head spun, the momentous decisions of her life flashing by at breakneck speed. Even small choices had consequences she could never have imagined. And many were on the verge of crashing down on her now.

One such decision came months after the first payment.

Her visit to the Alachua County courthouse now replayed in full color. The granite steps. The oversized oak door. The long, stately corridor. The friendly greeting from the deputy magistrate, who handed her three pieces of paper and a fountain pen.

And after a ten-minute wait, it was done.

Excited to have learned the name of her real father, appreciative of his life-changing generosity, Ginny formally changed her name to Virginia Gentry Milburn. That was when she began signing term papers and legal documents "G. G. Milburn," a small tribute to her generous father emblazoned on everything she did.

When she married Wally in law school, she changed names again, dropping the "Milburn" entirely to become Virginia "Ginny" Gentry Fox. And by the time law school was over, thanks to professors who insisted on using her first two initials as her classroom name, she was known by all but Wally as Gigi Fox.

But now, she feared, that name change might come back to haunt her.

She stood up from the lush king bed, walked to the bathroom, and pressed a warm, wet towel on her face. On her most restless of nights, this was the most effective way to induce sleep. She laid the towel on the marble sink and looked in the mirror. Her eyes were beet red, her haggard face framed by the long silver-and-black hair that fell halfway to her waist.

Every word of the phone call echoed now as if they had spoken hours ago, not decades.

"Senator?"

She could still hear his voice now. A Midwestern twang. So unsteady. Nervous.

"Yes. That's me."

The call had come in to her general Senate number. A relative, the caller had told her assistant. Intrigued, the first-term senator had the call patched through.

"I see your name is Virginia Gentry Fox."

Before that call, she'd had no reason to hide her real maiden name. How could she have known that her mother had changed it for such a profound reason?

"Yes. But people call me Gigi."

"But Gentry is your maiden name?" His voice skipped as he asked it.

"It is."

"And you are fifty-eight years old?"

"I am." She'd grown impatient. She had a hearing to get to, back when senators went to every hearing instead of bouncing between TV studios and fundraisers. "How can I help you, sir?"

"My name's Melvin Gentry. I'm a year older than you. And I believe we grew up together in Mansfield, Ohio—same father, same house. You were our baby sister. The youngest. Then you left. Dad too. I remember when you and he left like it was yesterday . . ."

He stumbled over his words. He was trying to hold back sobs but failing.

"Things were never the same for our family . . ."

He stopped talking, gathering himself.

"I saw your full name somewhere recently, saw a photo, checked your age, and knew it was you."

She skipped the Senate hearing as they talked for the next hour.

Two weeks later she visited Mansfield. And with the help of some old photos and papers, she and her half brother pieced it all together. The Gentry side of the family. Mother's side. She even drove through Mother's old neighborhood—what was left of it. Company Line, they'd called it. A strong community once. Now a lowly strip mall. Torn apart like too many other communities across the country.

Six months later, an envelope arrived at her Senate office from Mansfield. A card from Melvin Gentry's daughter. Melvin had succumbed to the cancer he'd been fighting for years.

"Talking with you made him feel whole at the end. You gave him a closure he'd always been seeking. My brother and I thank you."

Her staff did some research into Melvin's passing. He'd been unable to access treatment that might've saved his life. With little financial means, he'd died a slow and painful death.

And he hadn't even asked her for help.

A week later came her second and final visit to Mansfield.

Melvin's funeral was a modest affair. Only forty people attended. Only the son and daughter knew who she was.

She sat in the last pew of the church and cried the entire hour.

CHAPTER 69

Near Columbus

Senator Gigi Fox.

Amity dug up her basic bio in no time—a rags to riches story, from public defender, to prosecutor, to DA, to attorney general, to U.S. senator. All of it took place in Florida, except for her time at Duke Law School.

She'd married a law classmate who became a successful lawyer. Both from humble beginnings, they came into money over time. But her calling card never changed—she always fought for the little guy.

As Dexter navigated the northeastern outskirts of Columbus, Amity dug deeper into the senator's past.

And her name.

It always appeared as "Senator Gigi Fox." On her official Senate website. Her campaign website. Documents she signed. Bills she sponsored.

Just Gigi Fox. No reference to a middle initial. Or a maiden name.

Similarly, in her online bios, only vague summaries described her family, or childhood. Growing up in poverty in Florida, moving frequently, under the loving care of an unnamed single mom who died when she was young. Nothing more.

"Is Gigi a nickname for Virginia?" Dexter asked at one point.

"I guess it can be, but there's no indication that that's the case here."

"Amity, it's gotta be her. There are so many holes in her early years."

"She's clearly hiding something. But we need something definitive."

———

THE WELL-LIT SKYLINE of Columbus emerged through the dark, wintry sky. Minutes from home, Amity still hadn't found anything.

Gigi Fox had been a senator for so long, there were no stories online about her public service back when she started. So nothing appeared in searches except the carefully curated summary of her own past. Every bio was consistent—and consistently vague on her origins.

Dexter knew she was struggling. "We'll probably do better in the morning, with—"

"Hold on. This one's interesting."

Perhaps Fox had thought she was in friendly company. Or perhaps it was before she had become so protective of her past. But at some point, *Duke Law Magazine* had decided to digitize their old volumes. And that included one issue, from years ago—buried pages in the Google search results—in which they interviewed alumna Gigi Fox only months after her first election to the Senate.

There was a brief article about her win, a number of photos, and a recitation of the complete interview in Q & A format: "A Conversation with Gigi Fox."

"Almost there, Amity," Dexter said as they exited the highway.

Amity ignored him, not looking up as they turned right.

About a page in, the new senator explained how rough the Duke Law faculty had been on women back in her day: "We were so outnumbered back then. In each class, there were two or three women, and dozens of men. But those professors . . . for some reason, they were a lot tougher on us than the guys."

"Tough in what way?" the interviewer asked.

GF: In every way. The first question to start the class. More
    questions than the guys. Tougher questions. And they'd mock

our answers—openly laugh at us. And the guys would laugh
along.

DM: Did you resent that you were treated that way?

GF: At the time, I hated it. But I've got to say, it prepared us well for
the male-dominated legal world we were about to enter. After
three years of grilling, we women were ready for anything—
more than most of the men laughing at us. And that's why so
many of us were so successful.

DM: Do you think that was the professors' goal?

GF: I don't know. For some, I think it was their way of protesting
our presence there . . .

The car stopped.

"We made it," Dexter declared as a woman's electronic voice, emanating
from the center console, announced they'd arrived.

Amity looked up.

"I'm almost done. Let's park in the garage, then get you a cab."

He circled the driveway and entered the garage entrance.

"My spot is on the third floor."

Amity returned to the interview transcript. Gigi Fox talking about her
rude professors:

"For others, maybe they thought they were helping us. Either way, it
made a big difference. Believe it or not, it's even the reason I go by Gigi."

Amity's eyes flashed.

DM: Really? How so?

GF: For most of law school, I signed my papers "G. G. Milburn," my
maiden name. Like the authors I'd read as a kid, I thought using
my initials would impress people. Silly, I know. Well, my
professors used it as yet another reason to mock me. At first they
called me "Miss G.G." in a derisive tone. Then simply "G.G."
Before I knew it, everyone in school called me Gigi, and they
have ever since.

DM: And what did the "G.G." stand for?
GF: Everyone called me Ginny as a kid. Short for Virginia.

Dexter turned the corner on the second floor.

DM: And the second *G*?
GF: Gentry. It's an old family name.

"Gigi," Amity said, looking straight ahead. Beaming.
She had no middle initial because the letters *G.G.* were her initials.
Ginny Gentry.
Pulse racing, Amity mouthed the words "Virginia Gentry."
Like the senator herself, always there in plain sight. Right in her short and simple first name.
"I got it! It's her."
"Great work," Dexter said. "Now, which is your space?"
"Up there to the left. Spot 332."
He pulled forward and turned into the narrow space.
"They really squeeze you in here, don't they?"
"They really do." Amity laughed, thrilled at her find.
He looked back, reversed, straightened out, and pulled back in.
"We made it," he said, flashing her a thumbs-up as he opened the door.
As Amity reached down to remove her seat belt, the Jeep exploded all around her.

PART THREE

CHAPTER 70

———

Washington

As ALWAYS, EACH meeting of the president's afternoon was scheduled for fifteen minutes. No small talk, no chatter, all business.

FDA director Driscoll walked in at 2:00 p.m. sharp, two staff flanking him. The president sat behind her desk, reading from a national security briefing book as the trio approached. Three wooden chairs faced the president. Driscoll sat down last, in the middle seat.

Awkward seconds passed before Moore looked up from her desktop.

"So we bumped the vice president to meet with you. What's so urgent, Don?"

One of her weaker appointments, Driscoll had always seemed jittery in the Oval Office, but was even more so today. The pen in his right hand was shaking. She often wondered if he was up to this role. Too late now.

"Madam President, we are about to approve a new round of testing in cancer research the FDA has funded. I wanted to be sure you were aware."

"Testing on humans?"

He nodded. "Yes, ma'am."

"Under fifty?"

"Yes."

Her dark eyebrows shot upward.

"That's a big jump from the last time we talked. I thought that was years away."

"It was, but some impressive tests changed our mind. I think we're ready to take the next step."

"Don, there are some weighty considerations to balance. I would hope to hear more than 'I think.'"

She stared at him, sizing him up. Nominating him had been part of a political deal with the Texas House delegation, one she'd regretted almost immediately.

He stiffened.

"This *is* the right step, and there are robust safeguards."

The pen was still shaking.

"And where's China?"

"They haven't gone this far yet."

"Has anyone?"

"Outside of a few third world quacks going rogue, nobody."

She looked at his two staff, then back at Driscoll. Having witnesses was important. This was a big moment, and her next words were key.

"I've never pushed you or micromanaged you. Complex scientific and ethical issues like this are your domain, and I will not interfere. If you think it's time to move forward, then move forward."

"Of course."

She leaned in.

"How long will it take?"

"Done right, at—"

"Of course done right!" she interrupted. So much hemming and hawing for a Texan.

He nodded. "At least a year."

The president stood up. "Thank you for the briefing. Keep me apprised. And give your wife my best."

He did a double take. "Thank you, and I will."

Two minutes after the three left the room, NSA director Ellrod walked in. The president stepped around to the front of her desk, gesturing for her most trusted advisor to sit on one of two cream-colored couches while the president sat on the other.

"Good news, Sandra?"

"Very good. The combination of deepfake videos we've accumulated has done the trick. We've discovered numerous telltales of the new Saudi techniques."

"Excellent. So what do we do now?"

"We wait."

"Until?"

"Until they initiate a major deepfake operation. Then we expose them."

"Is that soon enough?"

"The way they're moving, my guess is it won't be long. But the best way to discredit them is to do it when they do something big. Let them stick their neck way out, then chop it off."

With her right hand, she cut through the air like a knife.

The president grinned.

"So you're saying the Senator Blue video isn't the one to respond to?"

"Madam President," Ellrod said, not returning the smile.

"Yes."

"We found no Saudi telltales in that video."

"You mean it's real?"

"I'll say this: we have yet to find any indication that it's a deepfake."

The president smiled.

"Oh, my. That won't play well in Alabama."

They looked at each other in silence before the president let out a long sigh.

"And how's that Ohio girl doing? The one who clerked for Ernest."

All of D.C. knew that any Supreme Court clerk of Ernest Gibbons was a superstar, especially the JAG slot.

"She's fine. Some cuts and bruises. Those shattering windshields are life-savers."

"And the reporter with her?"

Ellrod winced.

"Not well. Broken bones, some burns. But the head trauma and the internal damage are the biggest concern. He's still in a coma. It's touch and go."

"What the hell's the world coming to?"

"We've promised Ernest we'd get the girl to Walter Reed if she needs it."

"Good."

CHAPTER 71

——

Columbus

PAIN SCREAMED OUT from all corners of Amity's body.

Scrapes, slices, and cuts crisscrossed her face and neck, stinging whenever she changed expressions. Her Jeep's windshield had essentially exploded in her face.

She'd thrown her palms in front of her eyes as it happened, so her hands, wrists, and forearms were cut badly as well.

Her neck and back throbbed from two violent forces: whiplash from the explosion and the body blow of the airbag slamming her back against the seat. Days later, she still couldn't turn her head in either direction. And leaning forward or back triggered excruciating pain in her lower spine. Getting dressed required fifteen agonizing minutes on the floor, so she'd donned the same sweat gear for days.

Deep bruises ached up and down her legs and midsection.

"Think of it as a forty-mile-per-hour car wreck, straight into a brick wall," one of the doctors had said two days ago. "Every part of your body experienced trauma. It's going to take some time."

And she was the lucky one: Dexter's wreck had topped one hundred miles per hour. Upon opening the driver's-side door, he took the brunt of the blast from the car to the left of Amity's spot. And his body shielded her from the worst of it.

As Amity sat in an Ohio State hospital room, Dexter lay in the ICU, recovering from his fourth surgery in six days. Head trauma. Internal bleeding, and major damage to his lungs and spleen. Broken bones, including seven ribs, his left forearm and wrist, and his right femur and left ankle. Second-degree burns on his face, neck, and hands.

Of course her own pain was worsened by intense guilt. She was supposed to be the one in the driver's seat, getting out of the car. Not Dexter. Her last-minute obsession with tracking down Gigi Fox had probably saved her life.

Amity's phone vibrated in her sweatshirt pocket. She quickly reached for it. The woman—the doctor with the British accent—had not called since the explosion, which meant Amity had no idea what was happening with Mom. That silence was haunting—the guilt about the agreement she'd struck gnawing more deeply with every day that passed. She tried to tell herself it was what Dad would've done, but now she doubted it. At his funeral, his union buddies had all said that Gus Jones was best known for his unbending integrity.

It was Justice Gibbons. Again.

"Amity, how're you feeling?"

"Getting there," she lied. "The pain's diminishing every day."

"And your friend?"

"Not worse than before. Not better. But he's a strong man."

"Any progress in the investigation?"

"None."

"Well, please let me know if I can do anything."

For the past eighteen months, the justice had used that same phrase every time they ended a conversation. And this was no small offer: help from Justice Gibbons could move mountains in D.C. No one was more connected.

Amity had blown him off each time.

She was tempted to change that now but held her tongue.

CHAPTER 72

Columbus

AMITY OPENED HER laptop after the nurses had left the room.

Since her head had cleared, she hadn't stopped thinking about the tie between Senator Gigi Fox and Senator Shepherd Logan. It took only seconds of searching to uncover how deep their connection ran.

An entire generation of Beltway press had puzzled over the quirky duo. "The odd couple," they'd been dubbed years ago. Odd because Fox and Logan came from different parties and were opposites in almost every other way. Yet they were the closest of friends.

Senator Shepherd Logan was a no-nonsense, rock-ribbed Republican. A social conservative, Tennessee's senior senator was slow to embrace any modern notions of equality or civil rights. A hawk on war, taxes, and spending alike.

Senator Gigi Fox was the fiery populist from Florida. As the state's attorney general, she'd filed case after case to end school segregation and rocketed to national fame after personally arguing and winning a pivotal Supreme Court case. She'd brought equal vigor to the Senate, fighting for civil rights and equality in all forms. She'd opposed every war while supporting every minimum wage increase, pro-labor law, and voting rights bill that had come before her.

But somehow, from the day they were sworn in together, Gigi Fox and Shepherd Logan had remained best friends. They were often seen eating together around D.C., laughing. Leaving hearings together, yukking it up after having just disagreed. They made countless joint appearances, from Army bases to college campuses. They and their spouses traveled the world together.

Beltway columnists celebrated them as throwbacks, living reminders of the good old days when the denizens of the District disagreed during work hours but remained amiable. At key moments, those columnists opined, those soft relationships mattered.

And Fox and Logan had proven them right over the years.

When three Western senators got caught in an insider trading scandal, Logan and Fox together called it out—and that was the end of those senators.

When a South American terrorist attacked a U.S. consulate, killing five American diplomats and two Marines, all of D.C. bickered about who was to blame . . . until Fox and Logan came together and demanded that the families of the dead deserved unity. They called for an independent bipartisan inquiry into security at outposts around the world, and it soon came about.

And when presidents faced major decisions, particularly at moments of crisis, they'd often call Fox and Logan to huddle in the Oval Office. If those two could come together around a set direction, so would the Senate.

As they'd aged, slowing down and increasingly eclipsed by the hyperpartisan generations that followed, the relationship had gotten less ink than in earlier years. Although, weeks before, photos had circulated of the two sitting together at the funeral of Duke Garber, one of the other respected lions of their generation.

So they're friends, Amity thought. *How nice. But it doesn't tell us anything about the matter at hand.*

Dig deeper.

Did they at least share an interest in certain issues?

Nothing stuck out on the surface, but perhaps they served on committees together. So Amity eyed their webpages.

Again, Logan chaired the Banking Committee, a critical role in Washington. He also sat on Homeland Security and Government Affairs, Appropriations, and Veterans' Affairs.

Fox also sat on Appropriations, but that didn't mean much. Almost a third of the Senate sat on that committee.

Outside of Appropriations, Fox was on Judiciary, where she was the ranking member and prior chair, and that was where she'd fought so many of her civil rights battles. And she sat on Environment and Public Works, Energy and Natural Resources, and Foreign Relations.

Curiously, neither sat on the Health, Education, Labor and Pensions, which had direct jurisdiction over health care.

Amity stared blankly at her screen, plumbing other research options.

Even if the senators didn't share committee assignments, maybe they'd pushed major legislation together. Fortunately, an essential part of a Supreme Court clerk's duties was mining arcane legislative history, researching how laws before the Court had come about in the first place. Who had sponsored them? What was their intent? What was the testimony for or against? Was there other evidence in the record? Once at the Supreme Court, every word and data point of a law's legislative history became fodder for arguments between the clerks, and ultimately the justices, as they wrangled over decisions.

Amity dove into decades of that history to see what issues Fox and Logan had worked on together.

She found nothing.

Consistent with their polar opposite ideologies, Fox and Logan had appeared on almost no major bills together. Sure, they had joined legislation that enjoyed wide bipartisan support, but those bills included dozens of cosponsors. And ceremonial items that weren't controversial garnered unanimous support, including theirs. But when it came to meaningful, substantive legislation—laws that had required a fight, but accomplished something big—nothing turned up.

Stuck, Amity pulled out a legal pad and wrote down all she'd learned.

Good friends.

Traveled together.

No joint legislation.

No substantive committees overlap.

There had to be more to it.

As she often did lately when she hit a research roadblock, Amity thought back to her Supreme Court term. At a moment like this, jammed in a legal corner, needing to find a nugget to change a case's outcome, where had she turned?

To the justice himself.

Justice Gibbons was up there in age. His body was failing him. But his mind remained agile and chock-full of lessons—especially concerning politics, since he'd spent twenty years in Congress before becoming a judge.

What pearl of wisdom would he share at this moment?

She recalled one of her final cases—the one that had kept her up nights in the final weeks of the term. A critical voting rights case impacting millions of voters. The justices had been split 4–3, with two undecided. Her job had been to draft the dissenting opinion for Gibbons, but she'd held out hope she could swing the two final votes and write a majority opinion instead.

The record was scant. The briefs comprised hundreds of pages haggling over the meaning of five vague words in the contested statute. Oral argument, an hour of the same. The deliberations among the justices quickly broke down into the same food fight that the lawyers had been engaged in.

When she'd explained the dilemma, Justice Gibbons had asked a simple question.

"Did you go back to the committee testimony?"

"I did. Nothing helpful there," she'd said.

"Okay. Well how about the subcommittee?" he'd asked.

"The subcommittee?"

"Yes. No one ever looks there anymore, but sleepy subcommittee hearings are where much of the action takes place. Big decisions, along with testimony that might tell us what was behind the bill."

Lo and behold, in the transcripts of one of those subcommittee hearings, she'd found testimony that explained why the contested words were added and what they meant. Justice Gibbons's 5–4 majority opinion upholding the law made front-page news on the last day of the term—all thanks to the transcripts from some alphabet soup subcommittee.

A "sleepy subcommittee," Justice Gibbons had called it.

Amity quickly took a second look at both Fox's and Logan's committee assignments. Neither listed subcommittees on their official or campaign webpages, which was why she hadn't checked the first time.

She checked the website for the Senate Appropriations Committee, the one committee they both served on.

Twelve subcommittees were listed there, covering a range of topics. Agriculture and Rural Development. Commerce. Defense. Energy and Water Development.

The first one she opened was the Subcommittee on Labor, Health and Human Services, Education, and Related Agencies, which had jurisdiction over medicine and health matters. But neither Fox nor Logan sat on it.

None of the others jumped out, so she returned to the top of the list.

Going in alphabetical order, she first opened the Agriculture and Rural Development subcommittee.

As the new page opened, the committee's longer, formal title appeared on the top of her screen: Agriculture, Rural Development, Food and Drug Administration, and Related Agencies.

"Food and Drug Administration," she whispered.

She scrolled down, pulse quickening.

There they were. The odd couple.

The first senators to appear on the page.

Logan and Fox—the chair and ranking member of the subcommittee that set the budget of the FDA.

CHAPTER 73

Columbus

"I REMAIN DEEPLY disappointed. You're supposed to be the best."

They were speaking on Quinn's secure line. He was parked blocks from the Columbus hospital where Amity Jones was holed up. And ever since she'd arrived there, he'd been fending off nonstop criticism.

From all ends.

"I am," he said, trying not to sound defensive. "How was I supposed to know he'd drive the car?"

"Is he going to die?"

"It's touch and go."

"And the girl?"

Quinn fumed, tired of being yelled at for circumstances beyond his control. Balancing competing demands.

"Battered and bruised. But she'll be back on her feet."

"Perfect." Sarcasm oozed through the phone. "We'll need a plan B."

CHAPTER 74

_____

Columbus

ONCE AMITY IDENTIFIED the subcommittee, the contours of the broader plot emerged in plain sight.

Shepherd Logan and Gigi Fox reigned over the Senate subcommittee that funded drug research, perfectly positioning them to bankroll the testing of new treatments. And not long after the funds had started flowing, loved ones of both senators had been saved from bleak cancer diagnoses.

No way this was a coincidence.

In fact, it felt too familiar. Odds were they'd been offered a similar choice to her own: a favor to save a life. In their case, that favor had been federal funding. And, like her, they couldn't say no.

In between knocks on the door, nurse check-ins, and migraines, Amity downloaded every agenda and report that had passed through the subcommittee in recent years.

From her quick count, in the prior two years the subcommittee had approved hundreds of millions in research grants to a who's who of elite medical schools and research universities. At each hearing, the FDA director or a top aide appeared before the committee at the end of a dreary meeting to present a detailed report of upcoming research to fund. And with little or no discussion, often with only Logan left in his seat, other times Fox sitting next to him, the subcommittee approved the report to move the research forward.

Amity emailed the reports to the one person she knew who might glean additional tidbits of information: Simon, who'd been checking in daily. She followed up by phone an hour later.

"Did you total it up?" he asked, far more intrigued than in their initial call.

"Sure did. Harvard, Stanford, Yale, Columbia, and Johns Hopkins led the list. Followed by a bunch of major public universities. That's one big trough of dollars they're feasting from."

"Yep," he said. "But at least for a better cause than most Beltway spending."

"Maybe so. But somewhere in these reports, money is flowing to pay for that van and all the work and people behind it. Gotta give 'em credit. Trading government research funding to save handpicked loved ones is one heck of a pay-to-play scheme."

Amity's jaw clenched after she said the words. She and Mom had been desperately looking for help for almost two years. But relatives of the well-connected had jumped the line.

Then again, she reminded herself, so had she at the first opportunity.

"So how are you going to find out who's conducting the treatment?" Simon asked, passive as always about helping.

"Why do you think I sent them to you? You might find something in those reports that no one else could."

"Okay, I'll look through them."

Seconds passed, then Simon spoke again.

"By the way, did you notice who else sat on the subcommittee? Maybe he's involved too."

"Yeah. The other old-timers were Senator Blue from Alabama and Sam Ireland from Colorado. And a few junior members I don't know well. We definitely should look into them."

"Oh, Amity. You missed the big one." Simon loved when he was a step ahead of his older sister. "The guy who's been in the news a lot lately."

"I did? But I read the whole list from the website."

"Right, the updated website."

"Updated?"

"Yeah. You must've not looked at the roll call votes in the subcommittee."

"I dove straight into the reports themselves . . ."

He was enjoying this too much.

"Okay. You got me. Who was on it before they updated the website?"

"Another old-timer."

A long pause.

"Just tell me!"

"That senator from Maine."

Amity's face stung as her eyes widened, stretching any number of scars. "Duke Garber?"

"Yes. The one who jumped off the cliff."

"Oh my God! What are the odds? Maybe that had something to do—"

"Exactly what I—"

Another call came through. She held the phone away to see who it was. UNKNOWN NUMBER.

Finally.

"Let me grab this," she said, jumping over.

"I thought you loved your mother."

The woman with the British accent was back. But for the first time she sounded angry.

"Of course I do," Amity replied meekly.

"Then why end her life?"

"I was only—"

"We had an agreement. Your mother is receiving care that millions would do anything to receive. That care will save her life—end her pain and yours. And you did the only thing we asked you *not* to do."

"But—"

The woman hung up.

CHAPTER 75

——

Bethesda

OTHER THAN GETTING into the best shape of his life, Palmer Knight—holed up in a suburban Maryland hotel for the second week—was downright miserable.

Restless, his reputation in tatters, he'd passed the time watching TV, scanning social media, and working out twice a day. Ellrod had assured him they'd take action in a week or two, and his lawyer had kept up discussions with the lawyers at CNN. But nothing had changed yet.

Early in the afternoon, he'd lifted weights in the small motel gym, grabbed a turkey sandwich from a Subway down the street, and, returning to his room, checked Twitter as he ate.

In order to receive a constant stream of tips, he'd long kept his Twitter messages open to anyone. Most of what came through were cranks, conspiracy theorists, and a steady stream of both women and men coming on to him. Still, he looked through them all. Every once in a while some viewer or source or whistleblower had something real to share. Something big.

Two direct messages awaited him now.

The first was spam.

But the second one, coming from the Twitter handle @buckeyejag, tossed red meat his way.

"I've solved the riddle of Duke Garber."

He wrote back immediately.

"You have my attention. Do tell."

"Call me at this number. Ms. Jones. Room 342."

It was a 614 number.

He wolfed down the turkey sandwich, then dialed the number.

"Columbus Memorial Hospital."

"I'm looking for a Ms. Jones in room 342."

"One second."

He flipped a pen in his hand as he waited.

The phone clicked.

"Is this Palmer Knight?"

"It sure is."

"This is Amity Jones. So glad you responded."

Like a lot of his best sources, she sounded crazy at first, spewing a flood of names, dates, dollar amounts, and theories. But thirty minutes of conversation made it clear that she was anything but. Plus, any clerk for Justice Gibbons was legit. The guy was a giant in D.C., and the Knights and the justice went way back. This woman must have kicked ass at every level to climb to that highest rung on the legal ladder.

As Amity spoke, Palmer followed along online, conducting quick web searches to confirm things she was saying. They all checked out, including Senator Garber having sat on the Appropriations subcommittee alongside Logan and Fox. Heck, Sam Ireland sat on the subcommittee as well. He'd practically coughed up a lung during their interview weeks ago. Maybe he'd cut the same deal as the others, but to cure himself.

"Okay, you got me," Palmer said. "It's wild, but it's by far the best theory I've heard on what happened to Senator Garber. Now what do we do about it?"

"I'm hung up here for a few days, I'm afraid. But we need to get to Fox and Logan as soon as possible."

"Easier said than done. Those two hardly talk to the press anymore. And they're permanently surrounded by handlers."

"Well, you'll have to get to them some other way."

Palmer shook his head, thinking back to the protective press flack guarding Ireland. That was next to impossible these days.

Amity went silent for a few seconds.

"I know just the person who can help."

CHAPTER 76

────

Washington

THE MEMBERS OF their informal caucus looked like they'd aged a decade.

Gigi, who'd always appeared far younger than she actually was, was faring the worst. Her eyes were bloodshot, and her bun was uncharacteristically loose, stray hairs falling down below her shoulders. Wrinkles Shepherd Logan had never noticed before were carved deep into her neck, cheeks, and forehead.

They were back in the Marble Room for the first time since the explosion, but Shepherd Logan had no intention of broaching the topic.

No. Given the haggard looks on their faces, it was time for good news.

"Well, the FDA is moving forward on approval," Logan announced, forcing a smile. "We are closer now than ever."

Sam Ireland was leaning against one of the columns, standing behind his regular chair. "C'mon, Shep. It's Blackwood who's closer than ever. He's going to get all the attention for this. We'll have to stay mum the rest of our lives."

"I mean 'we' as in the human race, Sam. I'm not concerned about credit. This may be the greatest achievement any of us will have been part of. Think about how we each have felt in recent months. The relief. The security of a second chance. Now multiply that by millions, for generations. And we started all of it."

"Careful, Shep," Ireland said. "You're sounding a lot like Blackwood. That's not a good thing."

Logan knew not to respond, so they sat in silence for an awkward few seconds.

Ireland finally spoke up again, saying out loud what they all were thinking.

"I'm glad we're making progress, but did we have to go that far? That young woman clerked for Ernest, for God's sake."

Logan had been aghast at the news, yelling at Blackwood for ten minutes about it.

"It was rougher than we thought it'd be," Logan said, frowning.

"Well, at least they won't be back on it for a while," Blue said.

They all sat in silence again, knowing he was right.

CHAPTER 77

―

Boston

STUCK IN A middle seat between two snorers, Simon Jones hardly slept the entire six-hour flight. He usually rode first-class on JetBlue's red-eye flight from San Francisco to Boston, but he'd called too last-minute to snag a good seat.

With nowhere to go after landing at 5:40 a.m., he checked into a motel near the airport and lay down on the lumpy mattress of a closet-sized room. The roar of jet engines kept him up for some time, but exhaustion eventually knocked him out. After an hour of sleep, he woke, showered, and grabbed an Uber for the drive into Boston.

He loved the town but couldn't concentrate on his surroundings on the way in.

Since he'd been old enough to remember, Amity had taken on the world alone. Far more than Mom, she had led their small family. More than she needed to, even. By the time he reached high school, Mom was doing just fine. Tough and funny when she wanted to be, especially when his friends stopped by the house. But Amity was gone and never saw those sides. She only remembered the bad times.

His wife, Jenna, used to ask why Amity always did the heavy lifting. And Simon had explained she preferred it that way. *Don't worry about it,* Amity would always say. *I've got it all under control.* She seemed to worry more when Simon *got* involved than when he didn't.

That was why Simon had told her nothing about the last-minute trip.

But he felt compelled to go. Something serious was unfolding.

Serious enough that Amity's harebrained conspiracy theory—that someone was advancing gene research far beyond what had been approved—suddenly appeared to be very real.

And serious enough that Amity had almost been incinerated a week earlier.

The older sister who'd always been the rock of the family was in pain, in danger, and unable to respond. And of all topics, the one at the heart of things was in his wheelhouse.

He could help on this one. He *had* to help.

And the good news was that he'd already made a major breakthrough. The committee reports Amity had sent the day before revealed a suspicious pattern at one school. A major red flag.

"Harvard Square, buddy," the driver called out.

The car jolted to a stop. Minutes later, Simon sat down in a diner a few streets away from where the meeting would take place.

Waiting for his veggie egg white omelet, he took out the file folder full of the reports Amity had sent. He'd gotten through them once during the plane ride. With more elbow room now, he took out a fluorescent yellow marker and highlighted every word and number that drew his suspicion.

He'd have one chance at this. In an hour.

So, like a kid cramming for an exam, he committed every detail and every question to memory.

CHAPTER 78

—

Boston

"WELL, AREN'T WE honored to have you here! Welcome to Harvard Medical School."

The short, round gray-haired man with the loose tie and large glasses shook Simon's hand furtively. The two sat down on opposite sides of a desk covered in papers.

Simon flashed a playful grin.

"Thanks for meeting on such short notice."

Simon wasn't surprised by the quick response to the previous day's request. Even the nation's most elite schools moved mountains to connect with Silicon Valley venture capital. At thirty-four, Simon felt like a kid next to Harvard Med's director of research administration—a PhD in molecular biology with decades of cutting-edge research under his belt. But at this meeting Simon was the boss. Not only was he from Silicon Valley, his firm was one of the world's largest investors in biotech, investing millions while seating guys like this in lucrative advisory committee posts.

Two months ago Simon had been promoted to partner. He thrust his new business card across the desk to underscore the opportunity.

The director eyed the fine print, then looked back at Simon.

"Of course. We'd love to show you what we're working on right now."

"Go right ahead. We have a new fund we're raising for and we want to know the lay of the land. You're the first school we're meeting with. And that's not an accident." He winked.

Going directly after the information he needed would make him appear too eager. Better to warm the man up. So Simon listened attentively, taking copious notes as the director walked him through a dozen research projects. Covering everything from hemophilia and sickle cell disease to hearing loss and preterm labor, it was an impressive summary. He'd circle back on some of these down the road. But with little time, Simon cut the man off after twenty minutes.

"That's a wide body of work, Doctor. Not many places are tackling all these areas at once."

The man beamed, chin up.

"I can guarantee no one else is. We have the most talented group of researchers and engineers in the world."

Simon nodded, saying nothing. Given what he was after, it was better to play hard to get.

"Shall I proceed?" the doctor asked, breaking the awkward silence.

"Please."

Ten minutes later, Simon sighed loudly enough to cut him off.

"Doctor, as you can imagine, we like to leverage our investments. And we often come in behind major federal grants. Tell me about your past couple years of FDA support."

"Of course," the director said. "Give me one second."

Without standing, he swiveled his chair around and wheeled it sideways to a set of shelves behind his desk. Thick black binders took up the bottom three rows of shelves. He took one out from the far end of the middle shelf, wheeled back around, and opened it to its front page.

"Here we go. These are our FDA grants over the past three years."

"I've reviewed some of the reports from Capitol Hill. You guys have done well bidding against your rival schools."

The director grinned. "Yes, we have. No one's pulled in more."

Simon casually reached for the binder.

"Can I take a look?"

The director stared at Simon for a moment, lips pursed. Sizing him up. No doubt torn as the Silicon Valley business card stared up at him.

It proved too much to resist.

"Sure."

Simon turned the binder his way, then flipped through the opening pages. He reviewed an introduction for the most recent year, which included a chart of awards granted to Harvard. He recognized the numbers. Although in a different format, they matched up with the figures he'd committed to memory.

"You're right. This is definitely better than anyone else."

"As I said, we are strong competitors."

He paged through the rest of the binder, looking for a distinct set of numbers—a series of allocations that had drawn his attention the previous day. But they never appeared.

"Can I help you find something?" the director asked.

Simon looked up, stomach fluttering. This was the moment he'd flown all that way in the middle seat for.

"You sure can. You guys have done great in the competitive grant arena. I've also been impressed by what you've pulled down in the directed grant program I've read about . . ."

He gestured down at the binder.

". . . but I don't see those grants listed here."

The director's eyes squinted. Confused.

"Directed grants? I'm not sure what you mean."

Directed grants.

The term had raised Simon's suspicion the moment he'd seen it the day before. Amid hundreds of competitive grants listed in the subcommittee reports—grants totaling hundreds of millions of dollars—buried deep inside almost every report was the occasional mention of a "directed grant."

They were smaller than the competitive grant awards: $2.5 million here, $5 million there. Amid the entire federal budget, or even the FDA budget, not a lot of money. A rounding error. But, for a single lab focused on one line of research, that could fund a lot of work.

The term "directed grant" had struck him as odd not only because he hadn't heard it before but because government grants weren't "directed." Just the opposite. By law, they had to be awarded following an intensely competitive process through a morass of bureaucracy. Dozens or hundreds of rigid requirements. Thousands of pages of documentation for each bid. A highly formal scoring system. Multiple rounds taking months at least, sometimes longer. The payoff could be huge, but so was the investment in competing.

A directed grant appeared to bypass all that.

So he'd dug further, only to find an even stranger feature. Deep in the appendix of each subcommittee report—print so fine he had to look hard to see it—a second pattern emerged. These grants had been "directed" only to a single institution.

Harvard Medical School.

Even as other schools had pulled down millions in competitive grants, none had received a directed grant.

None but Harvard, every other month.

The puzzled look on the research director's face appeared sincere, confirming Simon's hunch that "directed grant" was an odd term.

Simon leaned in.

"I mean the directed grants that Harvard has received every other month for eighteen months. They've been a steady source of funds for research here."

The director swallowed noticeably.

"Again, I'm not sure what you're talking about."

Simon cast a wry grin.

"C'mon, Doctor. I can't imagine millions of dollars would show up here that you wouldn't know about."

The man laughed awkwardly while fiddling with Simon's business card.

"I agree with that. I know about them all. And they're all in these binders. If the money isn't reported in here, this institution hasn't seen a penny of it."

Simon reached into his laptop bag, took out some subcommittee reports he'd printed out, and opened to a few of the dog-eared pages.

"Look at the highlights, Doctor. Then flip to the appendix . . ."

As the director did, Simon grabbed another report.

"Now look at this one."

The director reviewed the highlighted portions, biting his lower lip. Embarrassed.

"Hand me that," he said, reaching for the binder. He then performed the same comparison Simon had just done.

He laid the subcommittee reports on the desk as his face brightened to a pinkish red.

"I don't know what those grants are. But I can tell you they didn't come to us."

"It's a lot of money. They must've gone somewhere around here. How do I find out where?"

The director shrugged. "I honestly don't know."

Simon went quiet for a few more seconds.

"You know what I think?" he asked.

"What's that?"

"This looks political to me. Some type of well-hidden earmark with a fancy name. And somehow Harvard is getting them all. So I imagine it's someone here with high-level political connections. Anyone come to mind?"

The director leaned forward, folding his arms. "Young man, I'm wondering what this has to do with your investment interest."

Simon had prepared for this moment.

"You're kidding, right?" He chuckled. "Whoever has a direct tie-in to this kind of guaranteed revenue from the feds is someone we'd eagerly invest in."

The man sagged in his seat, relieved.

"I see. I hadn't thought of it that way."

He picked up Simon's business card again and eyed it closely.

"Let me ask around and get back to you."

CHAPTER 79

———

Boston

THE BLACK PHONE on the corner of Dr. Blackwood's desk rang at the worst possible time.

Twenty minutes before class started, the professor was holed up in his cramped med school office. Distracted by the frenzy of activity occurring in Washington, Tennessee, Ohio, and his own private lab, he'd had no time to prepare for this morning's lecture. Therefore, he was reviewing his notes from the prior year: even a recycled Paden Blackwood lecture was better than most.

So he ignored the call. He'd get the message later. After six rings, it stopped.

He never took calls on that line anyway. His secretary would transcribe the messages that accumulated there all day, then email a summary right after five. Mostly grad students and other professors seeking face time. Or some nagging administrator complaining about his expenses or over-punitive grading. All unworthy of his time or a call back.

The phone rang again. He looked at it for a moment, then back at his notes from the last year's lecture. It rang five more times and stopped.

Seconds later it started up for a third time.

He glared at it, stewed through another two rings, then picked up.

"I'm ten minutes from speaking to a thousand people. Who is this?"

"It's Phillip Conte."

Blackwood clenched his jaw. Conte was the med school's useless research director. He had moved over to that dead-end administrative spot after his own research had failed to generate a single major breakthrough in twenty-five years of trying. Now he was a glorified grant writer and bean counter, always nagging faculty about project summaries and proposal deadlines.

"I don't have time, Phil. Can we talk later?"

"I only have one question. Do you know anything about something called a 'directed grant' coming from Washington?"

He froze, recalling the first time he'd heard the term.

It had been one of their only meetings in person. As a group.

The senators—even Duke himself—insisted that the money had to be formally approved by the subcommittee. It needed to appear to support a major research university as opposed to a private company. And they would have to call it something. So they had settled on the drab term "directed grant." From that point on, dressed in that label, they'd buried each allocation deep within the reports that passed through the subcommittee.

No one reads the reports, both Duke and Senator Logan had assured him. And certainly not the fine print or numbers that small.

"Dr. Blackwood?"

"Yes? What was the term? I'm not familiar with it."

"A 'directed grant.' We've had millions of FDA dollars come to Harvard in the last few years through so-called direct grants, but it's the first I've seen of it. Someone asked me about them this morning, and I had no idea what he was talking about. No one I've talked to did either."

Good thing this was a phone call and not a videoconference. Blackwood could feel his entire face heating up, no doubt turning red.

"Someone asked you?" he sputtered. "Who?"

"Do you know what they are?"

He lowered the tone of his voice.

"I have no idea. 'Directed' doesn't make any sense. Everything's competitive. But who—"

"I had no idea either. But he said maybe it was political. And then I remembered that time that Maine senator came through and thought maybe you—"

Blackwood's stomach quivered.

"Did you tell him that?"

"What?"

"About Senator Garber."

"Of course not. I only thought of that afterward. You were the only person I could think of who had any ties to Capitol Hill."

"You call that political?" He feigned umbrage. "We were friends. Our whole lives. Long before he was a senator. And until only a few weeks ago."

"I understand. And I'm so sorry for your loss. Like I said, I'm just looking into what these directed grants are and where they've been going. I mean, it's a lot of money."

"Well, I have no idea either . . ."

Still needing the name, Blackwood cooled down.

"Let me ask around a bit."

"That would be great, Doctor. Some people will take your calls who won't take mine."

Blackwood smirked. More like most people.

"And who did you say was asking?"

"Some biotech venture capitalist from San Francisco. They're putting a new round of funding together and looking for good investments. I think I impressed him, but maybe you've got something to share as well."

"That's wonderful. Definitely. You have his name and number?"

"Sure. Hold on."

A few seconds passed before he came back on and read out the 415 phone number. Blackwood grabbed a pencil and scribbled it down in the margin of his lecture notes.

"Yeah, he's a young guy, but I checked him out after he left. Some new partner at one of the biggest firms out there. Could be a good opportunity."

Blackwood looked at his watch. Only three minutes until class and now Conte was trying to impress him.

"Great. His name?"

"Oh, it's Simon . . ."

Blackwood wrote the name down in his notebook.

". . . Simon Jones."

He wrote the last name down.

Then looked at it.

Jones.

Jones.

"Jones," he said out loud as the pencil fell from his hand.

CHAPTER 80

Columbus

SITTING UP IN the hospital bed, Amity took stock of her recovery.

The stinging across her dried-out face was always more pronounced after a night of sleep, and this morning was no different. But other parts were on the mend. She could now swivel her head in both directions, lean forward and back, and bend and lift her legs. All of this came with pain, but it was much milder than in recent days.

At least she now had a partner in her quest: Palmer Knight seemed resourceful enough to do some of the work while she laid low to keep Mom safe. But Palmer needed a big assist.

She dialed the private number at 7:40, when she knew her old boss would be free. He picked up on the second ring.

"Amity, why are you up this early?" Justice Ernest Gibbons asked.

"You know me, I'm an early riser."

He laughed. "You sure are, but right now you need to stop worrying about anything else and rest."

"Justice, this is about my mother's health, so I can't rest until I get her well."

He didn't argue back.

"Justice, you've told me to ask you for help when I need it, right?"

"I sure have. But you've never asked—not one time."

"Well, I'm calling this morning because I need your help now. And I won't lie: it's a big favor I'm asking."

Without giving all the details, she explained that she needed to have personal conversations with Senators Fox and Logan.

"Those two?" he asked, chuckling. "Good friends through thick and thin."

He was one person who'd know how to track the senators down. He'd been in their club once and had remained close since.

"So that's not media spin?"

"Not at all. From the Kennedy Center to the Mt. Vernon Grill, those two are always together. I've joined them on occasion. I'm happy to set a meeting up with them. Not hard at all."

Amity needed to catch them off guard.

"Justice, I can't say much, but you don't want to be involved with this. It's sort of an off-the-record conversation. And since I'm stuck in bed, I need a friend to have it for me."

He coughed through the phone, a tic of his when he wasn't pleased.

"Young lady, what are you getting yourself into? We're talking about two United States senators—two longtime personal friends of mine. And they're both getting up there in age."

"I know. Which is why you shouldn't be involved in the meetings. But please trust me. The meetings need to happen. It's directly related to my mom's recovery."

He grumbled for a minute more, then gave in.

"Well, like all of us old-timers, they've settled into the same weekly routines for years."

He spent the next fifteen minutes walking through those routines. Amity asked for one more favor, then they hung up.

CHAPTER 81

Cambridge

TWO P.M. ON the nose. Boloco, the burrito place right off Harvard Square. The time and place he and the woman had agreed to.

Simon looked around, but no one matched the description she'd given him over the phone.

Instead, packs of students surrounded him. A rainbow of ethnicities, they looked like kids. Almost all thin except for those who clearly worked out. The most common outfit was the red sweatshirt with a big white *H* emblazoned on the front. That would've been Simon back in the day—the middle-class kid from Mansfield, on a full ride, who wanted to fit in. Other outfits were far more preppy: slacks, sweaters and blazers, puffy coats, jeans, and high-end boots. And still others were so grungy and tattered, they looked ready to fall off. If it was anything like campus in his day, the ones wearing the most ripped clothes were the wealthiest kids in the place. A fashion statement they paid top dollar for.

Simon waited in line to get a bottle of water, then waited again for a seat to open up. After several minutes, two did, on the end of a long table dominated by the red sweatshirts.

He sat down on one side and used his tray to protect the spot across from him.

Over the next fifteen minutes, waves of students passed in and out the front door. More red sweatshirts, pearls, and ripped jeans.

But none resembled the description the woman had given.

Hungry, when the line dwindled down to zero, Simon lined up to get a burrito.

CHAPTER 82

———

Washington

ONE SPLASH OF cold water washed it all away.

For six days, Gigi Fox had put on a brave face around her colleagues.

For six days, she'd worked to convince herself.

But as she washed her face in her Senate office bathroom, the truth revealed itself. Just as it had each time she'd looked in a mirror all week.

Her efforts at persuasion might fool others, but they weren't working on their most important target: her own conscience.

She'd hardly slept in days, and it showed.

A fist rapped on the door.

"Senator," her longtime chief of staff asked.

"One moment," she answered, never turning her gaze from the mirror.

She prided herself on having fought off the aging process since her sixties. So much so that people often underestimated her age by decades.

So the wilted visage now staring back at her came as a shock.

Dark circles hung under her eyes. Her complexion was a grayish pale. Wrinkles etched deeper into her skin than ever before.

She looked exhausted.

Ill.

Old.

Her insomnia's worst consequence yet had just occurred. For the first time in her life, she'd nodded off in a hearing. Her staff had noticed, but not soon enough. She'd been at the Judiciary Committee as its members considered a long list of the president's judicial nominees—the most important hearing on the Hill that day, so reporters were there. And within moments of her eyes shutting, they'd snapped photographs. No doubt those images would appear in next day's Florida papers, along with the inevitable question: Was she too old to be a senator?

The papers would have it wrong: her age wasn't the problem. Not directly, at least.

It was her conscience. Her guilt.

She'd never been the nostalgic type. But as the old, tired face looked back at her, she pictured her young self. When her hair was jet black and her skin a smooth, buttery tan. Dark enough to stick out in a room and beautiful to most who saw it. But also light enough that, along with her straight hair, she was able to live her lie.

She'd come so far in her long life. Done so much good. Fighting for the little guy and the defenseless. Challenging segregation in schools and then inequality wherever else she saw it. Shattering glass ceilings every step of the way.

There hadn't been a singular moment when she'd consciously decided to do all those things. From law school on, her course of righting wrongs and taking on injustices had evolved naturally.

But, with age, she had come to understand the true motivation.

Another knock at the door.

"Senator, if you don't return soon, they're going to report this as a health scare."

Better than falling asleep in a hearing, she thought. The most notorious D.C. symbol of having stayed in office too long.

"Two minutes."

She held her small, wrinkled hands under the faucet for a final splash of water, then studied her face again.

The young, parentless public defender and prosecutor had been too eager and ambitious to see it.

The attorney general challenging the glacial pace of Florida school desegregation had been too consumed with the cause to process it.

But in her old age she had time to look back. And the wisdom to analyze herself.

It was all compensation.

For an enormous lie. One initial untruth that had snowballed into a lifetime of lies.

She'd succeeded only because she'd stood on Mother's broad shoulders and short lifetime of sacrifice. The strongest woman she'd ever known.

But then she'd denied her. Concealed her. And, with her, her own heritage. Her identity.

She'd denied it all.

She'd done it to get ahead. To avoid the burdens Mother had endured and had spent her childhood warning Gigi about. And once she'd climbed that first rung of success—the lie no doubt playing an essential role—she'd had to keep it buried.

And every year the lie persisted, each higher rung she reached, the lie had became exponentially worse. A trap she couldn't escape.

She dried her face off with a towel. Wiped away the smeared eyeliner. Tightened the bun on top of her head. And reapplied the bold red lipstick that always set her apart, even after other women arrived at the Senate.

In modern times, things were different. The burdens less.

People would never understand.

The judgment would now come *not* from the fact that she came from a Black mother and an absent white father. That was okay these days. For most, at least.

No, the judgment would come from the opposite end. Why had she spent a lifetime hiding the truth? Denying her roots? It was an act—a life— that would be publicly interpreted and misinterpreted. Inevitably scorned by many, including those she'd fought for.

She wasn't ready for all the questions. She never would be.

Which is why, six days ago, desperate, against everything she'd fought for her entire life, she'd gone along with the unthinkable.

And she hadn't slept since.

She laid the towel down next to the sink and walked out the door.

CHAPTER 83

—

Boston

A PETITE WOMAN—shoulder-length black hair with thin streaks of gray running from root to end—entered the restaurant as Simon downed the first bite of the burrito. She appeared to be Indian. A large man, tall and thick, with light-blond hair, sauntered in behind her.

The pair walked past the line and right to his table. Several seats were now open, but the two remained standing.

"Mr. Jones?" the woman asked in a refined British accent.

"Yes."

"Please come with us."

His pulse quickened. She was altering the terms of their rendezvous from the outset.

"Why leave here?" Simon asked, leaning back in his chair. "This place makes a damn good burrito."

The woman glared back. "This is nowhere to discuss what you would like to discuss. Please come."

He staged a mild protest, remaining in his seat while pondering his options. If he said the wrong words or appeared too worried, it would belie the story he'd spun earlier: that he was at Harvard searching for new investments. But if they had ill intentions, they'd already seen through his story. And walking out the door with them would end badly.

Only one move felt right. Call their bluff.

So he took another bite, chewing for a good ten seconds before swallowing.

"Ma'am, I'm not sure if you've been properly briefed on my firm or my role. We're the largest private venture investor in how you and the big guy here make a living. So partners like me generally meet where we want to meet."

Mouths agape, the pair looked taken aback by the comment and the tone. So he milked it.

"You can grab a burrito or not. Maybe a drink. It's up to you. But you kept me waiting for twenty-five minutes and I'm gonna finish the fine meal I paid for."

Now they were the ones with a decision to make. And they did, sheepishly heading over to the line. They chatted as they waited, the big guy typing on his phone several times.

Minutes later, the two sat down, each with a drink in hand.

The aggressive posture worked once, so Simon doubled down.

"So you're the guys getting the directed grants allocated to you in Harvard's name?" he asked, waving the final third of his burrito in the air. "That's quite a coup. Well done."

The woman lifted her hand from the table, palm facing forward.

"Mr. Jones, we are both research fellows at the medical school. We can assure you the funds at issue are going directly to the school. And the research we are doing with these funds is respected around the world."

"Even when the school's research director was unaware—"

"Director Conte handles the basic grants. This is beyond his purview."

"That's not the impression he left."

"He is an administrator who holds a wildly inflated view of his role. Any number of researchers here will tell you that."

"So what's the money for?"

"We're not at liberty to say." The woman was doing all the talking.

"These are taxpayer dollars approved by a public body. I can't imagine it's a state secret."

"You imagine incorrectly. It is precisely that."

"I've never seen an instance where public research dollars were—"

"Mr. Jones, don't mistake my youthful appearance. I have been in this field for decades. You are by all indications quite new. There is a vast amount of research done in secret, at this school and many others. And that is exactly how the government wants it."

She was good, answering with a grace and confidence that would shut down nearly anyone. But as Amity had said in her JAG days, "Just keep peeling away."

"Other schools?" Simon laughed. "In nearly three years, only one school received these directed grants."

"Indeed. Harvard has unique strengths."

"Which is why I'm here to learn more."

She stared back, a lopsided grin frozen in place. Unflappable.

Her oversized underling shifted in his seat. And that was when Simon figured it out. As good as she was, the big guy hadn't said a word. He was the weak link, there because of his muscle, not his poker face. They were supposed to be in a car right now, not having a long, face-to-face conversation in a restaurant. And through the entire conversation, her companion had kept his eyes focused intensely on her, eager to hear her response while avoiding eye contact with Simon.

It reminded him of too many business pitches he'd seen. If one guy is doing all the talking while another looks lost, you should worry about the company.

So Simon turned to him.

"And what role do you play, big guy?" he asked.

He leaned back defensively.

"I'm a researcher too. I do my best to save lives."

Said with total sincerity. Credible.

"And do you agree with her that direct, secret grants that are not on the books here are normal?"

"Um, of course. Like she said, it's common."

The words came out right, but his face was all wrong. Twisted mouth. Dilated eyes. Neck tilted back. Uncomfortable in every way a person can advertise it. A bad bullshitter.

"Whatever, guys. I came here looking for a guaranteed revenue stream to invest in. If you can't give me information on that, I'm not interested."

She took the mic back. "Sir, we're not interested in your investment. But we are interested in our reputation. We hope we've disabused you of any impression that something untoward is happening at the med school."

Simon laughed again.

"Not really. You haven't been helpful at all, but I'm moving on. I got the rest of what I needed from your grants director. Off to Yale. My guess is they'll be more eager to work with us."

With that, Simon stood up, tossed his burrito wrapper in a garbage can, and left.

———

PANIC HADN'T SET in yet, but paranoia sure had.

Doubled over to protect himself from the frigid breeze blowing down Massachusetts Avenue, Simon paced quickly toward the congestion of Harvard Square.

His two visitors had wanted to grab him from the get-go, but he'd stymied the plan. Then they'd tried to convince him that nothing suspicious was happening. But that woman was sharp: she knew he'd seen through it. So they'd need to go back to their original plan—fast.

Gloveless hands buried in his suede jacket's pockets, he hurried past a small bookstore, an art gallery, a crowded coffee shop, a deli, and a shuttered bar. Except for the snow, not too different from his favorite street in San Francisco.

As he passed the next storefront, a small art gallery, a commotion erupted behind him.

"Hey!" The words came from a woman's voice, in an annoyed tone. "Excuse you!" Practically a yell now.

He glanced back.

Outside the coffee shop, the big guy's head and blond locks towered over a plump gray-haired woman who sneered from behind him. They must have run into each other, but the big guy wasn't stopping.

Simon sped up, jogging along the icy sidewalk amid an obstacle course of pedestrians, streetlights, and newspaper stands.

He looked back again.

The big guy was now jogging too. Gaining. As awkward as he'd been in person, he was running fluidly, clearly an athlete. In his hard-soled leather loafers, Simon knew this was a doomed footrace.

As he reached the curb of a busy intersection, the crosswalk light flashed red from across the street.

5 . . . 4 . . . 3 . . .

Seeing his chance, Simon dashed into the crosswalk. But as his right shoe hit the layer of slush coating the asphalt, he slipped, falling to one knee.

. . . 2 . . . 1 . . .

The crosswalk light now a solid red, he scrambled to get clear of two lanes of impatient Boston drivers taking off as if they were in a drag race. But as he reached the middle of the street, the traffic racing the other way was only feet to his right. He skidded to a stop, almost falling again.

Stuck between the two lanes, wet snow spraying him from both sides, Simon gathered his breath while stealing a glance behind him. The big guy was at the curb, looking at Simon while shifting his weight from foot to foot. He would quickly close the forty feet that separated them.

A cacophony of horns honked in front of Simon, to his left. Then a wave of flashing brake lights made its way toward him. The congestion forced the cars passing in front of him to slow down, then stop completely. Mercifully, a two-foot gap between a van and a sedan opened in front of him.

Simon slid between the two vehicles, then veered to his left, crossing in front of another idled car and reaching the far sidewalk.

The crosswalk light switched back to green.

Knowing his head start wouldn't be enough, he weighed his slim options for escape as he passed two more storefronts.

The third facade provided the best answer.

He wouldn't have recognized the three-story redbrick building on its own. But the red-and-white sign jutting out over the sidewalk advertised the only building on Harvard Square he'd ever heard of.

THE COOP

The storied bookstore offered a much better chance to escape than another block or two of sprinting down icy streets in his San Francisco–weather shoes.

He sprinted between two white columns and through the Coop's doors.

CHAPTER 84

———

Camp Springs, Maryland

PALMER CIRCLED THE suburban Maryland block for the third time, trying to figure out where he'd made the wrong turn. The second jet in minutes descended low overhead, so he knew he was close.

Five minutes later he reached the grounds of Andrews Air Force Base.

"Palmer Knight?" the security guard asked as Palmer held up his driver's license.

"That's me."

The guard typed on his keyboard, then looked at his monitor.

At least a minute passed.

Palmer maintained a smile, masking his worry that the message hadn't gotten through. What would he say next?

"The name's Knight, you say?" the guard mumbled without looking up.

"Yes."

He typed a few more keys, then scratched the back of his head.

"Starts with a *K*," Palmer added.

The guard nodded, typed again, then looked up.

"There it is. Come on in."

The gate opened and Palmer entered a long driveway, passing a large sign that would've struck anyone outside the Beltway as odd: *Welcome to the Courses at Andrews.* What would American taxpayers think if they knew that down the street from the hangar housing Air Force One, their dollars were bankrolling two eighteen-hole championship courses for the exclusive use of federal employees and their families?

The Beltway politicians certainly knew. From presidents on down, they played here all the time. Fortunately, Justice Ernest Gibbons was one of them—a long-standing member, he had a set date most Fridays.

And according to Gibbons, one of the courses' other regular visitors was Senator Shepherd Logan. He had a tee time every Thursday afternoon before flying back to Tennessee. With D.C. missing the cold spell farther north, if the justice was right, the senator was somewhere on the back nine as Palmer pulled into the parking lot.

Palmer walked into the course clubhouse, which had an odd combination of golf apparel and equipment mixed with aviation paraphernalia—including models of jet fighters, bombers, and Air Force One—on display. Four men in close-cropped crew cuts walked by, looking like they'd just finished a round. Two other groups were huddled in circles, about to head out.

As a foursome walked away, Palmer approached the counter with the attitude that worked for him ninety percent of the time in these situations: Act like you're supposed to be there.

The tall, thin kid standing behind the counter looked too young to be the head pro, which was a good thing. In his twenties, probably, he was there because of his golf skills, no doubt, not his security chops.

"You guys running both courses this afternoon?" Palmer asked casually.

"We sure are. The weather held off, so we're busy today."

Not the answer he was looking for.

Palmer weighed which was riskier: running around thirty-six holes, looking for Shepherd Logan, or asking someone directly. With this kid, asking seemed better.

"You know which course Senator Logan is on?" he asked in the most serious tone he could muster.

The kid's brow wrinkled.

"This is the Courses at Andrews, sir," the kid said, as if he were protecting Fort Knox. "We're not even supposed to say who's playing here, let alone where they are. You know, for security."

"Kid, this is indeed the Courses at Andrews. And if you check your computer there, you'll see that someone by the name of Palmer Knight was, not long ago, given permission to enter."

Turning toward the computer, the kid typed on the keypad.

"Now, you'll also see that the authorization came directly from the United States Supreme Court. And once you've worked here for a while, you'll learn that when the Supreme Court asks for something here or anywhere else in Washington, it needs to happen."

The kid clicked on the mouse, then leaned in to the monitor, right hand rubbing his chin. He looked up from his computer, lower lip quivering, looking at Palmer eye to eye for a second or two. Palmer stared right back.

"And you'll also learn that when there's a last-minute authorization from the Supreme Court to see a senior *United States senator* only a select few would even know is on this golf course, *your job* is to make it happen." He waited a beat to dig the knife in, then smirked. "You know: security."

His little speech chased the kid's gaze back to his monitor. He typed several more keys quickly.

"The senator's on course two, sir," he said, not looking up. "He started early today, so he's probably well into the back nine now."

"Thank you."

"You can take a golf cart if you want. Grab one from over there."

He pointed toward a door on the far right.

CHAPTER 85

—

Cambridge

SIMON SPRINTED THROUGH the long, narrow first floor of the Coop, dashing past the checkout line, four tables of books, and two groups of students. Once at the back of the room, he raced up a wide, semicircular staircase to the second floor, three steps at a time.

From the second floor, another circular staircase led up to the third, forcing a quick decision. The new flight would get him farther away from his pursuer, but it also might trap him on the top floor. So he opted to stay on the second, maneuvering behind some bookshelves to a spot with a line of sight back to the first-floor entryway.

The big blond guy jogged into the Coop and stopped a few feet inside the front door. While Simon huffed heavily—the mix of work and fatherhood had kept him from running or biking for a good six months—his pursuer's chest hardly moved as he stood ramrod straight. Clearly familiar with the store, the guy methodically glanced in all the directions in which Simon could have run. The second-floor steps. The third-floor steps. The back of the first floor. But he never looked directly Simon's way.

The guy looked down, taking his phone out of his coat pocket. He read whatever message had come through, then typed a response. He waited for a reply, read it, typed something back, then put the phone back into his pocket.

Then he did something unexpected. And smart.

Nothing.

He just stood there, looking around the place.

He'd clearly been told to wait there. Probably for backup.

Which wasn't good news. Two or more people searching the place dramatically reduced Simon's chance of escaping.

But the pause also gave Simon a moment to do the one thing he needed to do to make his cross-country trip a success.

He took out his phone and called the same number he'd dialed from California the day before.

The phone rang twice before picking up.

"This is Phil," the now-familiar voice of Harvard med's research director said.

"Hello, Doctor," Simon said, trying to speak quietly without being too obvious about it.

"Can you speak up?"

Simon took a couple steps back while still eyeing the Coop's front door. The big guy hadn't moved.

"Hi, Doctor," he said more loudly. "It's Simon Jones following up."

It was a risky call, but the research director seemed genuinely out of the loop. He had clearly called someone to look into Simon's questions, which had triggered the woman's phone call to Simon, then the scheduled meeting. But odds were Conte still didn't know what was going on.

"Hey there. You still in town?"

"I am. Thanks for making calls about my question. They reached out and we had a good chat."

"That's great to hear. Did you get to talk to Dr. Blackwood himself? He's a real icon around here."

Blackwood. Simon had heard the name before and mouthed it now so it would stick in his mind.

The woman he had met with could have been Dr. Blackwood, but his guess was that she wasn't. No icon was setting up meetings at a burrito joint.

"Not directly. But he had his assistant call me. My guess is she's Indian. She was really helpful, and so impressive."

"Must've been Neena Vora. She's a real gem. But careful—she's not just some assistant. She's a world-class researcher. The secret weapon behind much of his success."

"Right. Neena. She's great. Well, thank you again for putting us together. All of your information was so helpful. I'll be back in touch when we close the fund and start investing. Take care."

"Wonderful. Safe travels."

After hanging up, Simon immediately typed the two names into his phone so he wouldn't forget them.

Blackwood.

Nina Vora.

Then he looked up. On cue, she walked into the Coop.

Two men were with her.

CHAPTER 86

—

Camp Springs

THE KID AT the counter was right: They were busy.

Starting at the eighteenth hole, Palmer drove the course backward, coming across at least one foursome at every hole. He drove past each looking dead ahead, as if on an important mission.

Act like you're supposed to be here.

None looked his way.

As in the clubhouse, two types of teams were playing the course. Fit guys with crew cuts and less fit guys without crew cuts. The grown-up version of shirts and skins.

The first group to catch his eye was halfway through the par-5 fifteenth. Four non–crew cut golfers, looking older than the other groups, were scattered across the fairway of a long hole. He slowed down to take a close look.

Three were gray-haired and well-dressed, and the fourth was bald. They carried themselves with confidence, and any of the four could have passed for United States senators. But he didn't recognize any of them. None resembled the photos of Shepherd Logan he'd pulled up on his phone.

He drove on to fourteen, a par 4. Crew cuts all. And younger.

On to thirteen, a short par 3.

A small circular green sat well uphill from the tee, a modest fairway and oval lake separating the two. Two bunkers abutted the front of the green and another hugged up against the far side of the lake.

Palmer stopped the cart feet past the green with a direct line of sight to the tee below.

Four men stood around the tee. For the first time crew cuts and non-crew cuts mixed, chatting together amiably as they took casual practice swings.

The crew cuts took the first two shots, each hitting the green, one only feet from the hole.

The group's third member drove his ball into the bunker nearest the hole. He walked to his cart spinning his club and shaking his head.

The fourth member took slightly longer to step up to the tee. He was older than the other three—in his seventies at least. Wisps of white hair fell from beneath an old-school tweed golf cap, the kind you'd expect to see on the links of Scotland with matching knickers. Even from a distance, sticking out from his long face was a distinct, pointed chin. He was thin, tall, and impressively upright for someone his age. Even though he moved slowly, when he kneeled down to tee up his ball, he looked limber. Athletic.

Palmer looked at the photo on his phone—tall, white hair, long face, angular chin—then back at the golfer.

Definitely Shepherd Logan.

Palmer wasn't a golfer—he had played tennis and squash in high school and college—but he had wasted enough of his life watching it to know that Logan's swing was that of a scratch golfer. His ball arced higher than the others', cleared the lake comfortably, and landed on the green only feet from the flag. Backspin carried it even closer to the hole.

The old senator clapped his hands enthusiastically and walked with one of the crew cuts to a cart.

Keeping his distance, Palmer turned his cart around and followed the path back to the end of the fourteenth hole.

———

SHEPHERD LOGAN WAS indeed an ace golfer. He didn't hit a bad shot for thirty minutes, which kept him from straying far from the others.

But that changed on the sixteenth.

The other three had already driven their balls safely into the fairway, when the senator stepped to the tee. His drive carried longer than theirs but tailed to the right into a bank of trees. He'd have to separate from the group to hit his next shot.

Finally.

Logan dropped his cart-mate off on the fairway before heading to the bank of trees where his ball had landed. Palmer drove toward the same spot from the other direction, timing it so he'd arrive shortly after the senator.

Once Logan got out of his cart to search for his ball, Palmer pulled up from the other side of the trees.

"Senator, need any help?" he asked as he pulled to a stop, catching him off guard.

The old man looked up with a strained smile—the politician feeling the need to be polite while wondering who the hell had snuck up on him.

"Do I know you?" he asked in a low, gravelly voice.

Palmer pretended not to hear the question, got out of the cart, and stepped toward him.

"I think I saw it right over there."

The senator cocked his head as his smile faded into an uneasy half grin.

"I said, do I know you?"

Palmer was two feet away now, wanting to see his face up close for the impending discussion.

"You might. My name's Palmer Knight . . ."

The old man's jaw hung open.

"I'm a reporter for CNN, but we've never had the pleasure of meeting."

He nodded slowly.

"I've seen ya before," he said, any hint of friendliness gone. "Senator Knight's grandkid. You covered Duke's death and appear to be in some hot water. How the hell'd you get out here?"

"I'm known to be resourceful."

"I imagine so," he said before flashing a sarcastic grin. "And your last name must open a few doors for ya along the way."

Palmer grimaced. Even over-the-hill senators had a low view of his work.

The old man sighed heavily, eyelids drooping halfway down. He was exhausted, and this intrusion was adding to it. He turned back toward a tree, using an iron to push away some low-hanging branches.

"And I don't imagine you're here to help locate my cotton-pickin' ball," he said without looking back.

"My guess is you know why I'm here, Senator."

He stepped to his left, next to a thick bush.

"Can't say that I do."

"You sure, sir?"

"I'm sure, Mr. Knight. Not a clue and nothing to say."

He leaned over, reaching far into the bushes with the club as if Palmer would just walk away.

A side of Palmer felt guilty. This was a proud man, and he deserved to be. He'd spent his whole career avoiding the types of scandals that had toppled so many of his colleagues. In the mud pit for years but clean as could be. At the twilight of his career, that legacy risked being tarnished. The stress of it all showed in his haggard face.

But another side of Palmer thought of Amity Jones. Laid up in a hospital, pain everywhere. That side was angry and spoke next.

"Senator, I hear Mary's well on her way to recovery. That's wonderful news."

The club in his hand froze and he turned around, his cheeks and neck flushed.

"Don't you dare mention my wife." His head tremored as he spoke. "She has nothing to do with this."

"With what, Senator?"

Logan's eyes narrowed, boring into Palmer for seconds. But his closed lips didn't budge. He knew he shouldn't say a word. He turned back to the bush instead.

"Senator, we both know Mary has *everything* to do with this. You've spent your life in politics, doing everything by the book. You set the standard for good behavior, never cutting corners. We've all admired that. But who could say no to saving your wife's life? I know I couldn't."

The club stopped moving. But still he didn't turn around.

"Don't bullshit me, son. Are you even married?"

"I'm not."

The senator had something to say, so Palmer clipped his answer short.

The old man turned back around. He looked right at Palmer, damp eyes gleaming.

"Fifty-six years. Fifty-seven next month. In all that time, almost never a bad day. Best friends. And through it all, she was always there for me."

"So of course, when given the chance, you chose to be there for her."

He ground his jaw, then answered. "You bet I did."

He turned to the side, stepping toward a different tree. He raked the ground with the club's head.

"Well, it's great she's healing. A miracle, really. But, Senator, we need to talk about the rest of it. The parts that aren't so good."

"I'm not talking to you about a thing. And if you don't leave in the next thirty seconds, I'll ask the two Air Force generals down there to get you thrown off the grounds. Believe me, they'll get it done quick."

It was Palmer's turn to get heated, something he never did with VIPs—and potential sources—like Logan.

"Senator, there's a young woman in a hospital in Ohio. A young veteran, a brilliant lawyer, banged up pretty bad and lucky to be alive. I'm sure you know something about how she got there. For that reason alone, this story's coming out. You can help shape it or not, but it's running. And you know the drill: good sources get treated a lot better than the folks who clam up. We can leave Mary out of all of it."

Logan turned Palmer's way again, a look of disgust shaping every part of his face.

"Is that a threat?"

"Senator, you've been around long enough to know that that's how the game works. You can play or someone else will."

A yell came from behind. A booming Southern voice that sounded like an Air Force general.

"Senator, y'all good up there?"

Logan looked past Palmer's shoulder, down to the fairway. Then looked back at Palmer. Sizing him up. Deciding.

Palmer's stomach knotted. This was the old man's best chance to end the intrusion. They'd believe whatever he told them.

"All good. Still looking!" he yelled, eyes still on Palmer. "If I don't get back to them soon, this will end badly for you."

He was right. Time was running out. Palmer took a card out of his wallet and scribbled his cell number on it.

"Do me a favor, Senator. Take this. This is going to come out. We need to confirm some details. Think about my offer."

He handed him the card, which the old man studied.

Palmer then pointed a few feet to the right of where he stood.

"Oh, and there's your ball."

CHAPTER 87

——

Cambridge

Neena Vora and one of the men stood guard about ten feet from the Coop's entrance as the big blond guy and a second man searched the place. They covered every inch of the first floor, each taking one side.

Simon looked around frantically, knowing they were well on their way to snagging him if he didn't do something fast. The third floor was still an option, but that would only delay the inevitable. He took a closer look at the sizable room behind him, toward the front of the building. It appeared to sell clothes, not books. Maybe his only opportunity.

He made a beeline toward the room, heading right for the crimson hoodies, large *H* on the front, that took up a number of racks. He pulled out an extra-large and threw it over his suede jacket. Too bulky, and visibly so. He moved his phone, wallet, and keys from the jacket into his pants pockets and, using the hanger that had held the sweatshirt, hung his jacket in the back of the rack. Without the jacket under it, the hoodie now fit perfectly. He then grabbed a Harvard cap from a shelf a few feet away and pulled it low over his head.

He moved back to his old spot behind the bookshelves in time to see the big guy and his new companion lumbering up the stairs.

Even disguised in the most common outfit in the store, the odds of getting caught were high, so he took out his phone and pulled up Amity's number. He quickly typed five words:

```
Dr. Blackwood. Harvard Med School.
```

The two men reached the top of the stairs and split up, one heading right, the other left, in Simon's direction.

Time to move.

Simon circled around one of the bookshelves and walked deeper into the second floor, away from the staircase. He then turned right, walking alongside two more bookshelves, then turned right again, now heading straight for the staircase. This put him on course to pass between the two men, who were about fifteen feet apart and focused on the sides of the room as opposed to the wide-open middle, the last place a person fleeing would want to be.

He ducked his head and marched right past them.

From the corner of his eye, he could see that Neena Vora was peering around the first floor while her companion eyed the balconies on the second and third floor. Neither was paying attention to the staircase. So he circled down as briskly as any college student would attack a set of stairs, but not so fast as to draw attention.

Once on the first floor, he moved to the right edge of the room. Multiple bookshelves, laid out in rows perpendicular to the long room, obscured the view from the front. Facing additional shelves that lined the back wall, Simon now play-acted the most curious book browser he could, sidling toward the store entrance at a leisurely pace while examining books along the way, even pulling out a few.

He passed beyond where the two were standing, his back toward them, then proceeded ten feet farther, reaching the store's front corner. He pivoted 90 degrees left and followed more shelves, his back still facing his would-be captors, until he was only feet from the door.

The temptation was to look back, but he ignored it. Too risky.

He sidestepped toward the glass door, pushed the metallic handle until it opened, and walked through the doorway.

The high-pitched squeal exploded in his ears, so loudly that his entire body jolted. What you'd expect in a bank, not a bookstore.

"Hey, dude," someone said casually from behind him. "You need to pay for those."

He hadn't broken the law since college dorm room bong hits, so it violated his constitution to run. But he did, not looking back.

He darted left on the sidewalk outside, then broke into a sprint. Campus was dead ahead, and Harvard's multiple houses, greens, and courtyards would make hiding much easier now that the big guy was stuck somewhere on the Coop's second or third floor. Only one street to cross, and the crosswalk light had just turned green.

But that moment of relief ended fast.

He didn't hear the loud footsteps and heavy grunting until they were only feet behind him.

Far too late.

A hard mass collided into the small of Simon's back, throwing his torso forward as his feet slipped out beneath him. He thrust his arms forward to stop the impending fall, but both were suddenly caught in a tight grip and pulled back hard against his chest.

He could do nothing as his head crashed into the concrete of the Cambridge sidewalk.

CHAPTER 88

———

Columbus

Dr. Blackwood. Harvard Med School.

THE OUT-OF-THE-BLUE TEXT from Simon, which had buzzed through as a nurse was checking her vitals, struck Amity as odd.

She called him right away.

No ringtone at all. Straight to voicemail. Not good.

She immediately dialed her sister-in-law, Jenna.

"Amity, how're you feeling?"

She kept it nonchalant.

"Better every day, thanks. Jenna, I'm looking for Simon. Do you know where he is?"

"He had some last-minute trip to Boston. Took last night's red-eye. We talked first thing this morning for a couple minutes, but that's it. He was exhausted and said he'd be back tomorrow night."

"Was the trip for work?"

Jenna laughed as if it was a weird question. "Well, I certainly assumed so. He got home from work a little late, packed a bag, and drove right to the airport. He takes the red-eye a lot, so I didn't think much of it, except that it was so sudden."

A few seconds passed.

"Is something wrong?"

"Nah. He must be in meetings. I'll let you know when I hear back from him."

Amity's stomach churned. Simon must've jumped directly into her business, but he had no clue about the risks. At the same time, if he'd flown to Harvard at the last moment—leaving Jenna and his two boys, which he hated doing—he'd uncovered something worth looking into.

She looked back at the text.

Knowing he would be in the air soon, she immediately texted Palmer.

Ask about a man named Dr. Blackwood. At Harvard Med
School.

CHAPTER 89

Camp Springs

AFTERNOON TRAFFIC IN suburban Maryland moved like molasses.

When Palmer left Andrews, his GPS estimated an arrival time at Reagan National Airport eighty minutes before his flight's departure. After one street of standstill traffic, it was down to seventy minutes. Then, after another bout with congestion, it fell to sixty-five minutes. Ten minutes of construction delays took it down under sixty. And it kept plummeting from there.

There may have been a later flight to the same destination, and there'd definitely be a flight the next morning. But for his purposes this was the only flight that mattered. If he missed it, he'd have to wait a week for the next one. And, given his chat with Shepherd Logan, a week was far too long.

So he gunned through every intersection, cut off every driver impeding his progress, and tested his C-Max's upper limits at any instance of open highway. By the time he pulled into Reagan short-term parking, the flight was due to leave in thirty minutes.

Palmer moved as quickly as he could through the airport. *Act like you're supposed to be there,* he kept telling himself. And it worked. At each stage of the airport scramble—grabbing his ticket at a kiosk, pushing his way to the front of security, then sprinting through the terminal to the gate—people cleared the way, ogling him as he rushed by.

He reached the gate four minutes before the flight's scheduled departure.

The gate area was empty and quiet, like a cleared-out bar. Pieces of paper and food wrappers occupied some of the abandoned chairs. It looked just like the one other time he'd missed a flight. Worse, the monitor above the desk was already displaying the next flight, to Los Angeles, scheduled to leave an hour later.

A short gray-haired woman in a blue United Airlines uniform stood alone at the jetway entrance, the door next to her propped halfway open. Palmer jogged to a stop in front of her, huffing heavily.

"Did I miss it?"

She looked at her watch disapprovingly.

"You sure cut it close: I was seconds from closing the door." She winked at him. "Got your ticket?"

"Sure do," he said, beads of sweat dripping down his forehead. "And thank you for waiting."

"Oh, I wasn't waiting."

He handed her the thin printout from the kiosk. The attendant ran it through the scanner, then, after a beep, handed it back with a grin.

"Two A. At least you'll have a wider seat to catch your breath."

Palmer returned the smile.

"Thank you. Will be nice."

"And it looks like you could use some relaxation. Fort Myers should suit you perfectly."

CHAPTER 90

Boston

SIMON CAME TO, flat on his back.

On a bed of some sort.

A throbbing pain pierced deep inside his skull—a stiletto stabbing his brain again and again. A separate and intense pressure pulsed behind his eyes, like wide forceps pinching the backs of his sockets.

He opened his eyes to a dimly lit room. The blur of a gray or off-white ceiling danced and spun above.

As the rest of his body awoke, the pain pounding his head marked only the beginning of his problems.

Fatigue weighed down every part of his body. When he lifted his head to get his bearings, his neck could barely hold it up. He dropped it back down to the pillow quickly. His legs felt glued to the bed. Arms too. Even his eyelids felt heavy, begging to close again.

He rubbed his eyes to clear his vision, but the blur remained, like swimming underwater without a mask. General shapes and colors came through—ceiling and walls, along with a host of other darker shades, colors, and fuzzy objects all around him—but nothing was in focus.

A high-pitched buzz from within his ears drowned out whatever noise emanated in the room.

He tried to focus. Where was he? Where was Jenna? And the boys? What room was this?

He rubbed his eyes again, this time with his left arm. All still a blur. But a pinch on the top of his hand offered the first clue as to where he was. Something was sticking into him.

He moved only his pupils to see what it was.

A thin tube, taut against his skin.

An IV.

A faint beep sounded faintly above the ringing in his ears.

Two beeps. One short. One long. Then a pause. Then two beeps again.

His heartbeat.

Why was he in a hospital room?

He laid his head back down and gave in to his stubborn eyelids, letting them close. But the pounding and fatigue continued.

Then came a voice, muffled, as if it were coming from another room. Barely audible over the ringing.

But loud enough to project kindness.

A woman.

"Welcome back, young man."

He reopened his eyes, tilting his head slightly forward. A figure stood before him. Blurry, like a gray shadow. Small. Round.

"Thank you."

The two words sounded right in his head, but his ears told him they'd come out as a jumbled mess.

He said them again.

"Thank you."

The figure moved slightly.

"Don't say much. Lie back. Close your eyes."

He did.

"You've suffered a severe concussion. All that you're feeling is part of that damage. You also may feel nauseous, so we've got a bucket next to your bed just in case."

Simon winced, imagining what a round of puking would do to his already fierce head pain.

"What happened?"

The words still sounded off. Oral mush.

He slowed down. Concentrated.

"What . . . happened?"

"A campus police officer tackled you on the street with more enthusiasm than necessary. Your head smashed right into the pavement."

Campus. What campus?

"Why?"

"You didn't pay for a sweatshirt from the Coop and took off when they tried to stop you. We can't help you with those charges, but, for now, we're happy to keep the concussion from killing you."

Reassuring.

"The Coop?"

"Yes. The Harvard Coop."

Boston? How was he in Boston? Why?

Then he remembered the all-night flight. The Uber from the airport.

The Coop.

The words triggered an image of the large bookstore. Running in. The stairs. Hiding. Grabbing a sweatshirt. Sneaking out. But that was it.

But why had he been there? Who was he hiding from?

It hurt to do so, but he plumbed his mind for answers.

Amity.

She'd been hurt and was still in danger. He was helping her. Getting her information.

He remembered texting her right before leaving the store.

"My phone," he said. "Where's my phone?"

Too fast. Gibberish.

"Excuse me?"

"Phone?"

"Oh. It was smashed to pieces when you were tackled. We've got what's left in a bag over there." She pointed to the side of the room. "But you're in no shape to look at a phone right now. You need more rest."

"My wife."

"The doctor talked to her. She's on a plane now."

"Amity?"

"Who's Amity?"

"My sister."

The nurse shrugged. "No idea."

He had to talk to Amity, and urgently—but, for the life of him, he couldn't remember what about.

CHAPTER 91

—

Washington

PALMER WALKED RIGHT past her.

First row. Left side. Window seat.

As promised, the first passenger on the plane.

Her head was tilted down as she read from a file that lay across the small table. But her signature silver-and-black bun made clear who she was. The wrinkles and auburn skin on her hands, wrists, and neck only provided corroborating evidence.

Seat 1A on the 5:40 p.m. Thursday flight from Reagan to Fort Myers— the closest direct flight to Naples.

Senator Gigi Fox was sitting where she always did. Just as Amity had said. Just as Justice Gibbons had predicted.

Her weekly trip home.

Most politicians would shy away from sitting in first class. Word would spread quickly that they were living large on the public dole while the taxpayers footing the bill squeezed together in back.

But Fox's wealth was so vast and well-known, she had never concealed it. On the contrary, it was part of her brand. So wealthy, she couldn't be bought, liberating her to fight for the little guy. A modern-day Roosevelt. A Kennedy.

And she was so passionate in that fight, people believed it.

Palmer believed it. He'd long been a fan. Which was one reason Amity's story was so mind-bending. Unfathomable. Knowing what he now knew, he wanted to study her more closely. Every contour and feature. But he didn't want to stare.

Without a carry-on bag to store above, he slipped past the suited man in seat 2B and took his seat in 2A. His neighbor looked at him funny, just as the flight attendant had, reminding him that he was a sweaty mess. He also still had his belt in his hand—he hadn't had time to put it back on after going through security. So he used the initial minutes on the plane to clean up. To help, the flight attendant brought two glasses of water and five wet wipes—the benefits of first class.

A minute or so after he handed back the drenched wipes, a second attendant pulled the thick door shut and the plane backed away from the terminal.

Only then did he start brainstorming how to start the conversation.

CHAPTER 92

—

Boston

"YOU'RE AT MASS General."

A doctor had been examining Simon for minutes—shining a light into his eyes, examining the wound on the left side of his forehead, asking basic questions about his symptoms—when Simon asked where he was.

"Is that in Cambridge?" Simon asked.

"No, Boston proper," the bald man answered. "Why do you ask?"

The plastic bag the nurse had given him contained more than jagged pieces of his shattered phone. His wallet and keys were also in it, along with his business card holder.

The first business card on top hadn't been his own but that of a man named Phillip Conte, Research Director, Harvard Medical School. Those few words had unleashed a full flood of memories of the day's events. The meeting with Conte. The phone call from the woman. The meeting at the burrito place and the dash into the Coop. The call back to Conte, then the attempted escape.

"Just curious if you're affiliated with Harvard Medical School."

"Oh, yes. Mass General is Harvard's largest teaching hospital. I teach there along with most of the doctors around here. And there's a ton of overlap in our research."

Not the answer he wanted to hear.

He couldn't remember her name, but, like Conte, the woman he'd met with was tied to Harvard Med School. A researcher. Her large companion likely was as well. And now he was cooped up at the school's teaching hospital, right under their noses.

The doctor stepped in front of the bed, looking directly at Simon.

"Has any of your short-term memory come back? What you were doing before running out of the Coop?"

The question sounded basic enough—a doctor inquiring about his patient's symptoms. But it also was exactly what those who'd chased him would want to know: Did he remember?

Not being able to trust even those providing his medical care intensified the nausea already roiling Simon's abdomen and throat.

"No. Not a clue, Doctor. Last thing I remember is taking an Uber from the airport. Then waking up here."

CHAPTER 93

——

Over South Carolina

AFTER AN HOUR-LONG wait on a side runway, the 737 bounced and bumped through the entire climb out of D.C. and for some time after leveling out. The turbulence was so rough, cabin service didn't start until the plane crossed into South Carolina.

Which delayed Palmer's plan.

"Care for a drink?" the flight attendant asked once the pilot had okayed cabin service.

"Sure. I'll take a Sam Adams. And do you mind lending me a pen?"

"Not at all."

She handed Palmer a plastic cup of dark ale and a pen from her jacket pocket. He took two sips as he contemplated the words that would do the trick, then tore a piece of paper out of *Hemispheres* magazine.

SENATOR.

He wrote in large, block letters.

I KNOW ABOUT: MANSFIELD; THE GENTRY FAMILY; YOUR SECRET.

AND ABOUT COLIN'S TREATMENT.

LET'S TALK.

PALMER KNIGHT

He read over the words three times before folding the note in half.

Gripping it in his left hand, he reached up between the window and the senator's seat and held it there.

The seat back in front of him jostled slightly as the senator shifted in her seat. Then the note was lifted gently from his hand.

The seat back inched forward. Then froze.

A minute passed.

Then five.

Then ten.

He finished the entire cup and still no reaction. No movement whatsoever.

———

FORTY MINUTES TICKED by between the time Palmer slipped Gigi Fox the short note and the plane's initial descent over central Florida.

Forty minutes that felt like four hours.

If her seat had moved—if *she'd* moved—Palmer missed it.

He sipped from his second glass of Sam Adams, racing through his options as time ran out.

His plan had been to force a conversation at the elderly senator's most vulnerable moment—thirty-six-thousand feet in the air, with no staff around to short-circuit it. As with her Tennessee colleague, the goal was to spring the chat on her quickly—shock and awe—when she had no time to concoct a slick story explaining it all away.

But the wise, cool customer in Seat 1A didn't need a soul to help her. She was short-circuiting the conversation just fine on her own. Giving herself all the time she needed.

"You done with that? We're landing soon."

Palmer jolted up as the attendant reached over to grab his nearly empty glass. He passed it her way along with the pen.

"Sure. Thank you."

He pushed his tray table into the seat back and locked it in for landing. Out the window, a bright sheen on the Atlantic reflected the half-moon floating at a 45-degree angle above. The front of thick, uninterrupted clouds that had so jostled the plane down the Atlantic Seaboard was now well north, replaced by a clear Florida evening and the bright lights of Orlando below.

Whether it was the view or the final swig of beer, his mind slowed down. Relaxed.

His confidence grew.

She was playing her hand well, but the senator couldn't let him walk off the plane and leave Florida having written what he'd written.

She needed to have a conversation.

Yes, she was forcing it onto her terms. But for her own sake, the conversation had to happen.

Palmer leaned back in his seat, waiting for her to make her move.

Fifteen minutes later the plane headed southwest out over the Gulf, small lights lining the coast below. The aircraft then banked hard to the left, crossing back over land, flaps descending as the pilots lined up for their final approach.

And that's when it happened.

The seat back in front inched forward. Seconds after that, it tilted back again.

A magazine appeared to Palmer's left, below his window for a moment before dropping to the floor with a soft thud.

He picked it up.

Nothing was on the cover except a picturesque photo of a white-sand Caribbean beach. Looked nice.

He flipped it over to a full-page ad for Jack Daniel's. On the lower half of the ad appeared some large cursive letters—old-school and elegant, if shaky.

Her response.

We'll talk. Walk slowly to baggage claim. I'll find you.

———

FOR A WOMAN in her eighties, Gigi Fox moved quickly, scampering off the plane as soon as the flight attendant wrenched open the heavy plane door. She didn't look back once.

Half her age, Palmer's neighbor in Seat 2B took his sweet time, getting one bag from below and a second from above. He then politely let the passengers across from them exit their row, along with all of Row 3.

Walk slowly, the senator had written. He was off to a good start.

Palmer entered the terminal. It was crowded for a small airport, mostly people walking in the same direction he was, escaping to Florida for the weekend.

With Fox nowhere in sight, he followed the signs to baggage claim.

A thick crowd stood around the small airport's single oblong carousel. An Atlanta flight topped the list on the monitor overhead. Then Charlotte. Then a LaGuardia flight that had also been delayed by an hour. With each flight, a continuous line of bags circled the conveyor belt, passengers lifting and lugging them away amid grunts and "Excuse mes."

Without being too obvious about it, he glanced around the baggage claim area.

No senator in sight.

"Washington-Reagan" popped up on the screen and a new wave of bags rounded the carousel. He stood back, hoping to spot the senator grabbing her bag. She'd only had a large purse with her in the cabin.

His seatmate winked goodbye as he wheeled away a large leather suitcase. Other bags came and went, and he recognized a few other passengers as they walked away.

No Gigi Fox.

Ten more minutes passed, and "Washington-Reagan" disappeared from the screen. New luggage from Houston and Chicago circled the carousel.

He felt the same hollow feeling as someone who'd lost their bags—but in this case he'd lost a U.S. senator.

Two more flights went by. Another fifteen minutes. Then an empty carousel.

Still no senator.

Ten more minutes passed. Was it time to give up?

"Mr. Knight."

It was a British accent, a deep baritone, from behind.

Palmer turned around to see a slim brown-haired man in a dark suit smiling back at him.

"Yes."

"Please come with me." Not British, but Australian.

"Are you with the senator?"

"I am."

"Where is—"

"Come with me."

CHAPTER 94

Columbus

AMITY BREATHED A sigh of relief.

Her phone rang at 8:00 p.m. sharp. As it had done nightly before the explosion, but not once since.

UNKNOWN NUMBER

She took the call sitting in her law office—the only one in the firm with lights still on. They'd let her leave the hospital two hours before and she'd hobbled here for one more round of research.

"How's she doing?" she asked.

"It depends." The voice was less angry than before. "Have you learned your lesson?"

"I have. I'm done." She faked a mournful tone as best she could. "I don't care what's going on as long as Mom lives."

A long pause.

"How can we be sure?"

"Let me see: I can barely move without excruciating pain, you no doubt have people watching my every move, and you have the power to save my mom's life. I'll just sit pretty and be the good lawyer."

"And daughter."

"Yes. And daughter."

Silence again for what felt like a minute.

Finally interrupted.

"She's making progress," the woman said.

It was the first time she'd characterized the treatment as progress. Even if it was a ploy to buy her silence, Amity still thrilled at the word.

"What's that mean, specifically?"

"It means it's working. The prime tumor is now half the size it was, and the cancer cells are mostly gone in the places they'd spread. Her lymph nodes are one hundred percent clean."

Amity closed her eyes and let out a heavy sigh. This was the progress report she'd waited two years to hear. But she didn't want to cling to false hope only to be disappointed later. She'd ridden that emotional roller coaster for too long.

"Your mom is actually a very strong woman," the woman added, sounding sincere. Sounding like Simon and Sam Solomon.

"When can I see her?" Amity asked.

"Excuse me?" the woman asked.

"I'd like to see her. It's not right that she's all alone."

She was looking at her computer monitor as she spoke. In fact, she'd been staring at it even before the call. The image of the attractive black-haired woman looked back at her, taking up most of the screen.

The woman's name appeared in the upper-right corner.

Dr. Neena Vora.

In the past hour she'd discovered the identity of her mother's caregiver—and captor. And the woman she was talking to now.

Simon's text had led her to a Dr. Blackwood at Harvard. And only a few keystrokes had revealed that the Harvard doctor and researcher was one of the most important scientific figures on the planet. Headlines over the past twenty years, both in medical journals and mainstream newspapers, described the larger-than-life Scotland native on the verge of making medical history:

Harvard Study Cracks the Code

Harvard's Blackwood Makes Another Breakthrough

New Blackwood Technique Raises Prospect of a Cancer Cure

Blackwood had to be the person they were looking for—the one on the receiving end of the millions of federal funds flowing from Shepherd Logan's subcommittee.

Then Amity had dug deeper.

Beyond his Harvard duties, Dr. Blackwood had created a private biotech research firm called BioRevolution. The day-to-day leader of that firm was an Indian-born, Oxford-educated woman named Neena Vora. A star student of Blackwood's, she'd spent a lifetime making cancer breakthroughs.

Amity had hunted down several lectures delivered by Dr. Vora to be sure. Outside of genetic research, Vora was a leading thinker on how the Hippocratic oath should guide doctors amid ethical dilemmas. She spoke often on it, including a spellbinding TED Talk the previous year. And as Amity had suspected, the graceful, mellifluous voice in those lectures was the same as the one on her phone each night.

The same voice as the woman talking to her now.

"That won't be possible, Ms. Jones. Especially after what you've done."

"So when will I see her again?"

"When we're sure that we can trust you."

It wasn't subtle. Mom would be leverage for as long as they needed. Vora was still holding the immoral bargain over her, making Amity's stomach turn.

Until an hour ago, there was nothing she could do but sit tight. Trapped, waiting for her nightly update.

But now she knew. Mom was likely in Boston, somewhere near Cambridge.

And so was Neena Vora.

CHAPTER 95

Fort Myers

JACKIE O MIGHT have been impressed.

The jet-black circular lenses, twice as large as standard glasses, directly faced Palmer when he sat down in the back of the exquisitely detailed Escalade. The problem was, their reflection offered a clearer vision of his own face than any view of Senator Gigi Fox. Her famous steely eyes hidden, she already had the upper hand.

The oversized glasses also accentuated how tiny the senator looked in the black leather seat enveloping her.

"Good evening, Senator."

As the Escalade pulled away from the airport curb, a panel of thick, clear plexiglass silently lifted in front of them, presumably soundproofing the conversation.

"You don't know me well, young man." Her voice walked the line between somber and angry. "But rest assured, charm won't get you far."

"My granddad told me that once about you," he said, desperate to build rapport. "Good thing. I've never been much of a charmer anyway."

He was lying but aiming for a bit of self-deprecation.

"You have ten minutes," she said curtly. "What do you want?"

Palmer's heartbeat quickened as he sat face-to-face with a woman who'd spent a lifetime carving up foes far more powerful than him. "The single toughest person in the Senate, man or woman," Granddad had once said.

But Palmer had also jousted with all sorts of challenging figures, learning that people responded differently to different approaches: aggression, kissing ass, or something in between. Palmer had figured out over time what worked with whom, spotting early tells like facial expressions and body language. But since Senator Fox was belted into her seat, her constrained position and opaque glasses made her nearly impossible to read.

With VIPs like her, his default had always been kissing ass, because he never knew who might feed him his next big scoop. But that didn't feel right today.

"Ten minutes?" he asked, laughing. "We won't even cover Company Line in ten minutes."

The senator's mouth opened slightly as her small body stiffened.

He gave it a few seconds, then continued.

"Actually, I'm less interested in your past than about the plan you and Shepherd Logan cooked up through that subcommittee of yours. I've seen all sorts of pay-to-play schemes, but a 'friends and family' plan for lifesaving cancer treatment? That may top them all."

Fox waved her hand violently in the air, inches from Palmer's left wrist.

"Stop," she said slowly, the command piercing the air for seconds.

"Excuse me?"

"How dare you talk to me that way."

Palmer didn't respond. His whole goal had been to rile her up, to get her talking. And she was talking.

"You know nothing," she said. "About my life. About life in general—how tough it can be. About the decisions we faced."

Her wrinkled right hand reached up to her glasses, then brought them down to her lap.

"Look at me."

Palmer didn't move.

"Look at me!"

Palmer turned his head directly toward her, matching her stare.

"What do you see?"

She widened her eyes, inviting Palmer in. They were sad. Spent. Swirling tendrils of thread-thin veins formed clouds of crimson over her eyes' inner halves, the tear ducts in the corners so swollen and pink, they looked ready to burst.

"I know what you think you see."

"What's that?" Palmer asked, turning forward again.

"Age. Old, old age."

Palmer shifted in his seat.

"Honestly, Senator, you look tired more than anything."

"Don't patronize me. But what you see in these eyes, in these wrinkles..."

She held her arms up, leaving her glasses in her lap.

"... in this graying hair, are the physical scars of a long, complicated life. But with those scars come a lifetime of hard lessons. With those scars come wisdom."

She lowered her arms.

"And when you've lived as long as Shep and I have, there's one thing you come to see that children like you won't understand for a good long while— that you couldn't possibly know. Something your granddad wouldn't have had the heart to tell you."

"And what's that?" Palmer asked quietly.

"That life is a never-ending series of tragedies. Accumulating as you go, then exploding toward the end. When you're my age, almost everyone you've ever known is gone. Early in life, they die from accidents. Violence. Illness. Some take their lives. But later it's almost all from disease. Horrible, awful disease, eating away at humanity one soul at a time."

She took a deep breath and put the glasses back over her eyes.

"When you're young, when you hear names of those you know, you picture what they look like on their best day. You associate them with what they do. You imagine them surrounded by family, in their brightest moments. But at my age, when you hear a name, you associate them with how they died.

You remember how they looked at death's door, or after they crossed over it. In the hospital. In hospice. In the casket. Withered down to nothing."

Palmer thought of his granddad in precisely that state back in Rhode Island a decade ago. What the senator was saying had been true for the initial years that followed. But then the memories improved. The darkest images, of the great man's final days, had gradually faded, replaced by visions of him at his finest.

"I've had loss, too, Senator—"

"Just wait. You've seen nothing. Until you're my age—if you make it to my age—you couldn't begin to understand. Everyone is gone. You're a relic in a world of strangers who hardly know you. And whom you hardly know."

She paused again, looking forward. They were now driving south on a major highway. I-75.

"I've spent my career fighting injustice. Tackling inequality and discrimination. Opening up doors for your generation. For little girls like I once was to have a better path. And with all that snooping around Mansfield, you and that law clerk . . ."

She trailed off. She knew he knew her secret but didn't want to say the words. Words that would shock the nation.

He responded gently.

"You have an incredible record of service, Sen—"

"But seeing all I've seen, the opportunity that now presents itself is just as big."

"To cure cancer?"

"That's just the beginning. Over time, it's developing the tools to regenerate dying parts of our bodies, whatever they may be. I have only a few years left, so it's all too late for me. But I can't think of a more lasting contribution I could make, and I'm blessed to be in the unique position to make it. Senator Logan feels the same way."

"But, Senator, there are laws and protocols around medical research. My understanding is that you're violating a host of them."

She shrugged.

"In the past, our civil rights heroes understood the value of civil disobedience. When laws were written or applied in a way that impeded equality or progress, they stood up for the greater good. They pushed through those obstacles and changed our country, and we rightfully celebrate them for having done so. Well, consider this our own form of civil disobedience, from the highest level, to achieve a goal that will change mankind. What are they going to do? Lock up an old lady? Put Shep and Mary Logan behind bars? For curing cancer?"

For the first time, she laughed. A hearty, openmouthed laugh that Palmer could see lighting up a room in different circumstances.

"From what I've read, there are huge risks involved. Those laws are there to protect against unanticipated consequences and all sorts of misuse."

She shook her head.

"If you trust government to get that balancing act right, you haven't learned much in your years of reporting. These days especially, D.C. is a witch's brew of donations and lobbying, bureaucracy and politics. It's all broken. That's no way to make decisions as profound as this."

"So who should decide? You?"

"How about the experts? Doctors and scientists."

He looked down at his phone to recall the name Amity had sent before he'd boarded the flight. She'd sent it for a reason.

"You mean people like Blackwood?"

Gigi Fox didn't flinch.

"Sure. Dr. Blackwood knows better. Others too. They're in a far better position to make the call than Beltway bureaucrats and corrupt politicians."

"And you're prepared to accept the consequences if things go wrong?"

"We're grown-ups. We get it. Dr. Blackwood and his team explained the risks. And everyone they treated signed on. In fact, the purpose of this final phase of research is to learn how to minimize those risks. If something goes wrong in a case, then . . ."

She trailed off, the implication clear.

"And you and Colin Gentry's parents were prepared for that?"

"Why wouldn't we be? He had less than three months to live otherwise. It wasn't a close call. Now he'll live a full life."

She'd just admitted the entire connection without a flinch.

"Thank God it worked out for him. But how about others?"

"What do you mean?"

"Those not as fortunate as Colin or Mary Logan. Are they supposed to just walk off a cliff like Duke Garber?"

He was trying to bait her into saying more, but she stayed calm.

"Duke's case was sealed the day he got sick. Nothing's guaranteed, especially this early. But at least he and others spent their final days advancing something bigger than all of us. Just as I'm doing."

"Still, you don't find it problematic that you and Shepherd Logan were able to get your loved ones to the front of the line? That's a pretty blatant quid pro quo for your support of illegal research."

She shook her head, bringing Palmer back to the principal's office.

"Have you not listened to a word I've said? I would've pushed forward on the work regardless. But I don't apologize for a moment for doing all I can to help little Colin. Hell, some chose to help themselves. Not me. Saving Colin was the least I could do for a family that's been through so much."

———

THIRTY MINUTES LATER, they pulled off I-75 and turned west for Naples.

In a way, it had been an easy interview. She just kept talking—all a good reporter could ask for. And in the process—directly or indirectly—she confirmed everything. Her own past. Blackwood and his plan. Saving Colin Gentry. And even as she justified it with great moral certitude, she left no doubt they'd violated the law.

"Young man, our ride's almost done. Now we face the biggest question of all."

"And what is that?"

"What will *you* do?"

"What will *I* do?"

"Yes. I've laid it all out for you. Everything you wanted to know. And now you know that lives are being saved as we speak. Thousands more to come. Millions, ultimately. Are you prepared to stand in the way of all of that?"

"Senator, I don't start or stop anything."

The car turned left and headed south along a road that hugged the coast, past well-lit mansions and the silhouettes of palm trees.

"Don't play dumb with me. We both know that exposing this would shut it all down. At the very least, stop the research in its tracks or delay it for years, which would mean so many lives lost. Are you prepared to shoulder all that now that you know what's happening?"

"It's about exposing the truth, something you've spent your whole career fighting for."

She shook her head, casting a disappointed frown.

"Fine," she said quietly. "Your choice."

The car slowed down and turned into a long driveway. A few football fields in front of them stood the largest mansion yet.

She knocked on the plexiglass.

"Senator?" the driver asked politely after the panel descended a few inches.

"Drop me off at the front door."

"Okay. And Mr. Knight here?"

"Take him to the boathouse."

CHAPTER 96

Naples

EVEN THROUGH THE tinted windows of the Escalade, Gigi Fox's so-called boathouse was bigger than most actual houses Palmer had ever set foot in.

Stuck in the back seat, Palmer knocked on the plexiglass panel, but the driver didn't respond.

He checked his phone. No signal.

The screen showed that several messages had been left, but he couldn't access them.

Minutes ticked away in silence. He knocked some more.

With nothing else to do, he typed down notes from the conversation into the phone. The key facts the senator had confirmed. Every verbatim quote he could recall. Questions that remained.

Then he stewed for a few more minutes.

"Hey, buddy," he said, knocking on the plexiglass again. "I don't know how it works down under, but this is America. You can't just take people hostage here."

Nothing.

He pounded harder, the panel barely moving. He banged on the door to his right, throwing in a few elbows for good measure.

Visible in the rearview mirror, the driver's eyes stared straight ahead.

He hadn't smiled since that first greeting at baggage claim. But he didn't appear angry. Just tense.

A queasy discomfort churned Palmer's stomach, dampening his initial satisfaction with the conversation.

The long wait at baggage claim. The drive all the way to Naples. The fact that she'd shared so much, not at all concerned about what he knew. Now another long wait.

It had all been a stall tactic. But for what?

The driver's demeanor suggested it was bad news.

Palmer tried to buck himself up. *She's a United States senator, for God's sake. She'd never off a reporter. That happens in other countries. Not here.*

But two words kept ringing in his ears.

"Civil disobedience."

If that's how she viewed it—civil disobedience to achieve a far greater good—a death or two were acceptable roadkill. Heck, they'd almost killed Amity and that newspaper editor.

He pounded again. Yelled more. Swore.

Nothing.

CHAPTER 97

——

Columbus

AFTER DAYS COOPED up, it was time to hit the road. But because she was sure she was being watched, Amity knew getting away undetected would require a complicated exit plan.

Leaving her office lights on and her phone lying on the desk, she grabbed an Uber at the less-trafficked side entrance to her law firm's office tower. She had the driver drop her off at the nearest Budget rental car office, then rented a green Ford Fiesta and drove back to her law office. Parking the Fiesta in the garage, she took the elevator back to her office, grabbed her phone, and turned the lights off. Then she descended back to the garage, hopped into the Jeep she'd rented the day before, and drove back to her apartment complex. She left the Jeep in her usual parking spot.

Once in her condo, she changed into more comfortable clothes, pulled her hair into her road trip ponytail and tucked it under a Buckeyes baseball cap, then packed a small overnight bag. She sat down at her kitchen counter, laying her iPhone on the countertop's cheap gray tile. She looked up a few numbers from the iPhone—Palmer Knight's, Simon's, Justice Gibbons's, a few others she might need—then saved them into the burner phone she'd been carrying the past week.

She left the iPhone on the countertop to throw off anyone tracking her through the phone.

Twenty minutes and one more Uber ride later, she was back in the Fiesta and heading north in the fast lane of I-71.

She plugged her designation into the car's GPS.

Seven hundred miles. And the roads were finally clear of snow.

If she drove straight through, she'd be there by 9:00.

If she took a few catnaps, 10:30 at the latest.

They wouldn't know she'd left Ohio until it was too late.

CHAPTER 98

————

Naples

THE ESCALADE'S CABIN exploded in light, a bright beam from behind casting an oversized shadow of Palmer's head on the dashboard.

He whirled around.

Two squarish headlights jiggled in the distance, having just passed the mansion and turned toward the boathouse, now approaching directly from behind.

Squinting, Palmer watched as the headlights grew larger. Once they got to within two car lengths, they doubled in intensity, forcing him to avert his eyes.

Gravel crunched as the car stopped, then a door opened and slammed shut.

Seconds later, a fist rapped twice on the window to his right.

A large figure bent down, his broad, toothy grin gleaming in the light.

The bald head and pointed broken nose looked like Mr. Clean after a barroom brawl.

Palmer froze in his seat, stomach clenching tight.

The hulking man opened Palmer's door.

He considered running, but the man's thick body was positioned in such a way that he'd have to run through him to get anywhere. And there was no running through this guy.

"Come with me," the man growled in an accent that sounded Irish.

Light shining in their eyes, the man walked Palmer back to his car, also a dark SUV. An iron grip squeezed his right arm down to the bone.

He opened the back right door of his SUV. As Palmer ducked and then leaned into the cabin, the man's grip held firm.

His one chance.

Palmer reached across with his left hand and clamped the man's clenched hand tight against his arm. He simultaneously swung his legs in and fell into the seat, then yanked the door shut as hard as he could with his right arm.

A spine-tingling crunch followed by an earsplitting scream made clear that the thick door shattered something significant in the guy's left arm. Maybe his elbow.

Palmer slammed the door again, but the man jerked his arm out of Palmer's grasp and away from the door.

As the man howled, Palmer scooted over to the opposite door and leapt out of the car, sprinting across the well-lit driveway and into the darkness.

———

"KNIGHT, GET YOUR fookin' ass back here!"

Palmer couldn't see the man and barely heard him as the ocean breeze muffled his words. But the pain in his voice cut through the darkness.

Palmer hid while catching his breath, then sprinted toward the road. But, knowing that was where they'd expect him to go, he ultimately doubled back, running in a wide semicircle farther away from the mansion, beyond the shadow of the boathouse.

Behind the boathouse, the flat lawn abutted what looked and felt like the back side of a sand dune, the top of which was illuminated by the faint glow of the Gulf. He ducked low and made his way eight or so feet up the dune, over thick sand and tall grass while navigating among dense, large-leafed bushes. The bushes cleared out feet past the dune's top, but the sand was much finer and the incline steeper on the other side, causing him to slip a few times as he ran down.

Staying close to the dune, Palmer jogged north, counting on his would-be abductors to look for him along the road.

CHAPTER 99

Boston

THE NURSE ON call responded in under a minute.

"Could you turn the lights off?" Simon Jones asked quietly. "My head is killing me."

"Of course."

Two minutes later, with the door closed again, only the glow emanating from a monitor kept the room from being pitch-black.

But Simon didn't lay his head back down. He needed rest but wouldn't get any here.

Simon had scanned the room before calling in the nurse. His clothes were hanging in a vertical cabinet in one corner of the small room. His wallet and keys lay on a small table to the right of the cabinet, along with the plastic bag containing his smashed phone parts and business cards. His shoes were under a wooden chair next to the table.

He let another minute pass, adjusting to the light. Making sure the nurse wasn't coming back. Then he got moving.

The IV tube slipped right out of his left wrist with only a slight pinch.

He dropped his feet over the left side of his bed, gripping the bed's metal bar as he straightened his legs. A wave of pain flooded his head, an intense pressure pushing out against his temples and forehead, but he grimaced through it, refusing to sit back down. He could stand the pain much better than he could the knowledge that he was being watched.

He took slow half steps to the cabinet and let his hospital gown slip to the floor. Over five painful minutes, he put his clothes, socks, and shoes back on. With his jacket still hanging at the Coop, he jammed his keys, his wallet, and the small plastic bag into his jeans pockets.

He stepped to the door and opened it a crack. The light from the hallway blinded him, sending another wave of pain pulsing through his head.

Seeing no one in either direction, he hobbled out of the room and followed the exit signs to the elevator.

CHAPTER 100

Naples

WITH A HALF-MOON rising above the horizon and the soothing sound of small waves lapping against the beach, Palmer would have enjoyed the jog if he weren't running for his life.

He planned to head north for a mile more, find his way back to the main road, then take an Uber to the airport.

Ten minutes in, his pocket vibrated. He slowed to a walk and took out his phone. A 202 number.

He ignored the call, knowing the sound of the waves would give away his escape route.

He picked up his pace again, ignoring a second call.

Then came the distinct vibration and ping of a text message.

He slowed to look down. The same number had just sent him a message.

```
Knight. This fool's errand or Amity Jones. Your call.
```

He called Amity's Columbus number. It rang through to voicemail.

He texted her. No answer.

A second ping came through. A photo of Amity Jones getting out of her car. A time stamp indicated it had been taken earlier in the day.

"Shit."

Palmer didn't take another step. It was over. She'd been through enough already.

He texted the 202 number back: Heading back your way. He turned around and walked south.

Fifteen minutes later, the lights of the Fox mansion emerged in the distance. Next came the silhouette of the boathouse over the arc of the dune.

Drawing even to the boathouse, Palmer took a diagonal step up the dune. The thin, shifting sand got the best of him on the next step, and he slipped to one knee.

As he stood back up, leaves above him rustled. Then a branch snapped.

"Hello?"

No answer.

More rustling, then a burst of snaps.

A tall, dark shadow raced down the dune, barreling into him with a loud grunt.

Rather than tackling Palmer onto the beach, the heavy figure bear-hugged him, pushing his thin frame across the sand and into the Gulf. About five feet in, Palmer toppled over on his back and into the cold salt water.

He planted his legs to stand up, but three sharp punches to the side of the head knocked him back into the water, face-first. Two hands gripped his shoulders, pushing and then holding his head underwater as the man's full weight crushed down on his back. Palmer kicked and swung his arms wildly, but the man didn't move.

Muffled yells came from directly overhead.

As Palmer held his breath, his lungs grew tight, aching more with every second that passed. He went still for a moment, then thrashed around with all the force he could muster, kicking backward and landing some hard elbows into what felt like the man's chest and gut.

But the man still didn't budge. And now a knee pressed hard into the small of his back.

His entire chest felt on the verge of exploding as pain shot outward from deep within his skull.

CHAPTER 101

Cambridge

"You did the right thing, Senator."

In the library of his spacious condo—surrounded by books, awards, and photos with world leaders—Dr. Blackwood could hear the doubt through the phone's receiver. He was close to losing her.

Just like he'd lost Duke.

He shook his head thinking back to it. They'd been lifelong friends, and he'd saved the man's life. Yet Duke had still almost betrayed him and their glorious cause. It had started with quiet questions, followed by more strongly stated doubts. Then outright challenges. And then the decision to go public, which Quinn had passed along just in time. The final, unacceptable risk.

"Doctor, we have to get this done soon," the senator said quietly. "This is getting to be too much."

Blackwood replied gently.

"Senator, we're almost there. You have done all you need to do. Now it's on my team to prove our outcomes. Then we launch. We are so close to changing the world, the final piece of your legacy."

"And the reporter?"

He had to say something.

"You're better off not asking."

A long pause.

"Okay. Does Senator Logan know?"

"Of course he knows," he lied.

Senator Logan had not called him all day. No doubt the reporter had visited him in Washington, but he'd heard nothing.

Just like Duke. Unappreciative bastard. He'd pulled Logan's wife back from sure death, yet now he was considering turning on him.

He'd send Quinn his way in the morning.

CHAPTER 102

Naples

A HARD KICK struck Palmer's shin from the left, followed by another muffled yell.

The weight on his shoulders and back lifted.

He thrust his head out of the water, air exploding from his mouth before he could suck in a breath of fresh oxygen.

"What the hell are you doing?" a voice screamed amid loud splashes. Australian accent.

Palmer choked out some water, took a series of rapid-fire breaths as the pain in his lungs eased, then gagged some more.

"Jesus Christ," said a second man, in an Irish accent. "You were supposed to grab him, not drown him."

"I was holding him down until you got here."

"Right."

A large hand clutched Palmer's left arm and pulled him up out of the water.

"Come with me."

An airy whistle accompanied each of the big man's breaths, but he didn't say another word as they walked up the dune and back to the SUV. Holding his injured left arm up against his stomach, he shoved Palmer hard into the back seat with his right.

"Buckle up."

Dripping wet, Palmer did what he said.

They drove off the grounds.

"I should kill you right now for what you did to my elbow."

Shivering, Palmer said nothing. He'd lost all control. Apparently Senator Fox's civil disobedience included kidnapping journalists after all.

The only sound that followed, for a good ten minutes, was more huffs of breath whistling out of the driver's nose. He was hurting bad.

Then a deep ring sounded up front.

The car swerved as the man lifted a phone to his ear.

"Hello, ma'am," he said politely.

A few seconds passed.

"Yes. I got him."

More seconds.

"Thank you, ma'am. I sure can."

He shifted in his seat, grunted, then cursed.

"Knight!"

"Yes."

"I can't pass the phone back and drive at the same time. It's on the center console. Reach forward and get it."

"The phone?"

"Yeah, the phone. Someone wants to talk to you."

Fox, no doubt. Palmer racked his brain for a way to convince the old senator to let him go.

Unbuckling his seat belt, he reached forward and grabbed what felt like an original version of a car phone—far thicker than a modern cell phone, longer, with a small antenna rising from the top.

"Senator, this is completely—"

"Mr. Knight, I'm glad you're safe."

He held the phone away from his ear and looked at it. There was no mistaking the voice. And it wasn't Gigi Fox.

He took another glance at the bald man in the rearview mirror.

Who was this guy?

And how did he have a direct line to the president?

CHAPTER 103

Washington

"MADAM PRESIDENT. PLEASE tell me what's happening."

Only a marble-top coffee table separated Palmer and the most powerful woman on the planet. They were seated in the White House's Treaty Room, on the second floor of the residence. The big bald man had walked Palmer into the room, nodded at the waiting president—wrapped in a white robe with a presidential seal on its right breast, her hair pulled back in a ponytail—then left them alone. Palmer's hard brown leather chair felt a lot less comfortable than her plush tan couch looked.

She flashed a quick grin. "That's funny. We brought you here to tell *us*."

Palmer had stewed the entire private flight. Trying to make sense of it all, he never got close. His guess was the bald guy whose arm he'd smashed was the same guy who'd followed Amity in Ohio.

"Are you part of all this? The plot with this guy Blackwood and the senators?"

She shook her head.

"We don't know much except that some highly respected senators are up to no good. And we mainly know that because of you." She cocked her head. "Who's Blackwood?"

"If you don't know anything, then why did a guy who's been running around Ohio on their behalf just drop me off at the White House."

She flashed a quick smile.

"It's complicated."

"I'm sure it is. But I think you owe me answers."

She took a sip from a cocktail glass.

"Word was you didn't drink."

She laughed. "I didn't until my hundredth day here. Want something?"

"Just answers."

Expressionless, she took another sip.

"Palmer, I assume you know how close I was to Duke Garber."

"Of course."

"Not long before he died, he sat in that very chair. Without giving me details, he said he was involved in something he wasn't proud of but that he was going to end it. Some type of medical research."

"So Duke was a part of it too?"

"Part of *what* is what we've been looking into ever since."

"He didn't tell you any details?"

She shook her head. "One thing Duke knew was how to keep a secret, so we've been scrambling to figure it out. We basically know what you've discovered—that Senators Fox and Logan were also involved. Of all Duke's high-profile responsibilities, we never thought to look into that little sub-committee of Shepherd Logan's. But we are now."

Their prior conversation suddenly flashed through his mind.

"That whole deepfake thing. Was it . . . fake?"

"No. Just incomplete. Duke was looking into that, too, and the Saudis knew it."

"So you floated the deepfake theory to see which possible cause was true?"

He crossed his arms, body tensing—remembering that his career was in shambles. She had used him from the beginning. Ellrod too.

She cast a sheepish grin. "I'm afraid so."

"And?"

"Well, we now know all about the Saudis' deepfake capacity, thanks to you. But we never could connect the Saudis back to Duke's death."

"Which means his death was related to whatever he was doing with these other senators on cancer research."

"Exactly. The timing was too coincidental."

The president took a final sip from her glass and set it down on the table.

"Palmer, can you please tell me what else you discovered? Duke was right to be concerned. We want to shut this down fast, but we need all the details."

"You can't wait to watch it on television?" Palmer asked.

"You talked to both senators directly. They and whoever else is involved won't just sit still. We need to move now."

Palmer spent the next twenty minutes explaining all he'd learned. She listened attentively, taking notes and saying nothing. As Palmer described the essence of the deal—secretly sending money to Harvard in order to save loved ones and complete the research—she shook her head repeatedly.

When he wrapped up, she frowned for a few seconds before responding.

"Duke was a saint. I can't believe he ever went down that path to begin with. It's the most reckless thing he ever did."

"All three were saints. My guess is they let the goal of curing cancer overwhelm their usual good judgment . . ."

Palmer remembered Shepherd Logan on the golf course—those exhausted eyes welling up.

". . . And my guess is most people would choose to save a loved one from cancer if they could."

The president winced. "Maybe most people. But when you take the oath they did, you commit to putting that type of personal interest aside for the good of the country. Duke knew that more than anyone. Fox and Logan too. What a shame."

The president turned her head away for a moment, then turned it back.

"Palmer, after all you've learned, why do you think Duke took his own life?"

He thought back to his conversation with Gigi Fox. She'd said they all knew the risks when they signed on. That they were prepared for the worst.

"Who knows if he really did?"

"You think they killed him?" she asked.

"They certainly haven't shown any hesitation to kill others."

"True. But the FBI said they saw no evidence of it. Only suicide. And they were looking, believe me."

"Well, if he did kill himself, my guess is something went wrong with his treatment. Senator Fox suggested as much. So he knew his time had come to an end. She told me herself they were all prepared for the consequences."

The president nodded and closed her eyes, then looked down.

"God bless him," she said quietly, holding the sleeve of her robe up to her right eye.

It was a rare show of emotion by the president. Palmer allowed a minute to pass before switching topics.

"So tell me more about the agent who was keeping tabs on all this."

"His name's Pierce. Secret Service. Former FBI. Don't let the Irish accent fool you: he's as patriotic an American as they come. And the best agent we have. I asked him to look into this as soon as Garber walked out of the White House."

"So how'd he end up in Naples?"

"One of the generals tipped off the Secret Service about your little golf visit at Andrews, so we knew you were chasing down the story. We wanted to follow your lead, knowing you might get them to open up."

She took a deep breath.

"Plus, we thought they might try to kill you. Sounds like we were right to think so."

Palmer's stomach knotted as he pictured his head beneath the Gulf surf.

"Gee, thanks for cutting it so close."

The president smiled.

"Well, better late than never. Either way, we now have what we need."

"What's that?"

"The full story. Thanks to you."

"So what's next?"

"We've got to shut down this Harvard professor of yours. Seize his labs and his research. I'm going to call in the NIH and FDA to take what he's done and make the best of it for the country, then announce that publicly."

She smiled.

"And whatever we do, we can give you a heads-up before we announce it." She winked. "And maybe an interview back here soon. You've earned it."

The president knew the media game as well as anyone, tossing catnip his way.

"That'd be great. Thank you."

One other question came to mind.

"Madam President, what happens to the senators?"

"We'll see, but that's tougher. Maybe we get them to cooperate against Blackmore—"

"Blackwood."

"Right, Blackwood. We turn them against him, then ease them out of office as soon as possible."

"That's it? For all they did?"

"Palmer, you said it yourself: How are you going to take down two re-spected eighty-year-old senators who pushed for a cure for cancer?"

Palmer saw right though her. She had an election next year to worry about. Florida alone might determine the outcome.

"Madam President, not everything's about politics."

"Palmer, forget politics," the former Colorado attorney general said. "I don't think a jury in the country would convict those two."

CHAPTER 104

—

Bethesda

BACK AT THE motel room, Palmer called Amity from the landline.

As before, it rang five times before going to voicemail. He left a message, then called again ten minutes later. Voicemail again.

Maybe they'd taken her after all.

Five minutes later, just as he picked up the phone to dial again, his cell phone buzzed. Another 614 number.

"Hey there," Amity said after he picked up.

"Hold on, let me call from a landline."

"Where've you been, Palmer?" she asked after he called back.

"Florida and back. You? I've been calling nonstop."

"Just passed Buffalo."

She filled Palmer in on her research: more details on Dr. Blackwood and Neena Vora. The company they ran. All their breakthroughs. Some of her writings.

"It's definitely them," Palmer said, summarizing his conversation with Fox. "But what're you gonna do when you get there?"

"I haven't figured that out yet. But now that I know who has Mom, I can't sit around in Columbus doing nothing."

"I can't argue with that."

They talked through a plan for the next ten minutes.

After hanging up, Palmer booked a morning flight to Boston.

CHAPTER 105

Cambridge

SNOW PILED UP on the windshield as Amity Jones and Palmer Knight entered their second hour in her rented Fiesta. She flipped on the wipers every few minutes to clear the view.

Despite the cold, the streets bustled around them. Kendall Square, a block from the Charles River, occupied only a square mile of Cambridge real estate but generated more biotech patents than anywhere in the world.

Amity and Palmer ignored the hubbub and kept their eyes on a sleek twelve-story building—dark steel and tinted glass—across the street. Among a number of high-flying companies, Paden Blackwood's BioRevolution was headquartered inside. Which meant Neena Vora was likely inside as well.

Cafés and restaurants filled the streets around Kendall Square, and many of those leaving the building were patronizing them for lunch. So they waited, hoping Dr. Vora would do the same.

"So he's okay?" Palmer asked after Amity had filled him in on the painful end to Simon's sleuthing.

"He's getting there. It was a severe concussion, so he's woozy and in some pain. His wife's here and in touch with their doctor back home."

Jenna had filled Amity in that morning. Simon had hobbled from the hospital to a Holiday Inn down the street, with Jenna joining him two hours later. He'd slept for ten hours straight. Amity planned on stopping by later, assuming this attempted rendezvous worked.

"Boy, did he come through by pinpointing Dr. Blackwood. Just in time too."

"He sure did," she said, allowing a smile. "Simon saved the day."

The adjoining glass doors opened and a group of five women walked out. As with all the others, they were wrapped in thick coats, three donning winter hats. Amity strained to get a good look at each face, comparing them to a printout of Neena Vora's photo that lay on the dashboard.

"No. No . . . No . . . No . . . And no."

Palmer leaned forward, squinting. "You sure about the woman on the far right?"

"I'm sure. Completely different face."

"Okay," Palmer said, still studying the short brunette.

A mixed group—two men, two women—walked out next.

"Too young," Palmer said.

"Agreed."

The doors shut behind them.

"So you really think they're being honest about your mom?" Palmer asked. They'd spent much of the first hour together debating whether they could trust Dr. Vora.

"I know *she* is. Like I said, she's a real doctor. I got the same feeling from one of the guys in the van."

"I don't know, Amity. They're both neck-deep in some pretty twisted stuff."

Two women walked out briskly. One wore glasses and had darker skin, black hair curling at her shoulders. Amity and Palmer both leaned forward.

She grabbed the printout from the dashboard and studied it.

"Nope. Not her."

"You sure?" Palmer asked.

"Definitely not. You really do need those glasses back."

Palmer chuckled. His Ray-Bans were sloshing around somewhere in the Gulf of Mexico.

One o'clock neared. More people were now walking into the building than leaving.

"You sure there's not another entrance?" Palmer asked.

"Yep. I walked around the entire building when I got here. It's either the garage or this door, but it doesn't look like many cars are leaving midday."

Over the coming minutes, waves of pedestrians trudged through the cold, up the building steps, and back through its doors. Only two men—one in a suit with no coat, one dressed in a thick parka with a backpack over one shoulder—walked out, a minute apart.

The car's clock said 1:10.

"Maybe she ate lunch in the office."

Amity shrugged. "Who knows? If so, we'll have to go in. But let's give it twenty more—"

Two loud bangs shook Palmer's window, sending them both inches in the air. A large redheaded police officer hunched over, his nose only inches from the snow-caked window. He twirled his index finger.

"What's the matter, Officer?" Palmer said, cracking his window. "I believe the meter—"

"Snow's about to get worse, buddy," he said in a perfect Boston accent. "We're clearin' these streets of all parked cars"—*pahked cahs*—"so we can get the salt down."

Amity grimaced.

"Gotcha," Palmer said. "A friend's about to walk out. We'll only be a couple minutes."

"Ya can be here for as long as you want, but your car's gotta go. Whether you do it or we do it for ya is up to you."

"Okay. We're outta here."

The cop trudged on to the next car as they turned back to the building.

Two men in dark trench coats approached the entrance, the first man pulling the door open as the other walked through. The first man then took a step into the doorway but stopped short. A black-haired woman in a puffy white coat brushed by to his left, moving quickly, coming the other way.

"What are we—"

"Hold on! That's her."

"You sure?" Palmer asked, the woman's face looking blurry to him as she skipped down the steps to the sidewalk.

"Oh, I'm sure. Dead ringer."

Amity reached for the door handle as the woman crossed the street two car lengths in front of the Fiesta.

"I definitely need that eye doctor. You sure you're up to this?"

She opened the door, frigid air shooting through the car.

"Of course I'm sure. Just do what we talked about."

"But what about the car?"

"Leave it."

She shut the door and followed Dr. Vora.

Fifteen seconds later, the car door slammed behind her as Palmer got out of the car.

CHAPTER 106

Cambridge

CLUMPS OF THICK, wet snow plummeted diagonally down as a stiff breeze whipped Amity's face. The bone-chilling air pierced her fleece jacket and her jeans felt as if ice water were streaming down them. Leaning into the wind, she pulled her Buckeyes hat low over her head, tailing Neena Vora from half a block behind.

They covered a block, crossed a street, then another block.

Amity stole a glance behind her. Palmer was following well back, hands jammed in his pockets, looking every bit as frigid as she felt.

Dr. Vora turned left at the next corner, disappearing from view.

Amity broke into a jog, then turned the same corner.

With a large brick building across the street providing shelter, the wind died. But Dr. Vora was gone.

Amity rose onto the balls of her feet to scan the length of the sidewalk. No white coat. No Dr. Vora. She couldn't have covered the block that quickly or crossed the busy street, so Amity slowed down, scanning the storefronts to her left.

A deli came first, large windows providing a clear view inside. With lunch hour over, only two tables were occupied, each by two guys.

She moved to the next storefront, first passing a wide wooden door, then another set of windows with *Annie's* written across it in script.

A coffee shop. Almost every seat full.

Walking slowly, Amity scanned each table. No patron resembled Dr. Vora.

The far window provided a direct line of sight to the shop's back counter, along with the line of people waiting to order along the far wall. She stopped to take a closer look.

Third from the front was a dark-haired woman in a white coat. Same outfit, same woman.

Amity doubled back and entered, pulling her hat down farther as she stepped into line.

The woman in the white coat ordered, paid with cash, then waited at the side counter.

She was much smaller than Amity had pictured. Prettier too. But it was definitely Neena Vora.

"Excuse me," a raspy voice said from behind her. "You ordering?"

Distracted, she'd let a gap open up in the line in front of her.

"Of course," she replied, stepping forward.

Dr. Vora picked up her coffee and walked to one of only two free tables in the place. She sat down facing the back of the coffee shop.

Amity stepped out of the line and headed right for the table. She pulled out the metal chair facing Vora and leaned over.

"Mind if I sit here?" she mumbled, her eyes shielded under the bill of her hat.

"That's fine," Vora said in a tone suggesting the opposite.

Amity sat, then lifted her cap above her forehead.

"Thank you, Doctor."

Vora looked up, then leaned in closer as she recognized Amity, her emerald eyes flaring wide.

"Wait, what are you—"

Amity clenched her jaw, trying to suppress the butterflies fluttering in her stomach.

"I much prefer meeting with you this way over last time. You know, face-to-face and not tied up. Plus, wouldn't you visit your sick mother in person if you could?"

Dr. Vora shook her head. "Ms. Jones, you do not understand the circumstances. You should not be here."

Even with her eyes trained on Vora's, Amity could see Palmer enter the shop, joining the line.

"I'm sorry, Doctor, but I'm here to see my mother. We are blessed that she is in your care. But a good doctor knows that you can't shut out a patient's family. Family is an essential part of her treatment."

A Supreme Court clerk has a front-row seat to the best lawyers in the nation. In action. Not only when they argue before the justices themselves but at the lower-court level. Amity had reviewed hundreds of transcripts in her year of clerking. Depositions and trial testimony where the best lawyers did the most damage. And one thing all the best lawyers did: they knew their witnesses cold *before* the deposition.

So as she'd driven from Ohio, Amity had skimmed over a half dozen of Dr. Vora's medical journal articles she'd printed out at the office. Like her lectures, her writing went beyond genetic research, often addressing medical ethics. The Hippocratic oath. And her dedication to holistic patient care, which included family and caregiver well-being. That philosophy explained why she called every night, keeping Amity comfortable with the treatment. Amity now echoed those principles, quoting Vora's own words as well as she could remember.

Vora nodded her head fervently. "Of course. That is so important. But these are not normal circumstances. Let me cure your mother; then we will release her to you. You have my word it will be done. But that is the *only* way it will be done."

Her reaction caught Amity off guard. Not the words, but the tone and the look. Rapid blinking, thin lips trembling.

Fear.

"Doctor, what's wrong?"

"What would be wrong?" Vora asked too quickly.

Amity's JAG training had never left her, with one key lesson echoing now: the best lawyers were always prying open doors. Each door opened onto a new layer of facts. At every opportunity, open another door. Then walk in. Then open another. Always forward.

Vora's awkward question allowed Amity to open a new door now.

"You tell me."

"There's nothing to tell, Ms. Jones."

But her eyes looked away, making clear that there was.

"I don't believe you. You're an incredible doctor. Your care for my mother has been as sincere as any doctor we've ever had, and you hardly know her. So why are you so fearful? What has Dr. Blackwood done?"

"Dr. Blackwood?"

"Yes. Your boss. The world-class researcher. You're scared of him."

Vora laughed awkwardly, then sipped from her coffee mug, which shook in her trembling hand.

"Why would I be scared of Dr. Blackwood?"

Another door cracked open.

"I can think of any number of reasons. He's breaking the law and you know it. He's manipulating politicians to get what he needs. He's committing violent acts to cover his tracks. And you're caught up in it all."

Avoiding eye contact, Vora said nothing back.

"Can my mother be released soon?"

"She cannot."

"Can you transfer her back to Mansfield, where I can see her? Under the care of Dr. Stumbo?"

"I'm afraid not."

"You can't? Or you won't?"

No answer.

"Can I see her?"

She finally looked directly at Amity.

"You can't."

Amity's temper flared.

"Doctor, you don't know me. And you may have forced me into our horrific arrangement. But I know the law like you know medicine. Keeping my mother in this way is against the law. I'm going straight from here to the authorities if you don't provide me a different answer to my questions."

Vora leaned forward, sweat forming on her chin and forehead.

"Even if doing so risks her life?"

"Explain yourself, Doctor," Amity said, her cheeks blazing.

Vora looked around the coffee shop, then back at Amity.

"You may have discovered who I am—who we are—but nothing's changed. Stay quiet, stay away, and your mother comes home safe and sound."

Amity didn't move.

"I don't believe you."

"Pardon me?"

"I don't believe you. You wouldn't harm her." She recalled the TED Talk she'd watched the day before. The quote Dr. Vora had returned to repeatedly in her articles.

"You took an oath to apply, for the benefit of the sick, all measures that are required."

Vora stared back, taken by surprise.

"Didn't you?" Amity asked.

"I certainly did."

"Letting my mother pass away would go against everything you stand for. Against all you have done and all you have written. You wouldn't allow someone to die whom you knew you could save."

She sagged, her eyes meeting Amity's. Damp. Defeated.

"Ms. Jones, I'm not in charge."

Amity lifted her hat, tightened her ponytail, then pulled the hat back on.

CHAPTER 107

Washington

"SENATOR, THIS ISN'T fun for either of us."

The two rivals sat across from each other in the White House library, a fire crackling to their side. They'd never met face-to-face before. Still, the president was lying, and they both knew it.

Payback was loads of fun.

Senator Byron Blue had attacked her for years—on TV, in the well of the Senate, in committee rooms, and in stump speeches. Often in the most sexist of terms.

"She should know her place," he'd said.

"She's shrill," he'd said on another occasion.

"You'd think she'd be better in the White House," he'd said on yet another.

But now she had him by the balls, and his twisted frown made clear how tight her grip was.

"Madam President, you don't believe—"

She shook her head, frowning like a disappointed teacher. The truth was, when she'd first learned about the old senator's secret, she couldn't have been more pleasantly surprised.

"Byron, let's not drag this out. Our national security people investigated your claim that it was a deepfake attack. They've scoured the tape in every way. And our best people all verified, independently, that it was authentic."

Beads of sweat trickled down the Alabamian's pasty, oversized forehead.

"Here you go," she said, handing him the square paper napkin from under her glass of water.

He dabbed above the eyes.

"So what are you going to do?" he asked.

"It depends, Senator. You've been a thorn in my side for so long, I'm tempted to have our national security advisor hold a press conference announcing their finding."

She leaned back, savoring the moment. His career would be over the moment that press conference ended. He'd spent decades grandstanding on "family values"—the first one to attack others for any transgressions. If declared authentic, the tape of Senator Blue with the young woman would finish him in Alabama and in his party.

"'Depends'?" the senator asked, quoting her back. "Depends on what?"

He'd repeated the key word, but she continued as if she hadn't heard him. "Or we can always announce that we can't rule out that it's a deepfake. Thanks to all your bellyaching, the public already may believe that anyway. But that small lie on our part would probably bail you out."

"*Depends on what*, Madam President?"

She lifted the glass and took a long sip of water, grinning as she put it back down.

"I'm so glad you asked, Byron."

CHAPTER 108

Cambridge

AMITY LIFTED HER hat and fiddled with her hair. At last.

Seeing the signal they'd agreed to, Palmer made a beeline toward the table. The metal chair clanged as he pulled it back and sat down next to Amity, facing Dr. Vora diagonally.

Her jet-black hair and emerald eyes were striking, accentuated by a layer of mist on their surface. But she looked worn. Frazzled. Which was exactly why Amity had beckoned Palmer over—to play the bad-cop role at the pivotal moment.

"Good afternoon, Doctor."

"Who are you?"

"Just a TV reporter looking into why you blew up my friend here."

He passed a card across the table. Vora's pupils darted back and forth, then looked away.

"I simply oversee the research and work to cure people. I don't involve myself in Dr. Blackwood's security matters."

"Well, he sure as hell involved Amity. Look at those scars. And another reporter is still in the hospital, fighting for his life."

Her eyes dilated.

"I would never condone violence—"

"Well, it's been a prominent feature of your enterprise. Just look at what happened to Duke Garber."

Dr. Vora shook her head in protest. He'd struck a nerve.

"Senator Garber? Dr. Blackwood and I did all we could to save Senator Garber's life."

Palmer chortled, waving his hand dismissively. "Save it? You're kidding, right?"

"I don't joke about my patients. We cured him against all odds. One of our best success stories."

"Then why did he take his own life?"

"We were as shocked as anyone. I personally informed the senator six weeks prior to his death that he was fully clean. After having endured so much, he'd finally emerged from the long, dark abyss."

"Well, somehow he mistook it for the edge of a high cliff," he said. "It doesn't add up."

"All I can tell you is that I did all I could to heal Senator Garber—just as I am with Mrs. Jones. And what we did with the senator worked spectacularly."

She spoke earnestly, not budging. Palmer's gut told him she was telling the truth.

"Do you have any reports to back that up, Doctor?"

"Of course I do. But I wouldn't share them with you or anyone."

"Well, they may be the only thing that saves you."

"Saves me from what?"

He cast a wry smile, then lowered his voice.

"Doctor, it's all toppling down."

"What is?"

"Your work. Your world. Duke Garber's death. It's about to crash down on you and especially on Dr. Blackwood."

"How do you know this?"

"I know, and others do too. At the very highest levels."

"So why are you telling me?"

"Because you appear to be the only person involved who has a conscience," Amity said.

"All I've worked to do is save lives. To bring about miracles like Duke Garber and Mary Logan." She looked at Amity. "Maybe soon your mother."

She gained energy as she continued. "We are on the verge of perhaps the biggest medical breakthrough in human history. Why would they shut that down?"

"Oh, they won't shut that part down. But you and Dr. Blackwood may read about it from federal prison cells, if they let you read at all."

"What am I supposed to do?"

"We're happy to do what we can, but we need three things."

She stared back, waiting for the list.

Amity went first.

"Let my mother go. Send her back to Mansfield. As soon as she's up to it."

She nodded.

Palmer followed.

"Next, you'll need to cooperate. When they call, tell them everything. And I'll vouch for you."

"With who?"

"People that matter."

Her face froze as she considered it.

"And the third?"

"I need those Duke Garber documents. Anything verifying what you just told me."

She shook her head.

"I can't do that. That violates the most basic principle of patient privacy."

"You've cut corners throughout—"

"Not against a patient, I haven't."

"Your choice. I can't help you unless you do."

She looked back down at the coffee mug trembling in her hand.

Even without speaking, her body language told the story. She'd turn over whatever documents she had. But rather than relief, Palmer felt a surge of adrenaline rush through him.

Because if she was telling the truth—that Garber had been fully cured—then they were back to square one. Why would anyone end his own life only weeks after learning he'd beaten cancer?

CHAPTER 109

—

Washington

THE BLACK SUV left National Airport—Gigi Fox still refused to call it "Reagan"—and carried her north along the Potomac before crossing the stately Arlington Memorial Bridge. A stiff wind blew straight upriver, kicking up whitecaps and spray amid dark, turbulent water.

Once in the district, rather than looping onto Rock Creek Parkway, the usual route to her Georgetown town house, the SUV circled around the back of the Lincoln Memorial and headed up Constitution Avenue along the mall.

Like everything else, the drive reminded her of her age. Even into her early seventies, when the Senate schedule was more relaxed and she was still in shape, she would jog the very route they were driving. Even on cold, gray days like this. But this morning she'd barely made it through the airport terminal.

A mile up, with the Washington Monument looming over them, the SUV turned left. They drove past the circular park known as the Ellipse, then past the gargantuan side of what she considered the ugliest building in Washington: the Old Executive Office Building. Overdone in every way, the OEOB perfectly symbolized the inflated male ego tarnishing American government for centuries. Unless it was with the vice president, she refused to meet there.

Two blocks later, the SUV entered a cavern of new, sleek buildings representing the modern D.C. of lawyers and lobbyists. They turned onto H Street. Halfway down the next block, without slowing, the SUV turned again, pulling into an alley most cars would drive by without noticing. A second turn led them into an even narrower alley. Twenty feet in, they stopped, an ominous black steel wall blocking their way.

The thick-necked, black-haired driver, who hadn't said a word since picking the senator up at the airport curb, lifted his wrist an inch away from his mouth.

"Ranger. Here."

A loud metallic clang sounded, followed by a faint whir as the left side of the wall pivoted away like an enormous door.

They drove forward, then descended into a dark tunnel below the street.

It wasn't the first time she'd taken this route, but it had been years. Back in the day, it happened once or twice a year. When the country desperately needed the partisans of Capitol Hill to come together on something important: the budget, a foreign policy crisis, a natural disaster. When cross-partisan diplomacy was in the national interest. Those moments always involved an initial secret meeting—one the press wouldn't sniff out—and then she and Shepherd Logan would get it done. And those meetings always started with this drive.

The SUV stopped again. Except for two large diamond-shaped reflectors directly in front them, it was pitch-black.

"Ranger. Here."

Another clang, followed by an explosion of light from the left side of the tunnel in front of them. Another door opened, then the car pulled forward.

This meeting would be different from those of the past. She was arriving alone. And rather than coming to solve a problem, she suspected—from the mysterious call late Saturday requesting this Monday-morning meeting—that she *was* the problem.

Something also told her this meeting would be her last.

They hadn't talked, but she assumed Shep was having a similar rendezvous. And that he would be equally uncomfortable.

They entered a small, well-lit garage and pulled up to a short curb.

The door next to Gigi Fox opened as soon as the car stopped.

A wiry bald man in a dark suit peered down through the open door. He grinned politely as he reached his hand in to help her out.

"Welcome to the White House, Senator."

PART FOUR

CHAPTER 110

Pemaquid Point

IT ONLY TOOK a few steps for Amity to figure it out.

Why he chose this place, of all places.

It triggered all her senses at once. The up-close spectacle of the rocks and lighthouse, framed by the panorama of bright blue sky and deep blue ocean merging at the horizon. The cool, damp air. The repeated crashing of waves amid the airy whistle of a stiff breeze. Even the pungent scent of salt water refreshed her like a palate cleanser before a meal.

She closed her eyes and took it all in, swaying in the wind, almost weightless as the tension she'd brought to the place fell away. Her muscles slackened and her breathing slowed. A few seconds in, she laughed out loud for the first time in months.

No wonder Duke Garber, facing all the pressures he shouldered in Washington, returned here so often.

She couldn't imagine a better escape.

"Amity, over here!" Palmer yelled through the wind.

She reopened her eyes and followed his trail up the rocks.

Reality crashed back in, along with the same jarring question: On his last visit here, what had the senator been escaping _from_?

As of two days ago, they no longer knew.

———

AN HOUR AFTER leaving the coffee shop, Neena Vora had made good on her final promise. She'd handed them a file confirming Duke Garber's clean bill of health. The cancer he had fought for so long—gone. The documents also clarified that his treatment had begun well over a year before. This meant he'd been an early participant in the plot—perhaps the *first* senator on board—raising more questions.

But a weekend of calls and research had turned up nothing new. The senator's former chief of staff called Palmer back but offered nothing useful, claiming Garber's personal life had hardly overlapped with their D.C. work. Calls to his two children went unreturned.

Desperate for answers, they'd woken early this morning and driven from Boston to Maine. But before nosing around New Harbor, the town Duke Garber had called home for most of his eighty years, they stopped by Pemaquid Point so Amity could absorb the full picture of his final minutes.

Maintaining their balance was tricky as they stepped carefully from one rock to the next. Amity slipped a few times, catching herself with her right hand, then slamming her left shin against a sharp edge.

"Getting to the top must've been a real chore for an eighty-year-old with bad legs," Palmer said from a few steps behind.

"Amazed he made it," Amity said above the breeze.

Halfway up, one large rock stuck out from the others, rolling up and over like a frozen wave.

"I remember this spot!" Palmer yelled out. "It's where Duke Garber announced his endorsement of Janet Moore three years ago, essentially ending that election. Feels like only days ago."

As they neared the top, strong gusts of wind blew against Amity's torso, forcing her to lean forward as she walked. The hissing of the ocean air drowned out all other sound.

But that wasn't why most of Amity's body was tingling.

It was the thought of a statesman like Duke Garber jumping off from where she stood.

The jagged rocks, white foam, and crashing waves presented a violent scene below. But the true killer would've been the dark, icy water, shocking his timeworn body the instant he hit the surface.

Whatever had led the senator to leap from here must have been overwhelming.

CHAPTER 111

Cambridge

THE RECEPTION DESK sat empty, forcing Dr. Blackwood to swipe his key card to enter BioRevolution's headquarters.

Odd.

Everyone at the company knew his routine. On Mondays, when he walked over after his morning seminar at the med school, a receptionist always buzzed him in on sight.

But her absence didn't dampen his buoyant mood. They were so close, and the final obstacle was gone. On a phone call the night before, Quinn had assured him that he'd shored up both Senators Logan and Fox. And without giving details, he'd made clear that the CNN reporter was out of the picture.

Once inside the double glass doors, Dr. Blackwood walked past the empty reception desk and down the hallway to Neena Vora's office. He wanted to hear about the latest round of results, the final round before approval.

With his corner office the next one down, he walked past Vora's office multiple times a day. Visible through her office glass windows, she was always hard at work.

But this morning, off-white blinds were pulled down all the way to the floor, blocking any view of his top lieutenant.

Her office door was slightly ajar.

He knocked.

No answer.

"Neena," he said softly.

No answer.

He pushed the door open and stepped into the unlit room.

The instant he flipped the switch on, a knot tightened in his gut.

Something was off.

Not only was his research director not there, but her always orderly office looked different.

Medical books and research binders still packed the bookshelves behind her desk, but there were new, sizable gaps between them. Personal items—photos of her two kids, of her parents, of London, and the covers of journals featuring her work—were gone. And along the walls, only barren hooks remained where other photos and her framed degrees from Oxford and Harvard had hung days ago.

He stepped farther into the office.

Vora's oversized computer monitor remained against the back wall, between the shelves. The port that held her laptop was there too. But the laptop itself was gone.

"Neena!"

He was practically yelling now.

No answer.

He rubbed his forefinger along the front of the desk, turned around, and stepped back into the hallway.

His hands grew clammy as paranoia set in. Why would his top researcher pull out? They were too close to their goal to have things blow up now.

"Neena! Nathan! Is anyone here?"

Only silence answered his question.

He walked to his corner office.

Like Neena's, his door was ajar, which made no sense. He locked it whenever he left.

Through the crack in the open door, he could see that the lights inside were on.

He walked through the doorway. Nothing was missing, but one thing was out of place. His large leather chair, which always faced the mahogany desk, instead was turned toward the large tinted window overlooking Kendall Square below. The chair's high back faced him.

He took another step forward.

The chair squeaked loudly as it swiveled around.

"Hello, Professor."

The bald-headed Quinn looked up with a toothy smirk, his left arm in a cast.

His muscles tensed. For all the work Quinn had done for Blackwood, the professor had never allowed him into the actual headquarters. Yes, Duke had recommended him. But a henchman like Quinn was a brute—beneath the dignity of the weighty work his company was doing.

"What the hell are you doing here?" Blackwell asked. "Where is Neena? Where is everybody?"

Quinn leaned forward and reached into his jacket pocket. He pulled out what looked like a thin leather wallet, then laid it on the desk, allowing gravity to flip it open. On one side was a gold shield. On the other appeared the large letters *FBI* next to a photo of Quinn.

"What the hell is that?"

"Doctor, I'm a special agent with the FBI. You know what you've been up to, and you know I know all of it. It ends today."

"Is this some sort of joke, you Irish bawheid? You've been part of it all."

"I've been *watching* it all," Quinn said, winking. "*You've* been the one doing it all."

Quinn's gaze veered over Blackwood's shoulder, toward the door behind him.

"Boys!" he yelled out.

A door creaked open down the hallway, followed by the thud of footsteps growing louder.

Blackwood wheeled around to see two men in dark suits enter the door.

"Please stand up against the wall, sir," the larger one said firmly.

Blackwood looked back at Quinn, seething.

"You're arresting me?"

"You better believe it."

"This is a setup. You were part of it all."

"Did I tell you I'm from the FBI?" he asked, feigning an introductory bow. "That's what we do."

Suddenly light-headed, all Blackwood could think about was the cause. How close they were.

"But you know the breakthrough we're about to achieve?"

"Oh, it will be achieved. But properly. Not by breaking the law."

"But my work is the only reason we will be there."

"Maybe so. But the law is the law. And you've heard the old saying: 'It's not about who gets the credit.' I recall you telling the senators that a time or two."

With the second man blocking the door, Blackwood had no choice. He stepped toward the wall.

"Please place your hands behind your back," the closer man ordered.

"Okay, okay."

The wall became a blur as Blackwood's breathing exploded in small bursts. Seconds after he held his hands behind him, the cold steel of handcuffs sent a shiver up his forearms to his elbows. As the cuffs clamped shut, he winced in pain, the hard metal squeezing tightly through his flesh and into his bones.

"You don't arrest a scientist on his way to such a historic achievement."

"Try me." Quinn laughed.

CHAPTER 112

New Harbor, Maine

TWENTY MINUTES UP the road from the lighthouse, Amity drove them into the little town overlooking the small working harbor.

Even on this winter morning, trawlers were anchored in the little bay and others were cinched to docks. One boat, loaded up with nets, was steaming out to the ocean.

While yards and sidewalks were buried in snow, the streets were covered in a gray slush, giving the town a dirty feel. This was blue-collar Maine—not the tourism Maine touted in travel guides.

They spent a few minutes exploring the main streets, then drove up to Duke Garber's modest one-story home. A whiff of fish hit Amity as she got out of the car and took in the wintry air.

A For Sale sign stuck out through a foot of snow in the house's small front yard.

They walked around the outside of the house, peering into each window. Enough natural sunlight shone through to make clear that each room was empty.

Nothing around the small house's perimeter told Amity a thing except that Duke Garber had never let the trappings of Washington change him.

CHAPTER 113

Washington

THE PRESIDENT HAD come to love the East Room. It was regal, grand, but still small enough that a modest crowd made it feel packed and energized.

So she chose it for the biggest moment of her first term. The site where she'd make history.

She'd spent weeks handpicking every one of the men and women now standing to her left and right on the elevated platform. Members of her administration in suits, doctors and researchers in white lab coats, families in casual attire. To her right stood the spindly, hunched, and altogether unimpressive FDA director, Don Driscoll. As she'd requested, he wore a white lab coat instead of his usual suit.

The visual was key.

The entire Washington press corps looked up at her from the floor. History in the making, her press team had promised on background. An announcement of worldwide consequence.

As they'd intended, speculation was swirling. A Supreme Court retirement? Action against Saudi Arabia? Some had gotten closer, guessing that another round of a dangerous flu strain was making its way from overseas. Either it was coming back, or she was announcing a new vaccine.

Standing with Driscoll and doctors only heightened the anticipation in the room.

But her audience was far wider than the reporters and cameras before her. The White House had requested that the news conference be aired live to the nation, and the networks had agreed.

She stretched her arms diagonally toward the ground, maximizing her energy level.

A green light on her podium clicked on.

Go time.

"My fellow Americans," the president said somberly, looking straight ahead, pausing to enhance the drama. "I am here with FDA director Driscoll to announce a major development."

She glanced left and right, her lips pursed.

"A development of both global and historic significance."

Another pause.

"Under his able leadership, and my direction . . ."

She finally allowed her somber face to lift into a full, broad smile.

". . . we are today announcing perhaps the most significant medical breakthrough in a century. I daresay, one of the most significant in human history . . ."

Not a soul moved in front of her. This was bigger than they expected. Much bigger.

"It goes back to a central promise I made when I ran for office. And now, with good fortune and hard work and good ol' American ingenuity, I can announce that, at long last, we have discovered . . ."

She slowed to emphasize each word that followed.

". . . a cure for cancer."

The room gasped, then fell silent in collective shock. Within seconds a spontaneous round of cheers and applause erupted—not just among the staff and families to her left and right but among the press corps in front of her.

She basked in the celebration for a good ten seconds, beaming her well-practiced smile out from the podium.

But she knew she had to amp up the drama even more. Images mattered more than words in today's politics. With only one chance at this history-making moment, she needed a photo sitting atop every newspaper in the country the next morning. The *Orlando Sentinel*. The *Columbus Dispatch*. The Cleveland *Plain Dealer*. The *Detroit Free Press*. And all the smaller papers across the swing states essential for reelection.

The president reached out for Driscoll's hand and lifted it high in the air. The pose had its intended effect as the flashes and clicks of cameras exploded around them. She turned slightly right and left, pulling Driscoll with her, giving every camera a good angle for the iconic shot. The politician and the scientist, celebrating the historic breakthrough.

After another ten seconds, she lowered her hand and stepped back to the podium.

"Dr. Driscoll will provide a more detailed briefing later, but the approach has been tested thoroughly and approved to move forward under the oversight of the FDA and our National Institutes of Health. A panel of doctors and bioethicists, including some of the experts around me, will oversee its rollout across the country. But we've seen enough data to know that the results are nothing short of miraculous."

The feeling in the room was downright giddy—a collective, palpable release of pure joy. The sea of smiles and glimmering eyes and tears reminded her of the crowd in Denver the night she won the election. The difference was this was a room of hardened reporters, not supporters. Yet even they were moved to tears.

She knew why.

Cancer impacted every person in America. Every last American had a family member, a friend, a colleague, in the midst of the fight. Everyone had a memory of at least one life that had ended too soon—of a friend or loved one poisoned down to almost nothing through chemotherapy and radiation. At any moment, millions were fighting the disease themselves, or recovering and worried, always, about a relapse. There was no room in America, including this one, where her news would not hit home personally.

A cure for cancer was the moon shot of the twenty-first century, but with a more personal impact on each American than even Neil Armstrong's short walk.

And she had scored a perfect landing.

So perfect, she couldn't imagine any top-tier candidates challenging her reelection.

CHAPTER 114

New Harbor

AMITY AND PALMER watched the president's press conference on the small television of New Harbor's lone lobster shack. The few customers and staff gathered around the TV set spontaneously applauded the news.

"She's good," Amity said. "She just turned others' scandal into one hell of a political win."

"Masterful," agreed Palmer, who had donned a baseball cap to keep from being recognized. "That staged photo op will make the front page of every paper in America."

As promised, the White House had called the evening before with a heads-up about the announcement, giving Palmer permission to hint at the essentials thirty minutes ahead of everyone else. They even offered him the first question of the press conference. But he declined, instead locking in a time the next day for the president's promised interview. Beating an official announcement by a couple minutes didn't feel as important as it had a few weeks ago. Plus, his gut told him the real story—the final piece of it—was there in Maine, not Washington.

As the announcement wrapped up, Amity downed an early afternoon white wine, her first in weeks. Palmer drank a beer. But their attempt to relax ended the moment two actual lobsters were dropped on the wooden table. Having never eaten lobster before, Amity sliced two fingers on her right hand. Palmer, more skilled but out of practice since his summer camp days, slammed a finger on his left with the rough side of a wooden hammer. Within minutes, both had butchered the shiny orange beasts into inedible messes of shattered shells and meat.

On seeing them struggle, the stocky redheaded woman who'd set their plates down walked back over and barked orders in a deep, scratchy Maine accent.

"Split it right there . . . No, there! . . . Harder. Really hammer it."

Amity followed along as the woman pointed to different parts of the recently boiled creature.

"Sorry, Helen," she said, reading her name badge. "We Midwesterners aren't well trained in carving lobster."

"We call it shelling around here, but don't worry—you're doin' fine."

She pointed to the large claw Amity had successfully ripped off, now occupying her plate's right side.

"Reach right in there and you'll find yourself the world's finest lobster meat."

She pulled out a long piece of white meat, dipped it in butter, and took a bite.

"Wow. You're not kidding."

It really was the best thing Amity had tasted in a while, but neither the lobster nor the TV set were the reason they were there.

Internet searches had gotten them nowhere all weekend. So they'd walked into this place, figuring that small towns in Maine functioned like they did in Ohio—where the local diner served as the hub of community gossip. A handful of regulars, and especially servers, were the eyes and ears of towns like this, especially when it came to well-known members of the community.

Helen tutored them on lobster shelling for a few more minutes before opening the door.

"What brings you to New Harbor all the way from the Midwest? This isn't exactly tourist season." She gestured at the empty dining room.

Amity shrugged. "Work. We're reporters from Ohio. We were big fans of the senator from here: Duke Garber. Now that things are settled down, we wanted to write a profile about him . . ."

She left it hanging. Far better for Helen to volunteer something than for them to pump her for information, raising suspicion.

"Senator Duke?" Helen asked, looking up wistfully.

Palmer chimed in. "Yep. Sounds like everyone called him that, huh?"

"Oh, yeah."

Amity cracked open the other lobster claw and pulled out a huge piece of pink-and-white meat.

"You're becoming a real pro," she said as Amity nibbled for a few seconds, then swallowed. "What are you writing about him exactly?"

Amity took a sip of water, remaining nonchalant.

"We're from a small town. Looks a lot like this without the harbor. So we love that the senator never left the small town *he* grew up in. Our goal is to write a profile about the impact such an internationally important leader had on a town like New Harbor. But we've spent the morning here looking around and honestly haven't found much."

"That doesn't surprise me. Senator Duke kinda kept to himself. In his later years, only a few of us interacted with him much."

Amity raised her eyebrows. "Did you get to meet him? Talk to him?"

Helen's eyes gleamed. "We're the best lobster place in town. What do you think?"

"He came here?" Palmer asked, sounding impressed. "How often?"

"When he was here for the weekend, he would usually come in one night out of two." She laughed again. "Now, I'm not saying we don't have great lobster, but it's not like there's much else to do around here."

"Did he come here with others?" Amity asked.

"He and Mrs. Garber were inseparable when she was alive. So they'd come here as their 'date night,'" she said, making air quotes with her fingers. "It was so sweet to watch them." Then she frowned. "After she passed, he'd come by himself, always with a handful of books or papers. He'd sit over in that corner for hours, reading or writing. That man was always writing."

She pointed to a booth at the back of the room.

"And you talked to him while he was here?" Amity asked.

"Of course. He was such a gentleman. It was small talk, though. I figured he didn't want to be bothered by someone like me, being as important as he was. But he'd often ask me about my view on things. Others too. And he'd actually listen, sometimes writing what we said down."

"Anyone else around here know him?"

"Not really. His world, and almost everyone he knew, passed by long ago. He loved this town till the end, but it was a different place than when he grew up. Same harbor. Same lighthouse. Mostly the same buildings. Heck, he lived in that house for almost sixty years. But all the people were different. Those he knew so well were gone. And that hit him especially hard after his wife died. He still loved the place, but my sense was that he was living in his memories."

She went quiet. Amity, a big chunk of lobster in her mouth, said nothing.

Helen leaned against the table.

"You know, on your story . . ."

She paused for few seconds, building up the suspense.

". . . most wouldn't have known it, but Senator Duke kept things going around here."

"What do you mean?" Palmer asked.

"An old town like this? Going back to your original question, having a U.S. senator from here really helped us. And sometimes saved the day."

"How so?"

"Look around. It's not like we have a lot going on outside of summer. Whenever we needed help, Senator Duke pushed as hard as he could. He got money to spruce up our little harbor down there. That highway you drove in on? They should've named it after him, because he's the only reason it got built. And now we have internet service because of Duke Garber. Lots of Maine towns would love to have what we got."

"Good for him. Sort of like your patron saint."

"I guess so." She was on a roll now. "And the lighthouse, especially— maybe the most important thing he kept alive. It's why tourists come to the region in the first place. Then they stop through town on the way back and spend money."

"That important, huh?"

"Oh, yeah. That old lighthouse is our lifeline. And whenever they were about to close it down, Senator Duke would throw some money to the Coast Guard, and the lighthouse and its little museum would be fine. To tell you the truth, a few of us local businesses have been talking about how much his death might cost our area. That's a bad way to think, I know, but still. As you put it, we've lost our patron saint."

Amity nodded, focusing on one word Helen had said.

"Museum?" She'd seen the lighthouse, but that was it. "What museum?"

They talked for another fifteen minutes, Palmer paid the bill, and they hurried out.

CHAPTER 115

—

Pemaquid Point

THE LITTLE CARDBOARD sign flapped in the breeze, dangling by a string in front of the red wooden door. Its handwritten ink indicated the museum was open from 10:00 to 3:00 on Mondays, Wednesdays, and Fridays.

It was already 3:10.

But with a light still on inside, and an old pickup parked in a small driveway below, Amity ignored the sign and knocked on the door. Palmer waited in the car.

No one answered.

She knocked a second time, then twisted the knob.

The door opened.

Inside, the distinct smell of cedar wafted from the long beams of rustic wood running along the floor and walls. Like the worn floor, everything in the place looked a half century old.

Almost every square inch of the rectangular room's white walls was occupied. Navigational maps, old tide charts, and black-and-white photos of bygone boats, huge fish, lobster nets, and rugged, bearded men standing among them. A stuffed blue marlin hung above the entrance to a second room, while a small shark hung over the front door. Three smaller fish took up other spots on the walls, and nets and baskets hung from the ceiling. A large black anchor dominated one corner.

The floor creaked as Amity stepped into the room's center, where stand-alone folding panels displayed additional photos and fishing artifacts: rods, hooks, and old lures, along with ropes twisted in a variety of knots her dad had once taught her.

Two thuds and a creak from beyond the room broke the silence, followed by a high-pitched, groggy voice: "Hey, lady, we're closed."

An old man in dark blue corduroy pants and a thick flannel shirt stepped through an open doorway to another room. At least in his seventies, he had a straggly white beard to go with a buzz cut of thick white hair. A sharp chin jutted out from his long, thin face, and a bony Adam's apple protruded from his thin, pale neck.

Narrow, dazed eyes gave away that he'd been napping.

"The door was open and the lights were on, so I came in," Amity said, lightening things up with a laugh.

"This is Maine. We don't lock our doors. But we're closed. Winter hours."

He said it firmly, leaving no room for negotiation.

"Jimmy's your name?" Amity asked, eyeing the plastic name tag on his shirt, although Helen had already told her.

"That's me."

"I'm Amity."

She reached out to shake his hand, trying to win him over and buy more time.

His thin hand gripped hers weakly but he didn't smile back. Apparently enforcing winter hours was a serious matter.

Then she saw it.

Her life preserver. On the wall next to the doorway he'd walked through.

A framed photo of Duke Garber, looking much younger than she'd ever seen him. He stood next to Jimmy, also looking younger, with a thicker neck, a full mane of wavy blond hair, and a lot more muscle on his bones.

"Hey, that's you and the senator."

He laughed. "You bet it is! Two young stallions."

"Were you guys friends?"

Helen had said they'd grown up together.

"Duke and I—we went back a long way. Few of us old-timers left, y'know. What's it to ya?"

"I'm looking into Duke's hard work to keep this museum and lighthouse open. I'm a writer, and wanted to do a story on it as part of a tourism feature back in Ohio. For our summer tourism special."

He laughed out loud.

"On our museum here? We'll take it."

"That, and the fact that Duke worked so hard to keep it going."

"Well, he sure did that, and then some. He kept this place alive. And kept me in this job after I got too old to pull lobster nets out of the ocean."

"How did he help exactly?"

"As you could guess from looking around, we don't make any damn money. So first he got us on the quarter—"

"'On the quarter'? What do you mean?"

"Y'know that lots of quarters have state symbols on them, right?"

"Of course." Ohio's quarter featured an astronaut and the Wright Brothers.

"Well, Maine's quarter shows a lighthouse—and, thanks to Duke, it's *this* lighthouse." He gestured at one wall, where a framed wooden display featured a bunch of quarters. "Those are some of the first ones they made."

Amity nodded, impressed by the senator's handiwork.

"Not bad."

"Well, once he did that, it made it easier for him to score us Uncle Sam's funds as part of the lighthouse operations. Y'know, you can't exactly let your state's symbol get shut down."

Amity smiled. "No, you can't."

"So here we are, still standing!"

"Good for him . . . and you."

Jimmy looked at his watch, sighing heavily. As if he needed to go but had more to say.

"And we're hoping that Duke still keeps that money flowing."

Amity cocked her head at the odd comment.

"How's that? People in town are worried because he won't be able to help anymore?"

He lifted onto the balls of his feet, a broad smile revealing at least two missing teeth.

"Well, he found a way to help anyway. Maybe better than the quarter. We are going to be the official home of Senator Duke Garber's personal papers."

"Personal papers?" Amity asked, suppressing a grin as her pulse sped up.

"Yeah. For a small Maine town, not too shabby. Duke was famous for keeping notes about everything. The big shots in D.C. wouldn't know it, but he kept a diary since he was in college."

"And you have his papers now?"

"Sure do. A couple nights before that last walk of his, he brought a few boxes by and said he wanted them to be kept here. That he wanted *his* little museum to house his personal papers. That it would add to the history of the place and might keep the dollars coming." He frowned. "When he jumped, the conversation made a lot more sense to us."

"So sad," Amity said, her tone masking her growing excitement. "So they're here now?"

"In boxes in that back room." He pointed through the doorway, then glanced at his watch one more time. "The missus and I've been planning on going through them at some point."

Amity clapped him on his bony shoulder, grinning.

"I could have those papers be a big part of my story about this place—would spread like wildfire."

"Fantastic," he said. "But yer problem is, I've got a doctor's appointment. You'll have to come back another time to dig in."

Amity grimaced.

"My colleague and I have to leave tonight, Jimmy. Is there any way we can stay for a few minutes and let ourselves out?"

He eyed Amity for a good five seconds, his right eye squinting, sizing her up. Then he flashed his gap-tooth smile.

"I'll tell ya what. The missus and I stay just over there." He pointed down the back side of the hill, toward a tiny cottage Amity hadn't noticed before. "She's making dinner at the moment. She'll check in on you and lock up after you skedaddle."

"Sounds like a plan," Amity said.

As Jimmy drove away, Palmer joined her in the back room. Three hours later, after several spirited visits from Jimmy's wife, they finished up. Jimmy returned from the doctor in time to say goodbye, locking up behind them.

They raced back to Boston.

CHAPTER 116

Cambridge

OFFICER MAGGIE O'CONNOR tugged her coat sleeve up her wrist, taking another look at her watch.

Good. Only twenty minutes left of her Monday-night second shift.

A wave of recent break-ins and muggings not far from campus had all of Harvard buzzing, and as a result, Cambridge's mayor fuming. He'd demanded that the chief of police triple the number of visible walking patrols. In law enforcement circles, whether the patrols reduced crime or not was a hotly debated topic. But it made citizens—and Harvard—feel safer, and that served the mayor's purposes.

Either way, the tactical shift made Maggie O'Connor's job a lot tougher, especially amid the monthlong deep freeze Boston was enduring. After seven hours of trudging through ice and snow, she was ready to go home.

Her radio crackled.

"We've gotten a couple calls for a passed-out vagrant on the sidewalk at Main and Ridge. Possible overdose. Over."

She was only a few blocks away from a corner she knew too well.

"I'm right down the street. I'll check it out."

She cursed under her breath. Whatever the call was about, dealing with it and the paperwork that would follow would take her way beyond the end of her shift. Which also meant she'd be late for childcare pickup, risking her third late-pickup fee in a week.

She jogged to the location where the vagrant was reported to be, snow and ice crunching under her boots.

The intersection was one of the worst trouble spots left in Cambridge, where ever-expanding gentrification butted up against the edge of a tough neighborhood and its open-air drug markets—a combination that sparked regular overdoses and occasional violence. Most students knew to stay away. Those who didn't were there for one reason.

From a few yards away, she spotted the subject, lying facedown in a snowbank along the sidewalk. She breathed a sigh of relief: a shock of white hair indicated he wasn't a student.

The old man was lying right outside a dingy Irish pub. Harvard and the city had tried to shut the place down for years. Quiet in the afternoons, by evening the place would brew with trouble, which often spilled outside and generated regular police visits. Someone tumbling out of the place wasted, then passing out or overdosing, was common.

She approached the thin, lanky body and nudged it with her right boot. The man didn't move.

She leaned closer in. Still no movement.

Worse, no sign of breathing.

The department provided every officer with a small bottle of Narcan, the miracle overdose prevention drug. Having saved dozens of lives with it, she whipped the bottle out of her jacket pocket.

Narcan was administered as a nasal spray, so she rolled the man onto his back. He lay limp on the snowbank, his left arm hanging down as if broken.

"Fuck!" she yelled, leaping up.

A gaping bullet wound oozed blood and other matter where the man's right eye should have been. Blood also drenched the snow beneath his head, and more blood and white ice crystals were caked on his face and trim white beard.

She tossed the Narcan bottle to the ground and reached for her radio.

"This is O'Connor."

"Whattaya got?"

"Get Homicide here right away! This isn't a strung-out vagrant. It's a fatal shooting."

As she spoke into the mic, she spotted a dark object on the part of the snowbank where the body had originally lain. She unhooked a small flashlight from her belt, leaned over, and pointed the beam downward.

It was a black leather wallet. Nicer leather than she would've expected for patrons of this dive. There were empty spaces in front, on the left, where the credit cards would have been, and clearly all the cash had been taken.

"Looks like a mugging gone wrong," Officer O'Connor said into the mic.

On its right side, a photo stared out from some type of identification card. Same white hair and beard on a long, striking face.

But it wasn't a driver's license.

She looked closer. Her heart began racing.

The red *H* in the top right corner of the ID gave it away. Her night had just gotten far worse.

"Looks like he worked at Harvard. A professor at the med school."

The radio crackled back.

"Jesus. Sending a team right away."

Another mugging, and this one had turned deadly. Walking patrols weren't going away anytime soon.

CHAPTER 117

—

Washington

THE GROUND RULES were clear. And absurdly tight.

Fifteen minutes. Four questions.

Palmer had stewed all morning. Stick to the rules, or go rogue once the camera was rolling? Even as he entered the Treaty Room for the second time in two weeks, he hadn't made up his mind.

Once he and his cameraman had set up, the president whisked in from the side and sat down.

"How you holding up, Palmer?" she asked before the camera started rolling, smiling in her blue pantsuit.

The question left him seething. Ellrod and she had put him through hell—all to serve a purpose that, he knew now, had nothing to do with Saudi Arabia. Or national security.

"It's been a rough ride."

She winced empathetically. "But CNN's brought you back in, right? That's a start."

"Sure. But my integrity will always be questioned. You never get that back."

"Give it time," she said. "People bounce back—I've seen it many times. And my guess is this will help."

He looked down at his sheet of paper to avoid saying something he'd regret. They really considered him their errand boy—but talked as if they were doing *him* a favor by granting this self-serving interview.

"Anyway, I know our time is limited. Let's get started."

He asked the three questions they'd approved. Softballs all. The first was about her original pledge to find a cure for cancer. The second was about the crucial meeting when FDA director Driscoll informed her that they were on the verge of a breakthrough. And the third was how she felt knowing that millions of lives were about to be changed by that breakthrough.

Her answers were predictable. And, as always, perfect. The press conference all over again, close-up and personal.

Even though Palmer knew how she'd answer the final question, it was the one he most anticipated.

"Madam President, before we go, tell us more about Duke Garber. What did he mean to you? How has his loss impacted you—and this country?"

She closed her eyes, then looked down. Her lip quivered as she lifted the sleeve of her jacket up to her right eye. Almost an identical performance to the one he'd witnessed a few weeks back.

"God bless that man," she said quietly as she looked back up, eyes misty. "I've known no finer public servant. I daresay *the country* has known no finer servant. We miss him dearly."

This answer sealed it. No need to go rogue.

The president's answers—capped off with this moving display of emotion—were absolutely perfect.

CHAPTER 118

Columbus

"Amity? It's so nice to see you."

She could barely hear Dexter's voice as he whispered from the hospital bed, his bandaged head raised slightly by a small pillow.

It had been easier to look at him when he was in a coma. Eyes closed, he'd at least appeared at peace. Now he was lethargic due to heavy painkillers, yet still in obvious pain. His eyes were glazed over and his breathing heavy. Dark splotches on his face, neck, and arms indicated where his burns remained the most intense. In all, he looked and felt a decade older than a week ago.

"Not as nice as seeing you awake," Amity said.

He frowned, seeing right through her. "Not a pretty sight, I'm sure."

"Dexter, you're a tough guy. They're saying you're gonna recover fully."

His lips turned up slightly.

"I imagine you took that road trip for a good reason."

Amity nodded. He wanted to change the subject too.

"You better believe it. Do you remember all that we were up to before you got hurt?"

He nodded. "Of course I do. I may not recall the explosion, but everything that came before is etched into my memory. Can't wait to know what else you've found."

"I'm going to do more than tell you. I'm gonna read it to you, if that's okay."

"Read it?"

"Yeah. CNN is covering the story—and running it big online."

"Even better."

"But I'm reading it for your approval."

"My approval?"

"Yep. CNN is going to credit you for helping dig up the truth."

Amity pulled a chair up next to Dexter's bed, took out a draft copy Palmer had sent her, and began reading.

Still in a stupor from medications, Dexter kept calm at first. But as he absorbed the full, warped story, he couldn't contain his shock.

"Did he really write that?" Dexter asked as Amity read one excerpt of Duke's diary.

"He sure did, only a day after it happened."

"You think she told him that?" he asked after another damning passage.

"I see no reason to doubt him."

For twenty more minutes Amity read a paragraph or two, then Dexter would react.

"Stunning," he said when they finished, shaking his head as he looked up. "Just stunning. I'm so glad you're going for it, but they're going to come at you hard. You guys have backing for all of it?"

Amity held up a thick manila folder in her right hand, papers sticking out of its corners. Most of the pages were printouts of the photos she'd taken of Duke Garber's papers back in the lighthouse museum on Pemaquid Point. Fifty or so pages of the senator's notes and musings.

"Every word," she said. "Every. Word."

CHAPTER 119

Washington

A DARK SUV dropped National Security Advisor Sandra Ellrod off on Seventeenth Street, blocks from the White House and down the hill from the Washington Monument.

Palmer waited at the top, where they'd agreed to meet. From just within the wide circle of American flags—all limp on the windless, drizzly day—he watched as one of the president's most important advisors ambled up the hill like a tourist, shielded underneath a green poncho.

A half dozen men and women were walking in the vicinity. For his own security, Palmer had asked CNN to keep an eye on the meeting. And no doubt Ellrod had Secret Service watching as well. It was impossible to tell who was who. Still, being out in the open like this felt like the safest way to meet. What he and Amity had discovered in Maine underscored how dangerous this all was.

"Palmer, congrats on the big interview."

He couldn't even fake a smile. They were still playing him. And still thought he was going along.

She walked to his right as he took a step toward the World War II Memorial.

"Thank you."

"Palmer, we noticed the interview hasn't run yet. Are your bosses okay with it?"

He couldn't help but grin. The White House had of course assumed it'd be a stand-alone regurgitation of her every word.

"Oh, they're pleased, all right. But we decided to make a package out of it, and they wanted me to ask her a few more questions."

The truth was, while pleased, his bosses were also nervous as hell.

The morning after he'd returned from Maine, Palmer went back to the station and marched straight into the news director's office. He had the biggest scoop in his career, maybe in CNN's history, and all of it backed up with written documentation. He and Amity worked on it for the next three days, which included the interview with the president, along with a quick return trip to Pemaquid Point to get footage from the lighthouse. And the museum, where Jimmy stole the show.

After it was all put together, he'd interspersed clips from the president's interview at key moments of the broader story. The juxtaposition was so damaging, his bosses insisted that he give the White House the opportunity to respond. Hence this meeting.

Ellrod's pace slowed as she looked over at him. Confused.

"A package? What about?"

His heart pounded as he prepared to break the glass.

"The truth."

"The truth?" She laughed uncomfortably. "The president explained that quite clearly the other day. We should all be celebrating this historic moment for our country."

As much as she'd burned him, Palmer held out hope that Ellrod didn't know the truth. That she wouldn't have gone along with such a craven plan. Her reactions weren't clearing that up either way.

"Sandra, that's *not* the truth. And if she won't talk to me again, you need to pass along a message."

The splashing of the memorial's fountains grew louder with each step they took along the path down.

"I don't like your tone, Palmer."

Usually, this is when he backed off. After all, he'd built his career on being an "access" reporter—never pissing off his best sources. Sources like
Ellrod. Or the president.

Not this time. He'd stewed about it all week, embarrassed. If Amity
Jones had risked her life to get to the bottom of this story—and if she'd di-
verted from her sky-high professional trajectory to help her ailing mother—
he could burn through a source or two to get the ugly truth out.

They reached the memorial, then followed a granite walkway to within
feet of the oval pool at its center. Palmer turned to his left and walked
toward one end of the oval, passing the first of many pillars, each bearing
the name of a state.

"You need to tell the president that I know the truth on how the cancer
research came about. How it was funded. And the role she played . . . from
the beginning."

His blood boiled whenever he recalled the White House meeting after
Florida. When the president had stumbled over the name Blackwood. When
she'd asked him why Garber had ended his life. As if she knew nothing.

"What are you talking about? This was a promise she made to the voters,
and she's happy to have kept it."

Maybe Ellrod didn't know.

"Just give her my message," Palmer said, finally stopping. "Our package
will detail all of it. If she wants to comment now, we'll give her a chance. Of
course, it's her choice."

Her face was a bright pink. She was angry. Worried and angry.

"I'll pass it all along. Now, are we done?"

Palmer knew she meant permanently.

He looked up at the pillar towering over them. Ellrod followed his gaze,
confused. She had no idea why he'd walked her to this pillar in particular.
The one honoring veterans from Maine.

But she'd figure it out soon enough.

"Yes. We're done."

CHAPTER 120

Washington

PALMER SAT IN his small kitchen in Adams Morgan the morning after the story first aired.

He'd just finished his weekend-morning routine—workout, coffee, Cheerios. But his phone was blowing up as if it were a weekday.

Two calls rang through from the White House, just as they had the night before. Ellrod for sure. He usually picked those up right away, but he ignored them both. They'd had their chance but never called.

There was no point in answering now.

There was nothing to say.

———

THE ON-AIR VERSION of the story was devastating. And with links to all the diary excerpts, the online version delivered a second coup de grâce.

He looked it over once again at the top of CNN's website.

President Spearheaded Illegal Cancer Testing Scam

Moore Stopped Maine Senator from Revealing Plot

Palmer had insisted that one photo run under the headline: the eye-catching picture from four years back, when Senator Garber had endorsed Moore on that iconic Pemaquid Point rock, the lighthouse looming behind them. It was perfect—not only capturing the spot that locked in her presidency but possibly the one that would end it. One photo that summed up the disloyalty of it all. The betrayal.

Completely untouched, the boxes in the back room of the little museum had been a disorganized mess. Amity and Palmer guessed that Jimmy and his "missus" were nowhere near sorting through them. After arranging the wide variety of worn notebooks and beat-up binders into some semblance of a logical order, they began leafing through pages from a few years back.

Within minutes the president's first lie had emerged.

In their meeting after Florida, she'd told Palmer that Senator Duke had vaguely mentioned a plot he was uneasy with. But the senator's notes told a far different story. Long before that—eighteen months—he'd confided in the president about his own miraculous recovery from cancer thanks to his lifelong friend, Harvard's Dr. Paden Blackwood. The day after the meeting, he wrote what happened in his elegant longhand:

> *When I told the President the news about my recovery—and that Paden's gene treatment had saved me from my death sentence—she was fascinated. She immediately saw the potential to scale up the treatment for national use. We both grew incredibly excited about the idea. In my waning years, taking on this cause felt like the most important thing I could do. She heartily agreed, said I should take the lead, and we agreed to talk further.*

But that was only her first lie. On page after page, they continued.

The president and senator met again a week later. She encouraged Garber to move forward but was worried about politicizing the FDA. The request needed to come *from* the FDA *to* her, she insisted, and not vice versa. Especially given that Blackwood's technique was not yet approved, she couldn't be involved in the front end. And that meant sufficient testing had to take place to prove it out.

But she'd done some homework in the meantime.

The White House had looked into it. Because I sat on the appropriations subcommittee that oversaw the FDA, she recommended I earmark dollars to Harvard for Paden to advance his research to a point where it could be approved.

Two months later, another update:

It took some convincing of my colleagues, but we are moving forward on this historic endeavor. A majority of the subcommittee—old-timers like Logan, Fox, Ireland, and Blue—are on board with supporting Paden's research. We all see this as a cause bigger than ourselves. At long last, a noble bipartisan mission.

Nowhere yet did Duke Garber mention that Fox and Logan were securing special treatment for their loved ones. Either they'd all sworn one another to secrecy, or it happened without Garber knowing. Or it happened later.

Either way, as months passed, Duke Garber began to fret about the course the president had set him on. And amid many other issues—including his concern over Saudi Arabia's human rights violations—he expressed those doubts in his diary:

I've spent my entire career being forthright with my constituents and with the American people. So have my colleagues in this venture. This feels so at odds with that—the secrecy, the hidden funds, special access, the unanticipated consequences. Our mission is a noble one, but I'm not sure if the ends justify the means.

"Special access." This was the first time Senator Duke used the term. And he had to be referring to his colleagues curing loved ones with the treatment.

His doubts only grew. Then, as the president had told Palmer after Flor-ida, a meeting did take place where Duke first expressed them directly. But that meeting was more than a year ago, and she'd left a key part out:

> *Another meeting at the White House today about Saudi Arabia.*
> *After the others left the room, I had a private moment with the*
> *President. Told her that our approach on Paden's work was giving me*
> *great pause and it was time that America knew. She asked me to hold*
> *off. That it had to come from the FDA and that the FDA wasn't close*
> *to ready. That that was the only appropriate approach. Out of respect*
> *for her, I agreed to hold off.*

Not long after, he described an equally impactful decision—to seek some "special access" of his own:

> *I've referred Jimmy to Paden for treatment. The least I could do for a*
> *fellow old-timer who's been through so much. Seems to be off to a*
> *good start.*

Garber wrote about Jimmy the museum keeper quite often: he was his main connection back to the old days that he missed so much. Within months, Garber would refer two other townsfolk to Dr. Blackwood for treatment: an old boat captain and the woman who'd managed the town's general store for fifty years.

> *All three are doing better. Amazing! Paden really does have this thing*
> *licked.*

But despite these successes, his concern escalated, leading to two more meetings with the president. She talked him off the ledge each time.

> *"We're almost there," she told me. "It must come from the FDA."*

But Garber finally made up his mind. In his diary, the senator described a meeting months back where he'd told the president he planned to go public:

I've had enough. My conscience eats at me every night. The President was insistent that we keep going, but I told her I could no longer do so. That I hadn't spent fifty years in Washington building a legacy of integrity only to destroy it all at the end, even for a righteous cause. I told her I'd made my decision—I would raise this at an upcoming Intel meeting and call for a joint task force to examine the promise and risks of Dr. Blackwood's work. The President was not happy but she said she understood. And she appreciated me giving her time to prepare.

According to his diary, he'd told no one else.

But days later, his world came crashing down:

Paden flew to Washington today to meet me. Terrible news! My latest labs showed a dramatic relapse. There's a glitch in the treatment—always a clear risk of something this experimental. The cancer-fighting gene has itself become too aggressive. He believes he's caught it in time to still cure Jimmy and the others undergoing treatment, but for me it's spread too far. I only have weeks left.

Palmer felt sick the first time he read this entry in the museum, and worse every time after. Duke Garber's lifelong friend had told him he was on death's door—even though Dr. Vora's paperwork made clear he was perfectly healthy. But with others now getting treatment, Blackwood was insisting he needed more time to solve the problem. The implication for Garber was obvious:

I can't expose this. Paden has important work to do, and it would mean that the others would suffer my same fate.

In the days that followed, Garber filled pages with long, fulsome notes, capturing memories, philosophies, regrets. He shared quotes that meant the most to him. But even when facing certain death, he believed he was making a difference:

> *Paden assures me that, in time, my case will allow him to save others, far beyond his current subjects. It has given his treatment more precision going forward.*

His final entry came two days before his walk up the rocks of Pemaquid Point. And Palmer read it on the air to close out his story the evening before:

> *Too many are relying on Paden to stay alive. For them alone, his work must continue.*
>   *I have made my decision, and I am comfortable with it.*
>   *I have lived a life as full as anyone could imagine.*
>   *I have no regrets.*

Unlike any other entry, the senator signed his full signature after that final line.

———

THE WHITE HOUSE called a third time. Palmer still let it ring through.

Early on, he'd wondered why the president had let him walk out of the White House scot-free after Florida, knowing what he knew. At first he assumed they were gun-shy about getting rid of a reporter, especially after the explosion in Ohio.

But that wasn't it at all. It was worse. The interview had made that clear.

He'd become their useful idiot, an unwitting ally assisting the president in solving her problem. The one guy who knew the truth, helping the White House apply the best spin possible throughout. The president's offer of a heads-up, followed by the interview after, were just a continuation of the pattern, scratching his back again so he'd run a story in their favor. And, of course, that would secure continued access going forward.

And why not think he'd go for it? He always had.

He'd obediently chased Ellrod's every lead, amplifying the Saudi narrative and throwing the entire country off what had really killed Duke Garber. That was his kind of journalism. Lift a leak to the highest level and don't bite the hand that feeds you. Worked every time—for him and for the source.

So of course he'd do it again this time. They'd made a decent bet.

But in this case an American hero had walked off a cliff, wrongly believing he was dying for a noble cause. Pierce must have been the go-between—he clearly wasn't FBI but an elite Secret Service agent whom the president had enlisted to do her bidding throughout. Through him, the president got word to Blackwood that his old friend was about to go public and scuttle the entire plan. And Blackwood took care of it.

That betrayal, and what they put Amity Jones through, were too much.

And while the president had clearly used whatever leverage she had to coax the other senators into silence, Garber's notes were unimpeachable evidence proving it all. Fittingly, the guy who'd started it had ended it.

Palmer lifted his final spoon of Cheerios, chuckling.

The irony was that their cold-eyed assessment of his weakness sealed their downfall. Viewing him as a pawn, they didn't see it coming. The exclusive interview they had granted to secure good coverage—to keep him coming back for more—had let him lay the trap.

And now it had all come full circle.

He'd almost been destroyed by a video he had no idea had been recorded. A deepfake.

But he'd destroyed the president with a video she was fully aware of.

Her deepfakes were the old-fashioned kind. Blatant, shameful lies that were now airing on CNN every hour, rebutted instantly by Duke Garber's fastidious notes and Jimmy's down-home testimony about his old friend.

———

WITH BREAKFAST DONE and the sun out, Palmer donned a winter coat and took a long walk down Constitution Avenue, the Capitol behind him and the frost-covered mall to his left.

As he passed by one of the Smithsonian buildings on his right, his phone rang again, this time from an area code he didn't recognize at first.

In an elegant Southern accent, a low voice spoke through the phone.

"Mr. Knight?"

"Yes. It's me."

A pause.

"Thank you."

The words rolled out slowly, like separate sentences. As sincere as words could be.

"Who is this?" Palmer asked, playing dumb.

"It's Shepherd Logan. I'm here with my wife, Mary, in Tennessee."

"Hello again, Senator." It was their second call this week. The senator had contacted him from Old Town Alexandria several days before.

"Just calling to say I'm grateful."

"Grateful for what, Senator?"

"For leaving us out."

"I don't know what you're talking about."

"In your story. You mentioned our votes for the funding, mine and Gigi's and the others'. Which is fine. But you left out . . ."

He paused, not knowing how to say it.

"You left out . . . the rest. About Mary. And about Gigi helping someone. The others . . ."

He trailed off, not wanting to talk any specifics. He still felt shame for using his position to save Mary's life.

Which was exactly why Palmer had left that detail out, versus a president who'd done it for far less noble reasons: to assure reelection. A president who knew that even a Boy Scout like Shepherd Logan could never say no to saving his dying wife.

"I'm not sure what you're talking about, Senator. My goal was to cover the scandal, who orchestrated it, and why. And that's what I did."

"Well, thank you. I can tell you Senator Fox also appreciates it. And Mary the most."

"You're welcome, Senator. You're a good man."

Palmer paused a beat, distracted.

The White House itself was now visible to his right, beyond the Ellipse. He could only imagine the commotion taking place within.

But that wasn't what had thrown him off. It was a different image, inspired by the senator's mention of Gigi Fox.

Senator Fox's old, wise eyes were still staring at him. In the back of that fancy limo. The daughter of Mansfield's Abigail Bryant, who'd risen from nothing to engage in a little civil disobedience to cure the world of cancer.

"Please give them both my best."

CHAPTER 121

—

Mansfield

THE LIGHT AT the end of the exit ramp turned yellow at the worst possible moment.

Only two car lengths away, Amity was driving way too fast to stop.

As she veered left, the Jeep she'd rented for the week slid sideways on the icy road, slipping out of the turn lane. A quick pump on the gas and some sharp twists of the wheel kept her on the road, barely, as she completed the left-hand turn into town.

It was the third close call of her early morning drive up I-71 from Columbus. Not only was she rushing in wintry weather, but her attention had rarely been on the road at all.

More than a week after Boston, she still had no idea where Mom was. But bad news seemed imminent.

She'd put faith in Dr. Vora's promise to release her. And the doctor's caution that it might take a few days rang true. But Dr. Vora also didn't control everything; in fact, sitting in that Kendall Square coffee shop, she didn't seem to control much of anything. She'd cut a dirty deal with someone who couldn't even deliver.

And now, eight days later, Amity didn't know a thing. Her stomach had been churning with nerves for days. She'd hardly eaten or slept. She was gripping the wheel tight to keep her arms from shaking.

Overcast skies and piles of gray slush made the short drive into town more bleak than usual. Halfway in, a siren wailed behind her, growing louder. Flashing lights of an ambulance soon lit up her mirrors. She pulled over to let it pass. Chunks of ice pelted her side windows as the ambulance raced by, no doubt headed to the same place she was.

She maneuvered back onto the road, front tires clawing through a snow-bank.

Her phone rang.

Palmer. Again. He'd checked in at least once a day.

"Any news?" he asked.

"You're the news expert, not me." He'd been on TV around the clock since the story broke.

"I mean about your mom."

"Dr. Stumbo called last night. He asked me to come up to Mansfield to meet in person, so I'm just driving in now. But I know nothing specific yet."

She caught a glimpse of her thin, pale cheeks in the rearview mirror. She didn't want to say what she'd been thinking all morning: if it was good news, Stumbo would've said so on the phone, instead of letting her stew. Bad news? You have to share that in person. Just like the doctor had waited to tell Mom and her in person that Dad had passed. All these years later, every word of that horrible huddle in that little hospice kitchen still replayed in her mind.

"Palmer, this is torture."

She took the left into downtown. Despite the weather, more people were walking the streets than she'd seen in some time, heading into work. Another new coffee shop had apparently opened in recent weeks and was bustling with customers.

"Dr. Vora promised, Amity. And she said it would take a few days. Hopefully, this means she's back."

"I don't know. I think he would've told me if it was good news." She was too nervous to keep talking about it. "Any word from the White House?"

"Just that they're furious," he said, chuckling. "It's definitely the last time I'll have a story out of there until a new administration."

"Look on the bright side: that may come next week."

They hung up as she passed the old *News Journal* building. Dexter Mills, healing slowly, was still laid up in his Ohio State hospital bed, so some poor reporter had had to run the whole paper over the past two weeks. At least Dexter's spirits had been lifted by the explosion of hits the big story had generated on the *News Journal*'s webpage.

As she looked at the edifice, the word she'd used with Palmer echoed: "torture." Apt in too many ways. Not just her mom's condition but the guilt that still ate at her. Deep down, she still knew the original bargain to get her mom treatment hadn't been right. A rotten bargain with bad people. And now Mom still wouldn't survive anyway.

Did she go through all of this—sacrificing even her integrity—for nothing?

Another call came in. Justice Gibbons, later than usual.

"Hiya, Amity. Feeling better?"

His stately voice eased her frayed nerves.

"Almost there, Justice. You know me—I'm a survivor."

"Yes, you are."

"I'm even back to drafting a few briefs at work."

He laughed. "That firm of yours better count their blessings. Last year's sharpest Supreme Court clerk arguing appeals in Ohio!"

They chatted for a few minutes before hanging up. The justice never asked what she had done with the information he'd shared about his old colleagues. But he was the ultimate insider. She guessed he knew but wouldn't say a word.

Amity passed to the right of the abandoned Dairy Queen, her and Dad's go-to stop after Sunday fishing. The old sign shaped like an ice-cream cone had finally tumbled to the ground, so only those who'd once bought Blizzards there would appreciate the run-down building's past glory.

Amity pulled into the hospital's parking lot.

———

AMITY SPOTTED HIM as soon as she stepped into the third-floor waiting room. Sitting along a row of chairs, facing the door. A golf ball–sized black-and-purple bruise dominated the right side of his forehead. And while they had been prevalent in her East Coast days, she hadn't seen a crimson Harvard sweatshirt since returning home.

"Simon!"

He stood up as she hobbled across the room and the two hugged more tightly than she could ever remember, as much as it hurt to do so.

"Hey, Big Sis. Great to see you, although I don't know who of us is beaten up worse."

"Why didn't you tell me you were—"

"Dr. Stumbo called yesterday, and told me I should get here this morning. I wanted to surprise you."

"Mission accomplished. Did he tell you anything?"

"He didn't. But he said he didn't want to share the news over the phone. To get here if I could."

His lips pursed after he said the words. Despite the warm greeting, Simon also knew what an in-person visit meant.

They stared into each other's eyes for a moment but said nothing. Simon saw right through her.

"Don't give up, Amity. Mom's a lot stronger than you give her credit for." He smiled. "I just figured it was about time you weren't the only Jones doing all the caretaking."

She grinned back. They were words she'd waited years to hear, so they lifted her even amid the worry that hung over them.

"I like the sweatshirt," she said as they sat down, changing the subject.

He grinned. "I thought you would. Jenna figured I needed a souvenir from an otherwise painful trip. And, yes, we actually bought this one. I got one for you in—"

"Simon and Amity Jones," a nurse called out from the desk.

The siblings stood up and walked to the counter together.

"That's us," Simon said.

"Good, Dr. Stumbo is heading out now. He didn't want to keep you waiting."

The short, bespectacled doctor walked through the swinging doors and gestured toward the corner of the room. No one else was nearby.

"Hello to you both," he said after they sat in small chairs facing one another. His expression was as flat as always, lips pursed, jaw strained. If it was good news, he was hiding it well.

Simon's presence had calmed Amity for a moment, but her heart now raced again. Both her legs and arms were shaking.

"Hi, Doctor," she said. "What's the news?"

"Well," he said, a broad smile lifting across his face. "I've got some progress to report."

"What's that?" Simon asked, sitting higher in his chair.

Progress? Amity closed her eyes, preparing for the next words. She hadn't heard good news in so long. Not that she could really count on, at least. So she fought back against over-reading the lone word. For two years, she'd come to regret every sliver of hope she'd allowed herself to feel.

"The nurses are wheeling your mother down the hallway right now—"

"Wait," Amity interrupted. "She's back in Mansfield?"

Back home—away from that dark, bleak room where she'd last seen her. Where she'd left her alone.

"Yes. She's in Mansfield." He laughed. "Where else would she be?"

Tears welled up in Amity's eyes as a lightness lifted her whole body. They could at least see her now.

She grabbed Simon's hand, squeezing hard.

"And how is she?" she asked.

Dr. Stumbo reached out and grabbed Amity's other hand from where he sat. It was the first time he'd ever done that, or any comforting gesture.

"Amity . . . Simon . . . this is why I wanted to have you both here. Your mom is doing well."

"Well?" Amity asked, hope starting to burst through. "How well?"

Stumbo squeezed her hand.

"She's improving. She's getting better."

Tears flowed down Amity's cheeks as she began to bawl loudly.

"Amity?"

She looked down and took three deep breaths, trying to stop crying, wiping tears aside with her bare hand.

Then she raised her head back up, looking at Dr. Stumbo.

"Does she know?"

Dr. Stumbo nodded gently, smiling again.

"She does."

"Does she know how?"

"She doesn't. And she shouldn't. But she's processing it all now. She'll need your help in the coming days, but she's on her way."

Simon spoke up. "Doctor, that's great news."

"Yes, it is."

Simon looked over at Amity, beaming. "Told ya," he said, as if they were still kids. "Mom's faced some challenges in her life, but she's gutted it out every time."

Dr. Stumbo nodded as he, too, turned to Amity. "Your mother's tough, all right. Not sure anyone else I know would've gotten to this point. Not even close."

They filled out some forms as Dr. Stumbo instructed them on how to care for Mom in the coming days.

Whoosh.

The two swing doors flew open.

A nurse pushed a wheelchair through the doorway. Mom still looked pale and thin. But unlike at any recent hospital visit, she was sitting straight up. A faint smile lifted the corners of her wan lips.

But it was a confident smile. And sitting erectly in that chair, shoulders up, back straight, Mom looked as strong as Amity could remember.

"Amity! Simon!"

They leapt to their feet and ran to her chair. Unable to hug her, Amity gave her mother a light peck on the cheek as she grabbed both of her hands.

Simon pecked her on the other cheek, then stepped behind the chair. "I'll take it from here," he said to the nurse as he pushed Mom toward the door.

Amity held the waiting room door open as Simon wheeled her through. "We're taking you home, Mom," she said. "We're going home."

But in her mind, she was already one step beyond home. The cardinals would be waiting. And she couldn't wait to tell Dad the good news.

ACKNOWLEDGMENTS

WHILE ONE PERSON may capture it all on paper, a good story has so many who inspire and shape it along the way. And you never know when the most important moments might occur.

In this case, the spark came from a casual conversation in the Seattle living room of my friends Rich and Trang Tong. We were catching up on family. As soon as we were done talking for those thirty minutes, I knew what my next book would be about. I started writing on the flight back to Ohio, and *A Simple Choice* soon emerged.

A second key moment came when my mentor, former boss, and friend Judge Nathaniel Jones—a civil rights pioneer—gave brief remarks as we celebrated his ninety-second birthday. To a far younger audience, he shared a perspective I will never forget. I try to capture it through several of the book's more senior characters.

Numerous readers followed, including Sarah Landsman and her book club, Sherry Coolidge, Greg Landsman, Rachel Storch, and my parents, just to name a few. They all helped fine-tune the manuscript.

Then Mark Tavani and his team at Putnam—Ivan Held, Sally Kim, Katie McKee, Emily Mlynek, Aranya Jain, and everyone in art and sales—challenged me to lift the story and Amity Jones to their highest potential, which we did together. And Mitch Hoffman of Aaron Priest Agency patiently navigated the writing and editing process through thick and thin.

A Simple Choice is about many things—but none more important than the fight against cancer, a scourge impacting almost every family in America, my own included.

As this book is put to bed, I dedicate it to my own mom, Francie, and so many others waging that challenging battle as best they can.